Play 2 Win
Live 2 Serve
John 3:16-17

Donnie Prince

This book is dedicated to the memory of my father,
Thonie Travis Prince,
March 4, 1933 - January 16, 1981

Acknowledgements

A special thanks to Russell Rawlings, for all his talented work and time spent editing this novel.

To Linda Barnes, who encouraged me to keep working at this project, at times when I felt like giving up. And for taking my scribbled handwriting and typing these words.

To Sarah Hooper and Bruce Jackson, and all the people at A+ Graphics, who helped me lay out the cover design and format the book, making this novel a reality.

To Jesus Christ, for entrusting His words to me, and giving me the privilege to write them.

To my daughter Mary Katherine, and my nephew William Prince, for posing for the cover photo.

x

FOREWARD

Donnie Prince has been on an amazing journey. He has enjoyed the fruits of a successful marriage that produced two incredible, beautiful daughters. He has tasted success as an athlete, banker, insurance agent, real estate agent and homebuilder. And he has experienced personal and professional hardship in equal measure. He lost his beloved father way too early in life. He lost a new office building to fire. In the financial downturn of recent years, he lost everything.

Where lesser men have turned to the bottle – and worse – he has turned to the Bible. And the pen. He has leaned upon his faith and spiritual commitment to survive that which lesser beings have not withstood.

He has written a book – a marvelous book that tells of triumph and tragedy not unlike that which he has experienced. It is a story that draws upon the lives of those he has known the best and loved the most. In an account founded in fiction, he has taken the names of these "real" people and transformed them into characters whose actions and accomplishments are amplified beyond recognition. No disclaimer is required, for not only do these characters scarcely resemble their real world counterparts. Other than his daughters, Sarah and Mary Katherine, those of us whose names appear in the following pages are not accomplished athletes in any way, shape or form.

What we do represent is the past and present of Donnie Prince. We represent aspirations unfulfilled. We are not the people you are about to meet in "Play 2 Win – Live 2 Serve," but we would like to be.

Prepare yourself now for an equally remarkable journey. Prepare yourself to see Jesus Christ and the power of faith through the eyes and words of Donnie Prince. Prepare yourself to laugh, to cry, to smile, and most importantly, to cheer. As you prepare to meet Travis and MK and a supporting cast of individuals who maintain roles large and small in their lives, prepare to believe.

You're about to learn the secret and the story behind "Play 2 Win – Live 2 Serve." It is a story with which I am proud and humbled to be associated, written by a man who I am proud to call my friend.

I did not know Donnie Prince could write. I did not know Donnie Prince could preach. I did not know that Donnie Prince knew Jesus Christ.

I was wrong.

Russell Rawlings

INTRODUCTION

It was one of those moments. You feel as though you have been there before, even though you know you have not. You know it is your time to be right where you are. A handsome young man in his early twenties, sandy blonde hair, crystal blue eyes, tan skin with rugged features. He wears a dark pinstripe suit and tie that covers his 6 foot 3 inch, 200-pound frame. Shoes freshly polished, he is dressed for success. He has an important appointment, and he wants to make a good first impression. While he is waiting he paces quietly around the room. He has a lot on his mind. As he walks toward the large conference room window he looks across the parking lot to a sandlot field. The parking lot is filled with cars carrying little boys and their parents. Probably 10 to 12 years old. Bats and gloves in hand as they exit their vehicles and stroll toward the baseball field. As they walk, he remembers. He remembers back to those days when he was 10-years old and his first little league team. Those days when his father was one of the assistant coaches and they would ride over to the athletic park in his hometown of Wilson, North Carolina. On the way they would discuss important strategies and fundamentals like - catch the ball with both hands - run hard to first base - do your best no matter what - and whatever you do, don't sling the bat after you hit the ball; the umpire will call you out. He and his father also talked about other things. Things like what it was like to drive a car. How important it was to always tell the truth. That winning or losing was not the most important thing; it was how you played the game. That no matter what happened Mom and Dad would love him and they were proud of him. Just go out there and do your best. Relax, play fast and loose, and play to win.

Just then the door opens and he hears a familiar voice.

"Are you nervous buddy?"

"You bet I am," he replies. "You know I have never done anything like this before and I am scared to death."

"A sharp looking man like you, what have you got to be nervous about? Besides, I've seen you in a lot of tight situations, and you've always done okay."

"Yeah, but never anything like this, I'm out of my element today."

"Well Travis, I just wanted to come in here and tell you that I have never been prouder of you than I am right now. Just go in there and do your best. Remember who you are, and I love you."

"I love you too Dad, I love you too."

Then his father gives him a firm handshake and a hug, turns and leaves the room. It is a special moment between a father and a son. There are no more special moments than those shared between a parent and a child. Travis walks over to the chair next to the fireplace. He sits down. Puts his elbows on his knees, he bows his head, closes his eyes and he prays.

"Lord God of Abraham, Isaac and Jacob, I want to thank you Lord for this world you made, and everything in it. Lord, I want to thank you for all that you have created. I want to thank you for the life you have given me. The chance to be part of this creation, for my parents who love me, who have been beside me guiding me throughout my life, and the love and support they have always shared with me. I want to thank you for my sister Sarah and all the other friends and family that I love. Lord, you know that today is a new experience for me. You know that I am afraid. Father, I know that you will be with me today as I begin this new chapter of my life. Lord, you have already brought me so far. You have blessed me and shown me so many things I would have never thought were possible. I ask for your peace and confidence, that I would do my best, and in whatever happens, your will be done, and your son Jesus Christ will be glorified. In Jesus' name I pray. Amen."

As Travis opens his eyes he looks down at his hands. He gently rubs his palms together and a smile comes across his face.

"Lord I can't believe how you brought me here today."

And as he slowly rubs his hands together, he remembers, he remembers.

CHAMPIONSHIP ON THE LINE

"Welcome Ladies and Gentlemen, this is Alton Britt, the voice of Wilson Fike Baseball. We are coming to you from Doak Field on the campus of North Carolina State University where today the Golden Demons of Wilson Fike High School, will play the Burlington Williams Warriors, in the third and final game of the State 3-A High School baseball championship. The series is tied at one game apiece so today's ball game will decide the state championship. Today's game also features two of the nations top high school baseball players. For Burlington Williams today's starting pitcher will be hard throwing, right hander John Hudson. Hudson is 13-0 for the season. The 6 foot 5 inch Hudson has 173 strikeouts in 90 innings, allowing only 21 walks, with an ERA of 1.10 runs per game. Hudson's fastball has been clocked at 94 mph. Hudson has already signed a letter of intent to take his talented right arm to Clemson University in the fall. The Golden Demons are led by their own high school All-American, shortstop Travis Simpson. Simpson is also one of the nation's top high school football players as a wide receiver. He possesses great hands and blinding speed. This spring Simpson has led the Golden Demons with a .463 batting average, 12 home runs, and 34 stolen bases. Simpson has that rare combination of speed, power, and a great throwing arm. He has already signed a letter of intent to play football and baseball here next year at N.C. State. The big question for both of these young men is will they go to college or move straight on into professional baseball. Both of these kids are expected to be taken in the first round of this year's major league draft, but today we are here to decide the championship. These two young men are very familiar with one another. For the past two summers they have played summer baseball together representing the state of North Carolina, playing traveling baseball all across the southeastern United States. Today the head to head match up between these two is what everyone wants to see. There are at least two-dozen major league scouts in attendance today with radar guns and stopwatches. This is what championship baseball is all about. As the teams prepare to take the field, the two team captains, Hudson and Simpson are meeting with the umpires at the home plate to exchange lineups."

"Well Big John, you gonna take it easy on me today?"

"Well sure Travis, I'll take it easy on you, if you will take it easy on me."

The two friends shared a smile and a handshake. They had traveled the southeast together as teammates. They shared a great respect for one

3

another. Then Travis said, "Hey John, what ya' say we meet down the street at the Char-Grill after the game; winner buys, fair enough?"

"Yeah, that sounds like a plan. Good luck Travis, have a good game."

"Same to you John."

The boys shook hands and went back to their dugouts. It was time to play ball. The Golden Demons huddled in front of the first base dugout as Head Coach Gilbert Ferrell gathered his team together.

"Fellas, this is the last time this team will ever take the field together. Let's don't hold back, leave it all on the field. Win or lose, I love you guys. Now let's go out there and win this thing. Alright; on three, one, two, three." "Play to win!" "Go get 'em," and with that Fike took the field.

The stadium was packed. Parents, students, reporters, fans, scouts, and spectators, all anxious to see the match up of two championship teams and two superstar players. The atmosphere was electric. It was time to play ball. There is something special about a championship baseball game. Baseball is a game where it may not appear much is happening. Sometimes you can be lulled into the idea that the game is quietly moving along, then in the instance of one pitch, the outcome of a championship season is decided.

Pitching for Fike was junior left-handed pitcher Randy Prince. Prince was 10-1 with 87 strikeouts in 76 innings pitched. His ERA for the season was 2.18. Prince also would be a major college prospect next year. In the top of the first inning Prince retired the Warriors three and out. In the bottom of the first Hudson struck out the first two Fike batters on six straight fastballs, the fastest pitch was 93 mph. Then the stage was set for the match up everybody came to see, as Fike shortstop Travis Simpson walked to the plate. While Hudson stood atop the mound, Simpson settled into the batter's box, digging his spikes into the firm ground beside home plate. The left-handed hitting Simpson was set, scouts with stop watches and jug guns ready. The game was on. Hudson went into his windup and delivered a 95 mph fastball on the outside corner of the plate. Strike one. There was a movement amongst the professional scouts and fans in the stands. This was not your normal high school baseball game. These were two exceptional student athletes. Simpson again dug into the batters box, Hudson toed the pitching rubber, Hudson went into his windup, another fastball, 96 mph, right on the outside corner, strike two.

One of the Boston Red Sox scouts in attendance said, "Big John is really bringing it today."

Simpson again stepped back into the box, no balls, two strikes; he knew he was in a deep hole.

Travis thought to himself: "*I just need to protect the plate with two strikes.*"

Then Hudson again threw a fastball on the outside corner, this time Simpson was able to get the bat on the ball and hit a slow chopper toward the Williams' shortstop. In a blink, Simpson was out of the batters box racing toward first base. The Williams' shortstop made a clean play and an accurate throw to first base to get Simpson by half a step. Out three. As Simpson's foot hit the bag, the sound of stopwatches clicked in the stands.

The Atlanta Braves' scouts said, "3.3 seconds, man that boy is smoking!" and the row of teenage girls sitting behind him giggled and said, "You got that right!"

Over the next two innings the pitching continued to dominate the scoreless game. There is an atmosphere of tension that increases pitch by pitch in a classic pitching duel. Hudson was overpowering, striking out six Fike batters in the first three innings. The Fike pitcher, Prince struck out two while only giving up two hits through three and a half innings. In the bottom of the fourth Simpson came to the plate again; the score tied nothing to nothing, one out and nobody on base. Simpson again dug into the batter's box. Hudson then went into his windup and fired a 94 mph fastball on the outside corner. Strike one.

Simpson stepped out of the box and said to himself, "*If he is going to pitch me out there I've got to get a little closer to the plate.*"

Again Hudson went into the windup and threw another 95 mph fastball just outside, one ball, one strike.

Simpson's thoughts were, "*quick hands, line drive;* "*quick hands, line drive.*"

There is a unique sound to a baseball coming at you at speeds over 90 mph. You hear a hissing sound as the ball approaches, a swish as it goes by, and a "pop" as the ball hits the catcher's mitt. It is a special sound heard only by elite athletes. And right now these two friends were putting it all on the line in their head to head duel. Simpson again was ready. Hudson wound up and sent another blazing fastball toward the outside corner. This time Simpson's quick hands were ready, and he hit a bullet over the first baseman's head that took one hop and bounced off the right field fence. Simpson threw it into another gear as he rounded first and second base on his way to a standup triple, runner on third, one out. The two young men exchanged smiles; each had one win apiece. Then Hudson took the mound again, six straight fastballs, two more outs, inning over, at the end of four innings, no score.

Over the next two innings the game continued to be dominated by great pitching. With every pitch the intensity level grew. The crowd moved closer and closer to the edge of their seats. Everyone could sense the electricity in the air as the championship game moved toward its climax. Then leading off the top of the seventh inning Williams' catcher, Mike Edwards, worked Prince to a three-two full count. Then on the next pitch Edwards hit a Prince fastball 380 feet over the left field fence. 1-0 Williams, and the Williams crowd erupted!

Fike Head Coach Gilbert Ferrell called timeout, and walked to the mound to settle down his junior pitcher.

"Randy you've pitched a great game. Forget about that, that's over. Now let's get these next three guys out, and we'll come in and score you some runs."

Prince said, "Okay Coach."

Then the southpaw went back to work and set down the next three batters in order. After six and one half innings, Williams led 1-0.

There is nothing like the final at bat in a close, low-scoring baseball game. The dugouts on both sides and every person in attendance was at a fever pitch when second baseman Bert Ferrell came to the plate to lead off the bottom half of the seventh. Then, with a two-strike count Ferrell got his bat on a Hudson fastball and hit a single to right field. Fike suddenly had new life with a runner on first, nobody out, and All-American Travis Simpson coming to the plate. As Simpson made his way to the batter's box Williams' coach John Hackney called time out and went to the mound to talk with his senior right hander Hudson.

"Alright John, let's settle down now. Nobody for Fike has touched your fastball today except Travis. We've got nobody out and a man on first, we can't afford to put the winning run on base so we have got to pitch to him here. We need this out! We've been pitching him outside so Travis is crowding the plate. On the first pitch throw him inside to keep him honest up there. Don't throw him anything out over the plate, because if Travis hits one out of here we'll be on the bus heading back to Burlington, you got me?"

"Yes sir Coach."

And with that said, Hackney headed back to the dugout. As the Williams' coach reached the dugout steps, Travis Simpson said a silent prayer to himself,

"Lord may your will be done," and he stepped to the plate, one last time.

Alton Britt, the "Voice of Wilson Athletics", described the action.

"Well folks, this is the moment we've all come to see, the two All-

Americans face off with the game on the line. Separated by the most intense distance in sports, the 60 feet 6 inches between the pitcher's mound and home plate."

As perspiration poured from players and fans alike the crowd rose to its feet as a roar filled the stadium! Simpson's parents rose to their feet as well as Travis dug into the batter's box. His hands almost parallel to the inside corner of home plate. His older sister Sarah, a rising senior at East Carolina screamed out,

"Come on Travis, you can do it!"

His mother Kathy said, "I'm so nervous I can't look."

His father Ed said, "quick hands Son, line drive."

Second by second the crowd noise grew. The players' adrenalin increased. Their hearts began to beat faster, and then Hudson's right arm came toward the plate. He fired another blistering fastball, and then there was the crack of the ball hitting the bat. But this time the sound was different. This time between the ball and the bat were the million dollar fingers of Travis Simpson's left hand. And as the 96 mph fastball hit Travis' hand, the delicate bones in his forefingers shattered like broken glass. The crowd stood in silent horror as this All-American boy fell to the ground. Suddenly the championship was not that important. Coaches and trainers rushed to the field. Simpson's parents ran to be by their injured son's side. In what seemed like an instant, Travis lay on his back looking upwards toward the Carolina blue sky, his hand trembling uncontrollably from the excruciating pain. Above him were the faces of his parents, coaches and team doctors. Travis looked at his left hand, and he could see blood oozing through the white batting glove covering his twisted fingers.

His mother Kathy cried, "Travis, Travis, I'm here Son! I'm here!"

The next few minutes seemed surreal as the doctors worked to cut away the batting glove from Simpson's hand. Somewhere in the midst of the pain and confusion Travis passed out from the shock. The last thing he would remember would be telling his father Ed,

"I heard it coming Dad, I heard it, but it was too late."

WAITING AND WONDERING

By the time the Simpson family reached Wake Medical Center, Travis had already arrived, being transported by ambulance. He was being prepped for emergency surgery. The news of Travis' injury had quickly spread across the country. This young man's sports career had been closely reported over the past year. Featured in articles in Sports Illustrated Magazine and ESPN as America's top two-sport high school athlete. Ed, Kathy and Sarah Simpson, along with their pastor Jim McKinnon, were quickly ushered into one of the hospital's surgical waiting rooms as Travis' surgery was beginning. After a few minutes the family was joined by N.C. State University Athletic Director, Lee Matthews.

"Mr. and Mrs. Simpson, I wanted to come on behalf of all the athletic department and administration at the university to tell you our thoughts and prayers are with Travis and your family, we are all just so, so sorry that this has happened. I also want you to be assured that Travis and your family are all a part of our family at N.C. State. Travis will always have his athletic scholarship at N.C. State, no matter what injuries he may have. He will have the support of our team doctors and athletic trainers. We will provide him with physical therapy through our athletic department. The head of our Physical Therapy Department will develop a plan to assist Travis in his recovery. He will always, always be a part of Wolfpack Athletics, and we are here to support all of your family, anyway we can. Is there anything myself or the university can do for you, anything at all?"

Then an emotional Ed Simpson replied:

"No we are fine right now. Just keep Travis in your prayers, I cannot tell you how kind you all have been to our son. Your being here means more than you will ever know."

"Well, I will leave you now so you can have your privacy, I will be in touch, God bless."

Mr. Matthews then left the family alone with their thoughts. And as they waited, they wondered.

"Lord, why did this happen to Travis, and what now?"

Those are very hard questions. Unless you are a parent of a child who has battled a serious injury or sickness you cannot understand the depth of that kind of pain. The feeling of helplessness as your child hurts and you as a parent can do nothing to make it better. Ed Simpson would have taken a saw and cut his own hand off and given it to his son in an instant if he could have. But all the Simpsons could do was wait and pray. Over the next four hours as a team of vascular and orthopedic surgeons delicately worked together to reconstruct Travis's shattered hand, and while the doctors operated, the Simpsons sat quietly and wondered.

"*Why Travis Lord, why Lord why?*"

At 7:35, Dr. Jeff Hamilton, Chief of Orthopedic Surgery at Wake Medical Center entered the waiting room, introduced himself and sat down with the Simpsons to discuss Travis' injuries.

"Travis' surgery has been completed. We have been able to repair the damage to Travis' hand. When the baseball hit his left hand it broke the bones and dislocated the knuckles on Travis' four fingers. We were able to repair those fingers, and we have inserted pins to stabilize his hand. Travis will have quite a bit of swelling over the next few weeks. Once the swelling has decreased we will begin the process of physical therapy to help Travis regain the ability to use his hand again. Travis will recover from this injury. However, he will not have the strength or stability in his left hand that he had before the accident."

"What exactly are you saying doctor?" Ed asked.

"What I am saying is that Travis will be able to use his left hand the way most of us do, to perform normal day-to-day activities. However, Travis' current day-to-day activities are not normal. He is a highly skilled athlete, and this type of injury will not allow him to do many of the things he has been able to do in the past."

Ed then asked, "What things doctor, will Travis not be able to do?"

"Travis will no longer be able to hold a baseball bat, or catch a football. The loss of strength in those fingers will not allow him to do that anymore. I'm afraid Travis' football and baseball careers are over. I'm sorry."

With that said the emotion in the room began to swell. After a time Kathy Simpson asked,

"When will we be able to see him?"

"Travis will be in recovery for about 30 more minutes, then we will be transferring him to a room. I anticipate Travis will be in the hospital for three days. I will have a nurse come in and take you to his room. You can wait for him there."

Then Ed asked, "Does Travis know the severity of his injuries?"

"No, once Travis wakes up and has some time to rest I will meet with you all and we will discuss his recovery program together. I would suggest we do that in the morning once you and Travis have had a chance to get some rest. Again, I want to emphasize that Travis will regain the use of his hand. I am sorry that this has happened, I will do anything I can to help."

"Thank you doctor. Thank you for helping our son."

A few minutes later the Simpsons and Reverend McKinnon left the waiting room and walked silently toward the elevator. The only communication between them were the sounds of tears and deep breaths. As they entered the elevator Reverend McKinnon put his arms around Ed and Kathy and said,

"Ed, Kathy, I am so, so sorry."

Rev. McKinnon had married Ed and Kathy 25 years earlier. He had baptized Travis and Sarah. He was a close personal friend. Rev. McKinnon had been like a father to Ed since Ed's father died in 1981. Travis had been named after his grandfather, who died before Travis was born. In the elevator ride to the fourth floor it was the arms of Jim McKinnon that steadied the Simpsons through their trial. The arms of their minister, and their faith in God. When they reached Room 431, the family circled together with their pastor, they bowed their heads, and Jim McKinnon led the family in prayer.

"Dear God, we pray for your comforting hand, be with Travis, Ed, Kathy and Sarah. Surround them with your loving arms, God; be with them all today, tonight, and throughout Travis' recovery. Give them your strength and comfort. Assure them God, assure them that you are standing here with them, and you will be ever present, as they share their love for Travis and one another. Grant them your peace and healing comfort; in Jesus' name we pray; Amen."

Then as they waited for Travis, they all wondered what lay ahead. They waited, and they wondered.

The time was a little past 8:30 when the surgical bed transporting Travis Simpson arrived in his hospital room. The Simpsons were very emotional as their son entered the room. Travis' left hand was immobilized and in a cast. He was heavily sedated as he drifted in and out of consciousness. Kathy tried to speak with him briefly as he drifted in and out of sleep. After a few minutes Dr. Hamilton stopped in. He suggested the family get back to Wilson and try to get some rest. Then he would meet with them and Travis to discuss the extent of his injuries the next morning.

"Kathy and Ed, I know you want to be with Travis, but the best thing for Travis right now is sleep. We will closely monitor him tonight. You all have had a long day. Travis will be fine tonight."

After a short visit the Simpsons took Dr. Hamilton's advice. They left the room and made the quiet walk from Travis's hospital room out to the parking lot. When they reached the car the emotion of the day was too much for Kathy, and she broke down in tears.

"Why Lord, why did this happen Lord? Why?"

She had held it in as long as she could. Her hurt and frustration had to be released. Her son, her baby, who earlier in the day had the world by the tail, now lay in a hospital bed. It was more than any mother should ever have to bear. Ed, Sarah and Kathy stood together in the parking lot. They held on tightly to each other, the way families must in a time of crisis. Together they would make their stand against this trial, a trial none of them could have believed they would ever face. They had many questions about what lay ahead for Travis and their family. But they knew that they had each other, and that would see them through.

It was a quiet ride home that night from Raleigh to Wilson. They arrived home around 11 p.m., all of them exhausted from the day's events. Kathy and Sarah went to bed. Meanwhile, Ed went outside to get some air and try to collect his thoughts. It was a warm early summer night. Ed went and sat down on the back porch. He leaned against the rails on the side of the steps and gazed up at the sky. The moon was full that night, as Ed sat alone. He thought back to the night before, when he and Travis had sat outside and talked about the next day's championship game. They had discussed Travis' plans for next year. The decision Travis would have to make between going to college or opting to pursue a career in professional baseball. They had speculated about what pick he would be in this year's major league draft. Now as Ed sat here alone, he remembered back to the game. The moment when Travis was hit by the pitch, the sound of the ball hitting his hand, and then watching his son fall to the ground. It seemed as though Ed was watching a movie of someone else's life. Now all those options they had discussed the night before, were no longer options at all.

There would be no sleep for Ed Simpson that night. There would only be thoughts of what might have been for Travis and thoughts of what Ed and Kathy would say to Travis tomorrow. What do you say when your child's dreams vanish in an instant? What do you do when there is nothing you can do? How would Travis respond when he realizes that football and baseball are now just memories in his past? His future that yesterday seemed so clear and full of promise, suddenly is mired with uncertainty and disappointment. How would Ed stay strong for his son and his wife while his heart was broken too?

That night on those steps, the man of the house all alone, wept like a child. In the darkness, the father let his guard down. Alone, that's the way fathers face trials. Alone, because for everyone else's sake, the fathers have to appear to be strong, but a father's heart breaks too, and with only a rail to lean on and the stars to talk to, Ed Simpson bore his soul and shed his tears. There would be no sleep for Ed that night, only thoughts and questions about tomorrow.

The next morning the Simpson family was up early and on their way to Raleigh. Not much was said in the car that morning on the way to Wake Med. Kathy had packed a suitcase with some clothes for she intended to stay with Travis until he was released to come home. They arrived at Wake Med around 7:30. When they got to Travis' room he was already awake. There were hugs and tears. Travis had questions about what the doctors had said and they talked about the accident.

"I saw the ball coming at me but by the time I realized what was happening I could not get my hands out of the way. Then I felt this sharp throbbing pain in my hand, and then everyone was standing over me; that's the last thing I remember. Dad what did the doctors say? When will I be able to play again?"

Ed knew that question would be coming. He had sat up all night the night before wondering what his answer should be.

"Travis, the doctor is going to meet us here this morning at 10:00. When he gets here we will all talk about what happens next."

"Well I just want to put all this behind me and get back out there again, that's all I know."

For the next couple of hours the family made small talk about one thing or another. There were some phone calls from friends and relatives, calling to see how they all were doing, and what the news was about Travis' injury. Some of their friends told Travis that his injury had been reported as one of the lead stories the night before on ESPN, and that Travis was on the headlines of the sports page of The News and Observer. There was an article about it also in USA Today. All the calls were encouraging and they helped to lift Travis' spirits.

Then at 10 am Dr. Hamilton came into the room. He closed the door and sat down. It was time to talk.

Dr. Hamilton asked, "Travis, how are you feeling this morning?"

Travis replied, "Well, Dr. Hamilton, my hand is sore and I am tired, but I feel okay."

Then Dr. Hamilton began to tell Travis the bad news.

"Travis, when the baseball hit your left hand it compressed your four fingers on your hand, breaking your fingers and dislocating your knuckles. We were able to surgically repair your hand and over time you will regain the use of your hand. We will start you on a physical therapy program in a few weeks once the swelling goes down. You will have some scar tissue and there will be decreased strength and flexibility in your fingers."

"Dr. Hamilton, what does that mean? When will I be able to play football and baseball again?"

"Travis, I am sorry to tell you that with an injury like this, your hand will never regain the strength you had before the accident. I am afraid you will no longer be able to play football or baseball. I'm sorry."

With that said there then began a period of silence that lasted for a couple of minutes, but it seemed like hours. Travis then said,

"Dr. Hamilton, I'm only 18-years-old. I have been hurt before. This is only the fingers on one hand; surely you can operate again. Something can be done, can't it? Dad, Mom, surely this will get better; this can't be all there is?"

At that point the gravity of the situation began to sink in. Everyone knew that things for Travis were different now, and that for all of them, things would never be the same. What do you do when you see your son's life turned upside down in an instant? What does a young man think, what does he say?

One moment Travis was in his favorite place in the world, in a batter's box with the game on the line. The next minute he was in a hospital bed being told he would never play again. How can an 18-year-old superstar suddenly be sidelined permanently by those tiny bones of his fingers? Life can be very hard sometimes, and over the next few days Travis and his family would face the reality of how fragile life can be. There would be many phone calls and visitors over the next few days. Travis would soon leave the hospital and go back to his home in Wilson.

There would be the final exams to take before graduation. He would wear his cap and gown at his high school graduation with the rest of his classmates. Travis and his family remained strong in public in the face of their ordeal. But in their private moments alone, they would have their tears. They would express their sorrows to one another. Travis would lie in his bed at night and look at his bandaged hand. He would try to take it all in, to make some sort of sense of all that had happened. After all, he was only an 18-year-old kid with his whole life ahead of him, but now the life ahead of him seemed so, so different. He was confused. He was afraid. In the darkness he would do the only thing he knew to do. He did what he had always done since he was a little boy. He would pray.

"Lord, you know I am hurt and confused right now. I don't know what to say. I don't know what to do. Lord, I have given my life to you. Please be with me in this difficult time. Help me to see the plan you have for my life. Give me the courage to honor you in all that I do; and in all things may your son Jesus be glorified."

Then Travis would lie there and he would wonder, what was next?

THERAPY

Four weeks had passed since Travis' injury. The swelling in his hand had gone down. His stitches were removed when he had a follow-up visit with Dr. Hamilton at Wake Med.

"Travis your hand is healing nicely," Dr. Hamilton said. "The swelling has reduced. It's time for us to set you up a program to rehabilitate your hand. I will make an appointment for you with Dr. Stephanie Clauson. She is the physician in charge of physical therapy at N.C. State. Can you be there next Monday at 10?"

"Yes sir."

"Now that we've got that out of the way tell me how are you doing? This is a big change for you. Tell me how you are feeling?"

"Dr. Hamilton, my hand is sore and that is a concern, but I know in time my hand will get better. Not like before, but it will get better. But not being able to play ball anymore, that is very hard for me to accept. It just doesn't seem real. Sometimes, I get really down about it."

"Travis in my job, I meet a lot of people who have been involved in accidents. Sometimes like in your case, an accident can be life changing. And when that happens the changes can be very hard to understand, and even harder to accept."

"That's where I am Doctor. I feel confused by all that is going on. I just don't know what is next anymore. It is such a change for me."

"Travis; have you talked with your parents about it?"

"Yes sir; they are great and they have been so supportive, I have a wonderful family. But they really don't know what to say or do to help either."

Dr. Hamilton then asked, "Have you talked with your minister? Maybe consider some counseling to help you deal with these emotions of loss you are feeling?"

"Well, no I have not, but I would consider it."

"Just think about it Travis, we all need someone to talk to sometimes."

"Yes sir."

"Alright, go ahead to your therapy appointment next week and I'll see you again in three weeks."

The next Monday Dr. Stephanie Clauson met Travis at the N.C. State Training Facility.

"Travis it's nice to meet you. I am very sorry about your injury. I think we can get you started in some exercises to get some strength back in that hand."

"Thank you Doctor. I am just ready to get things back to normal, or as normal as possible anyway."

"Call me Stephanie. I'm not that old."

"Okay, Stephanie."

Stephanie was a young doctor who had been an athlete herself. She had played volleyball in college and beach volleyball while she was in medical school at the University of Florida. She was a Christian as well. She wore a cross around her neck.

Travis immediately felt a connection with Stephanie.

"I like your cross. I don't know where I would be now without my faith."

"I know Travis," Stephanie replied. "I lost my father to cancer two years ago. Sometimes things happen we just don't understand."

"I keep telling myself God has a plan for my life," Travis said. "But right now it is hard to keep believing."

"Just remember," she replied, "God is in control. He has a plan. We all have to keep reminding ourselves of that sometimes. But no matter what happens Travis, just remember God is in control."

For the next hour Stephanie did a thorough assessment of Travis' left hand. At times during the exam the tugs and pushes on Travis' fingers were very painful. During the exam Stephanie showed Travis some exercises to work on improving his dexterity, to strengthen his fingers. She gave him some clay and told him to take it home and work on massaging the clay with his fingers. Molding the clay into shapes or figurines would help Travis to learn to use his fingers again. Then after two or three months Stephanie would have Travis squeeze a tennis ball to improve his hand strength. Then bounce it and catch it to improve the coordination and regain the strength in his hand and arm. Over the following weeks Travis would spend many nights alone in his room. He would sit at his desk and work with the clay between his fingers. He could feel the sensation of the moist, cold clay as he molded shapes with his fingers. Although the exercises were painful, Travis found a sort of solace in molding the clay with his fingers. There is something very spiritual about working with clay. During those nights, alone in his room, Travis would pray. He would ask Jesus the recurring questions,

"Why did this happen Lord? And what do I do now?"

Over time Travis' frustration began to decrease, but his confusion would remain. Alone with his thoughts he began to realize how little control we really have over our lives, and how quickly life can change. For an 18-year-old young man he had experienced a great pain and loss. Yet in the midst of all his confusion Travis began to imagine himself as the clay, and that God was molding him for some other purpose. That God was in control. It would be a long time before the healing process was over but Travis was right. He was the clay being molded by the Master's hand.

BROKEN HEARTS

The next few days would hold many sleepless nights for Ed Simpson. Ed and Kathy would have many conversations about Travis' injury, their shared concern about their son. Concerns about the injury to his hand, concern about the devastation to his dreams. Parents are always worried about their children. Even in the best of times a parent is only as happy as his saddest child. While Travis did not complain he began to withdraw to himself. He stayed at home more. His appetite diminished. He began to lose a little weight. He just was not himself. The Simpsons had a family dog, Wesley, a West Highland White Terrier. Ed had bought Wesley for the kids one year for Christmas. Whenever Travis drove his car into the driveway Wesley would run to the door to greet him. Wesley always wanted Travis to immediately take him outside for a walk. It was a ritual the two of them shared. Whenever Travis lay down on the couch, Wesley would climb up on the couch as well and lay by Travis' side. Whenever Travis would go to lie down on his bed, Wesley would go lay under the bed until Travis got up.

In the weeks after the accident Wesley was a great comfort to Travis. When Travis was with other people they did not know what to say, but Wesley was always there. Dogs are very aware when the people they love are hurting. People tried to help Travis, but no one knew how. Over time Travis began to feel isolated by the awkwardness of the situation. It wasn't anyone's fault. It was just that the change of circumstances was so sudden and so dramatic, none of Travis' friends knew how to react to it. So Travis began to feel more and more alone. Travis came to rely on the consistency of his relationship with his dog. The saying, "a dog is a man's best friend," is so true. No matter how awkward or alone Travis felt, Wesley was always there.

At nights after supper Ed and Kathy spent many hours talking about Travis. They were watching him hurt inside and that was hurting them as well. The tension between the two at times would come between them. Neither one blamed the other for what happened, but they were both so frustrated with the situation they at times took their frustrations out on one another. When that happened Ed would often times leave the house and go visit his mother.

"Mom, I am just so overwhelmed by what has happened to Travis. I am mad about it. I am as 'ill as a rattlesnake,' and I just don't know what do to about it."

"Ed sometimes things happen that we just can't understand," his mother replied. "When your father died while you were in college I felt so overwhelmed. Your grandmother told me that when I got discouraged I just needed to get up and get busy. Try to help someone else; just do the best I could. That's what you and Kathy have to do now. Just remember this is something you are all going through together. You will get through this."

"Mom, I just don't understand why God would let such a thing happen to Travis? How can God be glorified if God allows Travis to be injured this way? God gave these gifts to Travis, and now God is not allowing Travis to use those gifts to honor Him. Travis has given his life to Jesus. How can Jesus be glorified if Travis can't use these gifts?"

"Son, sometimes bad things happen to good people. Now I know that's not what you wanted to hear right now, but you know it is true. Honey, we only see a small, small part of God's plan. God is in control. You believe that don't you Ed?"

Ed then reluctantly said, "Yes Mom, you know I believe that, but I have my doubts sometimes too. It is just hard to believe something good can come from this."

"Well Ed, that's what faith is. Believing in something when we don't have all the answers. Hold onto your faith! You hear me. Hold onto your faith!"

"Alright Mom, alright."

"Now come here and give me a hug. You're still just a little boy to me and I love you."

"I love you too Mom, I love you too."

When Ed got home that night he walked out to the back porch and sat down outside, leaning against the rails and gazing up into the stars. He prayed for answers. He prayed to the one who had the answers. But tonight there would be no answers. For now, they would all have to wait.

TIME FOR SCHOOL

For Ed and Kathy Simpson the days were passing quickly. Within a week it would be time for fall classes to begin at N.C. State. Their youngest child, Travis, would be going away to college. Ed and Kathy would be "empty nesters," not quite 50, and both of them were uneasy about all the changes in their lives. Travis' injury had turned the family's lifestyle and routine upside down. Before the accident they all had anticipated the upcoming college football season, but now they had no desire to watch a football or baseball game. Kathy and Ed also worried about how Travis would handle being away from home after the accident. How would he fit in now in the athletic dorm at State, now that he could no longer play the sports he loved? The family had always gathered together around sports activities. Ed had played baseball and golf as a student at Atlantic Christian College in Wilson. Kathy was a cheerleader and played college tennis. Sarah was a high school tennis player and a member of the swim team. The family had been actively involved in sports since the children were small. Ed coached the kid's youth teams. The family had spent countless days together going to ball games. Now that Travis could no longer play football or baseball, sports only reminded the family of Travis' injury.

It is very difficult for a family to adjust when the things that once brought such joy no longer bring a family together. Sports had been a common thread that connected the Simpson family. Athletic events now only reminded them of all that Travis had lost. The dynamic of the whole family changed. Travis leaving home was another change that Ed and Kathy now faced, and for Ed, it was especially difficult.

Ed was an early riser. He often would be up before sunrise and out the door to go to the gym or take a walk before work. That had always been his quiet time to pray and be with the Lord. Before the accident, Ed's life was great. He continually praised God for all the blessings in his life. The Simpsons were not extraordinarily wealthy people, but they were comfortable. God had blessed them with all that they needed. The children were everything to Ed. He lived for them and up until now neither of the kids had ever had a serious health problem. But now that Travis had been injured, all that changed. Ed was finding it difficult to be thankful. He was not able to pray as before. Being a father, Ed wanted to fix the situation, to make things better for Travis and the rest of the family. He wanted his son to be well again, to see his wife happy and smiling. Ed was upset with God. He felt abandoned and confused. He still believed in God. He knew that things like this happened, but Ed could not reconcile a loving God allowing such a tragic thing to happen to his child. Ed prayed. He read the scriptures. He attended church just as before. Yet no matter how hard Ed tried to accept the situation, the pain remained.

Those early morning walks and workouts became less frequent, and as the day for Travis to go away to school approached, Ed and Kathy were feeling lost and helpless. Their world was spinning out of control, and there was no way to slow it down. So Ed made a call to his pastor and went over to talk about the situation.

"Mr. McKinnon, Kathy and me, we are having a tough time right now. With Travis' injury and now him about to go away to school all of a sudden everything is so different at home. Kathy and I don't know how to make the situation any better. It is really testing our faith."

"Ed we don't understand all there is to know about God and His plan. But God loves you. He is standing right here with you. You and Kathy just need to hang on. Take it one day at a time. Just remember this is tough on both of you. I know you both want to make this better for Travis, and that things could just go back to the way they were before the accident. But that is not the reality of the situation. It's just something that only time will heal."

"I just don't understand," Ed said. "I am so confused by what has happened, I don't understand why there is so much pain and suffering in the world? How something like this could happen to our family? I know I shouldn't feel this way, but I am mad at God right now. I know it's wrong, but I can't help it. This thing has broken all of our hearts, and as a man and a father, I am mad about it."

"Ed, God never promises us that things will always be good. But God does promise us that He will stand with us in our trials. He is right there with you now. He is with Travis, Kathy, and Sarah. God loves you Ed, and He always will. There are some things about God and faith that we as humans cannot understand. But God is love, try and focus on that. Ed, try and focus on the truths, the foundations of your faith. God loves you and He is with you in this. Do not doubt God's love for you. You just hang in there friend. You take it one day at a time."

Mr. McKinnon had been like a father to Ed, talking with him helped Ed relax. It is a wonderful thing to have Christian people in your life that care about you. Over the next few weeks Ed and Mr. McKinnon would meet many times to talk about Ed's concerns for Travis and the family. Mr. McKinnon would always remind Ed that God loved him, and that God was ever present with the family during this trial. Mr. McKinnon would encourage Ed over and over to hang in there, and take it one day at a time.

So that's what Ed did. He got up every day and did the best he could for Travis and his family. Ed leaned on his faith, one day at a time. The family hung in there, and before you know it, it was time for Travis to go to school.

It is a day that every parent knows is coming, but nothing can prepare you for it, the day you take your child away to college. You pack your most cherished possession in the car, with all his clothes, TV, CD player and lots of money, and you go along as he leaves home to start a new life on his own. As Kathy and Ed made the trip to Raleigh, and the athletic dorm at State, they were doing all they could to be excited for Travis. But the trip was much different than they had anticipated it would be a few weeks ago, before the accident. If Travis had not injured his hand and had decided to play college football, he would have already been at State at summer football practice. They would have made this trip six weeks earlier with the rest of the incoming freshmen football players. The family would have been looking forward to the Wolfpack's home opener the following Saturday night against conference rival Virginia Tech. But instead, Travis and his parents would be going today to get him settled in along with all of the other "non-athletes." The idea of Travis no longer being an athlete was weighing heavily upon them all. When they arrived at the dormitory they all took Travis' clothes, and things to his room where they were met by Travis' roommate; Russell Rawlings.

"Well it's about time you got here, I thought I was going to have to go down to Wilson and get you myself."

Russell was a second-year student from Charleston, South Carolina. He was a red-shirt freshman quarterback. Russell was competing for the starting quarterback job at State that fall. Travis had met Russell a few times on recruiting trips to State, so the boys were very comfortable with one another.

"I know," Travis said. "I didn't think Mom would ever quit packing my suitcases, I think she washed everything I've worn since I was twelve."

"Now Mrs. Simpson," Russell said. "We only have space for so much stuff in this room. You don't want me and Travis to have to go stay in the girls' dorm do you?"

"Well I know that's what I would want to do if I were your age," Ed said, "but don't tell Kathy that or we'll never get out of here."

"Ed you better quit talking like that," Kathy replied. "Those young girls aren't interested in an 'old dog' like you, besides you've got a daughter of your own in a girls' dorm, remember?"

From there the boys, Ed and Kathy quickly got Travis situated. They then went and took a walk around campus. Afterward they drove over to the Char-Grill on Hillsborough Street and got a hamburger steak sandwich. Then they went back to the dorm and said their goodbyes. Kathy and Ed then made the lonely walk out to the parking lot to go home. Once they got back to the car and left the parking lot, Kathy began to quietly sob as she looked out the passenger window. Neither of them said a word the whole way home. There just wasn't anything to say. Their baby was gone.

Later that evening Ed went outside and sat out on the back porch. He was thinking back to when Travis was a little boy. He remembered the day he and Kathy took Travis to kindergarten at Wells School. Ed thought back to the days when he coached Travis' flag football team and they would play games on the fields behind the Wilson Recreation Department. He remembered taking Travis to Sunday school at First Presbyterian Church. Watching Travis play little league baseball, basketball, and soccer and traveling out of town to junior tennis tournaments. All those events that monopolize your schedule when your children are growing up. Sometimes they can be overwhelming when your kids are small. But when you take them off to college, you realize how much you miss those days. You just can't appreciate how important they are until they are gone.

While Ed was sitting on the porch, he looked inside the house and saw Wesley looking out the window. Wesley knew something was different. Whenever Travis was gone Wesley would always go to Ed. Ed went inside and looked down at Wesley.

"Well, I guess it's just you and me now buddy."

Ed put Wesley's leash on him, and the two of them went out into the backyard. They walked over to the hammock and Ed picked up Wesley. They got in the hammock together and laid down, looking up at the sky. It was a cool afternoon for late August. The sky was clear and the sun was setting in the west toward Raleigh. As Ed looked in that direction his mind was on his son. He wondered how Travis would adjust to going away to school after all that had happened. As Ed and Wesley lay there swaying gently back and forth in the hammock, the sky was beginning to turn from light blue to dark blue. The sun was dropping below the horizon in the distance. As the sky was darkening, Ed and Wesley could see the stars as they began to appear one by one in the Carolina sky. Then the sky turned black. Suddenly all the stars were visible, the eventful day was over. Wesley began to softly whine as he gently pawed Ed, he wanted to be rubbed. Wesley began to realize his best friend was gone. Ed put his hand on Wesley.

"I miss him too Wesley, I miss him too."

ALL ALONE

Moving days on a college campus are hectic. There are freshmen arriving on campus for the first time, trying to find their way to the cafeteria and the local nightspots. There are upperclassmen returning for their sophomore, junior and senior years. New people to meet, places to go, and things to do. For Travis it was a day he had looked forward to for a long time. He had long imagined what his first day at college would be like. That is the day every rising high school senior thinks about, thoughts about all the guys on the football and baseball teams. What would it be like to catch a pass over the middle and get tackled by a 245-pound linebacker? What would it be like to take the field with the Wolfpack opening night in Carter-Finley Stadium? To catch a pass and then race down the sideline for a touchdown, what would it be like to play shortstop for the Pack in his first Carolina-State game, or to play in his first ACC baseball tournament? What would it be like to go downtown with the players to meet all the college girls? There would be so many of them, and so little of him to go around. There were so many things that Travis had looked forward to, and now that his first day at college was here, everything was different.

Russell Rawlings was a very bright kid. He was a communications and journalism major. He wanted to go into sports broadcasting once his playing days were over. Russell had been a high school All-American quarterback. He was the future at quarterback for State. Russell was well aware of Travis' injury. The two boys had communicated many times by cell phone and text messages since the accident. Russell had attended summer school at State over the summer and he and a few of the other football players who were also on campus were there at the state championship game at Doak Stadium the day Travis was injured. Before the accident it had already been determined that Russell and Travis would be roommates, so Russell and Travis had been communicating over the previous weeks, getting acquainted. Russell had stayed in close contact with Travis over the summer. Russell knew Travis had been feeling isolated since the accident, so Russell was determined to get Travis involved in some campus activities.

"Travis, lets go over to Sorority Row and see if any of those girls need some help moving their clothes in their rooms."

"Russell, you know I am not much help moving things right now. I only have one good hand."

"That's alright Travis, I'll use you as bait."

"What do you mean, you will use me as bait?" Travis asked.

"We do it all the time. When one of the guys gets hurt in practice or in a game, we all use them as bait. Girls love a guy that's been injured. They want to comfort him. You know, an injury is a 'chick magnet.' Once those girls see you've been hurt, they'll be all over you, then we can meet them all. I'll do all the heavy lifting, you just carry some coat hangers, pillows, stuff like that. That injured hand is the ticket, I'm telling ya."

"Well, I'm glad it's good for something, let's go."

The boys took off by foot walking toward the girls' dorms and sorority houses. By the time they got there the place was crawling with coeds. Travis had never seen so many beautiful girls in one spot.

"I told you Travis, this is heaven."

Travis had always had plenty of girlfriends, the star athletes normally do. But since the accident Travis had not been comfortable around girls. He really had not been comfortable anywhere. But Russell, a seasoned veteran, knew that nothing cheers up a fella's spirits the way pretty girls can, so he quickly began the introductions.

"Hello, I'm Russell Rawlings, this is Travis Simpson. We thought we would stop by and see if any of you ladies needed some help getting your things up to your rooms?"

Within seconds the boys were busy meeting girls, moving armfuls of blue jeans and dresses. Russell and Travis were making plans, lots of plans.

Russell would say, "Travis' hand is a little beat up right now. He injured it playing baseball this summer".

With that the boys received a chorus of "oohs" and "aahs." All the coeds wanted to know, "Well how did that happen, tell me all about it?"

It worked like a charm just like Russell said it would. Soon Travis was surrounded on the sofa in the Delta Zeta house by at least a dozen sorority girls all trying to make an impression on this "wounded superstar." Russell meanwhile was over on the other side of the room talking with a beautiful blonde sophomore education major from Charlotte. He was feeling pretty good about his match-making skills. Russell knew that Travis needed a friend. He was determined to be there for Travis. Russell remembered back to the day Travis had been hit by the pitch. He imagined what he would have felt like should he himself be blindsided by a blitzing linebacker and have his career cut short by an unexpected injury. Over the next few days Russell spent every extra moment he had with Travis. They ate together. They hung out in the dorm room and at the fraternity and sorority parties. Russell did all he could to keep Travis involved, to keep him busy. Russell could sense a deep sadness in Travis. Even in a crowded room, Travis tried to maintain his distance. Only when the two boys were alone, would Travis later let his guard down and express his confusion about what happened, and what lay ahead for him.

Often times at night Travis would leave the room and go for a walk. He needed to be alone and try to make some sense of it all. Most nights he would put on his State baseball cap and walk around campus. He would walk past Doak Stadium, the baseball field where in a single pitch everything changed. He would make his way past the classroom buildings and student center over to the bleachers next to the tennis courts on the west side of campus. The bleachers at the tennis center were a quiet place where he could sit and be alone. There was no one around this time of night. There he could take off his cap in private. Oftentimes he would lean forward with his elbows on his knees, hold his hands together, bow his head and pray. He would pray for peace. Pray that he would be able to accept his injury. Pray that he would learn to live with the sadness he was feeling. He tried to remind himself that God was in control. That somehow God would work this for good, even though for now Travis could find no good in the pain he was feeling. Then when he would finish praying he would put his baseball cap back on. He would pull the brim down over his eyes. Alone in the darkness, the once shinning star would let his emotions flow. The tears of an injured and a confused young man in the quiet of those lonely tennis bleachers. Travis poured out his soul to the God he loved, but for now, he could not find.

HOME OPENER

The noise inside the tunnel was deafening as the team huddled together under the bleachers beneath the south end zone. Travis was in the back of the tunnel. He could see a glimpse of the field above the players' helmets. Then the fireworks went off and the team ran through the end zone toward the N.C. State sideline. The band played the Wolfpack fight song. The atmosphere was electric. The 9th ranked Virginia Tech Hokies were the opponent for the Wolfpack home opener. Travis was wearing the number 5 jersey he had been assigned before the injury. The N.C. State athletic department had made every effort to keep Travis involved in the football program. The coaches knew Travis would never play football again, but they were committed to his total recovery, so they did all they could to support Travis and his family. Travis ran to the sideline with the rest of the State offensive unit. Russell was in a heated competition for the starting quarterback position. The offensive coordinator for State was David Clark. Coach Clark was also originally from Wilson. Coach Clark had played for the Wolfpack in the early 70's. Coach Clark also was involved as a leader of the Christian Athletes Monday Night Bible Study at State. He had been very involved when Travis was being recruited to play wide receiver. Dr. Stephanie Clauson was also on the sidelines that night; and she approached Travis before the kickoff.

"Travis, how is your hand coming along?"

"It's getting better".

"I want to see you next week so I can set up a conditioning program for you, and give you some additional exercises to strengthen your hand. Will Monday at 3:30 work for you?"

"Yes," Travis said. "That will be fine. Do you want me to meet you at the training center?"

"Yes, I'll see you then. Let me go now so I can get my trainers set up before kickoff. It's good to see you, take care."

"I will, thanks."

Truth be known, Travis really did not want to be on the sidelines that night. He was not looking forward to being there knowing that he would never be able to suit up and play again. But the coaches, the players, and especially Russell, Coach Clark and Stephanie had been so good to him he found that he still felt a part of the team even though he knew he would never get to play. He especially wanted to see Russell do well. Travis did not have a brother, and he and Russell had only lived together for a week, but there was a closeness between the two boys. Maybe it was their love of sports? Maybe it was their shared belief in Christ? But somehow Travis knew God had placed him in that room with Russell. So tonight, Travis decided no matter what he was feeling, he was going to be on the sidelines to support his teammates and his roommate Russell.

State won the coin toss and deferred to the second half. Virginia Tech took the ball first as State kicked off to start the game. The coaches had already told Russell before the game that both the quarterbacks would play. Russell knew his performance tonight would go a long way toward determining who would win the number one quarterback spot. The first half was a defensive struggle. Neither team could get much going offensively, as Virginia Tech took a 10-7 lead into the locker room at halftime. During halftime Coach Clark came over to Russell.

"Russell, you are starting the second half. Go out there and believe in yourself. Trust your instincts. I have confidence in you, so believe you can do it!"

State received the second half kickoff and returned the ball up the State sideline until the ball carrier took a vicious hit at the 50-yard line right in front of the Wolfpack bench. Russell then led the offensive unit onto the field and immediately moved the Wolfpack to the end zone giving State a 14-10 lead. In the second half both teams' offenses got on track. Russell was 7 of 9 passing for 110 yards and one touchdown at the end of the third quarter with State leading, 21-17. Then later in the fourth quarter with 5:24 to play, Tech scored on a 5 yard run to regain the lead, 24-21.

After the Tech kickoff Russell led the Wolfpack back onto the field with the ball on the State 24-yard line. State proceeded to pick up four first downs that gave the Pack a first and ten on the Tech 27-yard line. Following a running play, State had a second and eight on the Tech 25, with 1:47 to play. Russell broke the team from the huddle. The Pack had an option play called toward the short side of the field. When Russell got to the line of scrimmage he could see that Tech was in a run defense. He looked at the Tech secondary and saw that All-American defense back James Branch was in one-on-one coverage with State's All-Conference wide receiver, Joe Moore split out to his right. Russell checked off at the line and changed the play to a fade route to Moore. Russell dropped back into a shotgun formation, and State snapped the ball. Moore raced down the right sideline, he and Branch stride for stride. Russell lofted a perfectly thrown pass just inside the back pylon. Both players leaped for the ball, the ball was tipped up in the air before finally being hauled in by the Tech defensive back. From there Virginia Tech took possession on the Tech 20-yard line and ran out the clock. When Russell came toward the sideline he was visibly dejected. The first person to meet Russell was Coach Clark.

"Russell, I want you to know I am proud of the way you played tonight. You made the right decision on that fade route. Joe is our best receiver, you made a good throw, the ball just did not bounce our way tonight. You made the right call. To win at this level you have got to take chances. I want you always to play to win, just like you did tonight."

Travis was very impressed by the way Coach Clark handled the situation. Travis had never stood on the sidelines and watched the other kids play. He had always been the one on the field doing the playing, while others watched him. He found that being on the sidelines gave him a different perspective of the coaches, the trainers, the managers, and the players on the sidelines cheering on their teammates. Not everyone played, but they all contributed to the success of the team. It gave Travis a new insight into what being a part of a team was really all about.

After the game Russell and Travis made their way back to the room around midnight. The boys sat around for a while, there wasn't much conversation, Travis got up and put on his baseball cap and looked over at Russell,

"Hey man, lets go for a walk."

"I don't think so Travis, I'm kind'a beat."

"Look Russell, I could really use some company tonight."

Russell then said, "Okay."

The two boys headed outside. Travis could see Russell was down, he had learned a lot about being down himself. Travis took Russell on his nightly trek around the campus until the boys reached the bleachers outside the tennis center. By then Russell's spirits were beginning to come back. They talked about the game. They talked about classes. They talked about girls. Then Russell asked Travis a question.

"Travis, I know you believe in God. You know I do too. I have seen you read your Bible, and I have watched you pray. I know all things happen for a reason, but do you believe God is in control of all things? Even bad things?"

"Yes Russell, I do believe God is in control of all things. Even the bad things like the interception tonight, or what has happened to me. I still have to believe God is in control."

" I don't know what it is like for you," Russell said, "because I have never walked in your shoes. But I want you to know I admire the way you have maintained your faith even through your injury."

"Russell, I have my doubts. I am confused and hurt by what has happened. I still can't believe four broken fingers on one hand could change so many things in my life. But I am trying to trust in God, the way I did before the accident. What else can I do?"

With that being said the boys began to ponder the questions teenagers face. They were both finding their way. They were both following Jesus, though they did not know where He was leading them. So the two of them sat quietly together, each one searching for faith, the strength and courage, that comes from hope.

NIGHT CLASS

"Yes, may I help you?"

"Yes Ma'am. I am Travis Simpson. I have an appointment to see Dr. Clauson today at 3:30."

"Alright Travis, have a seat and I'll let Dr. Clauson know that you are here."

After a few minutes Stephanie came out into the lobby.

"Hello Travis, come on in. Tell me, how is your hand?"

"Well, it's getting better. The clay has really helped loosen my fingers, but they are still sensitive. My hand overall is still pretty stiff."

"Tell me Travis, what have you been making with the clay?"

"Well mostly I have just squeezed it into balls, no particular shapes or figures. I have just mashed the clay in between my hands. Honestly, I have never thought of making anything. I have just used the clay to exercise my hand."

"Travis, one reason I wanted you to use the clay was that making things with clay can be very therapeutic for your mind as well as your hand. Do you have any ideas about something you would like to mold? Something you would like to make?"

"No, I never thought of myself as a potter," he chuckled. "What would you suggest?"

"Well that's up to you. Just keep working with the clay some everyday. Then think of something that is important to you. You'll come up with something."

Travis: "Sure, I'll try it."

"Also I want to add another exercise," Stephanie said. "I want you to take this tennis ball and squeeze it."

So Travis took the tennis ball and squeezed it with his left hand.

"Man that hurts. Wow! I had no idea my hand was that weak."

"Its okay, I know it's sore, so don't expect too much of yourself. Just gently squeeze the tennis ball. Then drop it and catch it with your fingers, three times, go ahead and try it."

Travis dropped the ball lightly, then he caught it.

"That's not so bad."

"Okay, let's toss it in the air, then catch it."

Travis again did what Stephanie asked.

"Okay, I can do that alright, but, that squeezing, man it's a killer."

Stephanie: "I know squeezing something with your fingers is the hardest part, but just start out slow and it will get better. You're doing great.

You should be very proud of how far you have come."

"Thank you Stephanie."

"Travis, how are you feeling about all that has happened? I was glad to see you at the game Saturday night. I'm sure this injury has been a dramatic change for you. I want you to know I am interested in helping you anyway I can."

"I wish things were different, no denying that, but I can't do anything about it. I feel like people are staring at me. I'm not really comfortable back home. I don't like people feeling sorry for me. Here at school I can blend in with the crowd so I am less self-conscious. My hand looks more normal now, almost like it did before the accident. But it feels so different. I am not comfortable touching someone with it. It feels strange. I am very self-conscious about it."

"Travis, those feelings are very normal. I know that doesn't make it any better, but things will get better with time. You need to trust me on that."

"I know things will get better," Travis said. "I'm just trying to hang in there as best I can."

"Travis, are you coming with Russell to the Bible study tonight?"

"Yes, Russell and I will be there."

"Good, that is a great program. Coach Clark is a wonderful study leader. Every year we take one of the four gospels and do a yearlong study on the life of Jesus. This year we are studying the book of Luke. Have you ever been involved in a Bible study before?"

"No, I have gone to church all my life, Sunday school since I was a little boy, but I have never been involved in a group study. I think with all that has happened, it will be very helpful for me right now."

"Good, I know you will enjoy the class. I am glad to hear you will be coming. Let's get together again in three weeks to see how your therapy is going, and I will see you at Bible study tonight."

"Thanks Stephanie, thanks for listening."

"You are welcome; my door is always open if you need to talk."

Travis left Stephanie's office and stopped by the library to study. Then he made his way back to the dorm room. Russell had already gotten back from football practice so the boys took their Bibles and went by the cafeteria to eat. When they got to Bible study, Coach Clark met them at the door.

"Hello guys, I'm glad you could be here tonight, come on in and take a seat."

Travis was surprised by the number of kids in the group, by the time they were seated there were over 150 students there already.

"Russell, I can't believe how many people are here."

"This Bible study is great Travis, we have this many every Monday night."

Coach Clark then made his way to the front of the room and opened the program.

"Ladies and gentlemen, please rise and let us pray, then remain standing for the Pledge of Allegiance."

"Father God, giver of all things, we come to you tonight to praise you for your goodness, the life you have given us to live. Lord, I thank you for all those young people who are here tonight. May you bless them as they seek to grow their knowledge of love for you and your son Jesus Christ, Amen.

"Class please repeat after me, I pledge allegiance to the flag of the United States of America, and to the Republic for which it stands, one nation, under God, indivisible, with liberty and justice for all. Please be seated."

After the Pledge of Allegiance Coach Clark began to explain the message of the gospel. He explained how the Bible is one story, that the 66 books of the Bible explain God's creation of man, and the world. That the Bible explains the relationship between God and man, that as people, we will never completely understand the complexity of God and the world in which we now live. But God came to earth in the form of a man, Jesus Christ. Jesus came to teach us all about who God is, and to offer us salvation by Grace, through His death on the cross, and His resurrection. Coach Clark explained that this year they would be studying the gospel of Luke. That every four years they rotated through the four gospels, they would also be studying sections of the other books of the Bible that identified Jesus as the Messiah.

As Coach Clark was speaking, Travis could sense a desire growing within him to learn more about Jesus. He had been a Christian all his life, but something in his spiritual life now was different. Since the accident Travis had been searching for answers to questions he never had before. Questions about pain and suffering, Travis was aware that there had always been people who found themselves in difficult and confusing circumstances. But now that he himself had experienced this painful and unexpected change, he felt the need to deepen his faith. After all, at this point, what else did he have to lean on? He looked around the room and saw the other kids carefully listening to the words Coach Clark was saying. Travis now began to understand the quiet confidence Coach Clark displayed. He could now see that Coach Clark had himself placed his trust in Jesus. It was apparent by the words he spoke, and also in the way he lived his life.

When the boys got back to the dorm that night, Russell began his homework, and Travis put on his baseball cap, picked up his tennis ball and went for a walk. Eventually he made his way around to the bleachers overlooking the tennis courts. The sky was clear, all the stars were out, the moon was full, there was a cool crispness in the air. That night as Travis sat alone on the bleachers, he could sense something was different, as he gently squeezed the tennis ball, he began to feel that things in his life were changing, God had His hand firmly on Travis Simpson, and Travis' lessons were just beginning.

LORD IF YOU ARE WILLING

The weeks quickly passed for Travis and Russell. Saturday would mark the eighth week of the college football season. After the loss in the opener to Virginia Tech, State had won five of the next six games. This week the Wolfpack would be making the 25-mile trip to Chapel Hill to play the Tar Heels. Carolina was also 5-2, and both teams were ranked in the top twenty. Carolina was ranked 15th, State was 19th. Russell had continued to play well, so well in fact, that he had been listed as the starter for this week's Carolina-State game.

Meanwhile, Travis had been diligent with his exercises. Dr. Clauson had designed a total fitness program for Travis. She wanted to make sure Travis continued to exercise just as he had before the accident. Dr. Clauson knew that it was important for Travis to stay active physically. She knew that Travis needed a sense of normalcy in his life right now, so she kept him busy with a very vigorous fitness program.

Travis also continued to attend Bible study. As the group met on Monday night, Coach Clark was leading the students through the fourth chapter of the Gospel of Luke, the assignment for the week was The Temptation of Jesus. As the weeks had passed Travis found himself more and more focused on the scriptures and the lectures of Coach Clark. After class Russell and Travis often discussed the lessons and the lectures, this week's lesson was especially meaningful to Travis, as he was going through a period of testing himself.

When the lecture began Coach Clark explained Satan's tempting of Jesus. He pointed out that Jesus' temptation came immediately following His baptism. Coach Clark illustrated the point that our times of testing often come after periods of great success. That Satan oftentimes attacks us the most when we are experiencing success. For one thing, Satan views the believer's success as a threat. Also, that when we are experiencing success we may feel that we have less of a need for God, that we can do things on our own. That is when we are most vulnerable to stray away from our faith. Coach Clark explained that Jesus had fasted for forty days. That Jesus had a very real need for food. Satan first tempted Jesus to trust in Satan's provision of food, instead of waiting on God to supply Jesus' needs. Secondly, Satan tested Jesus with worldly possessions and fame. Thirdly, Satan tempted Jesus to prove He was the Son of God. He questioned Jesus' belief in Himself, and who He really was, and who God was to Him. Coach Clark explained that Jesus triumphed in this testing by quoting the scriptures. Just like when we face Satan's attack today, our dedication to study, and our knowledge of the Bible, will take us through our seasons of testing that all of us will have to face.

After the lecture was over Coach Clark opened the floor, and the students discussed the text. This Monday Travis stood up and asked a question.

"Coach Clark, why would the Holy Spirit lead Jesus into the desert to be tempted by Satan?"

Coach Clark replied, "Jesus came to earth to demonstrate God's love. Jesus faced all the same struggles we face today. Jesus was tested so that He would know what it is to be tested. Jesus understands our sufferings because He has been tested too. That makes Jesus worthy to be our only judge, because He alone has overcome the world. Jesus stands at the right hand of God to atone for our sins. For that, we owe Jesus our lives."

Then Travis asked another question. "Coach Clark, I know that if God is willing He can fix all things. Isn't that true?"

"Yes Travis, that is true."

"Well Coach Clark, if God loved Jesus, why was Jesus forced to suffer temptation, and Coach Clark, if God loves us, why do people have to suffer, why do people have to be injured and hurt, and God does not heal them?"

At that point the room became very quiet. Everyone knew what had happened to Travis. It was a very heartfelt and difficult question. Coach Clark himself was moved by what Travis had asked. He prayed to God for the words to respond. Coach Clark then said,

"Travis, there are some things that happen in life that none of us can understand. Why some people get sick and recover, while others do not. Why one person's dreams succeed, while other people try just as hard, and they fail. While we are on this earth we only see a small part of God's plan, but God does have a plan for our lives. Even when we are confused and hurt by the things that are happening to us and around us. We must remember Romans 8:28,

'*That in everything God works for the good of those who love Him. They are the people He called, because that was His plan.*'

Remember God loves us Travis, He is working in all our lives, even though at times we don't see all of His plan."

It was an emotional moment as Travis sat down, and Russell was doing all he could to hold back his tears.

That night as the boys walked back to the athletic dorm Russell told Travis,

"Travis I can't imagine the courage it took for you to ask that question tonight. You will never know how much I admire what you are doing."

"What do you mean?"

"Travis, a lot of people would have turned away from their faith if they were faced with what has happened to you."

"I may appear to have great faith, but really Russell I am struggling every day with what has happened. I feel further than ever from God. I am just trying to make some sense of it all just like everybody else."

The boys quietly walked the rest of the way back to the dorm. Once they got back, Travis picked up his tennis ball, put on his baseball cap and headed out the door.

"Travis, do you need me to go with you tonight?"

"No thank you Russell, I need to be alone for awhile if that's okay."

Russell: "No, that's fine."

Then, as Travis was walking out the door, Russell said, "Travis, I'll have my cell phone on if you need me."

"Thanks Russell, for everything."

Travis then left the room, he began his walk around campus. As he walked alone in the darkness, he passed by boys and girls holding hands, kids in groups talking all over campus. There was an intramural flag football game being played on one of the lighted practice fields, people busily going about enjoying the crisp fall evening. Eventually, Travis made his way to the tennis bleachers. He looked over towards the stadium lights and the scoreboard at Doak Stadium. State's baseball team was playing an intra-squad scrimmage game. He could see the score was 5-2 in the eighth inning. Travis could hear the crowd noise and the crack of the bat as he sat there, wondering how did everything he loved go away so fast. He bowed his head and he prayed,

"Lord, I know that all things are under your control. Lord, I know I will never be able to play ball again, but please Lord, will you take away this doubt and pain that is in my heart? Please Lord, I beg you Lord; if you are willing; please take this pain away."

Then Travis put his hat back on, he pulled the brim down over his eyes to hide the tears. He gently squeezed the tennis ball in his left hand, and prayed for the strength to face what lay ahead.

STATE-CAROLINA

It was a cool crisp Saturday morning, not a cloud in the sky. Travis and Russell met with the rest of the Wolfpack players at the Football Center at Carter-Finley Stadium. There would be a team meeting at 7:30, then breakfast at 8:00. Then Russell and Travis along with the rest of the team would board the charter bus at 8:30 and make the thirty minute trip to Chapel Hill. By 10:00 a.m. the team was dressed in jerseys and pants taking a walkthrough of the field. Kenan Stadium is one of the most scenic settings in all of college football. The stadium sits in the middle of the University of North Carolina campus and it is surrounded by a backdrop of tall pine trees. Today, the second Saturday in October, the temperature was expected to be 60 degrees. Kickoff of the nationally televised game was set for noon. As Travis and Russell walked the field together, Russell was anxious about his opportunity to make his first collegiate start.

"Travis, I can't wait to get going today."

"I know you are excited, you will do great today Russell. I can feel it."

By 10:45 the team was dressed out in full pads and helmets, stretching and warming up. Russell and the other quarterbacks and receivers were running through passing drills, while Coach Clark looked on. Travis walked along side Coach Clark before games, assisting Coach Clark with whatever he needed. The two of them had known each other for a long time. Now that Travis was at State he was beginning to see the character and professionalism that made Coach Clark such a great offensive coordinator. After the game Travis would be leaving with his parents to go spend the rest of the weekend with his family. It would be the first time Travis had been to Wilson since he left for school.

"Travis is your Grandmother Prince coming to the game today?"

"Yes sir."

"Be sure and tell her I said hello. You know I ate a lot of food in her house when your parents and I were your age."

"She is bringing some food up here today. She is supposed to have some fudge for me."

"Well let's go out there today and give them all something to cheer about."

With that Coach Clark called the offensive unit together for some last minute review of the game plan. Then the team huddled outside the stadium field house, and at 11:40 the Wolfpack took the field to a chorus of "boos" from the sixty thousand Tar Heel fans. Coach Clark met with

Russell on the sidelines before the coin toss.

"Russell this is your game today. You are my starter. I have confidence in you, believe in yourself, and take your chances where you see them, remember, play to win."

Carolina won the toss, and they deferred to the second half. State took the opening kickoff and returned the ball to the State 24-yard line. Travis patted Russell on the helmet.

"You can do it Russell, have a great game."

After two successful running plays State had a third down and one at the State 33-yard line. The Wolfpack had called a running play off right tackle when they came to the line of scrimmage. Russell could see that Carolina was in a run defense. The Tar Heels were in man coverage, and the State wide receiver Joe Moore was one-on-one with the Carolina defensive back to Russell's left, right in front of the State bench. Russell changed the play at the line. The ball was snapped; Russell faked a handoff to the State running back then he dropped back to pass. Moore was running a go route down the left sideline; he had a step and a half on the Tar Heel defensive back. Russell planted his feet, pumped once to his right to draw the safety away from Moore. Then Russell quickly turned to his left and lofted a perfect spiral down the left sideline. Moore raced by the State players and coaches, then he caught the pass, and turned on the afterburners on his way to the end zone, 7-0 State. When Russell came to the sideline, Coach Clark put his arm around Russell and said:

"That's it Russell, great decision, keep it up, play to win."

From that point on the Wolfpack never looked back. Russell lit the Tar Heels up for 329 yards passing. He was 19 of 26 with three touchdowns as State beat Carolina, 34-21. After the game Travis met with his family outside the locker room.

"Hey what did ya'll think of Russell today?" Travis asked.

"Russell played great," Ed replied. "The whole team did."

Kathy then held out her arms and said, "You come here boy and hug your Momma."

With that there were rounds of hugs and kisses as the family went back to the parking lot to tailgate after the game. There they had Parkers barbecue, fried chicken, and fudge. Grandma Prince smiled at Travis and held out a plate.

"Travis, I made you some fudge."

Travis grabbed a couple of pieces and replied, "Thank you Grandma. I love this fudge, I think this fudge will cure about anything that "ails ya'.""

Grandma Prince then said, "You know Travis, when Ed would come over to see your momma, he always wanted some fudge."

"I know Momma, but Ed can't eat that fudge like he used to."

Ed: "I love that fudge!"

"I know you love it, but we've got to keep you around for awhile, you have to stay in some kind of shape."

With that said Ed ate two pieces of fudge. Sarah was also at the game and she brought one of her friends, Elizabeth, from Greenville. Sarah asked Travis, "Travis, how many girlfriends do you have now, ten, maybe twelve?"

"What do you mean by a girlfriend?"

Kathy: "You know what a girlfriend is Travis, how about it? Tell us, we want to know what you have been up to?"

"I have been out on a few dates."

Elizabeth then whispered to Sarah, "He is the most beautiful thing I have ever seen, those blue eyes look right through you!"

"Well what is a few," Sarah continued, "3, 10, 30?"

"Leave the boy alone," Ed said. "Sarah, how many dates have you had this semester?"

"40 maybe 50!"

They all had a big laugh and continued to eat and enjoy each other's company. They were a close family. They had been blessed. When they finished eating Kathy and the girls left in one car to go to Crabtree Mall and do some shopping on their way back to Wilson. Travis and Ed drove the truck back. On the way home father and son had some time to talk.

"Son it is good to see you. How is your hand?"

"It's getting better Dad."

"Well I really miss seeing you, I am glad you are going to be home tonight. Wesley and I have been lost since you have been gone."

"I am sorry I haven't been home Dad. It's been an adjustment going away for the first time. Since I hurt my hand it just seems a little easier to be around people who did not know me before the injury. In Wilson I feel like everyone feels sorry for me, like they are starring at me."

"Son, I know this has been hard on you. I wish there was something I could do to make it better for you. I just want you to know I am here for you if you want to talk. It's hard as a dad to sit back and watch your children grow up, I want you to feel like you have your privacy; but just remember I am here, if you need me."

"I know Dad, and I appreciate it, I really do. I am trying to find my way right now, I'll be okay."

The rest of the way home they talked about school, the new kids

Travis had met, Russell, some of the girls Travis had dated. They talked about the Monday Night Bible Study, Coach Clark and Dr. Stephanie Clauson. When they pulled in the driveway Wesley was looking out the window beside the front door. When Wesley saw Travis he leaped up on the side glass and started pawing at the door. When Travis opened the door Wesley was all over him.

"Wesley, how you doing buddy, how you doing! Come on, you want to go outside?"

Travis put Wesley's leash on him and they went out in the backyard. Ed grabbed two Pepsi's from the refrigerator and went out and sat down on the back porch. Ed thought back to the Christmas when he first bought Wesley for the kids. He thought about how good it was for Travis to be home. That night Ed, Travis and Wesley cooked steaks on the grill. They talked about all sorts of things. The girls were shopping, so the boys had the house to themselves until all the malls closed. The three of them stayed out on the porch late into the night. Ed slipped Wesley at little steak. It was a boys' night out. The Wolfpack had beaten Carolina, Travis was home, it just doesn't get any better than that.

POSSIBILITIES

"Hurry up Ed! We are going to be late for church."

"Alright Kathy, I'm coming."

 Ed then said, "Travis, are you ready Son?"

"Yeah Dad, I'll be right there."

"Alright you guys," Kathy continued, "it is 10:43 and we are going to be late, you two need to get going!"

"Kathy," Ed said, "It is 10:35, you need to quit telling stories about the time to scare Travis, the boy is 19-years-old, he knows what time it is."

Kathy then answered back, "Ed, it's you I'm talking to. You are the one who is always late."

"Travis, have you and Russell got any extra space in your dorm room?"

Kathy: "You boys better just get in the car."

With that the Simpsons were in the car, and headed off for church. It was an overcast cool October morning, as the family drove past the park at the Wilson Recreation Department. They passed the miniature train track that Travis and his family had ridden on when he was a small boy. The gymnasium where he had played basketball, the tennis courts were he had taken tennis lessons, and played junior tennis tournaments. Since the accident, Travis spent a lot of time thinking back to when he was a child. He tried to remember as much as he could about the way things were before. So many things about his life had changed so quickly. He tried to focus on his memories, to give him some sort of footing on which to plant his feet. It seemed the foundations of his life had shifted with his injured hand. His injured fingers had broken all their hearts. Travis was determined not to let it break his spirit as well.

By the time the Simpsons entered the sanctuary it was 10:50. The service started at 11, so Ed was off the hook. Once they got inside the church Travis was greeted by family and friends. They asked him, "How do you like school? What is it like?"

There were so many people he had known for years who were glad to see him, and offer him words of encouragement. Travis was still uneasy about his circumstances; he was uncomfortable talking about what had happened. He knew he needed to try and put it all behind him, but the wound was still so fresh, he just had to take "baby steps," one step at a time. Ed knew what Travis was feeling after their talk the day before. Ed tried to stand back and let Travis work things out on his own. Ed wanted so much to help, but he knew Travis had to sort things out for himself.

As the service began, Travis saw Joan Gibbs, the church music director. Travis and Mrs. Gibbs were very close. He had been in the children's choir and the middle school and high school chorus. He looked at the podium where he had stood on Youth Sunday and had given his testimony with the other graduating seniors, the Sunday before the accident. Everything, everyone looked the same, but Travis felt so different. He was clinging to his faith, telling himself that God was in control. But everything in his life seemed out of control. Somewhere he hoped to find the answers. The answers to why this had happened to him? How was he going to ever get comfortable again? He was scared. Scared of what might happen next. Scared of what was happening inside him. He was concerned about the nagging questions that were turning his once bright future, into shades of gray.

Travis stared at the stained glass window at the peak of the church chancel. The bright colors of the glass formed the image of a lamb, surrounded by angels and the lion representing the tribe of Judah. He focused on the symbolism of Jesus, he thought about his own life, his desire to use his talents, his gifts to glorify God. Now that his talents were gone, he wondered how God could be glorified. He wondered how he could still be useful to God. Why would God allow such a thing to happen to his children? What good could come from what had happened?

When Reverend McKinnon began the sermon, he instructed the congregation to turn to the gospel of John, Chapter 9, verses, 1-5.

As he went along, he saw a man blind from birth. His disciples asked him, "Rabbi, who sinned, this man or his parents, that he was born blind?" "Neither this man nor his parents sinned," said Jesus, "but this happened so that the work of God might be displayed in his life. As long as it is day, we must do the work of him who sent me. Night is coming, when no one can work. While I am in the world, I am the light of the world."

John 9:1-5

From there Reverend McKinnon went on to say that God uses all things and all situations to work in our lives. That in all things, our joy and disappointments, our successes and our failures, God continually working through us will demonstrate His power and grace if we will trust Him, that when we are most vulnerable, God is there with us. That God wants us to place our hopes, our trust, in Him alone. When we have nowhere else to turn, God is there. Jesus' statement about the man being born blind so that God's healing power could be displayed in this man's healing, demonstrated how God is working in all situations, the good, and even those things that appear to be bad. That when we learn to place our trust in Jesus, He may open our eyes to opportunities we never dreamed possible, but before that can happen, we must place our hope in Him.

Travis listened intently to the sermon. He wanted to trust Jesus with his hopes, and also with his fears. He could not see the good in what was happening, but he had always believed in God. Travis was so confident in his beliefs before the accident. He knew that God was the same now as before. But their relationship had changed. Travis was mad with God about what had happened. The trust in their relationship was gone, and Travis did not know what to do to get it back.

After church Mrs. Gibbs came out into the congregation and hugged Travis.

"I miss you so much Travis. This is the first time since you were six-years old that you have not been with me at choir practice. I just can't believe you are all grown up."

"I know Mrs. Gibbs, I miss singing. I miss a lot of things."

Mrs. Gibbs then put her arm around Travis and she asked; "Tell me Travis, how are you? I think about you all the time."

"I'm doing okay. I have a lot to be thankful for, I just feel confused right now; I'm not sure how to react to all this, I worry about what comes next."

"Travis your faith is strong. You are a fine young man. Just trust in yourself, trust in God. Also please call or come by if you ever need to talk. I love you, you know that don't you?"

"Yes ma'am, I love you too."

After church the family went out to lunch. They spent the afternoon together, and they enjoyed the rest of the day. By late afternoon Travis left to drive back to school. When he got back to Raleigh, Travis went to his room and sat down at his desk. He began to mold the clay between his fingers. He thought about the sermon, that God is shaping our lives in all our circumstances. He was still hurt that God, who was in control of all things, could allow such a thing to happen to him. But he tried to focus on the idea that there was a purpose for what had happened. That God was going to use this for good. Travis began to imagine what that good might be. So he worked with the clay, then he squeezed and tossed his tennis ball. He imagined Jesus being there with him while he did his exercises, and tried to imagine the possibilities God had planned for him ahead.

CHRISTMAS BREAK

The weeks passed quickly as the Wolfpack football team made its way through to the end of football season. Russell continued to improve and the Pack finished the regular season 9-3, and accepted a bid to the Peach Bowl New Year's Eve in the Georgia Dome in Atlanta. Travis was finishing up his final exams before Christmas break. He had a good first semester academically with a 3.2 GPA. Travis and Russell continued to develop their friendship. They became closer as the weeks passed. Travis had an appointment with Dr. Clauson on the Monday before he left school for Christmas break. He met her at the weight room in the athletic department field house to discuss a conditioning program she had designed for him for the spring semester.

"Travis, how are you?"

"Good, things are coming along; I am looking forward to having some time off from school, spending time with my family for Christmas."

"So am I, I am leaving tomorrow for Canada to spend Christmas with my mother. This will be the second Christmas since my father died. His not being there is still very hard for my mother. We are all still adjusting."

"I know, I am still adjusting myself, some things I guess we never quite get over."

"That's right Travis; I know my life, and my mother's life will never be the same without my father being here. Life can still be good, but it is different, it will never be the same. Okay, enough about that, let's take a look at that hand, have you been doing your exercises?"

Stephanie began to pull and maneuver Travis' fingers as she tested his hand strength and flexibility.

"Yes," Travis replied. "I have been doing the exercises with the clay and the tennis ball. The soreness is improving, but it is a slow process. I feel like I have a long way to go."

"Have you made anything with the clay? Have you molded anything yet?"

"I have not made anything I would want to show off! I'm not very good at pottery, but I have an idea of something I would like to make."

"Well," Stephanie asked, "tell me; what is it?"

"I don't want to say, I would rather make it, then I will show it to you."

"That's fine, I look forward to seeing it when you are through." Stephanie continued, "Now, I want to talk with you about a training program I want you to begin next semester. I have a conditioning plan for you to do four days a week, running, weight lifting, swimming, and agility drills. I want you to be in the best shape of your life by the end of next semester. Improving your conditioning will help you physically and mentally. I have outlined the workout plan in this folder. Once you get back from Christmas break we will get started."

"That sounds good, I need some structure to keep me going. Before the injury, practice and playing games kept me in shape. Now that that is over, I need something to keep me on track."

"Travis, I have something for you before you go." She handed him a small gift box.

"Stephanie, I don't have anything for you, I was not expecting a gift."

"That's okay Travis; this is just something I wanted you to have, go ahead and open it."

Travis opened the box and there was a small tool about the length of a pencil with a wooden handle, one end had a small flat blade, like a knife, and the other had a small blade that hooked upward like a spoon. Travis looked at it, wondering.

"What is it Stephanie?"

"It's used to carve clay," Stephanie replied. "When you are molding clay you use this tool to carve away the excess clay. You use it to prune away the clay so the details of your object can be seen."

"Thank you Stephanie, I wish I had something for you."

"Don't worry about that, you just make me something."

"I don't know if I'll ever mold anything worth having, but I will try."

"Alright then, you have done very well with your recovery program so far. You go home and have a wonderful Christmas with your family."

"Thank you, you too Stephanie." With that Travis left the training center and headed to Wilson.

Over the next few days Travis visited with many of his friends from high school. The college kids were back in town having conversations about their first semesters. Travis enjoyed the reunions; he was beginning to feel more at ease. He still had his doubts, the why me? What now questions remained. However, he was adjusting to his situation. Christmas Eve he and his family went to a candlelight service at church, it was something the family had done since he was a child. Afterwards they went to his grandparents' house where the family exchanged gifts. Before the accident he would have received a new baseball glove, football cleats, maybe a new baseball bat or football. This year the gifts were all clothes, gift cards, and a pair of dress shoes. Like his life, the gifts were different. Instead of talking sports, the family conversations were on other topics.

Travis knew they were all trying to focus on other things for his sake. He appreciated that they were all trying to help. He could sense that they were all still concerned about him. Being with his family again over Christmas helped him to see that there were some things that had not changed. His family would be there for him no matter what happened. The Christmas service was the same. Wesley still followed him everywhere he went. He thought about all of the things that really mattered, the love of his parents and his sister Sarah. His friends he had grown up with, his belief in God. Things were different, but like he and Stephanie had discussed, life could still be good. Travis began to think about all the new relationships that were developing in his life, Russell, Coach Clark, Stephanie. He began to see the blessings these new people were to him. He was trying to focus on the good things that were ahead of him. He missed football and baseball. He was proud of what he had accomplished; he wanted to hold onto those good memories. Now the time was approaching when another door would open. Travis knew God was in control. He was learning to trust again.

December 27th Travis, Russell and the rest of the football team left Raleigh on a charter flight to Atlanta. When the team arrived at the hotel in Atlanta the hotel was filled with Wolfpack fans. The team went to banquets, they toured historic downtown Atlanta, it was a good trip. The Wolfpack was playing Auburn in the Peach Bowl. Both teams were 9-3, and ranked in the top 20. The day before the game Travis got a text message from John Hudson. John had been drafted by the Atlanta Braves as the 23rd pick in the prior year's major league draft, so John had decided to sign with the Braves after high school. He had been playing professional baseball in Florida. John was spending the holidays in Atlanta, so he met Travis and Russell at the hotel. John and Travis had spoken many times since the accident. John was one of the first people to visit Travis when he was in the hospital. John had gone through a difficult period himself, as he had felt responsible for what happened to Travis. John had trouble pitching batters inside after hitting Travis. It was still bothering him, but he and Travis were good friends. Talking to each other helped both boys recover.

"Big John, it's good to see you."

"It's good to see you too Travis."

"John, you remember Russell?"

"Yeah, hey Russell, man you guys are having a great season, congratulations."

"Thanks John, we're all really excited about playing Auburn tomorrow night."

"Well good luck, I'll be pulling for you guys."

"John," Travis asked, "are you renting out a skybox with all that money you got from the Braves?"

"Come on Travis, You know I'm just a poor country boy."

"Enough of that John," Russell said. "We know what kind of money those first round draft picks make. I hear you have more money than Travis has girlfriends!"

"I don't know Russell, that Travis is a 'chick magnet,' my little sisters followed him everywhere we went when we played travel ball together."

"That's not true John."

"It is true! Russell I have two sisters, 18 and 16. They never went to our high school games, but they always went to watch our travel games, it was 'Travis this, Travis that.' I bet it's the same way at State; isn't it Russell?"

"It's amazing, I don't know how he does it. The less attention he pays these girls, the more they want to go out with him. I'm telling you it's a gift."

"Stop it please! Russell you are the starting quarterback, John you were the number one draft pick of the Atlanta Braves. You guys aren't having any trouble finding a date. Me, I'm just a ball boy for the football team. You guys are superstars."

With that being said, John sort of hung his head, he still felt bad about what had happened.

"Travis," John continued, "I was talking with the chief scout for the Braves last week and he was asking about you. He told me that the San Diego Padres had you rated as the top high school player in the draft, and the Padres were going to take you as the fifth pick in the first round."

"That's just a rumor John, who knows what might have happened."

"Well, I know I'll never be able to tell you how sorry I am Travis, if it had not been for me…."

"John, stop right there, it was just a freak accident, its nobody's fault. It's just one of those things that happened; I don't want you worrying about it. I could have hit a line drive that could have injured you. It's not your fault."

Russell spoke up. "You know every time I drop back to pass, or take off to run, I could take a hit that could end my career, you just never know."

"Enough of this kind of talk, Russell lets go downtown and 'Big John' can buy us lunch with all that money he's got. Besides, think of all those Auburn girls that need a date for New Year's Eve."

With that the boys took off. They had a great rest of the week. The

Pack beat Auburn, 21-17. Travis and Russell headed back to Raleigh with the rest of the team. It was time for spring semester.

MAN, AM I TIRED

Travis walked slowly up the steps, he opened the door to the dorm room, walked in soaking wet with sweat, sat down on the bed and leaned back against the wall.

"Man, what happened to you?" Russell asked.

"Russell, I have never been this tired in my life."

"What have you been doing?"

"Stephanie Clauson made this conditioning program for me; I'm telling you Russell it's a killer, but that's not the worst part."

"Travis, you look like you are dying, how could it be worse?"

"Stephanie did it with me, and she didn't even look tired, I mean she wasn't even breathing hard."

Russell laughed, "Travis you let a girl take you down like that, how hard could it be? What did she make you do?"

"She made me do all these volleyball exercises."

"Volleyball! Come on Travis, girls play volleyball."

"Russell, Stephanie is not a normal girl. She played professional beach volleyball. She had me jumping barefoot in a sandbox, sit-ups, leg kicks, jumping rope, running stadium steps, shoulder exercises and wind sprints. The whole time she was talking, explaining things, I couldn't catch my breath, it was so embarrassing."

Russell laughed again, this time a little harder, "Man, I love you Bro', but I'm glad it's you and not me!"

"The worst part was that Coach Clark was in there watching us. He just smiled at me the whole time. Stephanie ran me in the ground. Coach Clark loved it. He told Stephanie it was the best total body workout he had ever seen. I know he was laughing at me the whole time. You should have seen the grin on his face."

"Man I hate it for you, but you have to admit it is kind of funny." Travis then leaned forward and handed Russell a manila file folder.

"What's this?" Russell said as he opened it up.

"Russell, that's the conditioning drills we did today."

"Why are you giving it to me?"

"Well Russell, I told you Coach Clark said it was the best workout program he had ever seen, so he wants you to do it with me!"

"Wait a minute," Russell replied. "I already have a workout schedule with the rest of the team."

"Coach Clark wants to test Stephanie's program on you too, and then he may use it for all the backs and receivers next year. He told me to tell you to meet Stephanie and me tomorrow at 3:30. He had a big smile on his face, he said he would see you tomorrow, he will be there again to watch us."

Russell just sat there, it didn't seem as funny now that he was going to have to do the workout routine too.

Travis then asked, "Russell, what do you think now? I would have tried to talk Coach Clark out of making you go, but I was so tired I just nodded and said 'Yes sir, I'll be sure and tell Russell.'"

"Travis, are you shooting me straight, was this your idea?"

"Would I do that to you?"

"Yes! I know you would!"

"Well either way, you and I both have to be there tomorrow, so don't laugh too hard. We'll see how well you do with Stephanie."

"I don't care what you say, no girl can outwork me, I'll be there."

The next morning Travis could hardly walk, and Russell just kept on teasing him.

"Travis, are you going to make it to class. Do you want me to call some of those girls you've been dating to carry your books?"

"Laugh now Russell, while you can."

At 3:30 the boys met Stephanie and Coach Clark at the training center.

Coach Clark: "Russell, I want to see you go through this conditioning program with Travis and Stephanie today."

Russell was really a little nervous, so he just kept his comments brief with a simple, "Yes sir, Coach."

From there Stephanie put the boys to work. For the next hour and a half she ran those boys in the ground. When they finished Coach Clark walked over to Russell and said:

"Well Russell, what do you think; is it a good workout?"

Russell, gasping for air, "Yes sir."

"I agree, I want you to do this with Stephanie and Travis for the rest of the year until fall football practice, don't you think this would get you in shape?"

"Yes sir."

Stephanie then said, "I can't take all the credit for this program. I used to date a Navy Seal when I was in graduate school in Florida. Most of these drills are from the Navy Seals' conditioning program. We will add the swimming drills next week."

"That will be great," Coach Clark replied. "What do you think boys?"

Russell: "Oh yes sir coach, I can't wait."

Stephanie just smiled and walked off, "I'll see you boys tomorrow."

Once she left Coach Clark walked over to the boys and smiled as he said, "That Stephanie sure is fit isn't she?"

Russell still gasping for air said, "Yes sir, she's something alright."

"Travis, I am glad you suggested inviting Russell today."

Russell looked at Travis like he could kill him. Travis just smiled back at Russell.

"Yes sir, it's nice of Russell to volunteer to work out with us."

Coach Clark then asked, "Did you guys ever think you would see a girl wear you out like that?"

"No sir," Travis replied.

Coach Clark then said, "I'm glad it's you guys and not me!"

Then he smiled again as he turned and walked away. Then Russell said to Travis,

"You threw me under the bus this time."

"Well, at least I am under there with you, wouldn't you have done the same thing to me?"

"Of course I would have!"

By now Russell was beginning to catch his breath as his attention turned to food.

"Let's go take a shower and get something to eat."

Travis: "After that maybe we can find some girls to massage these aching muscles?"

"Yeah, just as long as they're not volleyball players."

They laughed and took off. They were worn out today, but before long the boys were giving Stephanie a run for her money. The semester seemed to fly by. Travis and Russell worked out, they went to Bible study, and they did their schoolwork and made plenty of time for all the social activities going on around campus. Before they knew it was time for Easter and spring break. So much was happening in Travis' life. Russell was the best friend Travis had ever had. The boys were closer than brothers. Travis decided he would stay in Raleigh for the summer. He got a job near the end of the semester as a waiter at 42nd Street Oyster Bar in downtown Raleigh, just a couple of miles from the State campus. Russell was going back to Charleston for the summer to work with his family's landscaping business. Travis' life was changing. Things were different, but they were becoming good again.

TABLE FOR TWO

"Yes ma'am may I help you?"

"Yes sir, table for two, we have a reservation for 7 p.m., Simpson."

"Yes we have you here Mrs. Simpson, we will have a table open in just a few minutes. Please have a seat here, or you can sit at the bar if you like."

"We'll be fine right here. I would like to sit in that section over there where that young man is standing."

"Yes ma'am; I see, well Mrs. Simpson, I will have a table for you, but these young ladies also have a reservation at 7, and they have requested a table in that section as well, and they were here first."

Kathy and Ed looked over their shoulder and saw four attractive college girls sitting waiting for a table. Kathy then told the maitre d',

"Let me talk with them and see if they will mind sitting somewhere else."

As Kathy began to walk over toward the girls, Ed could sense that Kathy had her "claws out," and having a teenage daughter of his own, he was not expecting either side to compromise and give up their table.

"Girls, my husband and I are here from out of town to have dinner tonight and we would like to eat in that section of the restaurant," as she pointed to where the young man was standing.

"The maitre d' told us that you girls had requested that section as well. I was wondering if you would mind if we took the next table. We have to drive back to Wilson after dinner, and we would like to eat and get back home before it gets too late."

Then one of the girls said, "I understand, but I have dated the guy who is the waiter in that section and I wanted to sit in his area so I could see him. I am hoping to go out with him again, you understand don't you?"

Kathy asked, "Are you are speaking about that young man over there?" pointing toward the waiter.

"Yes ma'am, we met last week and we really hit it off, I'm sure we will go out some more, I just wanted to see him again. Girls today have to go after what they want. You understand don't you?"

"Yes," Kathy replied. "I understand. Don't worry about me; you can have the next table."

Once Kathy and Ed took a seat in the waiting area Ed said, "Kathy, you took that better than I thought you would."

"Girls today, they just won't leave those 'poor boys' alone."

"Yeah," Ed said. "I know it, having girls like that chasing after you, what a problem to have."

The young girls got the next table, and then about thirty minutes later Kathy and Ed were finally seated in the table next to them. The girl Kathy had spoken to then leaned over to Kathy and said,

"That worked out fine, you see you all didn't have to wait too long. I'm sure he is going to ask me out again, isn't he gorgeous?"

"Yes he is, and who knows, before long he may be introducing you to his parents?"

The girl then said, "That's what I'm hoping for, you understand, you were once our age, remember?"

"Oh yes," Kathy replied. "I was once your age; and I understand."

Just then the young man returned with the girl's dinner. The girl said, "Travis, I was wondering what time you get off work tonight, maybe we could go out or you could come by the sorority house?"

"Well, I don't have any plans."

Then the girl said, "I was hoping we could spend some time alone together," as she rubbed her hand up Travis' right arm.

With that Kathy had seen enough.

"Excuse me, may we have some service please!"

Travis turned around.

"Mom, Dad, what are you doing here, you didn't tell me you were coming."

He bent over and hugged and kissed Kathy, and hugged his dad.

"You should have told me you were coming."

"Well, I know you are busy Son," Ed said, "and who could blame you," as he smiled at Travis and looked over at the girls.

"Yeah Dad, there are plenty of things to keep you busy at college."

Kathy: "I can see that."

"Oh yes, Mom and Dad, this is Jennifer."

Kathy said, "That isn't necessary Travis, Jennifer and I have already met, haven't we dear?"

Jennifer, who had unfortunately got what she hoped for, a little sooner than she expected said, "Mrs. Simpson, if I had known you were Travis' parents I would have let you all go ahead of us."

"That's alright Jennifer, I was young once. I see you don't mind going after what you want, you just didn't expect to meet the parents while you were doing it."

"Alright now," Ed continued, "down girls."

"Dad I'm going to get you and Mom a glass of water, I'll be right back."

When Travis got back to the table the fireworks had settled down.

"Dad, why didn't you tell me you were coming?"

"We wanted to surprise you," Ed said. "Russell told your mother you would be working tonight. Besides, I like the idea of you waiting on me for a change. Tell me Son, how are things going?"

"School is good, my hand is getting stronger, that is a good thing."

Ed said, "You look great. You look as fit as I have ever seen you."

"Stephanie has Russell and me doing that fitness program I told you about. We are stretching, swimming, jumping, the thing is intense. I believe I am quicker and stronger now than I have ever been."

"That's great Son, I am so glad to see you smiling again."

"I still have my moments, but things are improving. The Bible study has helped me a lot. I have learned so much in that class. Russell is the best friend I have ever had. I'm still unsure of what's ahead for me, but I know I won't have to face it alone. God has a plan. I am just learning to trust Him a little more every day."

Ed said, "That's wonderful Son, I can't tell you how proud we are of you. Just take it one day at a time."

Kathy added, "We love you Son, you are doing great."

"Thanks Mom."

"What day will you be coming home this weekend?" Ed asked.

"I have to work Friday night, so I will come on home Saturday morning, then I'll spend Easter Sunday at home and I'll come back Sunday night."

"That sounds good," Kathy replied. "Sarah will be home too, and I want us all to have dinner with your Grandmother Prince."

Travis asked, "Will you ask her to make me some fudge?"

"She will make some if you ask her," Ed said. "Your mother won't let me have anything good anymore."

"Ed, you have eaten too much tonight. You ate a whole basket of hush puppies, all that fried shrimp, and a steak!"

"Travis, can you set me up with one of Jennifer's friends, your momma wants to get rid of me, can't you tell?"

"Dad, there is no way I am getting in the middle of that; you are on your own."

Then Travis leaned over and put his arm around his mother and kissed Kathy on the cheek and said, "I love you Mom, you are still the only girl in my life."

Ed and Kathy finished their dinner. After some discussion, it was decided that for Ed, there would be no pecan pie for dessert. Then there were the goodbye hugs and kisses, and the Simpsons then got in the car and drove back home to Wilson. When they got home Wesley was waiting at the door to go outside and have his private time. Afterward, Ed and Wesley came back inside and lay down on the couch together. Ed told Wesley all about his visit with Travis. They talked about how much better Travis was doing. They both missed Travis terribly. Wesley and Ed agreed that Travis was growing up. They knew they had to accept it. They were thankful they had each other to lean on. After awhile they then decided to take another walk outside. Wesley and Ed then sat on the porch to ponder all the day's events. Things in their world were changing fast. Neither Wesley nor Ed knew for sure how to respond to all the changes, Ed looked down at Wesley.

"God is in control, like Travis said tonight, we just have to learn to trust Him a little more every day."

Wesley didn't say anything; he just climbed up in Ed's lap. After all there really wasn't anything else to say. They both agreed that God was in control.

LET'S HAVE A TALK

"Hey, is anybody home?"

Wesley came running to the door and jumped on Travis' leg.

"Hey buddy, what you been doing, you want to go outside? Come on let's get your leash."

Kathy said, "There's my boy," she walked over to Travis and hugged him. "How's my baby?"

"I'm good Mom. Where are Dad and Sarah?"

"Sarah is over at Anna's house, I think they are laying out working on their suntans. Your Dad went to Lowe's to get some paint. He is going to paint the storage building. It's beginning to rust in a few spots, and I think he wants to change the color of the roof so it matches the shingles on the house. How do you like the new roof?"

"It looks great, the yard looks good too."

"You know your dad is always up to something."

"Yeah, Dad loves a project."

"Are you still thinking you want to study engineering?"

"I think so Mom, I enjoy my math classes, they are not easy, but you know I have always loved math. I guess I got that from you."

Kathy was a high school math teacher; she had always been the one who helped the kids with their homework. She had been a personal tutor for the kids in math.

Travis said, "Engineering lets me use math to work on projects; so it has elements of all the things I enjoy. I also have learned so much in my Bible study class that Coach Clark teaches. I am beginning to see that whatever I do, I want to be able to witness my faith. To learn and teach others about the Bible and Jesus Christ."

"Travis, that is wonderful." She hugged him again. "I am so proud of you Son, it's great to have you home."

Just then Sarah walked in.

"Travis, what's up?"

She walked over and gave him a hug and kiss.

"I just got here Sarah," Travis replied. "It's good to see you. What have you got planned tonight? I know you're up to something."

"Yeah, Anna and I are going out to eat with Geri and Dillon, then we are going to hang out at Anna's. Why don't you text Joseph and Tyler and we'll all go out together?"

"That sounds good, I'll send them a message, we'll just plan on that."

"Alright," Sarah replied. "I'm going to grab some sunscreen and head back to Anna's. I love you, we'll see you tonight, bye Mom, love you!"

Kathy: "Love you too honey."

Once Sarah left Travis took his clothes to his room. He also brought a large duffle bag of laundry. Kathy quickly took the clothes and got the washing machine going. Travis sent out text messages and e-mails to his friends. The kids were making plans for Saturday night. Kathy saw that Travis was reconnecting with his friends. She remembered it had not been long ago that Travis was uncomfortable around people. She could see that his smile was coming back, she took a deep breath, thinking how blessed she was. There had been so many changes in their lives, but through it all, their family was growing closer. She remembered back to the day Travis was injured, seeing him in the hospital, the meeting when Dr. Hamilton told them that Travis would never play football and baseball again. To see Travis smiling, the kids home for Easter, she could begin to see things coming together, but still she was not completely over it all herself. She had begun to feel a cautious optimism about the future. She was unsure about what was happening, but she was beginning to believe, to trust in God's plan, Kathy too was learning to trust again.

Kathy said, "Travis, come with me outside and we'll have a glass of tea, I want you to tell me some more about school."

The two of them went outside and sat on the back porch. Wesley tagged along. They talked about Travis' classes, Russell and the kids he had met at school. Travis told her about the conditioning program Dr. Clauson had designed for him and Russell. Then Kathy asked Travis to tell her more about the Bible study.

"Mom, I have learned so much this year from Bible study. You know I have spent a lot of time with Coach Clark at football practice and games. I have always admired him."

"I know Travis, David Clark is one of you father's closest friends. David is a fine man."

"Coach Cark really lives out his faith. He is quiet, but he is very open about his faith in Jesus. Listening to him teach the Gospel of Luke has taught me so much about God. Being in the Bible study has helped me to focus on my faith while my circumstances have changed."

"Travis, what has happened to you has affected us all, as a mother it is hard to accept that your child, whom you have entrusted to the Lord could be hurt this way. Now that you are grown I know I cannot protect you from life's difficulties, but when you are a parent you spend your life loving and providing for your children, when they hurt, you hurt. Being a Christian I know God is in control of all things. It is confusing as a parent when you see your child hurting, both of your hearts are breaking and God seems to remain silent."

"I know Mom, it is hard to believe it's real when something like this happens to you. When I went to see Dr. Hamilton after the accident, there were so many patients there in the clinic, many of them with injuries more severe than mine. You see people all the time who are sick, they have disabilities, or some other form of hardship, but it is someone else and not you. But when it is you, you begin to see people who are hurting differently. You want to help them, to do something to make it better. Being injured has opened my eyes to the suffering of people around me. I am not sure what to do about it, but I want to do something."

"I know what you mean; since this has happened to you I am so thankful for all of those years you and our family has been healthy. I am so thankful that you are recovering from the accident. You don't know how many times I have thanked God that He placed you in that room with Russell. That you had signed to go to State and David Clark was there for you, that Stephanie Clauson is in charge of your physical therapy. God placed those Christian witnesses in your life to help you through this. I am convinced of that."

"I know Mom, they have helped me so much. I do not know what God has in store for me. I will tell you Mom, it scares me to think about the future, now that so much has happened, but I still believe God's plan for my life is the same plan He had for me before I was ever born. It is just a different plan than what I expected."

Just then Ed opened the door and walked out onto the back porch.

"Hey, Big Boy, how are you doing?"

"Hey Dad, I heard you went to Lowe's to get some paint."

"That's right, I've got some paint, I'm going to paint the storage building this afternoon. Guess what else I've got?"

"I don't know Dad, what?"

"I've got two new paint brushes."

Kathy quickly said, "Momma doesn't paint with oil-based paint."

"I know Travis, your momma doesn't like to put that paint thinner on her finger nails. Wesley said he would help me but he is still trying to get rid of those flees he's been fighting. So Travis, I guess the only one left to help me is you."

"Dad I just got home, I've got plans. Besides, I don't want to get paint on my nails either."

"Alright, you had me feeling a little sorry for you until you threw that nails line in there. Wesley, what do you think? You think Travis ought to help me paint?"

Wesley just lifted his head up, and then he laid it back down in Travis' lap.

Ed said, "Even the dog has turned against me."

Then Ed started walking toward the storage shed. Travis looked over at Kathy.

"Mom, I guess I better go help Dad so he doesn't make a mess."

Travis then got up and father and son walked over to the shed to start painting. Kathy sat on the porch and watched the two men in her life walking together side by side. She noticed how much they walked alike. The shape of their bodies, the way they laughed, and the way they smiled. Things were different, but things were improving. Kathy thought about the way Travis expressed his faith in God, his growing relationship with Jesus. Years ago she had prayed that God would use Travis' life as a witness, an instrument to lead others to Christ. She could see that God was leading Travis; even through this accident God was drawing Travis closer to Himself. She did not know where God was leading Travis, but she knew wherever God would take Travis, Travis would never be alone. Jesus would always be there too.

SUNRISE

"Sarah, have you got my black shoes?

"Yes Ma'am."

" I was going to wear them today," Kathy said. "I am dressed except for those shoes!"

"Mom, I'm dressed too, and I need those shoes, I left my black ones in Greenville!"

Ed quickly grabbed his tie and went down to Travis' room to get out of the way. "Travis, you dressed?"

"Yeah Dad, come on in. Sounds like it's going to get noisy over there."

"I know it, let's go ahead and take the truck to church. I'm not getting in the middle of those two!"

"Good idea. Let's go," Travis said.

Ed then yelled out, "Kathy, Sarah; Travis and I are going to take the truck and we will meet you at church!"

Kathy just stared at Ed as he and Travis went outside.

"Dad, which one of them do you think will end up with those black shoes?"

"I don't know Son, but I'm not sticking around to find out."

The boys got in the truck and started to church.

"What time are you heading back today Son?"

"I am going to hang around until after lunch, around mid afternoon, then I need to get going. I've got some things to do once I get back to school today."

"When do you start your exams?"

"My first exam is next Monday; my last one is next Friday. So I have a lot of studying to do this week."

"I'm sure you are going to do well, what about your Bible study, when does that end?"

"Our last class is tomorrow night, Coach Clark is lecturing on the angels who met the women at the empty tomb, and Jesus' ascension into heaven. I am anxious to hear what he has to say."

"That's great Son, tell me what he says and we can talk about it."

After awhile the girls met Ed and Travis at church. Ed thought about asking Kathy about the shoes but decided against it. Sarah was wearing the shoes. Kathy had changed clothes. Ed was used to these sorts of things so he just kept quiet. Once church was over the family had lunch together, and before long the kids were out the door, Sarah heading east to Greenville,

Travis heading west toward Raleigh. When Travis got back to campus he got started on his homework. Russell met him at the library and the boys spread out their textbooks, and got to work. Not much was said. They both were concentrating on the task at hand, preparing for final exams. This was the last full week the boys would be together before summer break. The rest of the night was spent studying for final exams and Monday's Bible study.

Monday night when the boys got to Bible study Stephanie and Coach Clark greeted all the kids as they entered the classroom. They thanked the students for their participation in class. They recognized students for their attendance. They encouraged them to continue their daily Bible study and prayer time over the summer. There was a special recognition of the seniors who had completed four years of study. The seniors then took a few minutes to talk about the impact the study of the gospels had on their lives, and how their faith had grown through increased knowledge of the scriptures. Travis listened carefully as the seniors expressed their faith in God and their growing personal relationship with Jesus. Travis had never been in an environment where people so openly discussed their beliefs. He thought back to the beginning of the year when he first arrived at State. How confused and hurt he had been those first few weeks. He listened to the seniors give their testimonies and imagined himself standing there, speaking to the class three years from now when he himself would be a graduating senior. So much had happened in the past twelve months. The seniors inspired him with their sincerity and passion for Jesus. When they finished speaking it was time for Coach Clark's lecture.

Coach Clark began the lecture in the twenty-fourth chapter of Luke. He spoke about the women who arose early and went to Jesus' tomb and found the stone rolled away and Jesus' body was gone. How two angels appeared to the women and said to them,

"Why do you look for the living among the dead? He is not here, He is risen!"

The angels reminded the women how Jesus had told them and the disciples how, *"The Son of Man must be delivered into the hands of sinful men, be crucified, and on the third day, be raised again."*

Then they remembered his words. Coach Clark went on to speak about Jesus meeting two of the disciples on the Road to Emmaus. How Jesus appeared along the road and walked with the two disciples. He hid His identify from them while they discussed Jesus' ministry and His crucifixion. The events of Jesus' teachings, in verse 21, the men said,

"They had hoped that He would be the One who was going to redeem Israel."

They expressed their confusion and doubt about what had happened. They went on to recount the story of the women and the empty tomb. Then in verses 25 and 26, Jesus again reminds them that the Christ must suffer to fulfill what the prophets had spoken about Him. Then again, while the disciples were all together Jesus appeared to the group of eleven,

"Peace be with you,"

He told them. He wished them *"peace,"* but in their amazement they were afraid. Their human minds could not comprehend all that was happening. Jesus again reminds the disciples of what had been prophesized about Him. He told them to touch Him. Then He ate food among them to calm their fears. Again Jesus reminded the disciples what He told them earlier, the prediction of Jesus' death and resurrection. He commissioned them to preach the gospel beginning at Jerusalem and then to all the nations. Then they went with Jesus out to the vicinity of Bethany. Jesus lifted up His hands to bless them, and then as Jesus was blessing them, Jesus left them, and was taken up to Heaven.

Coach Clark went on to speak about the importance of the empty tomb, Jesus' resurrection and His ascension into Heaven. Coach Clark explained that the entire Bible, the Old and the New Testaments, our faith in God and our home for all eternity rest on our decision about what happened that day. Early that morning, sometime around sunrise, the women, followers of Jesus rose early to go to the tomb to anoint Jesus body. It was an act of service. They got up early to fulfill a commitment, a commitment to someone they knew; someone they loved. Sometime around sunrise the women discovered the empty tomb. There, at the empty tomb, the women were greeted by angels who told them the *"good news"* of Jesus' resurrection. Then Jesus appeared to the disciples. He explained again the necessity for the Son of Man to suffer, to fulfill what had been written about Him in the scriptures. Jesus commissioned the disciples to spread the good news of the gospel, beginning in Jerusalem then to all nations around the world. Jesus then ascended into the Heavens showing the disciples that He was who He claimed to be; the Messiah, the Savior of the world, the Son of the Living God.

Coach Clark then reminded the students that the commission of the church today is the same as it was that day two thousand years ago, to take the good news of the resurrection and ascension of Jesus Christ and teach that message around the world, that every sunrise, every new day, is an opportunity for Christians to share the love of Christ. Wherever we are, wherever we go, we have a responsibility to our neighbors and to God, to teach the gospel to people who need the good news of hope. The good news of how each of us can choose to develop a personal relationship, with our Lord and Savior Jesus Christ.

When the class was over Travis and Russell headed back to their room. Once they got back, Travis grabbed his baseball cap and his tennis ball and went for a walk. It was a warm night; the moon was full, clouds drifting across the face of the moon, and between the stars. He took his seat on the tennis bleachers. He leaned back against the bleachers and looked up into the sky as he squeezed the tennis ball in his left hand. The pain in his hand was gone. He was stronger in many ways than he had ever been. He thought about all that he had lost, then, he thought about all that he had learned. He thought about all that God is. Travis imagined what God was capable of. That Jesus had created the world, and that God was in control of all things. Even though Travis had so many questions, he knew he had made the most important decision. Travis had accepted Jesus as his Lord and Savior. He did not know what God had planned for him. He was afraid to get his hopes up. He did not want to be hurt or to be disappointed again. Travis knew that God willing, there would be a sunrise tomorrow morning. Wherever God wanted Travis to go, whatever God wanted Travis to do, if Jesus would give him the strength, Travis would go. He bowed his head, took off his cap and said a prayer.

"Lord, lead me where you want me to go, show me what you want me to do. Lord give me your peace, that I might have the courage again to honor You in all things."

Then as he sat there in the moonlight, thinking about a sunrise, even though he was still afraid, Travis knew he was not alone.

MOLDING CLAY

"That's the last of it," Russell said. "I didn't think we would fit it all in there."

"I know Russell, I never thought you could fit all that stuff in a Nissan Sentra, but you did it."

Russell had finished packing his car. School was out for the summer and it was time for Russell to head home to Charleston.

"This time tomorrow my dad will have me in someone's yard planting bushes or pulling up weeds."

"Come on Russell, it won't be that bad. You'll find plenty of time for those 'southern belles' on those Low Country beaches, all those Charleston girls down on Market Street and Rainbow Row, it won't be so bad."

"I have to admit, spending the summer in Charleston is pretty nice, if I could just spend a few more days at the beach, and not so much time pruning azaleas, Travis, do you know how many azaleas are in Charleston? My dad is a slave driver, he works, and works, and works, he loves it. He tells me his dad taught him to work hard and now he's teaching me. The man loves to teach hard work."

"My dad is the same way," Travis said. "He loves projects; he is working on something all the time. The only time he rests is when he sleeps. He likes to be doing something all the time."

"If they only knew how many single girls there are, and that all we wanted to do was meet as many of them as we can, they might ease up on us so we could make ourselves more available to them, the girls I mean."

Travis said, " I think our dads remember what it was like to be our age, they know how good we have it, so they don't feel sorry for us. They know we have it made. They wish they were our age again too!"

"Yeah, our dads aren't dummies, they just like messing with us, I'm gonna do the same thing with my kids."

"Dad loves to tease me; he thinks he's tough. I just play along, he loves it."

"Yeah me too, we're lucky to have such good fathers, I guess I better hit the road, I don't want to keep Mom and Dad, and especially all those girls waiting."

The boys shook hands and said their goodbyes. Russell cranked up the Sentra and headed south to Charleston.

The next few weeks Travis stayed in Raleigh for summer school. With Russell gone Travis had the dorm room to himself. During the day he went to class. He took a business management class and physics. He continued to do his workout program. Stephanie was in Canada for the summer. Coach Clark was busy preparing for the upcoming season, and so the people Travis spent most of his time with for the past year were gone. At first Travis found it difficult to stay in a routine. He was alone a lot. He found himself out of sorts; it took a while to get used to the solitude. It reminded him of the time immediately following the accident, when people avoided him because they didn't know what to say. Now he was alone for a different reason, but the loneliness was the same. As the days passed Travis began to settle into a routine, his class schedule and workout routine came together. He worked at the restaurant at night. Often times at night he would take a walk, he read his Bible and concentrated on his schoolwork. He continued to work with the clay, molding it with his fingers. He began to focus on the creative aspects of the clay. He became interested in shaping images, things that were important to him. Travis began to explore the healing power of creativity. Learning new skills helped him to accept change. The changes we all face, people coming in and out of our lives, changes in our circumstances. During the summer Travis was growing. He was learning that his life, like the clay, was adaptable. Travis began to see that like the clay, his life was being molded, being shaped, but for what, he did not know.

The week before school was to begin, Travis went to Atlantic Beach to spend a week with his family. The family met in Pine Knoll Shores and rented a house on the beach.

"Mom, where do you want me to put this bag of ice?"

"Travis, just put it in the cooler on the deck."

"Kathy, is that everything, are there anymore suitcases?" Ed asked.

"No Ed, that's all of them."

Kathy then asked, "Sarah you want to take the lounge chairs and go over to the beach?"

"Sure Mom, let's go."

The Simpsons settled in. For the next week they cooked on the grill, slept late, stayed up late at night, talking and catching up with one another. Ed and Kathy lay in bed at night and talked about how quickly Sarah and Travis had grown up. Ed watched his grown children walk up and down the beach. He also watched the other small children and their parents making sandcastles, running in and out of ocean waves, and young boys and their fathers throwing football. He remembered back to all those days he and Travis had enjoyed playing catch together. Ed was so thankful for all the blessings in his life. The kids were all but grown, and he loved them more than ever, he could see that all their lives were changing, he was thankful for the memories; he just wished he could keep them with him forever, but he knew he could not. Parents spend their lives loving and nurturing their children, preparing them for a life of their own. Ed and Kathy were proud of their children, the adults they were becoming. They enjoyed the week that they had together; but just like raising children, the week went by too fast, and soon it was time to go home.

The night before they were to leave, the family went out to dinner. They drove over to Beaufort and ate on the waterfront at Clawson's Restaurant. The food was great, they all had a wonderful time.

"Sarah, when do you have your first day of orientation?" Ed asked.

"I meet the principal and all the other new teachers next Wednesday. I am so blessed to be able to get a kindergarten job in Greenville; it could not have worked out any better."

"I know Honey, we are so proud of you."

Kathy asked, "Travis, when will Russell get back to Raleigh?"

"A week from Monday, he says his dad has just about killed him this summer. Russell said football practice will seem like a vacation after a summer of pulling weeds."

"Russell told me you set a record at State last year for first dates. Lots of first dates, but almost no second dates. Why is that?"

"I don't know Mom. It just worked out that way."

Sarah: "Come on Travis, what gives? What do you tell all those girls, why no second chances?"

"I just don't feel that comfortable around girls."

"Travis, how can you feel comfortable enough on a first date, but not comfortable on a second or third date?" Kathy asked.

"I don't like to talk about it, it just doesn't feel right, that's all."

"What doesn't feel right," Kathy continued, "is something wrong will all of those girls?"

At that point Travis became very quiet. He put his fork on the table, his expression changed. Kathy sensed something was not right.

"Travis, is something wrong, have I said something to upset you? If I did I am sorry."

"No Mom, it's nothing you said, it's just that I have dated a lot of girls, they are all nice, most of them are great. It's just that once we go out, we start to talk, we begin to touch, it leads to holding hands."

"Well that's normal Honey," Kathy replied.

"I know it's normal Mom, but since the accident my hand feels different, not to the girls, but to me. I'm just not comfortable with a girl holding my hand."

With that said the mood at the table became very somber. Kathy then realized that although Travis had come a long way in his recovery, the emotional scars were still fresh, and the hurt Travis felt ran deeply, affecting all aspects of his life. Kathy's heart ached for Travis. She tried to compose herself as she sat there for a moment, but her feelings for Travis got the best of her, and she began to cry.

"I'm sorry Travis, please excuse me."

Then she got up and left the table. Sarah excused herself and followed her mother outside. Travis looked toward Ed.

"Dad, I'm sorry."

"Son, don't worry about that. Your mom loves you, she was just surprised, that's all. She'll be fine."

When the family got back to the house Travis went for a walk on the beach. The sun was beginning to set. The sky was turning purple, and across the shoreline rows of cottages were perched atop the sand dunes to the west, as the sun began to sink below the expanse of ocean on the horizon. To the east the moon was rising in the distance. The temperature was warm as the ocean breeze blew the clouds across the sky. As the ocean waves lapped against Travis' feet, he stood there, trying to take in all the beauty that surrounded him. The roar of the ocean, the salt air as it blew across his face, the consistency, the majesty of God's creation. That night, as he stood beside the ocean, he thought about the wonder of it all. In the midst of all the confusion, through all of his fears and doubts, Travis realized God was in control, and he prayed for the peace of mind to lay all the hurt of what had happened behind him, so that he could move forward.

"Lord, I have carried this burden as far as I can in my own strength. I know that I cannot overcome these fears and doubts on my own. Lord, all that I am belongs to You. Father, accept me as I totally commit my life to Jesus. Shape me into whatever you want me to be, and release me from this pain that is in my heart."

The sun set, the sky turned black, the stars appeared. Travis took a deep breath, as looked out into the darkness. He watched the moonlight as it danced atop the ocean waves, he felt God's Spirit of Peace wash over him, then he turned and walked back toward the cottage on the hill.

The clay was now ready, for the Master's Hand.

MK

"Travis, hurry up and get your shoes on, we've got to get going."

"Alright Russell, I'm ready."

The boys headed out the door; they stopped down the hall and knocked on one of the other dorm room doors. Joe Moore came to the door with his ankle wrapped in an ace bandage holding a pair of crutches.

Travis asked, "Joe, what happened to your foot?"

"Oh that, it's nothing; my foot is fine, I just have these for show."

Russell said, "Yeah Travis, Joe is the bait, remember? Last year it was your hand. Joe is fine, his foot is just a conversation starter, that's all."

Travis: "I don't know about that Russell, that's kind of sleazy isn't it?"

"Look Travis," Joe said, "not all of us are as lucky with the girls as you are. Some of us have to use whatever we can to get a date!"

Russell: "That's it."

Travis: "Alright, but I don't feel good about this."

The boys got in the car and headed toward the girls' dorm. Once they got there they went to work. Russell did the talking and the "bait" worked like a charm. Joe had all sorts of attention from the coeds. The boys were competing with two basketball players, one who had a shoulder injury, and some fraternity boys, one with a broken arm. Things were going according to plan when Russell said, "Hey man, will you take a look at that girl!"

She was walking up the sidewalk. She had on a tennis dress, her long brown hair pulled back in a ponytail. She was sweating, her athletic body had curves in all of the right places; she had a large tennis bag across her shoulders.

Russell: "Man that girl is as cute as a 'speckled pup.'"

She looked over and smiled at the boys as she walked in their direction.

"Hey guys, she's smiling at me!" Joe said.

She walked up to the boys and stopped. She was wearing a white tennis dress and a cross around her neck; then she looked at Travis and said,

"How's the fishing?"

Travis just stood there; for once he was speechless. Then she said again,

"How's the fishing?"

Russell asked, "What do you mean, how's the fishing?"

She said, "I see you brought your 'bait' with you; so, how's the fishing?"

Joe said, "Who me?"

"Yes you!" She replied. "You're just the 'injured jock,' you're probably not even hurt."

"Do you think we would have to stoop to something like that," Russell asked.

"Yes, I'm sure of it!"

"What would make you think a thing like that?" Joe asked.

"My mother told me guys would be out today, pretending to be injured; I guess she was right."

Then she looked at Travis, "You don't have much to say. What's wrong? Cat got your tongue?"

Travis just starred at her. He couldn't figure what to make of all of this.

"No, my tongue is fine. I'm just a little surprised that a girl as smart and pretty as you, would fall for a trick like that."

"What do you mean, fall for it, I'm on to you guys!"

"Well," Travis continued, "all we were trying to do is meet some new girls, and here you are."

"We haven't met, you don't know my name."

"My name is Travis Simpson; what's yours?"

"I know who you are," she replied. "I remember when you hurt your hand; I saw it on ESPN."

"Okay, you know who I am, so tell me who you are."

Then she said, "If you want to know my name, you're going to have to do some work first."

Russell said, "What do you have in mind?"

"Not you, Travis here."

Then she handed Travis her tennis bag.

"Come with me."

"Yes ma'am."

She then turned and they started walking toward the girls' dorm.

Joe asked, "What about us?"

The girl just raised her arm over her shoulder and waved goodbye, she never looked back.

"Travis has his hands full this time," Russell said. "Did you see how he looked at her?"

"No. I wasn't looking at Travis," Joe replied. "That girl is so fine, 'um, umm!' How does he do it?"

"I don't know, I've been watching him for a year and I haven't figured it out yet, but I'm going to."

Travis followed the girl into the dorm, as they walked he said, "You know some things about me, but I don't know anything about you."

She said, "I don't know too much about you, so tell me, where you are from?"

"I'm from Wilson, just about forty miles east of here. Where are you from?"

"I'm from Orlando, Florida. I am an athlete myself."

Travis then asked, "What sport do you play?"

The girl stopped, looked at the tennis bag, batted those big blue eyes and said,

"Tennis."

Travis looked down and smiled.

"Oh, I guess that should have been pretty obvious."

She cut him a little slack.

"Well, I have that affect on guys sometimes."

"I'm sure you do." Travis said. "I've never had much luck with girls."

She smiled.

"There you go playing tricks again. I know better than to believe that."

By now they had weaved their way through the students and parents moving clothes, TVs, and stereos into the dorm and made it to the girl's dorm room. She stopped and turned toward Travis.

"I'll take that now," she said, and he handed her the tennis bag.

"You still haven't told me your name."

"My name is Mary Katherine Outland, but my friends call me MK."

"MK, I like that"

"It's Mary Katherine for now; but we'll see."

Then she turned around and went into the room. Travis just stood there for a minute. There was something different about this girl. He smiled to himself, he wanted to knock on the door and talk with her some more. He felt a little anxious; he wasn't quite sure what to do. It wasn't like him to feel nervous around girls; not this way, so he decided to call it a day. He turned and headed back outside, when he got back to where Russell and Joe were standing, Travis could see the two of them were surrounded by girls. Travis could see a man walking up behind Joe and Russell, once he realized who the man was he quickly turned and walked the other way. Just then, Joe felt a tap on his shoulder, Joe turned around with a big smile on his face. The man asked,

"Joe Moore, how did you hurt your foot?"

Joe's smile quickly vanished.

"Coach Clark, what are you doing here?"

Russell turned around; he just stood there speechless.

Coach Clark: "Russell, what kind of injury do you have, memory loss?"

"Sir, sir"

"What's wrong fellas? Cat got your tongue?"

Russell said, "No sir"

"I didn't expect to see two of my offensive players out here, one of them injured, trying to pick up girls."

Joe: "Coach, you've got us, we shouldn't have…"

Coach Clark raised his hand.

"Look, I was your age once myself, being out here doesn't bother me, but that fake injury does."

Russell: "Yes sir."

"We'll just have to run 15 extra wind sprints after practice for the next three weeks to get Joe's ankle back in shape. Russell, that will help your memory too; won't it?"

Russell: "Yes sir"

Coach Clark then asked, "Russell where's Travis? I'm sure he's in on this too."

"I'm not sure where he is right now."

"I'll work something out with Stephanie Clauson to take care of Travis," Coach Clark continued, "so Russell you tell him he's not off the hook, I saw Travis turn and walk away as I was coming up behind you two."

Russell: "Yes sir."

With that Russell and Joe put their tails between their legs and headed back to the car. Russell said,

"Well at least Coach Clark got all three of us."

Joe: "I bet that Travis thought he was in the clear."

Russell said, "Whatever we have to do will be nothing compared to what Stephanie will do to Travis. Stephanie is tough, man!"

By the time Russell and Joe got back to the room Travis was already there.

"Travis what happened with that girl?" Russell asked.

"Which girl?"

"Come on Travis," Joe said, "you know which girl, the tennis player, what was she like, what's her name, where's she from?"

"She is on the tennis team, she's from Orlando, Florida, her name is

Mary Katherine; sometimes she said her friends call her MK."

Russell: "What did you say her last name was?"

"I can't remember, she said her nickname was MK, I got to thinking about that and I forgot her last name?"

"Travis," Russell asked, "a girl that looks like that! How could you forget her last name?"

Joe said, "If you said you got sidetracked by that tennis dress I would understand."

"I've been thinking about it ever since I left, I just can't remember, seems like Oswald, Outlaw, I'm just not sure. Anyway, I've got some time to check up on her, I'll figure it out before I see her again."

Russell: "Did you say she was on the tennis team?"

"Yeah, she said she was a tennis player."

Russell: "Then let's go to the tennis website, it should have the roster on there."

The boys cut the computer on and pulled up the tennis team website, the website showed the roster for the previous year's team.

Russell said, "She must be a freshman, we would have noticed her if she had been here last year."

Travis agreed, "You're right, no way she would have been in the athletic department and us not seen her."

"Let's look up the recruiting news;" Russell suggested, "maybe they have something about her there."

The boys then scanned the athletic department website.

Russell: "Right there she is, Mary Katherine Outland, freshman from Orlando, Florida."

"She must be good," Travis said. "It says she was the top junior tennis player in the country. She made it as a qualifier in last years U.S. Open."

Russell: "Travis, you better watch that girl; She's tough, she might just settle you down, boy."

Joe said, "Travis, I'll be glad to watch her for you if you need me to; she did smile at me first you know."

"You're right Joe, she told me she was interested in you, but that ankle injury concerned her."

"Russell, I told you that was a bad idea, then Coach Clark busted all our bubbles."

Russell then said, "Travis, Coach Clark caught us, he was not happy; Joe and I have to run 15 wind sprints after practice for the next three weeks."

"Oh no, sorry fellas,"

"He saw you too!" Russell replied.

"Man! I thought he did, what time do I have to be there with you guys?"

Russell: "He said to tell you that he will let Stephanie Clauson handle your punishment."

"No way! That's not fair!. Stephanie will kill me, especially for this!"

"Well Travis, I tried to protect you, but what could I say?"

Russell and Joe laughed, "Travis you did end up with the girl."

"Yeah, I hope she's worth it."

Later that night, Travis grabbed his cap and tennis ball and went for a walk. He walked his normal track around campus. He made it around to the tennis courts and took his seat on the bleachers. He squeezed the tennis ball in his left hand. His hand felt stronger, and so did he. He thought about the girl he met today. He wondered, how good a tennis player was she? He imagined sitting in the bleachers watching her play, how and when he would meet her again. He said; "Mary Katherine Outland, MK. I'll be seeing you soon."

NO MORE FISHIN'

Russell walked in the dorm room and sat down on the bed, then laid down with one arm hanging off the bed toward the floor. A few minutes later Travis came in dripping with sweat. He sat down on the bed and leaned against the wall. After a couple of minutes Russell said,

"That's the last time I'm going fishing, no more bait for me."

Travis: "I'm with you, what did Coach Clark make you do?"

"He made Joe and I run wind sprints, 15, after practice."

"That doesn't sound so bad."

Russell said; " The sprints were from the back of one end zone to the back of the other, 130 yards each!"

"Ouch, that is bad."

"What about Stephanie, what did she have you do?"

"Nothing any different, not yet. She didn't mention it, so I guess Coach Clark hasn't seen her to tell her. Today is my last day though."

Russell said, "Maybe not."

"Yeah today was it, you know they will talk about it tonight at Bible study."

"Oh yeah, you're right Travis, you're 'toast' man, you're done tonight." Travis just got up and went to the shower.

An hour or so later the boys headed out the door. On their way to Bible study they stopped by Joe Moore's room, and Joe was dragging too.

Joe said, "Russell, man, I hurt all over."

"I know man, I know."

The boys went to the cafeteria and grabbed a bite to eat, and then the three of them went on over to Bible study. When they got there Coach Clark and Stephanie met them at the door. Coach Clark said,

"Joe, Russell, I'm glad you guys could make it tonight, how are you feeling?"

Joe said, "We're fine coach."

Coach Clark said, "How's your foot, Joe?"

"It's fine Coach Clark, thank you for asking."

Coach Clark smiled at Russell, "Is your memory coming back."

"Yes; I will never forget this as long as I live."

Coach Clark: "Good, I'm glad to hear that."

Stephanie then looked toward Travis.

"Travis, Coach Clark tells me you boys were doing some fishing yesterday, did you catch anything?"

Travis knew she had him, so he tried to make the best of it.

"Actually, I did meet a girl who I liked very much. She surprised me."

"That's interesting. How so?"

"There was something different about her; I can't quite put my finger on it."

"That's alright Travis," Stephanie replied. "We'll have some extra drills to do tomorrow, we can talk about it then."

"Yes ma'am."

The boys went into the classroom and took a seat. The room began to fill. The boys were looking around checking things out, then something caught Russell's eye.

"Hey Travis, look at that girl. Is that who I think it is?"

Russell pointed to the girl talking to Stephanie.

"That girl with the baseball cap."

Travis looked up.

"It sure looks like her."

The girl looked around and saw the three boys looking at her. She just smiled and walked in their direction. She walked over to where they were sitting.

"Travis Simpson, funny meeting you here, in Bible study class."

"It's good to see you again. I enjoy this Bible study. I hope you will too."

Then Mary Katherine said,

"Aren't you going to introduce me to your friends?"

"Yeah sure," Travis said, "Russell Rawlings, Joe Moore, this is Mary Katherine…"

Travis paused, he could not remember her last name. Mary Katherine quickly caught on.

"Well, I can see I didn't make much of an impression on you, if you can't even remember my name. I guess it was hard to remember my name and the names of all those other girls you met yesterday!"

"I do know your name; it just left me for a moment, you've had that happen before. Besides, I even looked you up on the Wolfpack sports website."

Mary Katherine was impressed. He was honest, he was interested, and "boy was he cute," but she played it smooth.

"I see, well, Outland, Mary Katherine Outland."

Travis smiled and breathed a sigh of relief. He had dodged a bullet, and he knew it. Mary Katherine took her seat and Coach Clark called the meeting together. He started by explaining the gospel rotation of the Bible study. He talked about his expectations for the students. He told how Jesus had called Peter from being a fisherman, to be a *"fisher of men."* Coach Clark then took a glance toward the boys, they hung their heads, and Mary Katherine smiled. Coach Clark went on to say that we all as Christians are Disciples of Christ. That God created us all to fellowship with and work for Him, that no matter what our job, our circumstances might be, we will only find fulfillment when we are in fellowship with God. We find the pathway to God through our relationship with his Son, Jesus Christ.

When the class ended Travis reached over and tapped Mary Katherine on the shoulder.

"Mary Katherine, are you going back to the dorm?"

"Yes," she said.

"Would you like me to walk with you?"

"That would be nice."

"Russell, Joe," Travis said. "I'll catch up with you guys later."

Joe looked at Russell.

"How does he do it?"

"It's a gift," Russell replied.

Travis and Mary Katherine walked across campus. As they walked they talked about their families. Travis told her about his parents, his sister Sarah, and Wesley. Mary Katherine told Travis about her father Rudy, who was the new men's tennis coach at State, her mother Rita, and her brother Joe, who played golf at Florida State. Before long they reached the girls dorm.

"When will I see you again?" Travis asked.

"I have tennis practice tomorrow, it will be over at 3 p.m., why don't you stop by? Do you know where the courts are?"

"Yes, I've actually spent a lot of time there myself."

"Do you play tennis?"

"I played junior tennis until I was fourteen. After that I just focused on football and baseball, tennis is more of a girl's game anyway. My mother played college tennis."

"A girl's game! Well wear your tennis shoes tomorrow and we'll play a game or two!"

"I'm just saying girls play tennis, and not football or baseball, that's all. I didn't mean anything by it."

"I hear you, but you did say tennis is a 'girl's game!' So you just be ready to play tomorrow, besides I am just a girl!"

"Okay then, I'll see you about 3."

After they said goodnight, Travis circled back around to the tennis courts. He sat down on the bleachers, and as he looked at the stars, he thought about tomorrow.

"*I'll see you tomorrow Mary Katherine, I'll see you tomorrow.*"

STILL THE SAME

"Hi Travis, how are you doing? I haven't seen you in a while," said the lady in the reception area. "Do you have an appointment with Dr. Clauson today?"

"No ma'am," Travis said. "But I was hoping I could speak with her a minute. Is she in?"

"Yes, she is, she has someone with her right now. They should be out in a few minutes if you'd like to wait."

"I will, thank you."

Travis then sat down and picked up a magazine off the coffee table. It was a Wolfpack Alumni magazine with a picture of Russell on the cover. Travis read the article about Russell and the rest of the team. This was the football preview issue. State's first football game was a non-conference game against East Carolina University; it was on the road in Greenville, a week from Saturday. While Travis was reading Stephanie came out into the lobby.

"Travis, do you need to see me?"

"Yes, I don't have an appointment, but I wanted to talk if you've got a minute?"

"Sure Travis, come on in, have a seat. What's up?"

"I was wondering if I could be excused from my workout today, I have somewhere I need to be at 3 p.m."

"Well, tell me a little more about it. You know it's important that you continue your exercise routine, but you can miss a day if you need to. Where is it you need to be?"

"I met this girl over the weekend, the one I told you about, she was in Bible study last night."

"Mary Katherine Outland?"

"Yes, that's her. She has tennis practice today; she and I are going to play a few games after she finishes practice."

"Travis, you do know that Mary Katherine is one of the top women's tennis players in the country."

"Yes, I read about her on the internet. I played junior tennis until I started high school. I was invited to play in the Southern Junior Qualifier from the time I was 10 until I quit playing competitive tennis in the eighth grade."

"Do you think you can play with Mary Katherine? She's tough!"

"I know she's good, and it has been a long time since I played, but I am taller and faster than she is, and I've always had a big serve."

"3 p.m. at the tennis center?" Stephanie asked.

"Yes ma'am."

"That will be fine for you to miss your workout," Stephanie said. "And I think I'll come and watch. I want to see Mary Katherine play. Would you mind?"

"No, come on." Then Travis said, "Stephanie there is one more thing, I have something for you."

Travis unzipped his book bag and handed Stephanie a gift box.

"Travis, what is this?" Then as Stephanie opened the box she said, "Travis, it's beautiful, did you make this?"

"Yes, I made if for you, for all you have done for me."

Stephanie did not know what to say.

"Travis, I am speechless. Thank you, this is so special."

Stephanie took the gift and set it on her desk.

"This is where it will always stay. Travis, whenever I see it, I will think of you."

"I thought for a long time about what I wanted to make with the clay," Travis said. "What was important to me. I realized when everything else in my life changed, God was still the same. The cross was where I found my strength, so I made this one for you."

"It's beautiful, thank you Travis."

When Stephanie looked at the cross; it reminded her that she was making a difference. Not just in her job, but also as a disciple of Jesus.

She looked at Travis.

"Don't underestimate Mary Katherine today, she's something special."

"I know, I better be going."

Travis got up and left the room. Stephanie looked at the cross and thought, "*Travis is a special young man.*"

Stephanie had never thought about the possibility of Travis playing tennis. She knew Travis was a naturally gifted athlete, but she had no idea he was such an accomplished junior. Stephanie began to wonder just how much tennis talent did Travis really have? So Stephanie decided to make that 3 p.m. match, and find out for herself.

It was around 2:30 when Travis, Russell and Joe made it over to the tennis courts. Russell and Joe decided to tag along. The football team had a night practice scheduled to help prepare for their opening game on the road at night against the East Carolina Pirates. Russell and Joe wanted to see Travis play Mary Katherine, but more than that, they wanted to get a look at the other girls on the tennis team.

"There were some cute girls on that tennis website," Joe said, "and think about all those girls on those other teams too."

The boys took a seat and leaned back on the bleachers. They were sitting a few feet away from an attractive red headed lady wearing sunglasses and a tennis dress. Russell pointed at Mary Katherine.

"Travis, there she is, man is she hot!"

"Smoking," Joe said.

Russell: "I tell you what Travis, she hits that ball hard!"

"I know," Travis said. "She's better than I thought she'd be."

Joe then asked Travis, "Do you think you can take her?"

With that the lady sitting near them smiled, as the boys continued to talk about Mary Katherine and the other girls. After a few minutes the lady spoke up.

"Excuse me, aren't you Russell Rawlings?"

Russell turned and smiled.

"Yes ma'am."

The lady then asked, "Russell, are you boys tennis fans?"

"Well Travis is, or at least he is a fan of that girl over there anyway," as he pointed to Mary Katherine. Russell then said, "Travis is going to play her a match after the team finishes their practice today."

"Really, that girl is pretty good," the lady said.

"That's what I hear, but Travis played tennis growing up, and she is a girl."

"Russell, she is mighty good." Travis said, trying to lower the expectations a little.

Then the lady introduced herself, "My name is Rita, it's nice to meet you Russell. Who are your friends?"

"This is Joe Moore and Travis Simpson."

"I'm pleased to meet you boys. Travis, how do you think you'll do against Mary Katherine?"

Before Travis could answer for himself Russell spoke up again.

"I think Travis will beat her, he's bigger and faster than she is."

Travis then took the opportunity to speak for himself.

"I don't know; she's very good."

Rita: "I think I'll stick around and watch if you don't mind."

About that time Stephanie and Coach Clark came up.

Coach Clark said, "Travis, I hear you are playing Mary Katherine today."

"How did you know Coach?"

"Russell told me."

"Thanks Russell, who else did you tell?"

"I told your mother." And everyone laughed.

"Is she coming too?"

"No, but I do have to send her a text message after every game with a scoring update."

"Great."

The girls' tennis practice was winding down. The coaches dismissed the team and Mary Katherine motioned for Travis. He picked up his tennis racquet and walked out onto the court. While he was walking, an athletic man wearing tennis shorts and a State T-shirt came and sat down next to Rita.

"Hey Honey, how did practice go today?"

"Practice went good," Rita said. "The girls played hard. It looks like Mary Katherine is going to play a match with that young man over there," as she pointed to Travis.

Rita leaned over and whispered in the man's ear.

"That boy is Travis Simpson."

The man's eyes lit up.

"He played baseball and football."

"I know," Rita said. "I remember when he was injured. That was the saddest thing, but that's him. The boys were saying that he played tennis until he started high school. He made it into the Junior Southerns every year until he quit playing competitively."

"Does Mary Katherine know that?"

"I don't think so; if she did, she did not mention it."

The man then asked, "Did you know they were playing today?"

"A mother knows Dear, a mother knows."

Travis then walked onto the court. He met Mary Katherine at the net.

"You played really well Mary Katherine, I'm impressed."

"Thank you, I love to play. When was the last time you played Travis?"

"I haven't hit a tennis ball in a couple of years, but when I was younger I played all the time. My Mom made Sarah and me take lessons when we were younger. Sarah was a very good player until she started driving, then she got interested in dating; that cooled the tennis."

"That happens with a lot of us girls. You know a boy can ruin a girl, that's why I'm watching you."

"I like watching you too."

They smiled and chatted a little more; then they started warming up.

They started out playing mini-tennis, hitting short shots inside the service box. Then they moved back toward the baseline, forehands crosscourt, back and forth. It had been years since Travis had played tennis like this, but his hand-eye coordination was so good he quickly began to hit solid, deep spinning shots over and over. He moved quickly from side to side; he seemed to glide across the court. Then they switched to backhands. Travis hit a classic one-handed backhanded, with his follow through finishing high above his head. The more they played, the harder Travis hit the ball. After a few minutes, Travis was warmed up. Mary Katherine walked to the net, and again she asked,

"Travis, how long has it been since you played tennis?"

"It's been a while."

"Are you shooting me straight Travis, you hit it mighty good for someone who doesn't play anymore?"

"For the past year all I have done is work out, it seems good to get out and actually play something again."

Mary Katherine, still not totally satisfied Travis was telling her the whole truth asked, "Are you ready?"

"Let's hit a few serves; then we can play a set."

"Sounds good to me."

Travis went back to the baseline. Mary Katherine was on the other side of the court. Travis looked at the tennis ball, bounced it three times, tossed it in the air. "Pop." It sounded like a rifle shot. The ball exploded off his racquet, skipped in the service box and bounced against the screen behind the court. Mary Katherine didn't move; she didn't have time. The ball had gone past her in a blink. Travis bounced the ball again; then he tossed the ball. "Pop." Another bullet. The boys in the stands sat up, and Russell said,

"Did you see that?"

Rita: "It was moving so fast, Rudy how fast is that serve?"

Rudy didn't say anything, he just watched. Again Travis tossed the ball. "Pop," this was the fastest one yet. A well struck tennis ball has a unique "popping" sound; and when Travis served everyone around the courts stopped. Mary Katherine put her hands on her hips and scowled at Travis.

"Travis Simpson, are you lying to me?"

"What do you mean?"

"You know what I mean, you better not be lying to me."

Travis walked up to the net, then as he tapped his racquet on the top of the net.

"I am not lying, it's like I told you last night, I played tennis when I was younger, and I was successful with it, but football and baseball were my favorite sports. But I have hit some kind of ball since I was a little kid. I know how to play; I just haven't played in a while."

Mary Katherine looked at him hard.

"Alright then, let's play. But if I find out you're lying to me I'm going to be upset with you, do you understand?"

"Yes ma'am, I understand."

With that the match began.

COULD THIS BE REAL

"M OR W?"

Mary Katherine showed the handle of her Wilson tennis racquet to Travis.

"M," said Travis.

Mary Katherine spun the racquet on the court. The racquet spun to the ground W side up.

"I'll serve," Mary Katherine said.

The match was on. Travis gave Mary Katherine the three tennis balls. She slipped one in the side of her skirt, rolled one to the back fence; then she toed the base line. She had her game face on. Travis walked behind the baseline; he pulled the strings on his racquet with the fingers of his left hand. He knew Mary Katherine was a player. She had all the shots. He decided he would have to overpower her, or outrun her. Travis knew that if the points lasted very long Mary Katherine would run him out of position, he had to go for broke to stay with her, so that's what he decided to do. If he went down he was going to go down swinging. Travis assumed his position one step behind the baseline. He leaned forward with the racquet spinning in his right hand. Mary Katherine tossed the ball in the air. She hit a solid serve in the right corner of the service box to Travis' forehand. Travis hopped forward and to his right, planted his feet and took the serve on the rise and whipped a blistering forehand crosscourt winner, just inside the baseline. Love-15. Mary Katherine moved to the ad side. She did not look up. She bounced the ball and whistled a serve right into Travis' backhand. Travis blocked the ball back just past the service box. Mary Katherine raced toward the net, and then hit a spinning backhand winner off the back of the baseline. 15 all. She flashed a smile at Travis.

"So. I see we've both come to play."

Travis just smiled back and nodded. He knew girls liked to have the last word. From there on every point was close. Travis went for the winners, while Mary Katherine kept moving Travis side to side until she had an opening. Then she would hit the ball into the open court. The first game went to three deuces before Mary Katherine held her serve and took a 1-0 lead. The two walked to the net to change sides. They each grabbed a cup of water.

"You're going to run my legs off if you're not careful," Travis said.

"If you wouldn't hit the ball so hard, I wouldn't have to make you run so much," Mary Katherine replied.

"You know I'm going to keep hitting it hard."

"Then get your running shoes on!"

It was now Travis' turn to serve, so he took the balls and walked back to the baseline. He knew he had to win his service games to have any kind of chance. He toed the baseline, took a look at Mary Katherine and she nodded to let him know she was ready. He tossed the ball into the air. "Pop." The ball skipped in the service box and against the fence. Mary Katherine clapped her hand against her racquet.

"Good shot." 15-Love.

Again Travis tossed the ball, another serve out wide. Mary Katherine lunged to her left and the ball bounced off the racquet. 30-Love. Mary Katherine walked behind the baseline, starring at Travis. She had that, "*You better not be lying to me,*" look on her face.

Travis just looked at her and smiled, and thought to himself, "*Man, that girl is cute. I haven't had this much fun in a long time.*"

Mary Katherine backed up another step behind the baseline. Travis tossed the ball; then he hit a blistering serve up the "T" that landed just beyond the service box. Mary Katherine pointed up.

"Out."

Then she took a step inside the baseline. She hadn't seen him hit a single second serve. Travis knew he had to just spin the ball in there, and when he did Mary Katherine blasted a forehand winner down the line. 30-15. Mary Katherine then knew that if Travis didn't get his first serve in, that he was in trouble. So that's how the match went. Travis went for it, and when he made a mistake Mary Katherine made him pay. All the games were close. Great shot-making on both sides. Both Travis and Mary Katherine were quick on their feet and hit the ball with power. Mary Katherine was at the top of women's tennis, while Travis was a diamond in the rough, and now everyone could see it.

With the score 3-2 and Mary Katherine leading the players changed sides. Mary Katherine looked at Travis.

"It looks like we've drawn a crowd."

And pointed to the bleachers. Travis looked up and the bleachers were full. Around the edges of the court players of both women's and men's tennis teams were taking in the action. Russell had texted the football team, and even a few of Travis' girlfriends.

"I think all the guys are here to watch the 'next big thing' in women's tennis," Travis said. "Word is she's mighty pretty."

"Flattery will get you nowhere out here Buddy," Mary Katherine replied. "But it might help you later."

Then she tossed Travis the balls and headed for the baseline. By now the crowd was into the match. Russell yelled out,

"Come on Travis, you can get back even right here!"

Then one of the girls on the tennis team screamed.

"Go get 'em Mary Katherine, take that boy down!"

Then the crowd really got into the action. Rita leaned over to Rudy and whispered.

"This is the best I've ever seen Mary Katherine play."

Rudy nodded and agreed.

"I think you're right; she is getting better all the time."

"You don't have anybody on your men's team who can move like this boy," Rita said. "If he was playing tennis full time there's no telling how good he could be. How fast do you think his serve is?"

"110-120-mph," Rudy answered. "But I could teach him to hit a lot harder than that."

"If you had him to go along with those four freshmen you recruited this year, you would be in great shape this spring."

"Let's don't go jumping the gun, Travis may not be that interested in tennis."

"He's out here today."

"Yeah," Rudy replied. "But playing tennis isn't the main reason he's here."

Travis walked to the baseline; he looked around at the crowd. He felt the excitement of the competition. He remembered the electricity of being in a close ball game. He thought he would never feel this way again. He looked across the court at Mary Katherine. They were both playing to win, but now it was more than just a tennis match. There was chemistry there. Travis wanted to win, but most of all he wanted to be challenged. Mary Katherine was the thing Travis needed; she was a worthy opponent. He admired the way she played. Then as he focused on the action, Travis went into *"The Zone."* His pulse quickened. His eyes focused. Everything around him went into slow motion. He tossed the ball and pounded another ace; his fastest serve of the match. Then he hit three more in a row. Mary Katherine just stood there, amazed by what was happening. Stephanie leaned over to Coach Clark.

"I knew Travis was a great athlete, but I can't believe what I am seeing."

"I've known Travis since he was a child," Coach Clark replied. "He had the best arm I've ever seen for a shortstop, and he had blazing speed and great hands on the football field. I had always heard he was an excellent junior tennis player. But I have never seen him play before today, but with this athletic ability he would have been dominant in any sport."

"His injury has affected just the fingers on his left hand," Stephanie said. "Since he hits a one-handed backhand, tennis is the one sport his injury doesn't keep him from playing. I am so happy for him. Could this be real?"

"I remember when we were recruiting Travis, we rated him as one of the top all-around athletes we had ever signed at State. I wasn't expecting his tennis fundamentals to be this solid, but Travis could do anything physically, no question about that."

Mary Katherine knew that if she was going to beat Travis she had to step up her game, and Mary Katherine was used to winning matches. She knew how to get the job done. With the score tied 3-3 she again served to take the lead. Every point was close, Travis going for winners, Mary Katherine playing smart solid defense. The game went to deuce four times before Mary Katherine finally won the game and took the lead, 4-3.

Travis and Mary Katherine then changed sides with Travis serving to tie the match. Travis hit his first serve long. On the second serve Mary Katherine pounded a forehand by Travis. Love-15. Then again on his next first serve Travis faulted. On Travis' second serve Mary Katherine was ready, and she hit another winner off of Travis' second serve. Love-30. With that the girls' tennis team celebrated the good shot. Travis aced Mary Katherine on the third point. 15-30. Then Mary Katherine rallied in the next point. It was a long defensive point until Mary Katherine hit a short slice to Travis' backhand, bringing Travis to the net. Then Mary Katherine hit a high topspin lob just over the top of Travis' outstretched racquet landing the ball just inside the baseline. 15-40. The crowd then cheered the great shot-making. Travis looked at Mary Katherine clapping his hand against his racquet.

"Great shot."

Then he went back to the baseline, and blasted another ace. 30-40. Now the guys were giving it back to the girls.

"Come on Travis! One more ace and we're back to deuce."

The next point was another long point, but eventually Mary Katherine hit Travis another short ball well inside the baseline. Travis then stepped in on a forehand and hit a bullet crosscourt, but the ball clipped the top of the net and floated out wide. Mary Katherine had broken Travis' serve, and took a 5-3 lead. The next game was close. Every point was hard fought, but in the end Mary Katherine had too much finesse for Travis, as she took the set 6-3. After the final point the spectators gave both players a round of applause. Travis walked up to the net and shook Mary Katherine's hand.

"I don't like losing, but you played great."

"Thank you. So did you. Travis, I have played tennis with some of the top college men and professionals. I've never played with anyone who hits it as solid and runs as well as you do. I'm still having a hard time believing you haven't practiced."

"I have had so much happen in the last year," Travis replied. "Playing tennis again was not something I even considered. I'm glad you asked me to come out today. I'd like to play again sometime."

"What about tomorrow?" Mary Katherine asked.

"That would be great, around 3 p.m.?"

"Sure, I'll be looking forward to it."

After the match Travis and Mary Katherine walked over to the bleachers.

"Wow, you two are good," Russell said. "Travis, that serve of yours is wicked."

"I could hear it whizzing by me but I could barely see it!" Mary Katherine said. "Dad, how fast do you think Travis' serve was?"

"120-mph at least. Travis, I'm Rudy Outland, Mary Katherine's father. This is my wife Rita."

"We've already met." Rita said.

"Mr. Outland, these are my friends, Russell and Joe."

Russell quickly added, "Mrs. Outland; if I had known Mary Katherine was your daughter I would not have said how good looking she was, and that Travis was going to beat her."

"Russell, quit while you are behind," Travis suggested, and then they all had a good laugh.

Stephanie came over to Travis.

"Travis that was amazing; I had no idea you could play tennis like that."

"She beat me 6-3!" Travis replied.

"I won this time," Mary Katherine said. "But with some practice you would beat me 6-0. If you want to work at it, you could be a great player at any level."

After the group talked for a while the crowd began to disperse. Travis and the boys were about to head back to the dorm when Travis stopped.

"Give me a minute guys."

He then turned and walked back toward Mary Katherine.

"Mary Katherine, do you have any plans for later tonight?"

"I do have quite a bit of homework."

"I do too; normally after I finish studying I go for a walk at night, around 10. If you could finish your work by then or so, would you like to come along? I could swing by your dorm around 10 p.m."

"Yeah, I'd like that. I'll see you then."

"I'll be there at 10." Travis confirmed.

In the meantime Rita and Rudy had walked to the parking lot. Rita asked, "What do you think of that?"

"She played great."

"That's not what I meant." Rita replied.

"Travis is good, no question about it."

"That's not what I meant."

"I think if Travis practiced he could make the team and help us. He could be a great player, no doubt about it. He's a gifted athlete."

"That's not what I was talking about."

"What are you talking about then?"

Rita put her arms around Rudy and said, "I've never seen Mary Katherine look at a boy the way she looks at Travis. She told me that Travis reminded her of you. I think she's right."

Rudy gave Rita a kiss.

"Thank you Honey. Travis Simpson seems like a fine young man."

Rudy didn't say anything else, he just smiled as he turned and walked away. Rudy knew a great prospect when he saw one; after all he had once been one himself. Rudy could sense he'd met a special young man today. What would happen next, Lord only knows.

YES

Travis met Russell and Joe and the boys started walking back toward the dorm. Joe said, "This is one of the best days I have had in a long time."

Travis said, "Thanks Joe."

"Yeah, I enjoyed watching you play Travis, but I was talking about Alicia Garcia, the junior tennis player from Spain who sat beside me during the match, she is gorgeous."

"Yeah Travis," Russell added, "you and Mary Katherine played great, and Joe and I had a great day too, we realized that we haven't spent enough time watching women's sports."

"Russell's right," Joe said. "These girls are fit, they are outgoing, and they like sports. Man they are perfect."

"Travis you have opened our eyes to a whole new area of dating." Russell concluded. "Women's tennis, softball, volleyball, soccer, swimming, Joe and I are going to get schedules and rosters of all the women's sports teams. Man we are pumped."

Joe then gave Russell a high five.

"Alright," Travis said. "I'm glad I could help."

About that time a voice said, "You looked pretty good out there."

Travis recognized the voice and turned around.

"Hey Dad, when did you get here?"

Ed then said, "I got here about the time you started warming up; you hit the ball great."

"Thanks, she still beat me up pretty good; it's kind of weird, I've never lost to a girl before."

"Well Travis, that girl is one of the top women's players in the world, and besides, if you're going to get beat by somebody, it's easier to accept losing to a girl who looks like that!"

"She is mighty cute, and Dad, she is just as nice as she is pretty. I met her Sunday when she was moving into the girls' dorm. She has a great personality, she won't take any junk off me, I can see that already."

"That's a good thing, don't you think?"

"Yes Dad, she is a special girl. I've just met her, but there is something about her. I want to find out what it is."

"Travis, I've never heard you talk about a girl like that."

"I know Dad, I'm in uncharted territory."

"That can be a good thing too. So you really like her?"

"Yes Dad, I do."

"Travis, let's talk a little about the tennis. You popped those serves

Yes

pretty good out there today."

"I know, I just tried to think, 10 in a row for an Icee."

When Travis was small he and Ed would go practice tennis. Travis would try to hit 10 good serves in a row for an Icee. Ed and Travis had always practiced together. That was the time when father and son developed their relationship.

"I remember, you're a lot bigger now, but I still love to watch you play. When are you going to play again?"

"Mary Katherine and I are going to play tomorrow."

"Be careful playing with Mary Katherine."

"What do you mean?"

Ed then put his hand on Travis' shoulder as he began to explain the complexities of playing sports against a girl you're real interested in, interested in becoming more than just as a practice partner.

"Don't win the battle, and lose the war. Whatever you do, don't beat her!"

"Why not?"

"Son, if you like this girl; practice with her. If you have to play her, let her win."

"Dad, would you do that?"

"Son, I do it all the time. I've lost to your mother. I've lost to your sister. Travis, I've lost to you!"

"Dad, you've never lost to me on purpose, have you?"

"Remember, when it comes to Mary Katherine, "win the war, not the battle."

"Okay Dad, I gotcha."

"What are you going to do about tennis Travis, are you going to start practicing again?"

"I don't know, I really enjoyed today, I haven't thought that far ahead."

"Travis, I've never told you this, because I wanted you to make your own choices, but I've always thought tennis was your most natural sport. You were very good at everything you ever played, but when you were small, the first time you picked up a tennis racquet I could see that you could do anything you wanted with a tennis ball."

"Dad, why didn't you say something when I was younger?"

"Son, children have to make their own choices. That was your decision, and you were a football and baseball All-American, and you loved it. I just wanted to come up here today and watch. I wanted to see what would happen. Travis, your athletic gifts are still there, with some practice, you can play with anyone. You will know what to do, just pray about it, okay."

"Thanks Dad, I will."

"I've got to be going, your mother doesn't know I'm here, I left my cell phone at home so she couldn't call me. I hate that phone. Sometimes; I like to get off by myself once in awhile."

"Dad, do you want to go by the Char-Grill before you go?"

"I got a charburger steak sandwich on my way here. Son; you know my truck automatically turns in the Char-Grill whenever I'm in Raleigh. Your momma is cooking grilled chicken for supper, so I need to be hungry. She's had me on a diet for ten years now, so this is our secret."

"I hear you, thanks for coming today."

"I love you Son, just keep praying, the Lord will lead you."

"I will Dad, I love you too."

Ed then cranked up the truck and headed east to Wilson. Travis caught up with Russell and Joe, then the boys made their way back to the dorm. Once they got back to the dorm room, Russell said,

"Travis you really played great today. I had no idea you could play tennis, not like that anyway."

"Russell, didn't you play something besides football in high school?"

"Yes, I played basketball, but nothing like that. Travis how fast is your serve, do you know?"

"I've never had it clocked, it's been so long since I played like today. You use the same motion in a tennis serve as throwing a football or baseball. When my dad would take me to junior tennis tournaments, we would throw a football in the parking lot before my matches. People looked at us funny, but it sure works."

"Travis you move across the court so fast, and you seemed to always hit the ball so solid, then wherever she hit it, you just ran everything down. How did you do it?"

"It's just like playing short stop. You watch the batter swing, you can tell where the ball is going by the way he is swinging. If you look closely, watch the ball off the bat, you can get a good jump on the ball. It's the same with tennis. I watch the way she sets up to the ball then I start moving before she hits it. I can't explain it. I've just chased so many balls - footballs, baseballs, tennis balls, I don't think about it, I just do it."

"Travis, everyone there today agreed you are a natural tennis player; you do know Mary Katherine's father is the new men's tennis coach."

"I know now," Travis replied, "and her mother is the red-headed lady you told I was going to beat Mary Katherine, their daughter!"

"Yeah, that was not good, but I had confidence in you."

"It's alright, Mr. and Mrs. Outland were real nice. But Russell, these college tennis players are good, all these guys are fast, they all hit the ball hard. They have all the shots, it would take a lot of work to play with them, much less make the men's tennis team. Besides, Coach Outland might not be interested in me; today he saw me lose to his daughter."

"His daughter could probably beat all the guys on the men's team; she did qualify for the U.S. Open. Travis, all I'm saying is I know what I saw today, you are a natural, it's a gift to play like that, just think about it."

"It's 6:30," Russell said. "Let's go get something to eat."

With that the boys headed to the cafeteria. The conversation changed from playing tennis to the players on the women's team, not only their playing ability, but their potential "dating ability" as well. While they were eating Travis also thought about what Russell and his father had said. He knew in his mind they were right, but his heart wasn't so sure. He didn't want to go out for the team and get his feelings hurt. He was afraid to get his hopes up and be disappointed again. After supper Travis went back to the room and did his homework. Then about 9:45 he put on his baseball cap and headed to Mary Katherine's dorm. When Travis reached the dormitory Mary Katherine was sitting on a bench outside. She had on a t-shirt and gym shorts, flip-flops and her hair was pulled back in a ponytail.

"You're on time Travis, I like that."

"I'm trying to make a good impression."

"You're doing fine so far."

Then she got up off the bench and the two of them started walking.

"Where are we going Travis?"

"I have a spot in mind; I've spent a lot of time there."

The kids talked as they walked along, music, schoolwork, cars, this and that. They made their way past the baseball stadium to the bleachers at the tennis courts.

"Travis. You're kidding right?"

"No Mary Katherine, this is the most secluded place on campus. Whenever I go for a walk I always seem to end up here. Last year this time I spent a lot of time on my own. I would always end up here. I've spent many nights on these bleachers, thinking about what might have been, and what to do next."

There was seriousness in Travis' voice. Mary Katherine could sense his pain. She spoke up and said, "Do you have your own private seat?" easing the tension.

Travis smiled and replied, "Ladies first."

Mary Katherine took her seat. Travis then walked to her right and sat down beside her.

"This is a quiet spot," Mary Katherine said. "These oak trees are beautiful."

"This is the perfect spot to get lost in your thoughts. I love this place."

"Travis, I can't imagine what you've experienced with your injury. I twisted my knee in a tournament when I was sixteen. At first it looked like it might require surgery. I wondered for a few days when or even if I would be able to play tennis again. I remember how scared I was. I also remember when you were injured, like I told you, I saw the replay on ESPN. My parents and I talked about it, we were all shaken by it."

"It has been hard," Travis said as he looked down at his hands and rubbed his palms together. "At times I have been really down about it. I have said my prayers and shed my tears, many of them right here."

"I don't want to bring back bad memories; I just want you to know I admire what you are doing, the way you have bounced back."

"What do you mean?"

Mary Katherine went on to say, "Lots of people would have given up or been bitter if something like this happened to them. They would have been mad, maybe given up on God. When I saw you in Bible study after all that has happened, that told me a lot about you."

"After the accident my faith was severely tested. My injury hurt me, and also my family. I questioned God. I have had my doubts. I am not too proud to admit that at times I have been depressed. I have questioned everything I thought was real about myself, and God. Since the accident, I have found that my faith in God and my relationship with Jesus is the only thing that has remained the same. I don't know that I would have been able to make it without my faith. It makes me sad to think about people who try to live today, with all the struggles we face, without a relationship with Jesus. I have seen so many people who are struggling with things. Walking around campus, just going from here to there, now I notice people more. I wonder what burdens they are carrying; this injury has made me more sensitive to other people's pain. I notice it more, but I'm not sure what to do about it."

Mary Katherine asked, "Are you praying about it? Praying for God to reveal it to you?"

Travis was moved by the question, he sensed Mary Katherine's sincerity, the depths of her faith. Something was happening, his heart was moving, he was scared, but he was beginning to hope. Travis held out his left hand and said,

"My hand looks the same, but everything, my thoughts, my dreams, my plans are different."

Mary Katherine then reached out and touched Travis' left hand.

"Does your hand still hurt, does it feel different than before?"

When Mary Katherine held Travis' hand, he felt a sense of peace. His pulse was racing, he was so excited, for a moment he was well again. Travis didn't know what to say. Mary Katherine sensed the awkwardness.

"Is everything okay? I didn't mean to ask so many personal questions."

And she put her hand back by her side. Travis realized what had happened.

"No. It's fine, talking with you helps me feel better, and playing today was great. I like being with you, you can ask me anything you like."

Then he smiled at her and reached over and held her hand. Then Travis said,

"You holding my hand makes it feel normal again. Thank you for listening."

"Anytime."

Travis smiled and looked at her and said,

"I'm going to hold you to that."

"Good." She replied.

The kids leaned back on the bleachers, holding hands in the moonlight. Travis thought about how quickly his life had changed. A year ago he lay on the ground beside home plate in the baseball stadium just across the street from where he now sat. Looking up at the blue sky beyond his crying parents, and the doctors who where there by his side. Three nights ago he stood beside the ocean, starring at these same stars, wondering what God had planned for him. Tonight, as he sat beside this beautiful young girl, and poured out his heart, she took his hand, and calmed his fears. Travis then looked down on the tennis courts where earlier today he felt the exhilaration of competition again. For the first time in a long time, he dared to dream that good things could happen for him again.

Travis then looked over at Mary Katherine, and thought to himself,

"Could this be real, can this really be happening to me? Lord, can this be true?

Then, in a quite still voice, Travis heard Him answer.

"Yes."

HIS HANDS

"Travis, you're back again?" The lady in the reception area said.
Travis answered, "Yes ma'am."
"Would you like to see Dr. Clauson?"
"Yes, please."
Then the lady said, "I'll go get her."
Before long, Stephanie came into the lobby,
"Roger Federer, can I have an autograph?"
"Please, I got beat yesterday remember?"
"Yeah, but you played a pretty good player, besides, the way you ran and hit that ball; you'll be winning matches in no time."
"Mary Katherine invited me to play again today. I'd like to go again if you don't mind."
"Sure, go ahead. Travis, have you considered playing competitive tennis again?"
"Stephanie, so much happened in the last couple of days. I had a great time yesterday. But to tell you the truth, since the injury, I'm concerned about putting myself out there again."
"Travis, I understand, anyone who has experienced a loss like you have would feel this way. But Travis, God has blessed you with a special gift. The way you move on the court, the balls just explode off your racquet, God has blessed you with this talent, who knows where tennis may lead you. Trust in God, believe in yourself."
At that point Travis became emotional, as he began to fight back the tears.
"Stephanie, I want so much to believe again, to believe good things will happen for me. I am so amazed by all that God is showing me, to believe that this is really happening, and not just a dream."
Stephanie looked at Travis.
"Travis, give me your hand."
Travis gave Stephanie his hand, then they sat down and she looked him in the eye and said,
"Let's pray about it."
They both bowed their heads.
"*Dear Lord, thank you for our lives, the gift of life. Father, be with Travis, watch over him and keep him safe. Father, Travis has experienced so much change in his life. Lord, show him Your will for his life. Teach him to trust again. Lord, give him the courage and peace to use your gifts to glorify your Son Jesus Christ, in His name we pray. Amen.*"

When Stephanie raised her head she was crying. She reached out her hand and picked up the cross Travis had made. She held it in her hands.

"Travis, when I watched you yesterday; I could see God moving in your life. I even asked myself, could this be true? Lord, is this what Travis was created to do all along? Travis, we can't put our limits on God. You have a gift, trust in the God who gave you the gift. Remember Travis, with God all things are possible."

Travis was choked up; he didn't know what to say.

"God is with you, Travis. Follow your heart, He will lead you."

"Thank you Stephanie, you have been such a blessing to me,"

Then Travis stood up and he turned and walked out the door. Stephanie sat the cross back on her desk, then again she prayed to the Lord.

"Father, thank you for the miracle You are working in Travis' life, and thank you Father for allowing me to witness it."

Then she sat behind her desk and looked out her office window. She thought about all that had happened, and then she smiled as she thought about all the good things to come.

Travis got to the tennis courts at 2:30. Rita was already there watching the team practice.

"Hello Travis," Rita said. "I hear you and Mary Katherine are going to play again today. I was very impressed watching you play yesterday."

"Thank you Mrs. Outland. I really enjoyed playing with Mary Katherine, she is a great player."

"She loves to play, she and her father have spent so much time together playing tennis. It has been great for our family."

"My father and I have done the same thing. Dad taught me to play baseball and football. He coached my teams in little league. We practiced together. I've learned so much from the lessons my dad has taught me while playing sports."

Rita could see that Travis was close to his family.

"Travis, you obviously have talent. Have you considered playing college tennis?"

"Before yesterday I had no idea I would ever have a chance to play anything competitively again. I'm not sure what to do about it."

"What are you concerned about?"

Travis was hesitant, he was uneasy about sharing his feelings.

"I'm not sure I can do it. I'd like to play, but the guys who have grown up playing year-round tennis are so consistent. They have played so many competitive matches, I just don't know if I can make up that experience advantage they have.''

"Anyone can gain experience by practicing and playing matches,'' Rita said. "But the ability to run, to hit the ball with power. To anticipate where the ball is going to be hit, those are gifts, God given talents. They have been given to you for His pleasure. You believe that don't you?''

"Yes ma'am, I believe in God. I am a Christian. I believe God is in control. It's just hard for me to believe in myself again.''

"Travis, I know you have been hurt. Rudy and I as parents have talked about how we would react if something like that happened to Mary Katherine or our son Joseph. But whatever changes we face in our lives, God remains the same. He has good things planned for you, just like before. His love for us is unchanging. Trust in that. Travis, you have many gifts. You will discover what they are as you follow Jesus. He will teach you as He leads you. Have faith in that. I have watched a lot of tennis over the years. I know talent when I see it. Travis, you have the talent, the gift is there. Accept the gift and see where it leads you.''

Travis listened intently to what Rita was saying. He could sense the sincerity in her words. He immediately felt a connection to her. She and Mary Katherine displayed a sense of peace, the quiet confidence Travis had seen in his parents. He turned and looked out onto the court where Mary Katherine and the team were finishing practice. MK waved and smiled in his direction. Rita also smiled as she thought about the young man who had appeared in her daughter's life. She could sense a special chemistry between the two of them. For Rita to assist in her daughter's happiness was her mission in life. She wondered? Could this be the man God has planned for Mary Katherine? Is this the man who will be the father of our grandchildren? She had only just met this young man, but it was obvious that something was happening here. God was moving. Rita thought about the timing of the family relocating to Raleigh. Rudy's decision to make the transition from teaching at tennis academies, to coaching major college tennis, taking over a men's tennis program at a school with national title potential. Rudy had already recruited four freshmen from among his tennis academy students in Florida. Now this young man, a world-class athlete, suddenly walks into their lives. Travis has more natural talent than anyone she or Rudy has ever seen; he is a coaches' dream. Rita can see that Travis needs something to hang onto, an outlet to display these God-given talents. Soon she will sit on these same bleachers and watch her family's dreams play out on these courts. She wonders how much of a role will Travis Simpson play in their family, and if one day he may be part of their family. She smiles as she thinks about the possibilities. Only time will tell.

As the girls' practice was winding down, Rudy came walking toward the bleachers.

"Rita, how did my girl do today?"

"She did great, another solid practice. She spent a lot of time working on her serve."

Rudy then pointed to Travis.

"This young man has a great serve. Travis, I enjoyed watching you play yesterday."

"Thank you sir. Mary Katherine was the one who did the playing. She beat me pretty bad."

"She's mighty tough. I don't know if any of my guys could beat her. She beat all my men recruits from the academy last year; losing to her is nothing to be ashamed of."

That helped ease Travis' fears. Rudy was very approachable. Like Rita and Mary Katherine, Rudy exuded the confidence of faith.

"Thank you for telling me that. I've never lost to a girl before. I'm not so sure how to react to her beating me."

"Get used to it son. Dads lose to everybody; isn't that right Rita?"

"If they're smart they do."

Rudy looked over at Travis.

"Travis, let me know if I can help you with your tennis."

Travis' heart skipped a beat.

"Thank you sir. I'll take all the help I can get."

"Travis," Rudy said. "I like for Mary Katherine to hit forehands and backhands, crosscourt and down the line with a practice partner. Then they work on short balls, volleys and lobs. They practice serving and return of serves. After that they play some seven-point tiebreakers; that keeps her working on fundamentals. Organized practice builds confidence. I was wondering if Travis, you might consider being her practice partner?"

"Yes sir; that would be great."

"If you like, I'll sit over here and watch. I'll give you both some pointers as I'm watching you practice."

"Yes sir. Thank you sir."

Mary Katherine then looked toward Travis.

"Hey boy, who did you come to see today, me or my parents?"

Travis turned to Rita and Rudy.

"That's my cue, thank you again for your help, Coach Outland."

"You're welcome Travis, anytime."

Travis got up and jogged out onto the court. He stretched his legs and shoulder muscles. Then he and Mary Katherine jogged around the courts to loosen up. When they finished loosening up Mary Katherine said,

"Travis, I don't want to play today. I would rather practice, if that's okay with you?"

"Sure, that would be fine with me."

"Our match was pretty close yesterday; I don't know that I would have handled losing as graciously as you did."

Travis thought back to what his dad had told him.

"The longer I live the smarter Dad gets"

"Travis," Mary Katherine continued. "I'm not used to losing, and I don't want to be competing with…"

Then she stopped, she wasn't sure how to qualify their relationship. Travis saw her dilemma. He stepped in and said,

"The guy you are dating?"

"Are we dating?" She asked.

Travis stepped forward. He tapped his racquet onto the top of the net, then he smiled at MK.

"There are no other girls I'm interested in, and I would be jealous if I saw you with another guy."

Mary Katherine smiled. She looked down as she slid her right foot across the court in front of her. She then gazed back up toward Travis.

"I wouldn't want to see you with another girl either."

"So I suppose I would introduce you as my girlfriend? My only girlfriend?"

"And you would be my only boyfriend?"

"That's the way I want it," Travis replied.

"Me too."

Travis then said, "I wouldn't want to risk messing up something like that, just to win a tennis match."

"Well I guess we need to get to practicing then," she said. "Let's hit forehands first."

"Are you going to be my coach too?"

MK then walked up to the net, she leaned forward and kissed Travis on the cheek. Then she whispered in his ear.

"You better get used to me telling you what to do; you know all girls like to have their way."

"As long as you ask me this way, I will do anything you say."

MK smiled as she turned and looked toward her mother. There were also some of the other girls on the tennis team sitting in the bleachers behind Travis. He could not see them, but MK could. They stood up. Smiled, then silently clapped their hands, and gave Mary Katherine a thumbs up.

From there the lesson began. Mary Katherine was quickly putting Travis through his paces as Rita and Rudy looked on.

Rudy told Rita; "Mary Katherine is doing a good job coaching out there."

"She has had a good teacher."

Rudy smiled, "Thank you, Honey."

"Are you going out there?"

"No." Rudy said, "it looks like they are doing fine on their own. Besides, there's more happening out there than just tennis lessons."

"I like the way they look together, don't you?"

"Yes," Rudy replied, "they are both good kids. Everything I've heard about Travis Simpson has been positive."

"Travis reminds me of a young tennis player I used to know. That boy turned out to be a wonderful husband and father. I hope Mary Katherine will be blessed that way."

Rudy then said, "It's all in God's hands Honey, it's in His hands."

A GUEST FOR DINNER

"Hey Dad; How are you doing?"

"Fine Son. I got your message you called, what's going on with you?"

"I'm doing good," Travis said. "I wanted to see what you and Mom are doing for dinner tomorrow night?"

"We don't have any plans, not any that your mother has told me about. Why? Did you want to get together and do something?"

"Dad, I have something I wanted to talk with you about."

"Travis, do you need me to come to Raleigh; is something wrong?"

"No Dad, nothing's wrong. I just have something on my mind and I wanted to sit down and talk with you about it."

"That's fine Son, when do you want to get together?"

"I was thinking I might come home and have dinner tomorrow night, maybe we could cook out on the grill and we could talk then, just the two of us."

"That sounds great. You want me to cook us some barbecue chicken?"

"Yeah, that would be perfect. There is one more thing. I'd like to invite Mary Katherine."

"Mary Katherine. You mean that cute tennis player."

"Yes Dad, you know who I mean."

"You know that's fine with us. What time will you be here?"

"I thought we could get there around 5 p.m. so we could have time to visit before dinner."

"That sounds good to me. I am looking forward to meeting Mary Katherine."

"I really like this girl, Dad."

"I'm happy for you Son, I am proud of you. I'll look forward to seeing you tomorrow."

"Okay, I am going to invite her to come to dinner then; just plan on us being there tomorrow at 5 p.m."

"I'll see you then."

Later that Friday after the women's team finished practice, Travis met Mary Katherine at the tennis courts. Before they got started Travis asked Mary Katherine if her family had any plans for the weekend.

Mary Katherine replied, "No, nothing special. Why, what did you have in mind?"

"I was planning on going home tomorrow night to eat dinner with my parents; I was hoping you would come too?"

"What time?"

"We need to leave here about 4:00."

"What time will we get back?"

"I don't know for sure, but we could be back around 11:30."

"What would I need to wear?"

"Whatever you like."

"Who will be there?"

"My Mom, my Dad."

"Anybody else?"

"I don't think so."

"What will we be eating?"

"Barbecue chicken"

"Will we be eating inside or outside?"

Travis said, "I'm not sure, these sure are a lot of questions!"

Mary Katherine then explained, "I want to make a good first impression. A girl needs to know these things, especially before I meet your parents."

"So you will come to dinner?"

"Yes, of course."

"They'll love you, you don't have to worry about that."

"You know Travis, this is our first real date."

"I guess I'm a 'pretty cheap' boyfriend, our first real date and I'm taking you to eat at my parents' house."

With that being settled, the two kids each went to their side of the tennis court and practice got started. Mary Katherine took charge and they both went to work.

Later that night Ed got home from work around 6:30. Kathy was on the couch reading the paper. Wesley was lying on the top of the couch asleep.

Ed asked, "Kathy, what's for supper?"

"Whatever you want, K&W, Chick-fil-a, Western Sizzlin?"

"You don't have dinner ready? What do you think about that Wesley?"

Wesley just lifted his head then he laid it back down. Wesley knew he would have his dinner.

Kathy looked above the top of the paper, "I worked all day too, Buddy!"

"Alright, K&W is fine tonight, but what about tomorrow? What do you have planned to cook tomorrow night?"

"Since it's just the two of us, and the restaurants will be open for business, I'm not planning on cooking tomorrow night either."

Ed jokingly replied, "You're not!"

"No, I'm not! Do you want to cook?"

"I thought I might cook barbecue chicken on the grill tomorrow night?"

"Ed, why do you want to go to all that trouble when it's just the two of us?"

"Who said it's just the two of us?"

Kathy then pointed at Ed, then herself and said, "One, Two; Wesley doesn't count, he's got his own food."

Ed then sat down on the couch next to Wesley and picked up the sports page. He didn't say anything else for a while. After a few minutes Kathy asked,

"Are you ready to go to K&W?"

"Yeah," Ed said, "but we never finished talking about dinner tomorrow night."

"Ed, why are you so concerned about dinner tomorrow night? If it's just going to be the two of us, what difference does it make?"

Ed was holding the newspaper up hiding his face.

"Travis called me today and said he was coming home tomorrow, and he was bringing Mary Katherine Outland with him for dinner."

Kathy reached over and snatched the newspaper away from Ed and said,

"What did you say?"

"You heard me."

Kathy asked, "Travis is coming home to dinner tomorrow night?"

"Um hum."

"And he's bringing Mary Katherine Outland, the girl he's been playing tennis with?"

"Um hum"

"How long have you known about this Ed?"

"I just found out today."

"What time today?" Kathy asked.

"I don't know, around 9:30 this morning."

"9:30, and you have kept that a secret all day!"

"It's not a secret; I just got home to tell you."

"You go to K&W and get your own dinner you 'Old Bear.' I've got company coming tomorrow, you can take care of yourself."

"Wait a minute! What about my dinner tonight?"

"You're a grown man, you can take care of yourself."

With that Kathy grabbed the cell phone and called Travis. She wanted to get all the information she could about tomorrow night's dinner guest. Ed just smiled. After 25 years he was used to playing second fiddle to the kids. He didn't mind, he thought it was all kind of funny. Ed patted Wesley on the head and picked up his car keys. By now Kathy was on the phone with Travis. Ed asked her,

"Do you want me to pick you up something from K&W?"

"No, I'm too excited to eat."

Ed then replied, "I'm excited too, but I'm still going to eat."

So out the door he went.

The next day a little before 4 p.m. Travis arrived at Mary Katherine's dorm, he waited in the lobby reading the paper. After a couple minutes Mary Katherine came out of the elevator. She had her dark brown hair pulled back and braided. She wore a white and green floral dress and white sandals. Travis quickly stood up starring at Mary Katherine.

Mary Katherine asked, "Do I look okay?"

"You look great. This is the first time I've seen you dressed up this way; you look beautiful."

"Thank you, I want to make a good impression tonight. I am excited about meeting your parents."

"My dad is real laid back, he's looking forward to meeting you. My mom called last night and talked for an hour asking me all about you."

"My mom is like that too. She wants to know what's going on. I'm ready if you are, I don't want to be late."

"Me too, let's go."

The kids walked out to the car and headed for Wilson. When Travis pulled up in the driveway Ed was outside talking with their next-door neighbor Mike Richardson. Mike's six-year old son Ryan was riding his bicycle in the driveway. Travis parked the Jetta and then he and Mary Katherine walked toward Ed and Mike.

"Hi Dad, Mr. Richardson."

"Hello Son, who's this pretty girl you have with you?"

"This is Mary Katherine Outland. Mary Katherine this is my father Ed Simpson, our neighbor Mike Richardson, and Mr. Richardson's son Ryan."

Mary Katherine extended her hand, "Mr. Simpson, it is a pleasure to meet you."

"Mary Katherine; it's a pleasure to meet you. Kathy and I are excited to have you for dinner tonight."

"Thank you for inviting me."

About that time the front door opened and Wesley came flying outside, Kathy had Wesley on a leash but he was pulling with all his might to get to Travis.

"Hi Mom, looks like Wesley is in a hurry."

"Once Wesley gets his mind made up there's no stopping him." Kathy said.

Travis and Mary Katherine then walked toward Kathy, and Travis picked up Wesley.

"Mary Katherine, this is my mom, Kathy Simpson. Mom this is Mary Katherine."

Kathy was grinning from ear to ear, she didn't waste time on a handshake as she walked over and hugged Mary Katherine.

"Mary Katherine, we are so happy to have you for dinner tonight, and I love your dress."

"Thank you."

Kathy: "Travis she is lovely."

Mary Katherine was completely at ease around the Simpsons. They hit it off. Ryan then rode his bicycle up beside Travis.

Ryan asked, "Travis, is Mary Katherine your girlfriend?"

"Yeah Ryan, what do you think? She sure is pretty isn't she?"

Ryan just smiled and nodded, "Yes." Then Ryan said, "Mary Katherine, do you want to see me ride my scooter?"

Mike said, "Ryan, Mary Katherine came to visit the Simpsons tonight, she doesn't have time to watch you ride your scooter."

"It's okay." Mary Katherine said. "Let's see you ride it Ryan, I like to ride a scooter sometimes too."

Ryan then said, "I've got two scooters!"

He dropped his bicycle and ran into the garage. Ryan came running back with two scooters. Before you know it, Ryan and Mary Katherine were riding scooters in the Richardson's driveway. Mary Katherine had on a floral dress, braided hair riding a scooter. Mike looked at Travis and said,

"Travis, I think this girl is a keeper."

Travis replied, "She is something special alright."

Kathy and Ed just stood there smiling. They were both so happy; after about twenty minutes of riding the scooter Ryan had had enough.

"Mary Katherine, I'm tired of riding the scooter, do you want to go for a bike ride?"

Mike then said, "That's enough Ryan, are you trying to steal Travis' girlfriend?"

"No, I don't like girls."

Travis said, "You will Buddy, you will."

With that Ryan hopped back on his bicycle. Travis, Mary Katherine, Kathy, Ed and Wesley went inside. They all went into the den, sat down and got to know one another. Ed could quickly see why Travis was so attracted to Mary Katherine. She was polite, personable, beautiful, and very bright. She seemed completely comfortable, and Kathy loved her. Mary Katherine was exactly the kind of girl Kathy was hoping Travis would meet. After a few minutes Kathy and Mary Katherine were talking as if Travis and Ed were not even in the room. That's when Ed said, "It's time to get the grill started. Travis you want to come outside with me and Wesley?"

"Sure Dad."

Travis and Ed got up and started walking toward the door. Travis looked back; Wesley was lying on Mary Katherine's lap. Travis said, "Come on Wesley, let's go outside."

Wesley lifted his head, he looked at Travis and Ed, but he did not get up. Ed smiled and said again, "Come on Wesley, let's go outside!"

Wesley did not move.

"Wesley," Travis asked, "are you kicking me to the curb?"

"Wesley knows a good thing when he sees it," Kathy replied.

Mary Katherine just smiled. She had made a great first impression. The Simpson men, minus Wesley, went out in the back yard and lit the grill. Then they both sat down on the porch. After catching up for a few minutes Ed asked Travis, "Son, what is it you wanted to talk with me about?"

"Dad, there is just so much happening with me right now, I don't know where to begin."

"I'm listening Son; just tell me what's on your mind."

"Dad, since the accident I have lost a lot of confidence in things. No one particular thing. It's more like everything. I just expect something bad to happen. I've done my best in school, I've worked out, and I've worked at the restaurant. I've made some great friends. I have so much to be thankful for, God has blessed me; I know that. But honestly Dad, I am afraid. I am afraid of getting hurt again. I know I need to have faith and hope for the best, but I am afraid, and I don't want anyone else to know it, but I am. It makes me feel weak, and I don't know what to do about it."

Ed just sat there listening, he just nodded, and then he said,

"Go on Son, tell me, what are you having doubts about? How can I help?"

"Dad, I haven't played tennis in years. Back when I was playing junior tennis. I felt like I could have done more with it. If I had just played tennis and not played any other sport, I know I would have won more matches, played in the nationals. But now that I have been injured, I feel more vulnerable about so many things. Instead of believing in what is possible, I am afraid of something else bad happening. I don't want to feel this way, but I do."

"Travis, everyone is afraid sometimes, you know that don't you?"

"Yes Dad, I do."

"Travis, what has happened to you has been hard for me to accept too. But Travis, I have seen you grow so much though this trial. It's hard when we face difficult things; it's hard to believe in good things again. When your grandfather died, I was the oldest child, I was your age, and I was scared to death, but I had to go on. You're grandmother and your uncle Randy needed me. We needed each other. When that happened, I just did the best I could to accept it, but it took time for me to get my confidence back."

"Dad, in the past week I met Mary Katherine. I played tennis again. I feel like God is opening these doors in my life. He is teaching me to trust in Him again, but I don't want to get my hopes up."

"Travis, you're a good kid; you are everything I could have hoped for in a Son. I can see God is moving in your life. Continue to pursue your dreams. Things are going to happen in life, good and bad. Face the truth and do your best. Remember I love you and I am proud of you. Follow your heart. What does your heart tell you? What would you like to see happen?"

"I would like to play tennis at State. I want to be a part of a team again. I want to compete."

"Then set your sights on that and make it happen. Give it everything you've got, and then see where it takes you."

Then Travis said; "And Mary Katherine, Dad; I want to be with her every minute. I've never felt like this about a girl. She's funny, she's tough, she's beautiful. Mary Katherine is just a great girl. I've only known her a week, but I feel like I've known her all of my life."

Ed leaned back and smiled.

"Girls are a little more complicated than tennis!"

"I know," Travis said. "She is always a step or two ahead of me."

"Mary Katherine is a special girl, I can see that already. Just remember this Son; treat her the way you would want to see a man treat your sister or your mother. Treat her with respect and be honest about how you feel. Then pray about it. You won't go wrong doing that."

It wasn't long after that the barbecue chicken was ready to come off the grill. Travis and Ed went inside. They all sat down at the table to eat. After dinner the four of them relaxed in the den. Ed watched Travis. He saw the smile on Travis' face. Ed saw the way Mary Katherine lit up the room. How Kathy seemed so relaxed. Ed could sense a new hope. Travis was beginning to look toward the future. Kathy was also drawn to Mary Katherine, Ed could feel his own tensions drifting away as he saw his family laughing and smiling again. The man of the house began to see the joy come back in his home. The people he loved the most, his family, their security, their happiness, was everything to Ed. Now there was another person, a dinner guest, who had entered their lives. While Ed sat there quietly listening to the conversation, he looked over at Wesley. Wesley was listening intently to all that was being said. Ed thought to himself,

"Lord, I'll never figure out where You are leading me until we get there, but thank You for tonight."

Then the Voice inside Ed's head said,

"You're welcome."

HIS PLAN

It was around midnight when Travis got back to the dorm room. Russell was in the room studying when Travis arrived. It was unusual for Russell to be in the room studying on a Saturday night. Russell asked,

"How did it go tonight?"

"It went great. Mary Katherine and my parents really hit it off."

"What did you have for supper?"

"Barbecue chicken, man it was so good. My dad loves to cook on the grill."

"What did Mary Katherine have to say; did she have a good time?"

"Yeah, she really seemed to enjoy herself. I tell you Russell; I feel such a connection to Mary Katherine. I have only known her for a week, but I feel so comfortable around her."

"I am happy for you Travis. I agree, I have a good feeling about Mary Katherine."

"I've had a lot of things happen this week, meeting Mary Katherine, playing tennis again. Good things have happened to me that a week ago I would have never imagined."

"Travis, I have something I need to tell you."

Travis was suddenly concerned; Russell had a very serious tone in his voice.

"Sure Russell, what is it?"

"Travis, since I saw you play tennis with Mary Katherine last Monday, I have thought so much about what I saw, the way you played, all the things that have happened to you this past year. Watching you play tennis, you looked like you were born to hold a tennis racquet. I have had this feeling in my spirit. I have prayed about it. What to say to you; how to help you? I have something I feel led to tell you, but I don't want to overstep my bounds."

"Russell, you are like a brother to me, whatever you feel you need to say, I want to hear it."

"Travis, when I saw you and Mary Katherine last week, there was something between you from the moment you saw each other. Then when I saw you play tennis, I couldn't believe my eyes. After all that has happened, the way all the circumstances have come together. Your injury was only to the fingers on your left hand. Part of your therapy was to squeeze and toss a tennis ball. Stephanie puts us on this ridiculous fitness program so you're in the best shape of your life. Then up walks Mary Katherine, you and her play tennis and suddenly it's as if this tragic accident somehow positions you with this wonderful Christian girl on a tennis court. Then you play like you have been practicing and playing tennis every day, and you haven't played a match in five years. It just seems too good to be true, it's so surreal."

Travis just sat there. Russell was describing Travis' own feelings exactly. He just listened, wondering where Russell was going with this. Then Russell continued.

"Travis, I have prayed about this every night since Monday. I have this thought in my mind, I need to tell you, but I don't want to interfere."

Travis could see Russell was convicted by what he had seen and prayed about, then, Travis told Russell;

"Whatever it is Russell, say it. Say what is on your heart."

"Travis, do not be afraid. This is exactly where you are supposed to be, you are doing exactly what you were created to do. God is with you. Believe in your gift. This is real. God will be glorified by this, trust in Him. You know God is in control of all things. He has you right where He wants you. He will be with you every step of the way. I have felt convicted in my spirit to tell you that."

Travis leaned back on the bed, his back against the wall. The boys sat there for a few minutes, neither one said anything. After a while Travis picked up his tennis ball and put on his baseball cap, he looked over at Russell and said, "God bless you Russell, that is exactly what I needed."

"God is with you Travis; I can feel His presence whenever we are together. Is there anything I can do for you?"

"No Russell, you've already done more than I could have ever hoped for. You have been the best friend, at a time when I needed one the most."

Travis turned and walked out the door. He walked in the moonlight as he made his way across campus. As he reached the tennis courts he saw a figure of a person on the bleachers. When he got a little closer, he smiled as he recognized the attractive girl in her shorts, t-shirt, flip-flops and baseball cap.

"You weren't ready for bed yet?" Travis asked.

"No." Mary Katherine replied. "I had a big date tonight. I guess I was too excited to sleep."

"Sounds like you had a good time?"

"Yes, I had a great time. The food was good, I met some very nice people, rode a scooter. I didn't want it to end. It has been a wonderful day. I've been sitting here praying; thanking God for all these blessings in my life."

Travis sat down beside Mary Katherine and looked up into the stars.

"It is so incredible to think how awesome God is." Travis said. "He created and sustains this world. Yet somehow, in the midst of all this, He leads us and cares for us. God intended for you and me to sit here tonight on these bleachers together, before either of us were ever born."

Mary Katherine reached over and held Travis' hand.

"I love your parents Travis. I feel like I've known them all my life."

"Mary Katherine, in this past week, I have begun to hope again, you have been such an important part of that. I don't know where God is leading me, but I am so thankful He brought you into my life."

Mary Katherine looked up at the stars.

"It's funny," she said. "I was thanking God for the same thing. I'm looking forward to seeing where He leads us next week."

"Next week, together?" Travis asked.

"Of course, I could not imagine it any other way."

Then the kids leaned back on the bleachers, gazing at the stars. The Master gazed down from the heavens, pleased as His plan was unfolding.

It was 9:30 Monday morning. There was a knock on the door; then a voice said,

"Coach Outland, may I come in and speak with you?"

"Yes Travis, come in, have a seat."

"Is this a good time? I know you are busy, I don't want to interrupt?"

"Now is a good time. I have a meeting at 11 a.m., so we have plenty of time. What's on your mind?"

"Coach Outland, I know the tennis team has been practicing for three weeks now, and that I have not been at practice working out with the other players who are trying out for the team, but sir, I would like to come to practice and earn a spot on the team. I would be willing to do extra workouts to make up the time I've missed. A week ago I did not realize playing college tennis was a possibility for me. So much has happened to me this past week. Things I didn't believe were possible. I know it won't be easy. It will take a lot of extra work on my part to catch up with theses guys that have been playing every day. But I believe I can do it, but Coach Outland, I need your help. Coach Outland, would you work with me and give me a chance to earn a spot on your team?"

Rudy sat there for a moment; he had hoped Travis would come to him. Now Travis was here, Rudy searched for the right words.

"Travis, I want you to know that I will do anything I can to help you. I would do that for any of my players. I cannot promise you that you will make the team. If you do make the team, I cannot promise you that you will play. But I will promise you that I will give you every opportunity to prove yourself. I will give you an opportunity to compete. I treat all of my players the same. I will treat you all the way I would want a coach to treat my son. I will tolerate no profanity or unsportsmanlike behavior from my players. I expect all of my players to conduct themselves at all times, in public, and in private, as representatives of this tennis program, and the university. These are my rules, and they are not negotiable. Do you understand and agree with these rules?"

"Yes sir, I do."

"Travis, I have four freshmen that I coached at the tennis academy in Florida. These four kids were all ranked in the top 100 USTA rankings in the nation last year. I have one returning junior who was second team All-ACC from last year's team. I feel as though I have five solid players, the sixth singles spot is up in the air. I have four returning players from last year's team. I will keep twelve players on the team roster. During practice I spend a great deal of time teaching doubles. The doubles point is critical in college tennis. If you start out one point down after doubles it is very difficult to take that momentum back in singles. Every week, all season, I will schedule challenge matches to determine the lineup. I believe competition develops talent. I myself love to compete, I expect my players to compete at all times, and we never give up, until the last point is finished. Do you understand?"

"Yes sir."

"I can see you have the athletic skills to compete Travis. Tell me about your tennis experience, how you learned to play, what kind of coaching you have had?"

"My mom played college tennis and my sister Sarah was a very good junior player. I started playing junior tennis when I was 10, and I had lessons and went to tennis clinics. My mother was very focused on the fundamentals. She spent most of the time teaching me the proper techniques. By the time I was a teenager my game had progressed to the point I didn't have anyone to play with who could give me a competitive match. In Wilson we didn't have tennis facilities like they do in Raleigh or Charlotte, and I reached the point where I had to always travel to find a match. There just was no one else for me to play in town."

"That is a real obstacle in tennis." Rudy said. "If you don't have other players to push you, you can't improve. Somebody has to hit the ball back, don't they?"

"Yes sir, it's just like baseball. You have to see good pitching to stay sharp; if not, when you face a good pitcher you're not prepared. That's what happened with my tennis. I only played matches in tournaments. Once I reached the Southerns I played the kids who played tennis year round. I could hit with them, and often times overpower them and outrun them, but they made fewer mistakes."

"Also, my father played college baseball and football. We spent so much time together. He coached my teams and we went to games together. Sarah spent more time with Mom. I spent more time with Dad. That time I was able to spend playing baseball and football with my dad, versus all the travel involved in tennis, led me toward football and baseball. I love to play all sports, as you said; I love to compete."

"Travis, you have a gift. I could see that the moment you hit your first serve to Mary Katherine. The talent is there, you can be confident of that. What you do with it is ultimately up to you. I know you have experienced a great loss, Travis. I am sorry that happened to you, but in life we have to move forward. Take advantage of the opportunities that present themselves. As a coach, I see a talent in you Travis. I would like to help you develop it. So you be at practice today at 1p.m."

"Yes sir. Coach Outland, what do you want me to do to make up the time I missed?"

"You continue to practice with Mary Katherine as her practice partner. I can give you some extra help then. Besides, I've already had to make an exception to one of my rules for you."

"What's that sir?"

"I told the team that none of my players could date Mary Katherine."
Travis: "I see."

Then Rudy said, "Don't worry, I'd rather have peace in my home than not bend a rule, especially if the girls in my life are happy."

Travis just nodded and said, "Yes sir, I'll see you at one; again, thank you sir."

"You're welcome. Just remember you will have to earn your way, but I am always here to help."

With that Travis walked out of the office and Rudy leaned back in his chair. He thought about all that had happened in just one week. Then he thought back to the years when he struggled through the confusion of his own injury, the pain in his knee, the physical therapy, and then the difficult road to recovery. The second surgery, and then the third. The dark period while he struggled to stay out on the professional tennis tour, and then, the realization that his playing career was over. Now he sat in his office, two beautiful children, a wonderful wife, Rudy's coaching career was about to take off. He loved what he was doing. He knew the Lord had blessed him. Now along comes this young man, this great talent who needs his help.

Rudy smiled as he thought to himself, "*Lord, thank you so much, help me Lord to see your will.*"

Then he leaned back and imagined, he imagined and he hoped, for what was next.

"FIRST DOWN PIRATES"

It was 1 p.m. sharp when Coach Outland called the team together for practice.

"All right guys, let's get started. Men, today we have another young man here to workout with us. Travis Simpson will be joining us beginning today. He will be competing for a spot on the team. Travis, these are my assistant coaches, Charles Strader and Bobby Taylor, the rest of the players, you guys, introduce yourselves to Travis during the course of practice. Coach Strader, get the drills started."

That was the beginning of Travis' first day of college tennis. Once the stretching drills were completed, Coach Taylor lined the boys up on the baseline and put the players through an intense 30-minute session of footwork and agility drills. By the time the agility drills were over, the players were ringing with sweat. Travis excelled in the agility drills. His footwork from years of football and baseball practice was excellent. Also, the conditioning program Stephanie had designed for him had increased his total body strength and stamina. Travis was clearly the quickest and physically strongest player on the court.

Once the agility drills were over Coach Outland paired the players up, each with a practice partner. Travis was paired with Jim Rose. Jim was a rising junior from Winston Salem. Jim had been the number one singles player on last year's team. He was second team all conference as a sophomore. Jim was the only returner from the previous year's team that Rudy felt could help him in the future. Jim did not possess the physical skills to become an elite college player; he did however have a tremendous work ethic. He played like a coach on the court. Jim was a born leader. Jim got every ounce out of the talent he had been blessed with. Rudy also paired his four freshman recruits together. John Stone and Steve Anderson, both of the boys were from the Orlando, Florida area. Rudy had coached both the kids for the past eight years since Rudy had joined the staff at the tennis academy. The other two kids were twins, Carlos and Juan Garcia. The Garcia twins moved from Brazil to Florida when they were 15 to live year-round and study at the academy. The Garcia's had been one of the top junior doubles teams in the world. They were also both excellent singles players, but while playing doubles, they were all but unbeatable.

Rudy's coaching philosophy was based on technique, fundamentals, and conditioning. His practices were physically intense, and everything during practice was competitive. The playing partners played against each other as individuals, and then played against the other teams in doubles. All

123

the results from the practice matches were recorded, and those competitive matches would determine who would play, and who would not. The fall tennis season is a short season in college tennis. Rudy's plan, as was the case with most college coaches, was to use the fall matches as a way to determine his lineup for the conference season in the spring. Rudy organized every practice to evaluate all the areas of the player's games. From serving to forehands, backhands and volleys, the players were constantly competing with one another to improve their skills. When practice was over, the coaches met with each player individually to discuss what they observed. This kept each player focused on his improvement, and helped improve everyone's performance.

After practice Rudy met with Travis.

"Travis, I was impressed with your effort today. Your agility and footwork were excellent. I thought you gave it everything you had today."

"Yes sir, thank you sir."

"Travis your strokes are very solid. You hit the ball with power and your serve is excellent. I believe as a coach my job is to work with our players to improve all areas of their game. We want to eliminate the areas you are weak at. We want to turn your weaknesses into strength. Let's use a baseball analogy. When you were playing baseball, what was your favorite pitch to hit?"

Travis said, "A low fast ball out over the middle of the plate. I could really go down and drive that ball."

"What was your least favorite pitch to hit?"

"A curve ball that moved away from me. It was hard to hit that pitch with power."

"In tennis," Rudy said, "you are like a pitcher when you hit balls to your opponent; you try to figure out what type of ball the other player doesn't like, then you hit that ball to him. When the ball is hit to you, then you are the batter and your opponent is trying to expose your weaknesses. So we want to turn your weaknesses into strengths. We are going to focus on developing your ability to hit heavy top-spin shots and slices to keep your opponents off balance. We will also work to improve your consistency in your power game, your forehands, backhands, and serves. You have great hand-eye coordination. Those are God-given gifts you were born with. You have worked hard to develop those gifts; and you are in excellent physical condition. We want to help you develop all of your skills to make you a complete player. Do you understand?"

"Yes sir."

Then Rudy went on to outline Travis' schedule for the next week.

Travis continued to meet with Rudy, Coach Strader, and Coach Taylor every day after practice to keep track of his progress.

Each day after the men's practice, Travis would meet Mary Katherine and she continued to give Travis private lessons. The kids worked on tennis, and they also continued to develop their relationship. Then at night after tennis practice and schoolwork was complete, the two kids would get together and hang out. They discussed tennis, schoolwork, family and faith. Their relationship was growing. Travis could see the pieces of his life fitting back together.

Over the next few days Travis began to settle into a routine. He quickly became comfortable with the other tennis players and coaches. Travis was so thankful to be able to compete again. There were however some aspects of Travis' tennis game that were behind some of the other players. He had been away from competitive tennis for several years, so it would take some time for his consistency to return. Although the other players did not possess Travis' combination of foot speed and power, they all knew how to win matches. They quickly exposed Travis' weaknesses and pushed him to improve. Just as Rudy had explained, the competition with the other players made it obvious to Travis where he needed to improve. So the coaching staff and Travis began to concentrate on his areas of weakness, helping Travis to develop to the best of his ability. Mary Katherine and Travis worked with each other after practice to hone their skills, and Travis became totally infatuated with Mary Katherine. The two of them quickly became inseparable. There was romance in the air on and off the court. It was a soothing remedy for Travis' soul. His heart was mending with each passing day. He thanked God for these new blessings in his life. He began to believe again. It was a wonderful time for both of them.

As the days passed, the date soon arrived for the start of the college football season, and the Pack opened up their season with a road game against East Carolina. It was the first Saturday in September when the Wolfpack football team loaded up the buses and headed east to Greenville. The Pack had a Saturday night date with the ECU Pirates, it was the featured ESPN game of the week. The Simpsons and the Outlands met outside Dowdy-Ficklen Stadium, and tailgated with Parker's barbecue and fried chicken. It was the first opportunity for the families to get together. Ed and Rudy, as well as Rita and Kathy immediately hit it off. Travis was inside the stadium with the football team so Mary Katherine and Sarah, along with some of their friends from State and ECU, all got together and hung out before the kickoff.

Travis was with Russell and Coach Clark warming up before the game on the State half of the field. The ECU fans were out in full force in their purple and gold. It would be a vocal and hostile crowd. The Wolfpack players and coaches knew it would be a tough, hard-fought game, and as expected both teams came to play. The first half was an offensive showcase as Russell and the Wolfpack offense came out firing on all cylinders. Russell led the Wolfpack offense to touchdowns on their first three possessions. Then on their fourth possession, they settled for a field goal. On their next possession they scored another touchdown as Russell hooked up with Joe on a 37-yard touchdown pass just before the end of the first half. The State offense scored on every first half possession, and Russell was brilliant with three touchdowns and 268 yards passing.

The Pirates' offense also moved the ball at will in the first half as ECU picked up twelve first downs. With every first down the ECU field announcer and the Pirate fans would repeat the words; *"First Down... Pirates."* By the end of the first half the Pirates had scored 24 points of their own, and the Wolfpack took a 31-24 lead into the locker room at halftime.

When the Wolfpack entered the visitor's locker room, the offensive coaches made minor adjustments before the start of the second half. The defensive coaches had more than minor adjustments in mind. Defensive football coaches in college football are an intense group of individuals. The 24 ECU points sent the State defensive coaches into a frenzy. The atmosphere was intense as Joe Starling, the Wolfpack defensive coordinator, spelled the situation out for the defensive unit.

"I am so disgusted with you guys. You are playing soft. We are getting our butts whipped. I am not going to get embarrassed over here, especially on national television. I am so sick of hearing *"First Down... Pirates,"* and that cannon going off every time they score. Fellas, I'm going to make it real plain to all of you. We gave up twelve first downs in the first half. That's too many first downs for a whole game! For every time I hear *"First Down... Pirates,"* in the second half we are going to run five extra wind sprints after practice. If you guys can't play defense, I'll turn you into a track team. If you think I'm in a foul mood tonight, you play like that again in the second half; you'll think tonight was a church social compared to the way I'll treat you guys next week. Now be sure and take your 'skirts off' before we start the second half and get out there and PLAY LIKE MEN! or Monday you'll wish you'd never seen a football. You got me!"

Travis looked over at Russell.

"Whoa, coach Starling is hot!"

"I know. I'm sure ECU is going to come after us hard in the second half. Giving up 31 first half points is going to fire them up too. We need to jump on them early and take control of this game."

When the second half started, ECU received the kickoff and the Pirates went on offense. On the second play from scrimmage the Wolfpack defensive end put a hard tackle on the ECU quarterback, forcing a fumble that State recovered on the ECU 34-yard line. Then on the first down Russell found Joe open in the left corner of the end zone to extend the State lead to 38-24. After the State touchdown the rest of the third quarter was dominated by the defenses. Then, just before the end of the third period Russell led the Pack to the end zone again to take a commanding 45-24 lead.

On State's first possession of the fourth quarter State had the ball second and five on the 37-yard line, and the Wolfpack ran an option pass play toward the State sideline. Russell faked a handoff and rolled out to his right to pass, he was looking down field, waiting for his receiver to break free. Russell was still focused down field as the State receiver broke toward the sideline. Russell pumped a fake throw to his left to draw the ECU safety away from the receiver, then he planted his feet, and his arm began to move forward to throw the ball. Just as Russell began to deliver the pass he took a vicious hit in the back from the ECU defensive end who was rushing from Russell's blind side. Russell's body was driven forward while his head snapped backwards; the football fell to the ground as the 285-pound defensive end slammed Russell to the turf. Russell lay motionless, face down on the 30-yard line. Stephanie and the team doctors and trainers rushed onto the field. It was a serious collision; it was a clean hard tackle. Travis stood there in disbelief on the sideline. The whole team took a knee as Coach Clark led the players in prayer as Russell was being treated by what had now become a team of doctors and emergency personnel from the ECU and State medical staffs. Travis could not believe his eyes. One moment Russell was having the game of his life, then suddenly he lay unconscious on the field, and all Travis could think of was,

"Oh Lord, not again. Lord please, not Russell."

After a few minutes the doctors had immobilized Russell and loaded him on a stretcher and into an ambulance. He was taken to Pitt Memorial Hospital, and after x-rays and a CT scan, it was determined that Russell had strained muscles in his neck and right shoulder. He had also suffered a concussion; however, in time he would make a complete recovery. He was kept in the hospital at ECU overnight for observation. It would be three weeks before he could go back to practice and play again.

On Sunday Russell was released and he came back to Raleigh. Russell had a severe headache, and he and Travis spent Sunday together lounging around the dorm room. Later Sunday night Russell began to feel a little better.

"Russell, you feel like getting out for awhile, go get some fresh air?"

"Yeah, I'm so stiff; I need to get out and move around some. I think a walk would do me good."

The boys got to moving, and the fresh air lifted Russell's spirits.

"Russell, my heart skipped a beat when I saw you get hit."

"Travis, I heard that guy breathing right before he hit me. I flinched when I realized he was there, but that's the last thing I remember. I was out cold."

"It scared me to death. After what happened to me, then to see you get hit like that, it really made me think how fragile life really is."

"Travis, when I began to come to and get my wits about me, I was in the hospital and the doctors were all telling me to lay still while they did all these tests. Travis, I was thinking about you, thinking Lord, could something like what happened to Travis happen to me too, or something even worse. Am I going to be able to get up off this table? I was scared, I am not ashamed to admit it."

"Russell, we all know that life can change in an instant, but when you have a scare like this, it really makes you count your blessings."

"You are right. I know I am going to get better, and I'll be playing again in a few weeks. But when I was lying on that X-ray table I wasn't thinking about football, I was just praying I would be able to get up and walk again."

After a while the boys made their way back to the room. They were both exhausted from all that had happened. When Travis lay down to say his prayers, he thanked God for all the blessings in his life. His family, Mary Katherine, Russell, the opportunity to play tennis again, and that Russell would be okay.

"Lord, there is so much that can happen to us in this life. Lord, give us all the courage to keep believing, the hope to keep pressing onward in the face of the uncertainties and dangers that are all around us every day."

Travis was learning early in life that bad things can and do happen to all of us, and also to those we love. Seeing this happen to Russell brought back so many painful memories for Travis. Yet in the face of all that, Travis began to realize that you cannot protect yourself from all the trials and dangers of life. To live life to the fullest, the way God intended for us to live, we must pray for peace and protection, then boldly pursue our dreams as we venture out into the unknown. Travis thanked God for Russell Rawlings and his friendship, and that this time Travis was able to be there to help Russell. As Travis drifted off to sleep, he prayed for the courage to face tomorrow. The next morning, Travis and Russell would get back up again, to boldly tackle another day.

FEARS AND DOUBTS

"Russell, you feel up to going to Bible Study tonight?"

Russell was having severe headaches since his injury Saturday night. He was having trouble sleeping and he was still sore, especially in the neck and shoulder area. Travis was concerned about Russell. Russell had been quiet and subdued since the injury. That was not normal for Russell. Russell was always upbeat. Travis could sense that the mental scar of what had happened was still there, as well as the physical pain.

"Yes, I want to go," Russell said. "I haven't completed my assignment, but I want to hear Coach Clark tonight, just get out and move around."

"I'll text Mary Katherine and Joe. Are you ready to go get some supper?"

"Yeah Travis, that's fine, give me about fifteen minutes."

Travis sent out the text messages and within minutes the boys and Mary Katherine were on their way. When the kids got to Bible study, Coach Clark and Stephanie met them at the door.

"Russell, how are you feeling?" Coach Clark said.

"I hurt all over, but I'll be fine."

"Russell, are you taking your pain medication?"

"Yes Stephanie, but I haven't slept well, my neck is stiff, I can't seem to get comfortable."

"Stop by my office tomorrow and we'll work on some exercises to reduce that stiffness."

Russell's eyes opened up wide. "Now, you've got to take it easy on me, no more Navy seal training, I'm not ready for that."

"No, just some stretching. That's all."

Everyone smiled and the kids took a seat. Travis then saw that Jim Rose was in the class. Travis and Jim had seen each other around campus, but until Travis began practicing with the tennis team the boys really didn't know one another. Attending a major university like N.C. State with over 30,000 students, often times students pass by one another without ever getting a chance to talk. Since Travis and Jim had become practice partners, Travis had quickly come to respect Jim. Jim was a disciplined, intelligent young man. Jim was a believer and he was very open about his faith. Jim led by example, he was a wonderful witness of encouragement to others. Jim walked over to Travis and the other kids.

"Travis, you had a great practice today." Jim said.

"Jim, I appreciate your being so patient with all my mistakes."

"You're playing better every day, we will get there, you just hang in there."

"Jim you know Mary Katherine," Travis said. "This is Russell Rawlings and Joe Moore, guys this is Jim Rose."

"Russell, I was at the game Saturday night," Jim said. "You guys played great. How are you feeling?"

"I'm still sore, but I'm going to make it."

"I'm glad to hear that. It looks like class is about to start so I'll catch you all after class."

With that Jim went and took his seat and Coach Clark began the lecture. The students had reached the fourth chapter of the Gospel of Matthew. Coach Clark's lecture was on Jesus choosing some of his disciples. Jesus called two sets of brothers, Simon, who Jesus later would call Peter, and his brother Andrew. Then Jesus later called James and his brother John. Jesus told the brothers,

"Follow me and I will make you fish for people."

Coach Clark told the class that these pairs of disciples were siblings, brothers from birth, the first birth, the natural human birth. He explained that unlike the natural human birth, believers are born of a second birth, a spiritual birth. That Christians are brothers and sisters born by faith. As brothers and sisters in Christ, we belong to God's family, and that Christians need to bond together with one another. That the love between believers should demonstrate that love of family, as we live and interact with one another."

As Coach Clark was speaking, Travis began to consider the Christian believers God was bringing into his life. Travis thought about his new friend Jim, who was witnessing his faith while encouraging Travis as well as the other players. It was obvious that Jim's role on the team was changing. These four new freshmen were all exceptional players, and Jim would no longer be the number one singles player. Yet, Jim accepted his new position and he was leading by example as he witnessed his faith in the midst of his changing circumstances. Travis thought about Mary Katherine, this warm breeze that was blowing new life into his broken heart. Travis reached over with his left hand, the injured hand that led to so many changes in his life, and took hold of Mary Katherine's hand. Mary Katherine smiled at him, Travis leaned over and whispered in her ear:

"I will witness whenever Jesus asks me to go, but I'm through fishing."

Mary Katherine whispered back, "So am I. I have found what I was searching for."

As Coach Clark continued the lecture he explained the significance of the disciples immediately leaving their nets and everything to follow Jesus. That Jesus' call on a person's life can be so powerful that once they have experienced an encounter with Jesus, everything changes. A person's past becomes irrelevant. The new person, through a spiritual rebirth moves into a new life, the life of Christ. From there Coach Clark told of Jesus traveling throughout Galilee, preaching the *"good news"* and healing the peoples' diseases and sickness. Some had demons, some were epileptics, and some were paralyzed. Coach Clark emphasized that God was in control of all situations, that through our personal relationship with Jesus, Christ is closer to us than a brother. That after we are called by Christ, we are commissioned to be our brother's keeper, as we share the light of Christ together.

After class was dismissed the kids took off heading in all directions. Travis walked Mary Katherine back to her dormitory. Once they reached her dorm, they talked for a while, then they said goodnight and Travis headed back to his room. When he got to the room Russell was already there. Russell was lying on his bed with his left arm covering his face. Travis quietly put his Bible and notebook down on his desk, and then he sat on his bed.

"Russell, are you okay?"

"Yes, I'll be fine; it's just that I am really washed out right now. Not just physically, but mentally exhausted. I know I am going to be fine now, but it could have been so much worse."

Travis was well aware of the seriousness of Russell's injury. When the lineman tackled Russell, Travis could clearly see that Russell had been knocked unconscious and lay there motionless for over five minutes.

"Once I came to," Russell said. "I could hear the doctors and trainers talking. They were telling me not to move. They were talking about spinal cord injuries. Then when they all came together to move me onto the board to immobilize my back and neck, Travis I began to cry. I was so scared I could not control myself. Then at the hospital while they were taking the X-rays and CT scans, I was just numb all over. I honestly thought, 'I may never walk again.' Then tonight when Coach Clark spoke about Jesus healing people with diseases, epileptics and some who were paralyzed, I thought how God had chosen to spare me, to heal me. I am so thankful to know that I will recover. I almost feel guilty that God has chosen to heal me, when some other people do not recover. I feel so blessed, so undeserving. I am emotional now just thinking about what could have happened, how lucky I am."

The boys just sat there for a while, neither one knowing what to say, there just were not words. After a few minutes Russell said, "Travis, I'm going to hit the sack, try and get some sleep."

"That's fine, I've had a long day, I'm ready for bed too."

The boys got ready for bed, and then they cut the lights out. Travis lay there quietly thinking about his friend Russell, laying in the bed across the room. They too were closer than brothers.

"Russell, are you asleep?"

"No, not yet."

"Russell, when I injured my hand I thought God was through with me. I did not see how God could use me after my injury. That everything about it was bad, that nothing good could come from it. But it has. God is using me for good. I don't understand it all, but I believe it. God has begun a good work in you Russell. No matter what happens in your life, God will complete the work He has begun in you. You can have faith in that."

"Thank you Travis, God Bless you."

"God bless you Russell. Good night."

Travis lay there in the darkness. He could see his friend Russell lying there across the dimly lit room. He thought back to the nights when he laid alone in this bedroom in Wilson after his accident. He could sense the fears and doubts Russell was feeling. Travis remembered the times that Russell had been there for him. Travis quietly lay there, realizing that Russell had deep emotional scars from what he had been through. The team leader, the star quarterback, and the one everyone looked to for leadership and courage was fighting his emotions. Travis prayed that God would give him the wisdom to help him and Russell face the battles of doubts and challenges that lay ahead for both of them.

PRIVATE

The weeks quickly passed, as time so often does, especially during a sports season. Russell had recovered from his concussion as the Wolfpack prepared for their sixth game of the season. The Pack stood at 3-2 as they prepared for a Saturday afternoon game on the road against the Clemson Tigers. Russell has been involved in passing drills for the past two weeks, but this week he was scheduled to return as the starting quarterback when State faced the 13th ranked Tigers in Death Valley. Russell was physically healthy again, but the fear from the experience was still dogging him. Russell was having trouble planting his feet when he dropped back to pass. Russell had been tackled from behind, so he found it hard now to relax. Whenever he dropped back to pass, he found himself concentrating on the pass rushers, instead of focusing downfield on his receivers. Russell was losing his confidence, and Coach Clark could sense it. Coach Clark quietly reassured Russell that the position as starting quarterback was his job. Coach Clark exuded a calm demeanor of confidence that aided in Russell's recovery. However, they both knew that the Clemson defense would throw everything it had at Russell on Saturday. Clemson would come after Russell hard and fast, and that if State had a chance of leaving Clemson with a victory, Russell would have to step up and face the Tigers head on.

Meanwhile, Travis was fighting for a spot in the singles lineup on the tennis court. Rudy had five solid players; the sixth singles position was up for grabs. Rudy had penciled Travis and Jim in as the number three doubles team. Rudy knew that playing doubles with Jim would help Travis learn the strategy of doubles, and help Travis develop the finesse shots he needed to go along with his power game. The men's tennis team was 4-2 with a home match against Vanderbilt on Monday. Travis was 3-3 in singles while he and Jim were 5-1 in doubles. Travis' athletic talents were obvious, and he was making progress, but there were three returning starters from last year's team who were challenging Travis for the sixth singles position. Travis was feeling the frustration of his position, he was not used to getting beat, and it showed. Mary Katherine meanwhile had fallen into a familiar routine. She won matches, she was so accomplished that she was finding little competition in women's college tennis. Mary Katherine was undefeated in eight matches. She again had qualified for the U.S. Open, and she advanced through the qualifying and into the third round. The only question for Mary Katherine was when she would leave school to pursue her lifelong dream of playing professional tennis. She had already received inquiries from sports agents, endorsement contracts for equipment, clothing apparel, and modeling opportunities. All those things were in her future. The question was not if it would happen for Mary Katherine, only when?

Jim had taken the initiative to ask Coach Outland to schedule doubles matches for he and Travis after practice. The doubles teams that State had faced had realized Travis' weakness in his net game. The other teams were hitting the ball away from Jim and attacking Travis, so Jim wanted to help Travis work on his weaknesses. Friday after the men's practice, Jim and Travis were set to play a doubles match against Rudy and Mary Katherine. Ed and Kathy came up to Raleigh, the families were going out to dinner after practice. Rita met Ed and Kathy at the tennis bleachers to watch the match. Things started out well enough, the tennis was well played on both sides, and the match stood at two games a piece with Mary Katherine serving. That's when things got interesting. The Outlands did not like to lose. So they decided to go after Travis. It quickly became apparent that Rudy and Mary Katherine felt they had a better chance of winning by hitting the ball at Travis, and away from Jim. Just like the teams Travis and Jim were facing in team matches, the Outlands were going after Travis. Travis knew it, and he didn't like it, and it showed on his face. Travis became confused and frustrated, he was tired of getting beat. Now with Rita and his parents watching, Rudy and Mary Katherine playing, his frustration was getting the best of him. With the score 30-15, Jim hit a short ball to Mary Katherine, she quickly came up and hit a blistering forehand passing shot that Travis got his racquet on but the ball ricocheted well off the court. In his frustration, Travis slammed his racquet on the top of the net and glared at Mary Katherine, Mary Katherine then starred back at Travis, no way she was backing down. Travis and Jim won the next point to make the game score 40-30. Then with Mary Katherine serving and Travis again at the net, Mary Katherine stepped in on a short ball and drilled her hardest forehand of the match right at Travis' head. Travis had just enough time to get the racquet in front of his face as the ball careened off the racquet knocking him to the ground. Travis stood up, looked at Mary Katherine and said, "What is that all about?"

"What?"

"You know what! You almost took my head off!"

Ed looked at Kathy and Rita.

"Uh oh, here we go."

Mary Katherine walked straight up toward Travis with her brown ponytail bouncing behind her; she looked Travis straight in the eye and said, "You need to quit playing soft! When are you going to step up and be Travis Simpson? You have more talent that the three of us put together. When are you going to get the courage to use it?"

Then she turned around and walked back to the baseline. She put her hands on her hips and starred at Travis. She meant every word she said, and she was not about to apologize for it.

Kathy thought to herself, "*You go girl, that's exactly what he needed to hear.*"

Travis' blood pressure was off the charts. He felt his heart about to beat through his chest. He could feel the pulse in his neck as he starred at Mary Katherine. Rudy and Jim just stood there. The "love birds" were having their first fight, and nobody wanted to get caught in the crossfire. Travis walked back to the baseline; it was his turn to serve. He looked across at Mary Katherine and said, "Playing soft, uh?"

"Yes," she replied, "do you need any help adjusting your skirt?"

Jim thought to himself, "*Man, this girl is some kind of tough.*"

Rudy didn't say a thing. Travis' adrenaline was on overdrive. He was so mad he was crushing his racquet in his right hand. He bounced the ball three times, tossed it in the air and "POP!" It sounded as if the ball exploded when he hit it. No one said a word, they just moved from one side of the court to the other as Travis hit four aces in a row! From there on Travis completely dominated the match. He took his game to another level and beyond. He was attacking on every point as he and Jim won the next three games to win the set. When the match was over Mary Katherine shook Jim's hand and walked off. She didn't even speak to Travis. She walked straight over to Ed, Kathy and Rita, greeted them and told them she was looking forward to dinner. Then she walked off toward her dorm. Travis didn't know what to think or say. Rudy shook Travis' hand.

"Great match Travis, that's the best I've ever seen you play."

Rudy smiled as he walked off. He thought about all those times he'd seen Rita get upset with him, he knew that more than the seafood would be hot at dinner tonight!

Travis got to Mary Katherine's dorm at 6:30. When Mary Katherine stepped out of the elevator she was wearing her favorite black dress. She was gorgeous, and she knew it. She acted as if nothing had happened as she got in the car. When they reached the restaurant MK was her radiant, captivating self. She spent her time talking with the parents. She was polite with Travis, but the conversation was short, the atmosphere between the two was tense. Travis felt like the "odd man out." Especially with Kathy, the girls were on the same team together, so he just sat there biding his time, waiting for a chance to turn the tide back in his favor.

After dinner everyone said their goodbyes, Kathy and Ed walked back to the car.

"Travis has his hands full don't you think?"

"Yes, Mary Katherine is quite a young lady." Kathy replied. "She will not back down with him, and I like that."

"Travis won't walk away from a challenge either. Life with those two will be very interesting."

When the kids got back to the dorm, Travis parked the car and the two of them began to walk inside. The conversation was at a minimum when Travis decided he had had enough.

"I see that you have decided to make some points today Mary Katherine."

Mary Katherine stopped, turned in Travis' direction and said, "Well somebody had to."

"Had to what?"

Mary Katherine replied, "Somebody had to light a fire under you so you could show yourself and everyone else what you are capable of."

"I see. So is it the same with that black dress?"

"What do you mean?"

"You are obviously trying to light a fire in me by wearing that dress tonight."

Mary Katherine smiled and asked, "Is it working?"

Travis stepped toward Mary Katherine and pulled her close to him. "Yes, it is."

Then Travis said, "You didn't play nice today Mary Katherine."

"All is fair in love and war."

Travis then asked, "Is that what this is?"

"We'll see."

The rest of the conversation was private.

DEATH VALLEY

It was a beautiful fall morning in Clemson, South Carolina, as Russell and the rest of the Wolfpack football team took their pre-game walkthrough of the Tigers' football stadium. When Russell was in high school he had been heavily recruited by Clemson before he made the decision to leave his home state of South Carolina to play football at N.C. State. As Travis and Russell walked across the large orange tiger paw on the center of the 50-yard line, the boys looked around at the sea of orange bleachers that would later be filled with 80,000 rowdy Clemson fans. Clemson was a perfect 5-0 on the season and ranked 11th in the nation. The Tigers were led by their outstanding defense. They were aggressive and very physical; the Tigers' game plan was to attack defensively with blitzes and a very large and quick defensive line. The Tigers were a very difficult team to run the ball against, so State's offense would have to complete some passes to move the football, and that responsibility rested squarely on Russell's shoulders.

"This place is going to be noisy this afternoon." Russell said.

"You guys put some points on the board," Travis replied, "and that will keep them quiet."

Travis could see that Russell was still not himself. Russell was normally upbeat and talkative on game days. But today he was quiet and reserved. Mentally he was not over his injury. Travis knew that Clemson would play to win. They would come after Russell with all they had to try and shake Russell's confidence. As the two boys were standing there at the 50-yard line Coach Clark walked up and joined them.

"These folks sure love orange don't they?"

The boys smiled, but the tension was still there.

"Russell, you ready to go?"

"Yes sir Coach."

Coach Clark could tell that Russell was doing all he could to get over his injury and remain positive for his teammates. Russell had been severely injured. The only way for him to get over it would be to get back up, and try again.

"Russell, I recruited you because of your toughness, because I could see that you were a leader. Sometimes even the leaders need help. Rely on your teammates today. Let the game come to you, and play to win. Everything else will take care of itself."

Outside in the parking lot the Simpsons, the Outlands, and Russell's parents were tailgating along with some of the Wolfpack faithful before the kickoff. Sarah and Mary Katherine were there too with some of their friends.

All the girls were wearing their red and white. The girls were attracting a lot of attention from the Clemson fraternity boys. Sarah especially loved college football. She and Ed had been going to the Wolfpack games together since she was big enough to walk. Ed had bought Sarah a little N.C. State cheerleaders' dress when Sarah was a child. Sarah had always drawn a crowd when she was a child, and now that she was a young lady, she was still attracting attention. It was just a different kind of fans. One handsome young man from Clemson walked over to where the girls were and asked Sarah a question.

"You sure are a pretty girl to be at the ball game by yourself?"

Sarah, always the outgoing kid replied, "Well, nobody said I have to stay that way."

With that the handsome young men came from everywhere. Ed looked over at Kathy.

"Those girls can sure draw a crowd."

By now the boys were all introducing themselves to Sarah and Mary Katherine as well as the other State coeds with them. With the grills cooking in the parking lot, and the football players simmering inside the stadium, everything was in place for an exciting afternoon. By the time Mary Katherine and Sarah took their seats inside the stadium, the Clemson fans were rocking.

"I have never seen so much orange," Sarah said. "These fans are intense!"

"They call this stadium Death Valley." Ed replied. "It may be the toughest place to play in college football."

The girls looked around at the crowd; they felt the vibration of the crowd noise in the stands. The vibration literally trembled the concrete bleachers beneath their feet.

"Can you imagine how loud it is down on the field?" Mary Katherine said.

"No, I can't." Sarah replied. "I hope Russell has a good start today. We need to keep this crowd out of the game; or it's going to be mighty tough to leave here with a win."

"Travis is concerned about Russell." Mary Katherine said. "Russell has not been himself lately."

"That Russell is a fighter!" Sarah concluded. "He and Travis are just alike. Once Russell gets his buttons pushed, he'll be fine."

Mary Katherine then thought back to her and Travis' "little battle," and their make-up. She knew Sarah was right. Sarah was like the big sister Mary Katherine had never had. The girls rose to their feet with the 80,000 screaming Clemson fans. It was time for the kickoff.

Clemson received the opening kickoff and returned the ball to their own 37-yard line. From there the Tigers methodically began to establish their running game. Clemson picked up 5 first downs before the drive stalled at the State 19-yard line. Clemson had run 8:32 off the game clock before settling for a 36-yard field goal and a 3-0 lead. The game then turned into a defensive struggle. Neither offense could get anything going. Then with 4:32 to go in the first half State recovered a Clemson fumble on the Clemson 43-yard line. State picked up 2 first downs, then with second and six on the Clemson 18-yard line Russell dropped back to pass. Russell set his feet in the pocket. He was looking to throw a crossing pattern over the middle of the field, but the receiver was covered. Russell then looked out to his right, and threw a pass toward his secondary receiver near the goal line. Just as Russell released the pass he was drilled by the Clemson strong safety that had blitzed from Russell's blind side, knocking Russell to the ground. Meanwhile one of the Clemson defensive backs has broken across in front of the State receiver, intercepted the pass, and then raced 97 yards down the sideline in front of the Clemson bench for a touchdown. The Clemson crowd erupted! The rest of the half continued to be dominated by defense, as Clemson carried the 10-0 lead into the locker room at halftime.

When the Wolfpack offensive unit entered the locker room Russell was visibly shaken by what had happened, and the other offensive players could sense it. Russell's ears were still ringing from the hit he had taken and the crowd noise. Coach Clark called the offense together.

"Alright men, we're only down ten points. Our defense is playing great. They are keying on our running game and coming at us with blitzes. They want to force us to throw, so let's throw it. Russell, we're going to drop you in a shotgun formation, you call the plays at the line. Read the defenses and throw the football."

Russell thought to himself, "*Oh my God, me, now!*"

"Yes, sir, Coach."

Travis patted Russell on the shoulder.

"You can do this Russell; believe in yourself."

State received the second half kickoff and ran the ball out to its own 19-yard line where the State return man was buried under a host of orange jerseys, and the Clemson crowd went nuts. Then on second and nine on the State 20 Russell tried to force another pass that was almost intercepted, and he took another hard hit after he had thrown the ball. When the offense huddled before third down, Russell could feel his confidence slipping away. Just then Coach Clark called time out and waved for Russell to come to the sidelines. Coach Clark took off his headset, and then he walked out onto the field toward Russell so the two of them alone could talk. When Coach Clark reached Russell he put his hand on Russell's shoulder and looked him in the eye.

"We don't have a lot of friends in this stadium today, do we?"

"No sir."

"Those ten guys in that huddle are looking for a leader to take them through this battle today. Russell, there is no one I would rather have leading them than you. Take a deep breath, go back in that huddle, and lead, just like you have always done."

Russell smiled. "Yes sir!"

When Russell reached the huddle the players had begun to hang their heads; everyone's confidence was faltering. Russell walked into the middle of the huddle and took a knee.

"I am tired of picking myself up off the ground. When are you guys going to block somebody? Receivers, run hard through your routes! We are getting our tails whipped! It's embarrassing!"

The other players came closer; they were being challenged by their leader.

"Put your hands in here!"

The troops came together; then Russell said, "Let's kick their butts!"

With that the Pack broke the huddle with new life. Russell's swagger was back. The Pack lined up with five wide receivers. The ball was snapped, Russell's feet planted firmly in the turf as the receivers ran their routes. Russell could see the Clemson strong safety blitzing, coming straight at him full speed. One of the State receivers was breaking across the field to the open area vacated by the charging Clemson defensive safety. Russell stood his ground in the teeth of the pass rush, and then at the last possible second he fired a strike to the open receiver. When Russell released the pass the Clemson safety blasted Russell backwards and onto his back. Meanwhile the State receiver caught the football and streaked down field before finally being tackled on the Clemson eight-yard line. Russell lay on his back, cobwebs in his head, his legs twisting as he tried to get his wits about him. Stephanie and the team trainers were about to run onto the field when Coach Clark put his hand on Stephanie's shoulder.

"Wait." Coach Clark said, "let Russell get up on his own."

They all stood there watching as Russell slowly rose to his feet. Russell jogged across the field; then he walked into the huddle as all the guys were looking at him.

"Haven't you guys ever seen anybody get hit before?"

The tension eased, then the star quarterback said, "Men, let's stick this thing in the end zone."

On first and goal Russell whistled a pass over the middle, touchdown Wolfpack! When Russell reached the sideline the team was in a frenzy. Russell looked to Coach Clark, they simply smiled and nodded at one another, enough had been said. From there Russell put on a passing clinic for the Clemson fans as he threw for 285 yards and four second-half touchdowns. The only thing dying in "Death Valley" today would be fears and doubts as the Pack put a 28-13 whipping on the Tigers. Russell had rid himself of his demons today, and as Travis watched his friend from the sideline, little did he know that his turn would be next.

"THAT WAS ALL HE NEEDED TO HEAR"

"Are you nervous about tomorrow?" MK asked.

"Yes, I am." Travis said, "I know I have some good tennis in me, I just need to make it happen."

"You're right, you have some great tennis in you, but you have to let it happen. The harder you try to make it happen, the longer you will have to wait."

"I know you are right. It's just that playing sports has always come easy to me. I hate losing. It's not easy to be patient."

"Travis, you know that having good things happen requires hard work. Take me for example, I'm good for you, but I will require a lot of attention. You already know I'm a high maintenance girl. I like to have my way, but you wouldn't change that about me, would you?"

"No, I wouldn't. Surprisingly, the more I'm around you, the less I understand, but the more I learn about myself."

Mary Katherine snuggled up next to him.

"You see, you're getting smarter all the time. If you get your feathers ruffled in that match tomorrow, you just pretend it's me over there on the other side of the net, and if you're going to beat me, you're going to have to work for it. Then play like you did Friday. If you do that nobody will beat you!"

Monday afternoon was a warm humid day for early October with the temperature in the 80s. Vanderbilt was 6-1 on the season. They had an experienced team of returnees with the one exception being an incoming freshman high school All-American playing number six singles. He would be Travis' singles opponent in today's match. The match began with doubles and the Garcia twins were in a dogfight at number one. The match was hard fought, but in the end the Garcias prevailed. Travis and Jim were also involved in a close match, but Jim's steady play, along with Travis' powerful serve and ground strokes eventually wore down their opponents as the Wolfpack took the doubles point for a 1-0 lead. Rudy was ecstatic! He knew he had a talented team, but today against 9th ranked Vanderbilt, he began to see his young players come together as a group.

By the time the singles started the stands around the tennis courts were filled to capacity. Kathy and Ed were there, along with Sarah, MK and Rita. By now the local news media had heard that Travis Simpson, the once injured football and baseball superstar, was now playing college tennis. The other big story was MK. Fresh back from her successful performance at the U.S. Open, the sports reporters were anxious to get information on her future plans. There was also the rumor that MK and Travis were now a couple, that they had become more than just practice partners. These two kids had lived much of their lives in the public eye, so the media attention around them was buzzing when the teams took the court for singles. By now Stephanie, Coach Clark, Russell and Joe were there as well. The capacity crowd in the tennis bleachers and lounge chairs encircling the tennis facility cheered on the Pack when the two teams took to the courts to play the six singles matches. Travis played well in the first set. His serve was on, and his groundstrokes were solid. Travis played solid consistent tennis as he won the first set 6-4. On the other courts the Wolfpack men won the first set on one singles, they lost the first set at number two, four and five. Jim meanwhile cruised to a 6-2 first set win at number 3 singles.

In the second set Travis began to lose his focus. His opponent had found the chink in Travis' armor, and he began to draw Travis to the net with spinning slice shots, then hitting lobs or passing shots by Travis for winners. Travis became hesitant. His inexperience was showing. It began to affect his confidence and the Vanderbilt freshman was feeling his oats as he whipped Travis 3-6 to force a deciding third set. Meanwhile, the other matches concluded in straight sets with State winning at number one and three singles. Vanderbilt won at two, four, and five. With the match score now tied at 3-3, the third set of Travis' match would decide the winner. As Travis' freshman opponent won the second set, he pumped his fist in celebration of his victory. Then with the courts surrounded, he yelled out loud,

"Come on, you can beat this chump!"

Travis didn't say a word. He had seen this kind of rude behavior before. He didn't like it, he wanted to go over and rip the kid's head off, and after all, he was only half Travis' size. The State fans in the crowd booed the crude behavior, and the Vanderbilt coach was visibly disgusted with the unsportsmanlike conduct of his freshman player, it was a "freshman mistake."

In sports, like in life, you need to let sleeping dogs lie, as this young freshman would soon find out. The crowd cheered as Travis and his opponent took the court to begin the third set. Then everything got quiet as Travis prepared to serve. Travis was stepping to the baseline when a voice screamed out of the crowd,

"Come on Travis, kick that boy's butt!"

Travis looked over and smiled at MK. She was wearing her flip-flops and baseball cap, she had on her game face as she scowled at the Vanderbilt player on the other side of the court. With that the State crowd really got rowdy.

Travis said to himself, *"Lord, ain't she something."*

Then Travis calmly bounced the ball, tossed it in the air, and then blasted 130-mph serve into the service box and up against the fence. 15-love. From there he never looked back. Travis attacked at every opportunity. With the stands packed, his teammates, friends, and family watching, Travis Simpson "stood up;" and once he did there would be no turning back. Travis answered every question he himself had about his own abilities, as he pounded the freshman All-American 6-0, giving State the victory at 4-3.

After the final point, the State players and coaches stormed the court. It was a huge win for this young talented team. Rudy and the coaching staff could see that Travis along with these four talented young recruits and one experienced all-conference performer had united as a team. After the celebration Travis walked to the net and shook his opponent's hand. The young man from Vanderbilt, showed grace in his defeat, as he said,

"Travis, congratulations. You played very well today. I want to apologize for what I said today. I should not have done that, I am sorry."

"Hey, we all say things sometimes we regret. I have done it myself plenty of times. We'll just forget it happened. Good luck to you on the rest of your season."

The young man turned and walked away. He and Travis had both learned a valuable lesson. After the match Rudy gathered his excited team together.

"I am so proud of you guys. Your hard work is paying off. We got out front after doubles and we carried that momentum over into singles. Celebrate this win tonight. Then be ready to get back to work tomorrow."

Once the team meeting was over Travis was greeted by MK, Kathy, Ed, Sarah, and Rita.

"I told you, you could do it!" Rita said. "That third set was spectacular Travis!"

Kathy: "I always knew you were a great tennis player!"

"I am so proud of you Son." Ed said. "Congratulations!"

Then Travis received what he wanted the most, a hug and a kiss from Mary Katherine.

"I am so proud of you, you stomped that boy in the third set. You keep playing like that and you'll be playing number one singles by the spring!"

"I am just thankful to be playing."

Then Rita said, "MK is right, Travis, nobody in college tennis will beat you if you play like that! Remember, the farther you progress up the singles ladder, the easier it makes it for everyone below you. Because as you slide up to face the tougher competition, your teammates move down to play against easier opponents. It's a team game, so if one player improves and moves up the singles ladder, all the players will benefit. If you can move up to the top of the singles ladder, the other five players will win more matches."

"In junior tennis you just play for yourself," Travis said. "So I never really thought about it that way. I've just been trying to get a spot in the lineup."

"Team tennis is different," Rita said. "You play individual matches for team points. So when a player improves and moves up, that strengthens the whole line up."

Later that night, Rudy sat out on the back porch alone, looking out across the yard. Rita came outside, holding two glasses of lemonade.

"Would you like some company?"

"Yes, that would be nice."

Rita pulled up a chair and sat down.

"Today was a great win. I am so proud of you Rudy."

"I didn't hit a single shot today."

"You've done a great job with those kids; they are going to develop into an excellent team."

"Thank you Honey. I am so proud of them. They have come a long way in a short period of time. We all have. Moving to Raleigh, the kids growing up so fast, I feel so blessed. I just want to give back for all that's been given to me. God has blessed me in so many ways."

"You are giving back, to your players, to your children, to your other coaches, to me. You're a good man, and a great father and husband."

"I know every gift, everything is a gift from God. I love you all so much. No matter what I give to others, it will never be enough to repay God for all He has given me. When we were out on the professional tennis circuit, I thought I would be able to give you everything. When all that ended, I thought God was through with me. When I was playing professional tennis I thought I was in the midst of God's will for my life. Who would have ever thought we would be sitting here tonight in Raleigh, N.C., drinking lemonade."

"Jesus did." Rita replied. "He had it planned all along. Who knows where we may go, or what He may call us to do."

"Honey, you know I have given my life to the Lord. I have prayed that He would make His presence felt in my life. But I still worry that I am not the man God created me to be. I know that I have failed Him at times. I have made so many mistakes. I see so many people in need. Often times I feel as though I do so little to make a difference."

"Rudy, you have a compassionate heart. You love the Lord, and you share God's love with the people around you. This is all God requires of anyone. You are setting an example for your players and your family. God loves us Rudy. We are all His children. You have accepted the gift of salvation. By accepting Jesus' gift, you are blameless in God's eyes. When God sees you, He sees the Holy Sprit living inside you."

Rudy and Rita sat there in the moonlight. They had been married for over 25 years. Rita's voice was the voice inside Rudy's head, and his heart. No matter how long the two of them had been together, her approval was the "north point" on the compass of Rudy's life. While the two of them sat there quietly together, Rita thought about all of the blessings in her life, her two children, and her husband. She tried to soak it all in. She tried to savor every second of the blessing of time God had given them to share. They both were wise enough to know by now, that in every life, there is happiness and sorrow. The two of them were thankful to God that He had given them each other, to share their lives together. Then Rita reached over and held Rudy's hand.

"I love you Rudy."

Rudy smiled.

"I love you too Honey."

That was all he needed to hear.

IT DOESN'T GET ANY BETTER

The Wolfpack football team finished the regular season at 8-4 and accepted a bid to play West Virginia on New Year's Day in Charlotte. Russell had regained his form as he was named second team All-Atlantic Coast Conference quarterback. Mary Katherine meanwhile was her usual self, winning matches as she breezed through the fall tennis season. She had been invited to play in the Australian Open, and would be traveling to Sydney in January. Mary Katherine was seeing all of her dreams develop before her eyes. Her window of opportunity was open right in front of her. Now however, there was also a door that had opened, the door to her heart, and Travis Simpson had stepped into it. Mary Katherine had fallen head over heals for him, and so had her parents. Rudy and Rita welcomed Travis in as a part of their family. For nineteen years Rudy and Rita had prayed that the Lord would bring the right man, at the right time, into Mary Katherine's life. Travis was the right man, they were all certain of that. The timing however was complicated. Mary Katherine was the right age to begin a serious relationship, but with the travel and commitment involved in a professional tennis career on the horizon, they were all concerned how Mary Katherine's career plans would affect her and Travis' relationship. Mary Katherine's heart was torn between her dreams of playing professional tennis, which had been the love of her life, and how she and Travis would balance pursuing her dreams and continue to develop their relationship.

On the tennis courts Travis was hitting his stride. Since the Vanderbilt match he had regained his belief in himself. On the tennis court his physical skills were now ignited by his new found confidence. Off the court, he was totally captivated by MK. He adored her, and it was obvious to anyone who saw the two of them together that they were made for each other. So with the end of the fall semester quickly approaching, State's men's tennis team had one more fall match to play on the road against the University of Florida in Gainesville. By now Travis had rocketed up to the number two singles spot. Just as Rita and Mary Katherine had predicted, Travis' skills were being refined, and as he improved, the rest of his teammates were benefiting from being paired against lesser opponents. The State men's team had risen into the top 25 in the national ranking as they prepared to visit perennial power Florida. They knew a win over the Gators would send shock waves through the college tennis world, and Rudy and his team were up for the challenge.

The team was waiting for the noon American Airlines flight that would be departing Raleigh-Durham Airport for Gainesville. Rita was traveling with the team and she and Rudy were sitting together in the terminal with the rest of the players and coaches.

"Charles, Bobby, and I have been talking about the idea of moving Travis to the number one singles position." Rudy said. "I know that is going to happen at some point. This is our last match before spring so if we did it now it would solidify the lineup before Christmas break."

"I think that's a good move." Rita replied. "Travis obviously has the most physical skills, and you're right, it's going to happen. It's just a question of when."

"I am curious to see how Travis would respond to playing Steve Sloan." Rudy said. "After Steve won the NCAA men's singles title last year, he is probably expecting an easy match tomorrow. When I coached Steve at the academy he would get down on himself if you pushed him hard enough. He's never faced a player with the foot speed and power Travis has. I want to see how Travis will respond against that kind of an opponent. I've got to make a decision. What do you think I should do?"

"You know what to do."

"What?"

Rita reached over and patted Rudy's hand.

"Pray about it."

Rudy smiled and said, "You sure are a smart woman."

"I was smart enough to marry you."

Rudy looked over at Travis talking with Jim Rose before the flight. He knew there was something very special about Travis. Rudy could see the explosive talent below the surface, and he had an idea about how to get it out of him.

The Wolfpack arrived in Gainesville and checked into the hotel at 3:30. Then they went over to the University of Florida tennis center and had a light workout. They ate dinner and gathered for a brief meeting to discuss tomorrow's match. After the meeting Rudy asked Travis to stay, he had something to discuss with him.

"Travis, you have played some great tennis these last few weeks, I am proud of you."

"Thank you sir."

"Florida has a heck of a tennis team. Their number one player Steve Sloan won the NCAA men's individual singles championship last year. I coached Steve at the Academy. He's a great player. Knowing Steve, I'm sure he's thinking there's no way he can lose tomorrow. What do you think about that Travis, do you think Steve Sloan can be beaten?"

"On a given day, anybody can be beat."

"I agree, I think Steve can be beat. Tomorrow afternoon, I think you will be the one to beat him. I'm looking forward to watching you do it."

Travis' eyes lit up as a smile came on his face.

"Yes sir, I'm looking forward to it too."

Rudy shook Travis' hand as he smiled.

"Alright then, you're my number one singles player tomorrow. Congratulations, you've earned it."

"Thank you sir."

After their talk, Travis went outside the hotel to get some air. He sat down in a lounge chair by the pool and dialed a number on his cell phone.

"Hey Dad, what are you and Mom up to tonight?"

"Your mom is watching TV, and me and Wesley are reading a book."

"What are you two reading Dad?"

"Peace with God, by Billy Graham."

"How is it?"

"It's great. I've read it before, but I get something new out of it every time I pick it up. Besides, Wesley really likes it."

Wesley lifted up his head as he heard his name.

"Dad I've got some news, I'm going to play Steve Sloan at number one singles in the match tomorrow!"

Ed sat up on the couch. "Is that right? That is great Son. Congratulations!"

"Steve's a great player. I remember him from the Southerns back when I was a junior. I played him once in Columbia. Do you remember him Dad?"

"Yes, he was a pretty self-confident kid as I remember. He was sort of loud, pumped his fist a lot. Seems like he questioned some of your line calls. But as I remember it, he was the one calling all your serves out."

"Yep, that's Steve alright. I don't think I'll ever forget him. It will be nice to play him with an umpire in the chair watching him this time."

"Does Coach Outland know you've played Steve before?"

"No, I didn't mention it. Tomorrow is another day. But I sure am looking forward to getting another shot at him. I'm a different player now."

"Yes you are, but you were always the better athlete. Go out there tomorrow and show him."

"I will Dad. I better go. I want to call MK and tell her the news. Tell Mom I love her."

"I will Son. I love you, and I am proud of you."

"I love you too Dad."

Ed hung up the phone then he looked at Wesley and said, "Come on Buddy, let's go outside."

Ed and Wesley walked outside and sat down on the porch. It was a cool December night. The sky was clear; Ed could see his breath as he exhaled the cool night air. He thought back to the time when Travis had played Steve Sloan in junior tennis. Ed remembered how frustrated Travis was playing the Southerns against kids like Steve who went to tennis academies and only played tennis, while Travis had to travel out of town to find a match. Ed always wondered how Travis would have done against the academy kids on a level playing field. Now that the injury to Travis' hand had changed things, Ed smiled and said to Wesley,

"I sure would like to see Travis whip that Sloan kid tomorrow Wesley, how about you?"

Wesley sat up and wagged his tail.

"Yeah, I think you're right Wesley, Travis is going to give that boy a free tennis lesson tomorrow. A lesson that Steve Sloan will never forget."

The next day the team was quiet as they met for breakfast. The boys were focused on the task at hand. Then they got back together at 11 for a stretching session on the courts at the tennis center. Before their warm up the team huddled together; Jim led them in prayer as they prepared to take the court. Rudy knew that his four freshmen were now attending the Monday night Bible study with Jim and Travis. He noticed that in addition to the black shorts and white N.C. State shirts that signified team unity, his players were all wearing crosses around their necks. Rita looked on from the bleachers as Rudy and the team held hands and bowed their heads together in prayer. She could see that there was more than just a shared love of tennis uniting the group. There was a growing knowledge and love of Jesus that was molding these men together. She smiled with anticipation, and whiped a tear from her eye as she thought of the blessings in her life. She bowed her head herself and prayed.

"Thank you Lord for Your blessings, and may Your Son Jesus be glorified, Amen."

She opened her eyes to see the team break the huddle. Then she heard Rudy tell the team. "Believe in yourselves. Believe in each other. Play fast and lose, take advantage of your opportunities and play to win."

It was time to play tennis.

When the doubles matches began it was obvious that the young Wolfpack team was not intimidated by the Gators, as State jumped out to early leads in all the doubles matches. The Garcias were fantastic as they made quick work of their opponents taking the win at number one doubles. Travis and Jim were also playing excellent tennis. Jim was coaching Travis through the match. There was an obvious chemistry between the boys. Travis had the flash of brilliance in his game, while Jim had a calm comforting influence with his solid steady play and confident demeanor. Then when Jim hit a backhand winner down the line on match point, the Pack had secured the doubles point before the Gators knew what happened. The Florida faithful sat there in disbelief as this upstart bunch of N.C. State underclassmen had shown no fear in taking an early 1-0 lead.

After a short intermission, Rudy huddled his troops together before the beginning of the singles matches.

"Alright, we have to stay focused. These guys are a great team. They are not going to roll over for us. Stay in the moment. Encourage one another up and down the line. This match is far from over, together on three. 'One, two, three,' then in unison the team said, 'play to win.' Then the Wolfpack took the court for singles.

There wasn't much conversation between Travis and Steve Sloan as the boys warmed up before their match. Rita was sitting in the front row of the bleachers right beside the number one court. Rudy was sitting on the bench just in front of her. As the match began Steve was serving. The game went to three deuces before Steve held serve to take a 1-0 lead.

Now it was Travis' turn to serve. Travis toed the baseline and hit his first serve out wide to Steve's forehand, which appeared to be an ace, but Steve called the ball out. There was movement by the chair umpire but the call was not overruled. The call made Travis uncomfortable; he kept his composure, but lost his focus. Eventually losing his service game to fall behind 2-0. Steve then served again, and with the aid of two more questionable line calls Steve was up to his old tricks and a 3-0 lead. Travis sat down beside the chair umpire at the change over, his blood was boiling, while Steve sat there across from him, smiling that smug smile he was noted for. Rudy sat down next to Travis and said,

"Looks like Steve has 'hooked' you on some of those line calls."

"I'd like to take this racquet and cram it down his throat!" Travis said.

Rudy then calmly said, "Well, that sounds nice, but I've got a better idea, why don't you go out there and whip his butt with that racquet! Show him you're better than he is!"

Travis and Rudy looked down the line. State was behind on every court. Rudy said, "Travis, we need something to turn this momentum around. You got any ideas?"

"Yes sir."

"Well get to it then, I'm going to sit here next to the court and watch for a while."

Travis went back out on the court. He was trying to calm down. Then he thought about MK standing on the other side of the court glaring at him with her hands on her hips. A smile came on his face. He looked at Rita sitting in the bleachers; she smiled at him, clapped her hands and said,

"Come on Travis, let's get going, right here now!"

Travis tossed the ball in the air and whistled a 130-mph serve, his fastest of the match into the service box and past Steve for an apparent ace, but Steve again called the ball out. This time however, the chair umpire interrupted.

"Overruled. Mr. Sloan that ball was in, 15-love."

Steve didn't say anything, but he was visibly upset at being overruled. Travis proceeded to easily hold his serve to make the score 3-1. Steve then served and with the score 30-40 Travis hit a forehand crosscourt winner to win the game that Steve called out. Again the umpire overruled the call, and Steve went off. He verbally challenged the umpire's authority. It was an ugly display of poor sportsmanship, the kind of thing seen all too frequently in sports today. Travis quietly stood there as Steve had his temper tantrum in full view of everyone in attendance. Once Steve finished, the chair umpire calmly called Steve and Travis to the chair.

"Gentlemen, I am the official in this match; I will be treated with respect. If either of you have a problem with that you can hit the showers. Mr. Sloan, another outburst like that and you will be finished for today. That's all, now play tennis!"

Travis walked over and sat down next to Rudy. Rudy leaned over and whispered in Travis' ear, "I taught Steve a lot about tennis at the academy, but Steve didn't do too well in sportsmanship class."

Travis chuckled and said, "Yes sir, I can see that."

"Why don't you go out there and teach Steve how to take a beating like a man!"

Travis smiled and said, "Yes sir, I'll be happy to."

So that's what he did. With the home crowd watching Travis put a 6-3, 6-2, whipping on the NCAA defending national singles champion. In doing so, his inspiring play sent electricity down the line as the young Pack pounded the Gators on their way to a 5-2 victory.

Later that night when the plane touched down in Raleigh, the team was greeted by friends, fans, and the local media. Mary Katherine threw her arms around Travis' neck, with the local television cameras rolling. Paul Durham, a local reporter whom Travis had great respect for, asked Travis a question.

"Travis congratulations, I know it's been a great day for you and the team. What was the best part?"

"Beating Steve Sloan was exciting, the team winning was great, but being with Mary Katherine, it doesn't get any better than this."

Mary Katherine smiled and turned her head away from the cameras, as she leaned her head on Travis' shoulder. She could see her parents, Rudy and Rita, in the distance smiling back at her. She raised her head and whispered in Travis' ear for the first time,

"I love you Travis Simpson."

Travis whispered back "I love you too, and I will love you forever."

"Do you promise?"

"Yes, I promise. I will never let you go."

DOWN UNDER

Travis was running late as he pulled into the driveway to pick up Mary Katherine. She was sitting on the front porch waiting for him, and she was not happy about it.

"If we are late you are taking the blame for it!"

Rita walked out onto the front porch, "Merry Christmas, Travis."

"Merry Christmas Mrs. Outland. I don't think MK is in a very merry mood right now. I'm late."

MK gathered her gifts.

"I don't want your Mom and Dad to think it was my fault that we are late for church."

"I understand. They will not blame you if we are late, but I think we can make it on time."

"We better!"

"Travis, I'll let you go," Rita said. "You kids have a good time tonight."

Travis put Mary Katherine's gifts in the back seat and they pulled out of the driveway, headed to Wilson. They reached the First Presbyterian Church a little before 6 p.m. Just in time. They met Sarah, Kathy, and Ed, along with Travis' grandmother, and took their seats. The sermon was on the birth of Jesus, from the second chapter on the Gospel of Matthew. The children and adult choirs sang anthems. Then at the conclusion of the service the congregation lit candles while they sang "Silent Night." After the hymn the congregation walked quietly from the sanctuary and gathered on the steps and on the front lawn to receive the benediction. Then the congregation blew out the candles and greeted one another for Christmas. There were hugs and handshakes, lots of introductions, as everyone wanted to meet Mary Katherine; after all, she was a celebrity. Later the family gathered to open gifts. Mary Katherine was prepared with everyone's present accounted for. Ed sat there taking it all in. Wesley meanwhile, was ready to assist in opening all the gifts. Travis was smiling again. Ed remembered back to the awkwardness of the previous Christmas. So much had happened in the past year. They had all grown so much. Ed could have never imagined the turns that their lives had taken. Sarah was happy teaching school. She had met a young man and they were also developing a relationship. Things were coming together, although Ed could not understand exactly how all this had happened. Ed was thankful. Ed realized God was in control and that God's plan would be fulfilled in all their lives. Just like Ed's mother had told him those sixteen months ago, Ed had held onto his faith and God was providing for them all. It was better than Ed could have hoped for.

Christmas and New Year's quickly came and went. Soon it was time for Mary Katherine and Rita to board the plane to take them to Sydney, and the Australian Open. Travis and Rudy took the girls to the airport where they said their goodbyes. Travis and Mary Katherine had spent a part of almost every day together for the past six months, so neither of them wanted to see Mary Katherine board the plane.

"I am going to miss you these next three weeks."

"I'll miss you too. I didn't think leaving was going to be this hard."

"You'll have a great time; I know you're going to play great. But I'll be glad to see you come home. I already miss you and you haven't even left yet."

Within a few minutes the steward called for the passengers to board the plane. MK and Rita walked past the flight attendants and entered the terminal ramp as they waved goodbye. During the flight, Mary Katherine and Rita talked about tennis. They talked about school. They talked about shopping in Australia, but mostly, they talked about the men in their lives.

"Mom, how did you feel when you met Dad? What was he like?"

"Your dad was very handsome. He was very self-confident. He was kind, he made me feel special, and he made me feel safe. I was crazy about him from the moment I saw him, but I didn't tell him that of course!"

"When did you know Dad was the man for you?"

"I couldn't stand to be around him at first, but I couldn't stay away from him either. He could make me so mad, but my heart pounded every time I was near him."

"How did you two meet?"

"Your dad was playing tennis at UCLA. I went with a girlfriend to watch a boy she was dating on the tennis team, and there he was. Your dad was the handsomest thing I had ever seen."

Rita's eyes lit up as she described Rudy to MK.

"He was tall, tanned, let me tell you, he was a pretty thing."

MK laughed and said, "Mom, that's gross to hear you talk about Dad like that!"

"Well you asked me, and the truth is what it is! He had a whole bleacher full of girls watching him play, and they were not there for the tennis! After the match was over my friend introduced us, and it went from there."

"How old were you when you met Dad?"

"I was nineteen."

"How old where you when you got married?"

"I was twenty-two."

Mary Katherine said emphatically, "You dated three years! That's a long time."

"No, that's pretty normal."

"That seems like a long time to me!"

Rita could sense where the conversation was going. She just listened while Mary Katherine sorted things out in her mind.

"I tell you Mom, three weeks is a long time to be away from home."

"Yeah, I'm going to miss your dad, but I know we'll have a good time. It's a great accomplishment for you to be invited to play the Australian."

"I am thrilled to be playing, but I am really going to miss seeing Travis for three weeks."

"Does he know that?"

"Yes, I told him I would miss him."

"Does he know you love him?"

Mary Katherine said, "Is it that obvious?"

"Of course it is Honey; it looks to me like the feeling is mutual."

"It is. We've both said our 'I love you's,' but Mom I am crazy about him. He has changed the way I think about so many things."

"Like what?"

"I don't like being away from him, so travel is different. Tennis used to be the number one love of my life, but now I would rather be with Travis than travel and play tennis. I've started to think more about family. Being a mom myself. Having a life like you and Dad have together, being married and having children. Travis is the man I want to spend my life with and I don't want anything to come between us, not even tennis."

Rita was not surprised by what she was hearing, after all, "a mother knows." She had felt these same feelings herself. She remembered what it was like to meet the man of her dreams. To have your priorities change when a tall, dark, handsome man walks into your life. She chose her words carefully.

"Mary Katherine, all your father and I ever hoped for you was that you would be happy. Whatever and wherever that takes you. You are a smart girl with so many wonderful gifts. You're a great tennis player, great student; you have given your life to the Lord. You are everything a mother could hope for in a child. I love you, and I am proud of you. You will make a wonderful wife and mother. Whenever that day comes, your father and I will support whatever decision you make. Let's just you and I commit to pray about it. God will know when the time is right."

Mary Katherine smiled and said, "I love you Mom."

"I love you too Honey."

Then MK said, "But there is one thing I don't agree with you about though."

Rita looked at MK with a puzzled look on her face.

"What's that Dear."

"Three years is too long to just date!"

"We'll see MK, we'll see."

A few days later Ed and Wesley were sitting on the couch on a Thursday night watching the Australian Open when the phone rang.

"Hey Dad, what are you doing?"

"Me and Wesley are on the couch watching TV, the Australian Open, what about you Son? What have you been up to?"

"I don't know, this and that. I was thinking I might come home this weekend if you're going to be there?"

Ed could hear the loneliness in Travis' voice.

"Sure Son, why don't you get here tomorrow around 6 and we'll cook a steak on the grill. Your mom is going out to eat with your grandma so we can catch up."

"That's perfect Dad, I'll see you tomorrow at 6."

"I'll be looking forward to it."

It was about 6 p.m. Friday when Travis pulled up in the driveway. Ed and Wesley were outside in the Richardson's front yard. Ryan and his sister Madeline were kicking a soccer ball back and forth. Ryan had on his winter boots and a bicycle helmet; he was prepared for anything. Travis got out of the car and started walking toward Ed. Wesley ran toward Travis dragging Ed behind him.

"Hey Dad, Mr. Richardson"

"Hey Son, it's good to see you!"

Ed then gave Travis a hug while Wesley jumped up on Travis' leg.

"Wesley, it's good to see you buddy."

As he leaned over to pick Wesley up, Travis then looked over at Ryan and Madeline and asked, "Are you two playing soccer?"

Ryan yelled out, "Yes! Watch me kick the ball Travis!"

Ryan ran and kicked the ball. After kicking the ball all the way past the end of the driveway and out into the street Ryan adjusted his bicycle helmet and walked in Travis' direction. He looked up at Travis and asked, "Hey Travis, where is Mary Katherine?"

"She is in Australia."

Ryan asked, "Is she coming too?"

"No, she will be gone for ten more days. Australia is on the other side of the world. They call it 'Down Under.'

"Is she your girlfriend?"

"Yes, she is my girlfriend."

"Well, why did she go 'Down Under?'

Mike said, "Ryan, Mary Katherine went to play tennis."

"She is good at riding a scooter." Ryan said, " I like her."

Travis then said, "I thought you didn't like girls Ryan?"

"Mary Katherine is big, like a mommy, but she is cool."

"MK said you were a cute boy Ryan."

Ryan smiled, and then he said, "I've got to go ride my bicycle."

Just like that, he was gone; no grass can grow under Ryan's feet. With that, the three Simpson men turned and went inside. Ed put some baked potatoes in the oven. Then the three boys went outside and lit the grill.

"Pull up a chair Travis and tell me what you have been doing?"

"School, tennis practice. Russell and I went to see a couple of girl's volleyball games. Jim's girlfriend, Joanna, plays on the volleyball team. She introduced Russell to this girl from California who plays on the volleyball team with Joanna. I'm telling you Dad she is a spitting image of Stephanie Clauson. She could be her twin."

"Stephanie is a beautiful girl." Ed said.

"Russell really likes this girl, Dad. He's with her all the time."

"I see, so I guess they are out on a date tonight?"

"They are. Since Mary Katherine is gone, I am kinda like the third wheel."

"I see."

"Dad, how did you know Mom was the girl for you?"

"Well, she made me feel good when I was around her, then when she wasn't around, I was thinking about her. I didn't want to go out with anyone else, and I did not want to see her with another guy. The main thing was that I could see her as the mother of my children. I started thinking about having a family. That's when I knew she was the one for me."

"Dad, I have been miserable since MK left. I know professional tennis is going to be a part of her life. I want to see her travel and do all the things she wants to do. I just don't want to lose her."

"I see. Have you told her?"

"She knows I love her. But I haven't told her I'm scared of losing her. I'm just afraid that her playing tennis may become an obstacle. That she may meet someone else. I just want to know she will always be a part of my life."

"So you told her you love her. That's the first time I've heard you say that about a girl."

"I've never felt this way. I am happier than I have ever been. A year ago I would have never believed all this could happen, but it has. God has blessed me Dad, and I am so thankful. But I know what it is like to lose something you love. I would never want to keep MK from pursuing her dreams, but the thought of losing her is more than I could bear."

Ed saw concern on Travis' face. Travis was in love, no doubt about it. Ed thought for a few minutes.

"Travis, you know your heart is the best compass you will ever find. You need to tell Mary Katherine exactly how you feel. Follow your heart; be honest with her and yourself about your emotions. Do not leave important words unspoken. Then pray about it. Ask her to pray about it. The Lord will deliver the answer, and His timing is perfect."

"I want to spend the rest of my life with her, but I don't want to hold her back."

Ed smiled as he reached over and patted Travis on his shoulder and said, "Travis, Mary Katherine is a smart girl. She's a young woman who will make her own decisions. You need to be honest and tell her how you feel. Then the decision will be hers to make, but if you love each other, you can work it out. You have to tell each other how you feel. Okay?"

"You're right. I will tell her. I will do whatever it takes. I'm not going to risk losing her if I can help it."

"That's good; you won't go wrong with that."

Later that night Travis got back to the dorm room and Russell was still out on his date. Travis put on his coat and ball cap, grabbed his tennis ball and went for a walk. When he got to the tennis courts he took his seat. It was a cool, crisp, January night. The sky was clear, not a cloud in the sky. There were no leaves on the trees. The moon and stars were suspended against the pitch-black darkness of the night sky. The temperature was in the low 30s. Travis thought about MK. It was summer in Australia, on the other side of the world. She could not be any farther away from him. He thought about all that had changed in a year. It seemed like another person's life. Travis had found happiness again, something a year ago he thought might never be possible. That night beneath the stars, Travis set his mind to what was truly important to him. He decided that he would do whatever he needed to do, to show Mary Katherine how much she meant to him. He would never hold her back from her dreams, but he would fight for a place in her life.

Meanwhile, "down under" on the other side of the world, there was a beautiful young girl who wanted nothing more than to be sitting on a set of empty tennis bleachers in North Carolina. In the excitement of the Australian Open, Mary Katherine found her heart had never boarded the plane to Sydney. It belonged to Travis Simpson, and wherever he went, her heart would be there as well. Above it all sat the "Master Matchmaker." While the kids wondered what to do, the Master's plan had already been set in motion, and nothing was going to change it. Not distance, not careers, not a trip half way around the world. God knew what He had in store for Travis and MK. And is always the case with the Lord, the best was yet to come.

ANSWERED PRAYERS

"Ladies and gentleman, this is your captain. We are beginning our descent into Raleigh-Durham. The skies are clear. Temperature in Raleigh is 34 degrees. We ask that you secure all loose items in the overhead compartments, and turn off all electronic devices. We hope you have enjoyed your flight. Thank you for flying with American Airlines."

"Mary Katherine," Rita said, "you are going to have carpal tunnel syndrome in those thumbs if you don't stop some of that text messaging. My goodness; what is it about text messaging that fascinates kids so much?"

"I don't know Mom. We just like it."

Mary Katherine turned off the cell phone. She then looked out the window as the plane banked to the right and she heard the landing gear lowering and being locked into place. She could see the lights of the city as the houses and treetops clearly came into view. Then the plane touched down to a picture-perfect landing as the passengers clapped in appreciation of the captain's skills. They were home.

The plane taxied to the runway gate. Rita and Mary Katherine gathered their onboard luggage and made their way to the exit. As they were exiting the plane one of the stewardesses said, "Mary Katherine, congratulations on your wins at the Australian Open. What was it like to play on Center Court?"

"It was exciting, but she beat me that day, 6-3, 6-2. It was a great trip though. Thank you."

Mary Katherine had won three matches in the tournament before losing to the number two seed in the fourth round. That was by far the best showing she had had in a professional event, increasing the speculation that she would soon be leaving N.C. State to join the professional tennis circuit. When the girls entered the airport terminal, they were greeted by teammates, friends and family. In the midst of them all, stood Rudy and Travis. Mary Katherine's smile lit up the room as she ran to put her arms around Rudy's neck.

"I missed you Daddy. It is so good to be home."

"I missed you too Baby. I am so proud of you Mary Katherine."

Then, MK moved toward the place her heart and thoughts had been for the past three weeks. She stepped into the waiting arms of Travis Simpson.

Travis said, "I didn't think you would ever get back."

"I know, this has been the longest three weeks."

"Yeah, going to Australia, playing on Center Court on ESPN with all those 'Aussie Boys' hanging around. It sounds rough; I was worried you might not come back."

"Yeah, it's a tough life, but hey, somebody's got to do it. There are a lot of guys at those tennis tournaments, but not any more than there are girls here in Raleigh. I see how they all wait for a table in your section at 42nd Street Oyster Bar. I don't even like to go in that place when you're working."

"What do you mean? That's my job. Those girls don't mean anything to me. I'm just working for tips to make some extra money."

"Well, you seem to like that attention. How would you like to see guys hanging all over me after a tennis match?"

"It's not that bad, besides you are the only girl I am interested in."

"I believe you, but I still don't like it."

With that, the subject changed to a lighter note and they all gathered their luggage and headed home.

Soon the college tennis season was in full swing. Mary Katherine swept through her matches like a spring breeze. Rudy and the State men's team also started strong. The Wolfpack men, still riding high after their upset wins over SEC powers Vanderbilt and Florida, were 10-2 and in the thick of the Atlantic Coast Conference race at 5-1. The team was at practice on a Tuesday afternoon. It was a warm breezy day in Raleigh, the temperature in the upper 70s. Jim and Travis were in a close doubles match with the Garcia twins. Rudy and Rita were on the bleachers enjoying the action. Near the end of the first set Jim began to tell Travis that he wasn't feeling right.

"Travis, my head is killing me. The back of my neck is so stiff. It has bothered me for the last two days."

Travis, who had never once heard Jim complain about anything, could see Jim was hurting.

"Jim, let's just take a few minutes and sit down."

The boys sat down on the bench beside the court and Jim leaned forward putting his face in his hands. His complexion lightened as the color left his face. Travis leaned over and placed his left hand on Jim's shoulder.

"Jim, how long have you been feeling this way?"

"Two, maybe three days. I have felt rundown, like I was coming down with a cold. I haven't had any appetite and I haven't eaten or drank much of anything. I kept thinking I would just shake it off. But since practice started today I've felt a lot worse."

Travis could hear that Jim was having trouble breathing and that Jim was beginning to become disoriented.

"Jim, I'm going to walk over here for a minute and get you some water."

By now Rudy could tell that something was wrong with Jim. Rudy knew that Jim was a tough, competitive kid, so if he was sick he was obviously in pain. As Travis got up to walk to the water cooler, Jim then began to slowly lean to the right onto the bench, then his body turned forward as he rolled onto the court. Jim had passed out cold. Everyone ran in Jim's direction. Rita immediately dialed 911 as the trainers rushed to attend to Jim. Within minutes the rescue squad had arrived on the scene while Jim still lay passed out on the court. Jim was loaded onto a stretcher and taken by ambulance to the emergency room at Wake Med. For the next thirty minutes Rudy and the rest of the team waited anxiously at the hospital for news on Jim's condition. By now Mary Katherine had arrived along with Joanna, Jim's girlfriend. Rudy was on the phone with Jim's parents who were in the car on the way to the hospital when the emergency room doctor entered the waiting area.

"Are you all here with Jim Rose?" the doctor asked.

"Yes Doctor, I'm Rudy Outland, Jim's coach."

"Coach Outland, I am Dr. Glover, we have Jim on some IVs to get his fluids up. Jim is suffering from dehydration. We have run some blood work and I have ordered a CT scan to make sure we eliminate any neurological problems. It appears to me that Jim may have mononucleosis. That would explain his muscle aches, dehydration, and fatigue, but we are going to run tests to make sure."

"What will happen next?"

"We will keep Jim overnight for observation. He will be assigned a room within the hour. We will notify you at that time, you can see him then."

By the time Jim's parents arrived he had been admitted to the hospital and transported to his room. After his parents and Joanna had an opportunity to visit with Jim alone, Travis and MK went into the room. By now Jim's color had returned and he was conscious.

"Travis, it wasn't very polite of me to pass out before you came back with my water."

"No it wasn't! When I turned around and saw you fall out on the ground, I almost passed out myself. That's not the kind of thing you see happen every day."

"I hope you never see me do it again."

"Well, have you heard any news on your test results?" Travis asked.

"It looks like mono. If that's the case my tennis season is over. It could be a lot worse though, so I will be thankful if it's nothing more serious than that. But I hate to let the team down. Especially you Travis, we have been partners all year."

"We will be partners no matter what." Travis assured him. "The main thing is that you get better. That's all I care about."

Travis and Jim had become great friends. Jim had spent so much time practicing with Travis. Travis knew that Jim's help had played a large part in his improvement. Travis then asked, "Is there anything I can do for you, anything you need?"

"No, I'll be fine. Dr. Glover said I should be able to go home tomorrow. I'll give you a call once I know for sure."

Travis and MK said their goodbyes and then they made their way to the elevators and out to the parking lot. As they walked down the sidewalk towards MK's car, she could sense that Travis was upset. He was very quiet. There was a deep sadness in Travis that she had never seen before. Mary Katherine was not sure what to do or say, but she knew Travis was not himself. She unlocked the car and the two kids got inside. Mary Katherine looked over at Travis, and then she saw Travis wipe a tear from his eye. MK reached over and put her right hand on Travis's shoulder.

"Travis, Jim is going to be fine."

Mary Katherine did not know what else to say, she simply put her arms around Travis and did not say anything. Travis then composed himself. He forced a smile and looked in Mary Katherine's direction.

"I'm sorry you had to see that. I guess I'm not so tough after all."

"That's okay. I'm here for you, whatever you are feeling you can share it with me."

Travis took a deep breath.

"When I saw Jim pass out like that today, it scared me to death. Then when they loaded him in the ambulance, none of us knew what was wrong. When we got to the hospital, I was okay. But when we got to his room and I saw him in the hospital bed with his parents, it brought back all of those memories of when I was here, seeing him loaded in the ambulance, being in the hospital room. This is the first time I've been back here since I was here with my family. That was a very dark time for me. I don't like to think about it."

"Travis, you wouldn't be human if you didn't have strong feelings about being back here, especially with a close friend like Jim passing out the way he did. It was scary for all of us."

"Life can change so quickly." Travis said. "I know God is in control, but still I am afraid sometimes. I know how fragile life can be. It just hurts me when I see people I know hurting. I know what that is like. It scares me that something like that could happen to me again, or someone I know."

"I understand," MK replied. "I feel so blessed in so many ways. I thank God for all the blessings in my life, yet I know I can't control the future. That is just a part of life that none of us can change."

The kids made their way back to campus. MK dropped Travis off at the dorm. When Travis got to the room Russell was already in the room studying.

"Travis, how is Jim?" Russell asked.

"He is going to be okay. It looks like he has mono. If it is mono he will miss the rest of the tennis season. That will be really tough on the team. Jim is such a great leader on and off the court. There is no way to replace a teammate like Jim."

"Man, that's tough. I'm really sorry Travis."

Travis then sat down on the bed and leaned back against the wall.

"Russell, I need some advice."

"Sure Travis, what's up?"

"Russell, I am crazy about Mary Katherine. I know she is the girl for me, but she is such a great tennis player. She could turn professional today and every dream she has ever had would come true. I love her and I want to spend the rest of my life with her. But I do not want to hold her back. I could not live with her if being with me kept her from pursuing her dreams. I love her too much to do that to her. I'm just not sure what to do about how I feel. What would you do?"

Russell closed his notebook. He leaned back and thought for a minute. Russell could see that Travis and MK were made for each other. He prayed for the right words, then he said,

"Travis, everything you just told me is the truth. That's what you need to tell Mary Katherine. Tell her the truth about how you feel. Then the two of you need to talk about it. I can see it is weighing upon your heart. Tell her the truth. Then both of you place it in the Lord's hands. But I would tell her, I would tell her as soon as possible. I don't think you will be happy again until you have told her how you feel."

Travis sat there quietly absorbing in his mind all that Russell had said. Then he picked up his cell phone and dialed a number.

"Hey, Travis, are you feeling better?" Mary Katherine asked.

"Yes, I'm fine. There is something I need to talk with you about. Do you have time to take a walk?"

"Sure, come on over."

"Russell, thanks man. You are the best friend; you have helped me so much."

"Alright now, save that mushy stuff for Mary Katherine. Go tell her how you feel. I suspect she'll be happy to hear what you have to say."

Travis got up and grabbed his baseball cap and headed out the door. When he got to MK's dorm she was waiting outside. By now it was dark out. It was a mild spring night. The two of them walked around campus, talking about Jim's condition and the effects losing Jim would have on the tennis team. After awhile they reached the tennis bleachers. The two of them sat down, then Travis reached over and took Mary Katherine's hand. He looked her in the eyes and said,

"Mary Katherine, there are some things I need to talk with you about."

Mary Katherine could tell this was important, she took a deep breath, and then she asked,

"Okay, have I done anything to upset you?"

"No! Not at all! I just need to tell you something that has been on my mind."

"Mary Katherine, I love you. I am crazy about you. I can't imagine my life without you in it. When you were in Australia I was miserable. Mary Katherine, you are such a great tennis player. You have so many great things ahead of you. I want you to pursue your dreams. I want you to travel, to play tennis. I want every good thing for you. But I do not want to lose you. I would never hold you back; I could not live with myself if I did. But, I want to be part of your life wherever that takes you. I love you. I know what it's like to lose something you love. No matter what it takes, no matter what I have to do, I don't want to lose you."

Mary Katherine leaned forward and put her left hand over her face and she began to cry. Travis did not know what to say. He thought for a moment and then said the only thing he knew to say.

"I'm sorry Mary Katherine, I didn't mean to upset you."

Then Mary Katherine leaned forward, still crying she put her arms around Travis's neck, and then she kissed Travis and wiped the tears from her eyes.

"These are tears of joy, Travis. You don't know how many times I have prayed to God that I would one day hear you say those words. I love to play tennis, I always have and I always will. But nothing, not even tennis will keep me from you. I am yours for as long as the Lord will let me keep you."

And as the breeze gently blew amongst the oak trees, the scent of jasmines and roses filled the air. Above it all, the One who hears and answers all prayers took pleasure in the joy and love that was growing amongst two of His creations. Then as Mary Katherine leaned her head on Travis' shoulder, they both thanked God for answered prayers.

SUMMERTIME

The weeks quickly came and went as the Wolfpack men's tennis team approached the end of the regular season and began preparing for the ACC tournament. Over the past six weeks State had faced the meat of their ACC schedule, compiling a record of eight wins and five loses. The Wolfpack men stood at 18 and 7. It was the best regular season record the N.C. State men's team had complied in several years, and a great beginning to Rudy's coaching career at N.C. State. Still, even with the success the team had enjoyed there were the lingering questions of what might have been had Jim Rose stayed healthy and not contracted mono. During the time Jim had been sidelined he had continued to attend practices and team matches. Jim was a constant encourager of the younger players. He worked with Travis and his new doubles partner on doubles strategy and assisted Rudy and the other coaches, never once complaining about his circumstances. It was obvious to Rudy and the other coaches and players that Jim was a person of great character, and he was totally committed to the team. Jim displayed the Christian witness of placing the needs of others above his own. Jim was a leader, no question about it. Jim's example of grace in the face of adversity made a large impression on everyone, especially on Travis.

It was Wednesday afternoon, the team had just finished practice, and two days from now the Pack would face the University of Maryland in the first round of the ACC Tournament. Travis was relaxing on one of the player's benches between the courts when Jim came over and took a seat beside him.

"I'm not crazy about sitting on this bench," Jim said. "You remember this is where I passed out on you."

"Yeah I remember, but you promised not to do it again."

"Don't worry, I won't."

"Jim, you are setting a great example of leadership for this team. I am thankful for what this year's team has been able to accomplish, but I am so excited about what we can do next year with you back and healthy again."

"Thanks Travis, that really means a lot, especially coming from you. You have experienced your own disappointments. I believe this situation is an opportunity for me to witness my faith. I want to glorify the Lord by being faithful and continue to praise Jesus during this personal trial, remembering all He has done for me. Travis, I know you have been on a workout program that Dr. Clauson set up for you and Russell. If you would, tell me a little about it?"

"Stephanie played professional volleyball while she was in graduate school in Florida. During that time she dated a guy who was a member of the Navy Seals, he shared parts of their training exercises with Stephanie. She developed an exercise program using jumping drills, wind sprints, weight training, stretching exercises, and swimming. The thing is intense! The first time I did it I thought I was going to die. Coach Clark liked it, so he had Russell do it with me. After about thirty days I was in the best shape of my life. Russell and I still do it three days a week. Russell said Coach Clark was going to have all of the offensive backs and receivers doing it over the summer to get them ready for football season."

"Next year is my senior year," Jim said. "I know I am not going to play professional tennis, so this will be the last real competitive tennis season for me. We have everyone coming back next year. I believe if we all committed to stay in Raleigh over the summer, work out and practice together, we could compete for a national championship next year. What do you think about that Travis?"

"I think you're right. It's hard to stay focused on your own. If we all worked at it together this summer, and we did Stephanie's conditioning program, it would improve everyone's strength and agility tremendously. We would have to play better; no question about it."

"Also, playing singles and doubles against each other would keep us sharp." Jim said. "It's hard to find a competitive match when you're at home for the summer."

"I know, there's no one at home for me to play. I think it's a good idea. I'm all for it. Why don't you talk to Coach Outland about it? I'm sure he'd be in favor of anything that would be for the good of the team."

"I will, if nothing else Travis, you and I can do it together. But if everyone would commit to it, that would be awesome."

In the first round of the ACC Tournament the State men defeated Maryland 4-2. Then in the second round the Pack beat the University of Miami 4-3. That set up a match against the nationally fifth ranked Duke Blue Devils. The young Wolfpack played inspired tennis, but the talented Blue Devils were just too much for State and handed the Pack a 4-2 defeat. During the tournament Jim had approached Rudy with the idea of the team using Stephanie's conditioning program and the players committing to stay in Raleigh over the summer. The team discussed it during one of their team meetings and to Rudy and Jim's delight, every player bought into the idea and agreed to spending the summer in Raleigh and working out together to prepare for the upcoming season. After State's strong performance during the ACC tournament the team received a bid to the NCAA tournament and advanced to the regionals in Santa Clara, California before being eliminated by Rudy's alma mater, the UCLA Bruins. UCLA had an outstanding team as they handled the Wolfpack 4-2. The Wolfpack men finished the season 22-9 and ranked 18th in the nation. The Bruins would go on to win the Men's NCAA team championship.

On the women's side Mary Katherine had completed an undefeated singles season. Capped off with a 6-2, 6-3 straight set victory to claim the NCAA Women's Singles Championship. She had achieved every goal she had set for herself. There was nothing left for Mary Katherine to accomplish in college tennis. With her professional career on the horizon it was obvious to everyone, especially Travis, that it was time for her to move on. The spring semester was over and Travis and Russell were loading up Russell's car for the trip to Charleston.

"Travis, this time tomorrow I'll be trimming rose bushes."

"What makes you think they'll be rose bushes?" Travis asked. "You might be pulling up weeds?"

"No, rose bushes. My dad called last night and told me all about it. He has started planting rose bushes all over Charleston, in people's yards, parks, office buildings. He's got them in our yard at home and at our nursery. Now he goes around cutting the rose bushes back, then he sells the roses at the nursery and the farmer's market. He is so excited about it. Mom calls it an addiction. It just sounds like a lot of work to me."

"You have to admit that sounds like a good idea." Travis said. "He's got to cut the bushes anyway, so selling the roses makes a lot of sense."

"It does, dad's always up to something. He is up and working outside by 7 a.m. every day. He stays outside digging up or planting something every night until Mom drags him inside to eat. If I don't stay out there with him, I feel kind of guilty about it. The man never stops. He loves it."

"My dad's the same way. He's always got something going on. If he doesn't have something to work on he's miserable."

"Besides," Russell said, "I need to make some time for all those single girls this summer. You know those girls are mostly tourists. I told Dad that making sure the girls enjoy their trip to Charleston was a part of my civic responsibility. It was my way of helping to stimulate the local economy."

"I'm sure your dad agreed with that."

"Actually he did. He said that's how he met my mother. He said that by keeping me busy during the day he was helping me stay single a little longer. That would keep me out there to perform my civic duty. The man has an answer for everything."

Travis just smiled.

"Those 'Old Guys' are smart. The best thing is to just not to say too much."

"You're right. Look now, you and MK are coming to Charleston the week before school starts back, right?"

"You bet, the week before that Mary Katherine and I will be at Atlantic Beach with my family. Then we will come and spend the week with you. I am looking forward to those two weeks with her. I know it won't be long before she makes her decision about turning professional. I want to spend as much time with her as I can."

"Alright then, I'm counting on you coming. Look, I've got to hit the road. I want to get home in time to eat and get down to Market Street before Dad takes me on his 'roses tour.' Take care of yourself, I'll see you in August if not before."

"Drive safe, and tell your parents hello for me."

The boys shook hands. Russell cranked the car and headed to the low country.

As Travis watched Russell drive away, he thought about all that had happened in the past year. Another school year had come and gone. Travis had rediscovered his talent for tennis. Over the past year he had made new friends and accomplished many new and wonderful things. Then, at the center of it all he had met the girl he wanted to spend the rest of his life with, to be the mother of his children, to build a life together.

Travis thought to himself, *"Lord, what a wonderful year this has been,"*

Now it was summertime, and what an eventful summer it would be.

LIVE 2 SERVE

It was a Monday morning, the second Monday since the end of final exams. Travis, Jim and the rest of the tennis team met with Stephanie at the N.C. State training center. Joe Moore along with some of the other offensive backs and receivers were there too, as were Coach Clark and Rudy. There were over thirty athletes total who had volunteered to meet at 9 a.m. to begin Stephanie's conditioning program. Stephanie began to explain the conditioning drills to the guys. She told them she would be participating in the training with them. One of the incoming freshmen receivers, Jordan Smith, told Joe, "This can't be too hard if a girl is going to do it."

Coach Clark overheard what his new recruit said, then Coach Clark took a hard look over at the freshman and replied, "Son, we'll see if you feel that way in a hour or so."

Once the stretching exercises were over, Stephanie led the boys through the drills. Within thirty minutes the boys were totally exhausted while Stephanie looked as fresh as a daisy. Joe looked over at Jordan and asked, "What do you think now, Rookie?"

Jordan gasping for air and bending over at the waist didn't say anything.

"If you think this is tough," Joe said. "Just wait 'til we start jumping up and down in the sand for fifteen minutes nonstop, then we will swim 50 laps. Welcome to college football."

Coach Clark and Rudy just stood there enjoying it all.

Rudy looked over at Coach Clark.

"David, sometimes I wish I was a young man again, but this is not one of those times!"

Coach Clark laughed.

"Yeah, this is embarrassing for those boys. Stephanie looks like a supermodel, so you don't realize how great an athlete she is until you see her exercise. I'm glad I don't have to try and keep up with her."

It was about an hour later when Stephanie finished up the last of the drills and the boys, all of them gasping for air, "thanked God" that it was over. Coach Clark walked over to Jordan.

"Jordan how have you enjoyed your first exercise class with Stephanie?"

"It's tough Coach," Jordan replied. "That's the toughest woman I have ever seen."

"It's a good thing for you she isn't in charge of the passing drills you guys will be working on this afternoon. But since you didn't think these

179

exercises would be so tough, why don't you run some extra wind sprints after you all finish your practice?"

"Yes sir."

Meanwhile Jim and the tennis team were worn out as well. The tennis players were hurting in places they had never hurt before. Jim told Travis,

"I didn't think I could get this tired and live to tell about it."

Travis, who had been doing the training for over a year now replied,

"I told you it's tough, but all the stretching she makes us do will help you get over the soreness quicker."

Jim said, "Jumping in that sand just takes all the energy out of your legs, and the swimming takes it out of your arms and shoulders."

"The jumping in the sand strengthens your feet and ankles, as well as your legs. That has really helped me jump into my serve more. The swimming has strengthened my shoulders and hands, which has given me more power on all my shots. Running all those wind sprints has helped me run down balls better. The plan she designed uses every muscle in your body. We only do it three days a week so you can recover and still practice tennis. Stephanie is a brilliant trainer."

"You were right Travis, this has got to help the whole team play better tennis."

Afterwards Travis and Jim made their way out to the parking lot and they called it a day. The next morning the team was scheduled to meet at the tennis courts at 8:30. When Travis got there Jim had already arrived. Jim had a large cardboard box and big smile on his face.

"Hey partner, what ya' got there?"

Jim smiled and said, "I got you a T-shirt, come check it out!"

Travis walked over to Jim and Jim then handed Travis a shirt.

"I had these made for all the guys. I am the only senior, so it really means a lot to me that all the guys agreed to stay and practice this summer."

"Jim, you didn't have to do that."

"I know I didn't have to, I wanted to. How do you like the shirt?"

Travis held up the shirt.

"Man this is neat Jim, who designed them?"

"I did. Well the girl at the T-shirt shop helped lay it all out, but I wrote the logo."

Travis said, "Play 2 Win-Live 2 Serve; John 3:16-17. Man, that's neat. Why did you use the number 2 instead of the word to?"

"Because we all have two choices, we all either choose to accept Jesus, that Jesus is God; or we will reject Him, and there are two lives for the believer. The first life we are born with, and the second life we choose to live once we have accepted Christ into our lives. I thought by having the number 2, instead of the word to, people would ask what it stood for, just like you did. That would give us a chance to begin a discussion about faith and Christianity."

"That is awesome Jim! What a great idea! I like the American flag on the sleeve, and the Ichthys Symbol, the Christian Fish on the front. This is a great gift Jim, thank you."

By now the other boys had arrived along with Rudy. Jim had a shirt for everyone, and he had one for Rita and MK too. When everyone got there they changed into the shirts Jim had made and then they all sat down and talked for a few minutes about their expectations for the summer practices and the upcoming season.

"I want you guys to know I am so proud of what this team accomplished last year," Rudy said. "We had a great season. We have everything in place to take N.C. State to the top of men's tennis next spring. I appreciate all of your commitment. Being willing to come out on your own and practice together over the summer. I am also so proud of what you young men are doing off the court. Jim, I want to thank you for these shirts. I know we all have made the decision to accept and serve Jesus Christ."

Then Rudy held up the T-shirt.

"If we all commit to do what this shirts says, "Play 2 Win-Live 2 Serve," I believe we will see God use our efforts to honor His Son Jesus, and lead others to Christ. I am just so, so proud of you guys."

For the next two and a half hours the team practiced agility drills, serving, forehands, backhands, volleys. Then they played singles and doubles against one another. It was an intense, spirited practice. Once practice ended, the boys were ready for something to eat.

"Jim, you want to go down the street to the Char-Grill and grab a Charburger Steak sandwich?" Travis asked.

"Yeah man, I love those things."

The boys hopped in the car and headed off down Hillsborough Street. When they got to the Char-Grill they filled out their order ticket and stood outside in line waiting for their food. While Jim and Travis were talking, there was a man with his two young sons standing behind them. After a couple of minutes Jim felt someone tap him on the arm. He looked around and it was one of the young boys. The boy was ten, maybe twelve years old. The boy looked up at Jim.

"I like your shirt, where did you get it?"

Jim smiled at the boy.

"I'm on the State tennis team. We had them made for practice."

Then the boy said, "My dad asked why is the number 2 on the shirt?"

From there Jim introduced himself to the boy's father. Travis listened as Jim began to tell the father about the inspiration behind the number 2, about the team dedicating their season to the service of God. The man and his sons were Christians. The boy's father was intrigued by the message of the shirt, and that the N.C. State tennis players were openly expressing their Christian beliefs. The man also coached youth sports teams. He asked Jim if he could have some more of the shirts made so the father could purchase them for himself and his family, and also his youth league baseball team. Travis and Jim could quickly see that there was an interest among other believers who were also looking for ways to set an example for their friends, family, and children. That as college athletes they were more than just players on a tennis team, they had a unique opportunity to be Christian role models for others. Travis and Jim both began to wonder how God might use this simple message on the back of a T-shirt, to help lead others to Christ.

Later that day when Rudy got home Rita and MK had gone shopping. He hung around the house most of the day. The girls got back home about 6:30. When they came inside Rudy proudly handed them their T-shirts,

"Look at what Jim Rose had made for the team. Isn't that the neatest thing?"

"I love it Dad; what does the 2 stand for?"

Rudy beamed as he said,

"The number 2 stands for the 2 choices, to accept Jesus; or reject Him. Also the two lives, the life before we accepted Jesus, then the new life of the believers."

"That is a great message, what a witnessing tool!" Rita exclaimed. "That Jim Rose is a fine young man. What a wonderful disciple he is for the Lord."

"These kids are so special." Rudy said. "I am so proud of these boys. I can't wait to see how God will use these young men."

Rudy didn't know it, but God was about to use them all in ways they could never have imagined.

MISSION ACCOMPLISHED

"Travis, look at those two little boys over there, the ones in the State baseball caps. Do you see them? Look at their T-shirts."

Travis said, "Hey, they are wearing the 'Play 2 Win-Live 2 Serve' shirts."

"I have never seen my Dad as proud of anything as he is of those T-shirts," MK said. "He is so proud of you guys, the way you are all working together this summer, attending the Bible study. He and Mom love those T-shirts. I can't tell you how many people Mom and Dad have shown them to."

"Jim told me he has made over 300 shirts so far: little league teams, churches, youth groups," Travis said. "I sent one to Russell and his parents and they've had people in Charleston asking them where they can buy one. Jim said one of the ladies who bought some from him for her church group asked Jim if he had considered selling them in Christian bookstores. Coach Clark wants to sell them through the Bible study class, and Jim is going to try to get them in the campus bookstore and gift shop. These shirts have taken on a life of their own. Who would have thought those shirts would have gone this far so fast?"

"I saw two teenage girls at the pool wearing them. The shirts have such a simple, yet powerful message. They are spiritual and patriotic. They let you express your belief in God and country. I've had I don't know how may people ask me about the '2.' It's such a neat idea. Who knows how far they will go."

Over the next four weeks the faith of the kids and the public's interest in the shirts continued to grow. Meanwhile, the men's tennis team continued working with Stephanie's fitness program and practicing tennis. The team's fitness level improved week by week. There was also a noticeable change in the physical appearance of the players. All the boys became leaner and more muscular, some of them adding 10 to 15 pounds of muscle. Their flexibility improved, their hand-eye coordination got better. Their endurance increased.

With improved fitness came an increased mental toughness, the confidence that comes from hard work, and working together. On the tennis court each player worked diligently improving the weak areas in their games, as Jim and Travis continued to focus on improving Travis' all-court game. The increased strength and agility gave Jim more power and accuracy on all his shots. Jim had always been a very fundamentally sound player. He possessed a wealth of knowledge on the strategy and execution needed to hit all types of shots, especially heavy topspins and slices. Now with the increased strength and agility, Jim was adding power to his shot making. He was simply a much-improved player, and as Jim improved, he was also teaching Travis. Jim worked with Travis teaching Travis how to control the ball with spin. Jim helped Travis develop the skill to hit varying types of topspins and slices. Allowing Travis to open up the court more, to move his opponents farther to the side while creating alleys for Travis to then use his powerful ground-strokes to hit passing shots for winners.

Jim also taught Travis to use his strength and hand speed to hit serves with heavy topspin. At the same time Rudy taught Travis to hit his serve with more accuracy. With Rudy's and Jim's help, Travis was now more consistently hitting his serves over 130 mph. Travis' accuracy and velocity made his serve a dominant weapon.

During the summer break Travis and Jim also entered and competed in some men's professional tour event in doubles, while Travis competed in singles too. The boys participated as amateurs, so they were not eligible to receive prize money. But they gained valuable experience, and Travis was beginning to make some noise among the professionals as a singles player. Travis possessed a unique ability to hit the ball with power; his agility and foot speed, along with the pace that Travis had on all his shots, especially his serve, caught the eye of the other professional players, coaches, and sports agents. It was quickly becoming apparent that Travis himself had a potential career in professional tennis. It was just like Mary Katherine had said; Travis had all the ability in the world, and it would be up to Travis how far he would take it.

Mary Katherine meanwhile spent most of the summer traveling with the professional women's tour. Practicing and playing with the professional women helped her develop her game. Off the court she was constantly being recruited by sports agents, advertising executives, clothing companies, and equipment manufacturers, it was obvious that it was time for MK to turn pro. With all the activity the summer days quickly passed and before you knew it, it was the first week in August. Mary Katherine had just gotten back from playing two weeks on the Women's Professional Tour in Los Angeles and Cincinnati. It was a Thursday night and Rita and Mary Katherine were getting ready to go out to dinner. Meanwhile Rudy was in Florida on a recruiting trip.

"Mary Katherine, let's go down to 42nd Street, I want some seafood."

"Let's don't go there Mom. Travis is working tonight."

"That's good, we can eat at one of his tables."

"I don't like eating there when he is working. Those girls there are all over him."

"Oh Honey, it can't be that bad, let's go."

Mary Katherine didn't say much; she was mad, and it showed. The girls got to the restaurant around 6:30, and they requested a table in Travis' section. In a few minutes they were seated. Mary Katherine was still not happy. There were young attractive girls all over the restaurant and at the bar. Travis was waiting tables. He was polite and courteous to all his customers, but it was obvious that many of the girls in the restaurant had more than food on their minds. They were young women out for a night on the town. They were out meeting people, the way kids that age do, and Travis was a handsome young man, working for tips. So it was his job to take care of the girls and be nice, but Mary Katherine didn't like it. After a few minutes Travis came over to Rita and Mary Katherine.

"Hey, thanks for coming out tonight. It's good to see you Mrs. Outland. I had a good talk with Coach Outland after practice yesterday; did he tell you?"

"Yes Travis, he did. That was very good news."

"Yes Ma'am, thank you, I'm glad you approve. Mrs. Outland, Mary Katherine, what can I get you to drink?"

Rita said, "Ice water for me."

"I'll take ice water too," MK said.

After Travis left, Mary Katherine looked over at Rita.

"These girls are all throwing themselves at those waiters. I can't stand it!"

"Calm down Mary Katherine. Travis is just doing his job."

"I still don't like it."

"Well let's talk about something else. I know you and Travis are looking forward to going to the beach for two weeks. What time are you leaving Saturday?"

"10."

"What are you having for dinner?" Rita asked.

"Salmon."

"Did you have a good time at the pool today?"

"Yes."

Rita leaned over.

"Are you going to speak to me one word at the time tonight?"

"Yes."

About that time Travis came back to their table with the water and a basket of hush puppies.

"Mary Katherine, you look real pretty tonight." Travis said.

"Thank you."

"Is something wrong?"

Mary Katherine "growled" back at Travis.

"You know I don't like to see all those girls flirting with you."

"Mary Katherine, you know I need this job."

Mary Katherine then took the opportunity to again express her frustration.

"You wouldn't like to see guys hitting on me at my job; it upsets me."

"I'm sorry. What do you want me to do about it?"

"Go work in the kitchen with the cooks, or get another job!"

"Does it really bother you that much?"

"Yes! It does! You would feel differently if the shoe was on the other foot, if you were watching guys flirting with me."

Rita changed the subject and got Travis off the hook, for the time being anyway. Once Rita and Mary Katherine had finished dinner; Travis came back to the table.

"Can I get you anything else?"

Rita said, "No, it was delicious Travis."

MK didn't say anything. She was not happy.

"Mary Katherine, I'll come by after work," Travis said. "You are not still upset are you?"

"You'd be upset too."

"Well, I'm sorry it upsets you."

Then he said goodnight to Rita, and went about his work. Not much was said between Rita and MK on the way home. When the girls got back to the house MK walked straight up the stairs toward her room.

Rita asked, "Where are you going?"

"I'm going to change clothes. I've got somewhere to go."

"MK, you weren't very nice to Travis tonight. That's a mighty sweet boy. You need to remember that."

"I know Momma, but I want him to quit working as a waiter; that's all there is to it!"

Later that night, about 10:30 the restaurant and bar was packed when one of the waiters walked over to Travis.

"Travis. Man, have you seen that girl at the end of the bar?"

"No, I've been busy since 6."

Then the waiter said, "She is gorgeous, there must be ten guys over there talking to her."

"That's great, but Man, I am swamped with orders, and besides I have a girlfriend already."

"You need to see this girl, just turn around and look, over there, there she is."

As the waiter pointed toward the end of the bar, Travis turned around and looked.

"All I see are guys, where is she?"

Then the waiter pointed again.

"Just wait until they move, okay, there she is!"

Travis said, "Wait a minute, that's …"

Travis started walking toward the bar.

"Excuse me, pardon me," as he made his way through the crowd.

"Mary Katherine, what are you doing here?"

"I decided to come down here and wait for you to get off work."

"I thought I was just going to meet you at your house after work tonight."

"I thought I would come by and surprise you."

Mary Katherine was wearing a new dress she had bought for a "special occasion." By this time Travis began to get the picture.

"That is a pretty dress. Is it new?"

"Yes. I bought it just for you, how do you like it?"

"I love it. It's the kind of dress that would attract a lot of attention. Especially if you were trying to prove a point."

"I was hoping you would think so."

"I guess you are putting the shoe on the other foot?"

MK smiled.

"Yes, something like that."

Travis smiled back, then he leaned over and kissed Mary Katherine. It was the kind of kiss that makes a point.

"Well, that's what I call 'customer service' I'll have to come here more often."

"Not alone and wearing that dress you won't!"

Then he said, "You stay here, I'll be right back."

"Yes sir."

Travis then turned and walked into the back of the restaurant. In a few minutes he returned.

"Where have you been?" MK asked.

"I've been applying for a job as a cook!"

MK's eyes lit up as a big smile came across her face.

"Did you get it?"

"Let's just say we will always have someone in the house who knows how to clean fish."

MK jumped up and threw her arms around Travis' neck.

"That means a lot to me." She said. "I owe you one."

"You already owe me a lot more than one, but that's okay. I've got something I want you to do for me too."

"What is it?"

"We'll talk about it while we're at the beach."

"Well after tonight, whatever it is you want, the answer is "Yes.""

"You promise?" Travis asked.

"I promise."

"I'm going home now." She continued. "I'll see you in a little while." Then she was out the door and headed home.

Mission accomplished.

NO YOU DIDN'T

"Mary Katherine, you're joking right?"

"What are you talking about?"

Travis said, "There is no way we can get all these suit cases in my car. I don't think all that stuff would fit in a Suburban."

Mary Katherine said, "We're going to be gone for two weeks."

"You went to Australia for three weeks, and you didn't take half this much luggage."

"Well, I need all this stuff. We can get it in there. Where there's a will, there's a way!"

About that time Rita walked outside.

"Travis, how are you doing?"

"Hey Mrs. Outland, I'm fine. I'm just not sure how I'm going to get all of Mary Katherine's 'necessities' in this car."

"Mary Katherine started packing last night," Rita said. "She finished just before you got here."

"Mom, you are just as bad as I am; maybe worse!"

"I'll give you that." Rita agreed. "Okay, let's get to packing."

After a few minutes Travis could see that Rita and Mary Katherine had done this before. They took all of Travis' two bags out of the car. Then they proceeded to fill every square inch of Travis' Volkswagen Jetta with suitcases and dress bags. Having Sarah for a sister, he had seen his Mom and Sarah do this sort of thing before. He just stepped back and stood in amazement as the two women went to work. After about fifteen minutes Mary Katherine was smiling as she had just enough room to slide into the passenger seat.

Travis got in the car then he looked over at Mary Katherine.

"Have you got everything?"

"Ha, ha! I told you I'd get it all in there."

With that, they headed to the beach. A couple of hours later, Travis and Mary Katherine were driving across the Emerald Isle Bridge. Mary Katherine looked down at the Intra coastal waterway as the boats and jet skis maneuvered between the sand dunes and small islands lining the waterway. She could see the ocean above the rooftops in the distance. Seagulls flying in the bright blue sky, the salt air blowing in the passenger window. The smell of salt water, every young girl's paradise, they were at the beach. Once they crossed over onto the island, they turned left, continuing north on Highway 58, Emerald Drive. They passed shopping centers, restaurants, amusement parks, condos and cottages. They drove through Emerald Isle and Indian Beach, on up into Pine Knoll Shores, then they turned left into Beacon's Reach. An ocean and sound side community where the Simpson's had rented a house for the week. There were swimming pools, marina, and of course tennis courts. The townhouse in Fiddler's Walk was directly overlooking the sound, and just a short walk to the ocean. It didn't take long, with everyone toting suitcases to get all of Mary Katherine's things up the steps and into the house. Everyone, especially Wesley, was glad to see Mary Katherine and Travis.

"I wasn't sure the house was big enough to hold these three girls and all their clothes." Ed said. "I thought for a minute I was going to have to leave Wesley and his bed back home in Wilson."

Wesley's ears perked up when he heard his name called.

"So I left some of my stuff so he could come too." Ed said. "It just wouldn't be the same around here without him."

After awhile the luggage was unpacked and things calmed down. Mary Katherine, Kathy and Sarah were soon making plans to head over to the ocean. The coolers were filled and the bathing suits were on, it was time for the girls to hit the beach. Ed and Travis grabbed the coolers and sun umbrella, and the girls took the lounge chairs as the family and Wesley headed across Highway 58 toward the ocean. They walked down the shaded tree lined path between the cottages and through the sand dunes, up the steps to the community beach access, then across the wooden deck with benches atop the dunes. From there, the wide sandy beach and beach houses stretched north and south as far as you could see. Travis felt the warm breeze blowing against his face. He saw the waves roll ashore, one upon another. He looked forward and saw the girls walking down the steps and onto the sand, with Ed and Wesley close behind. Travis could see his past and his future right in front of him. He had been coming to this beach since he was a little boy. Watching his parents and his older sister reminded him of his childhood. Now he was here again as a grown man with his family, and this young woman who only a year ago had walked into his life, and helped him put the pieces of his broken heart back together. As a smile came across Travis' face he remembered all that had happened in the year since he had last stood in this spot and looked out into the ocean. The beauty, the majesty of it all reminded him that God was in control. That God had great plans for him and his family. Then as he walked down the steps and onto the sand he took comfort in the knowledge, that throughout all his past, as well as in the future, that God and his family would always love him and that he would never be alone.

As Travis walked across the sand with the sound of his flip flops flapping beneath his feet, the warm sand between his toes and splashing against the back of his legs as he toted the cooler. Before long he had caught up with everyone. The cooler was put down. The sun umbrella was lifted into place. Then with beach chairs and towels unfolded and sunscreen applied, the vacation was officially under way.

"Travis," Ed said. "We're going to have our hands full trying to beat the guys off these pretty girls this week."

Travis smiled as he looked towards Mary Katherine.

"I had to do that all by myself just two nights ago!"

"That's not exactly true," Mary Katherine replied. "I was just trying to make a point."

Sarah then added, "You were just putting the shoe on the other foot."

Mary Katherine said, "So he told you already."

"Oh yeah," Sarah replied. "I hear from my brother whenever he needs girl info."

"Yeah, me too." Kathy added.

"Wait a minute," Travis said. "Whose side are you two on?"

"Travis, girls have got to stick together," Sarah replied. "Besides Mary Katherine is family, we're sisters! What makes you think she didn't tell me before you did?"

"No! I don't believe it."

"Whose idea do you think it was for Mary Katherine to go back to the restaurant?" Sarah asked.

"No!"

Sarah then said, "Oh yes! I helped her decide which dress to wear."

"I don't believe you."

"It's true." Mary Katherine replied. "Sometimes I talk to Sarah and your Mom to get 'classified information.' It helps me accomplish my plans."

Travis asked, "Sarah, how could you help her pick out a dress while you were in Greenville?"

Sarah didn't say a word. She just picked up her cell phone and scrolled through the uploaded pictures on her phone's camera. Then she handed it to Travis.

"See for yourself."

There on the camera was the picture of Mary Katherine holding the dress up in front of her in the mirror.

"That's wrong," Travis said. "Mom were you in on it too?"

"I liked red dress myself," Kathy replied. "But Mary Katherine made the final decision."

Then Sarah reached over and took her phone back.

"Isn't technology amazing?"

"Dad did you know about this?"

"No Son, I'm technologically challenged. Besides, it's them against us; remember?"

Sarah then said, "Travis, Mom and I, we did you a favor anyway. You and Mary Katherine are made for each other. We're just helping you along a little, that's all."

Then Sarah said, "Mary Katherine, did you know you are Travis' first girlfriend?"

"No I didn't. I heard Travis had more girlfriends than Casanova!"

Sarah said, "Travis has had more girls chasing after him and more dates than Casanova, but you are his first real girlfriend."

"Really? Is that true Travis?" MK asked.

"Yep, you are my first, and my last."

Sarah said, "Whoa! That's saying something. How do you feel about that Mary Katherine?"

"That sounds good to me."

Ed just leaned back in his beach chair and smiled. He knew Travis Simpson "the bachelor" was officially off the market. He could see his Son was head over heels for Mary Katherine, and Ed knew once Travis made up his mind there would be no changing it.

The next few days consisted of time spent riding jet skis, deepsea fishing, long moonlit walks on the beach, and lounging in the sun. It was a time for the family to catch their breath, and catch up on the past year's events and changes. Sarah was becoming serious with her boyfriend of almost a year. During the day she and Mary Katherine shopped together and spent countless hours on the beach, talking about all the things young women their age have on their minds. Meanwhile Travis and Ed talked about the upcoming school year, the goals for the tennis team. They discussed Mary Katherine, the choice she would soon have to make about whether or not to return to State for her sophomore year or turn pro. Then during the afternoons before dinner Travis and MK got in their tennis workouts to keep their games sharp. There was so much going on in Travis' life now, things that a short time ago no one could have predicted.

It was a little before 6 p.m. on Friday night, the family was about to leave the house to go out to dinner when Travis' cell phone rang.

Travis answered, "Hello."

Then the voice on the other line said, "May I speak with Travis Simpson?"

"This is he."

"Travis, my name is John Stone, I am the section chief for the United States Tennis Association. I am calling to inform you that your application has been approved and you have been selected as a participant in the qualifying rounds of this year's U.S. Open. Congratulations!"

Travis stood there for a moment in shock.

"I'm sorry, could you repeat that please?"

Mr. Stone then said again, "You have been selected as a qualifier for the U.S. Open Tennis Championships. Congratulations!"

"I don't know what to say; thank you."

"You will be receiving an e-mail with information on match schedules and the qualifying draw. I look forward to meeting you in New York."

The rest of the conversation was a blur for Travis. After a couple of minutes he hung up the phone. Travis stood there, mouth open with a confused look on his face. Everyone was staring anxiously at him.

"What is it Son, is everything okay?"

"Yes, everything is fine."

"Who was that Travis?" Ed asked.

"His name was John Stone with the United States Tennis Association. He said I had been accepted as a qualifier for the U.S. Open."

Everyone leaped to their feet.

Sarah said, "New York, New York! Wow! That is so cool!"

Ed and Kathy just stood there speechless. Sarah and Mary Katherine were jumping up and down screaming. Wesley was excited too, running in every direction.

"I don't understand how they chose me, I didn't apply to be in the tournament."

Then a voice said, "Yes you did."

Travis asked, "What do you mean?"

Then the voice said, "I signed you up."

"You did not!"

"Yes I did, I told you I didn't like to travel to tournaments on my own, so I signed you up."

"Mary Katherine, what am I going to do with you?"

"Kiss me I hope!"

And with that the celebration was on. Later that night when the family reached the restaurant they were seated at their table, the dinner conversation was much different from what they all expected only an hour ago. Sarah and Mary Katherine were discussing all the stores and sights they would visit on their trip to New York. Mary Katherine told Sarah about the cocktail parties and dinners for the players and their guests. The celebrities they would meet and all the other players Mary Katherine had met on the women's tour over the summer. Mary Katherine told Sarah how "gorgeous" the men players were, although they both quickly agreed that neither of them were interested in looking at other guys. Meanwhile Kathy and Ed were busy making travel plans and hotel reservations, scheduling time off from work and substitute teachers. Travis just sat there in the middle of it all, trying to convince himself that this was real and not a dream. Just then, Mary Katherine leaned over and whispered in his ear.

"You don't know what to do with me; do you Travis Simpson?"

Travis just smiled and looked her in the eye.

"Yes I do; I'm going to hold on tight to you, and never let you go."

"You better. You promised me, remember?"

"Yes, I do."

Later, once the family got back to the house, after everyone else had called it a night. Travis lay awake in his bed, unable to sleep from all the excitement. He got up and slipped on his shorts, T-shirt, and put his flip-flops on and headed downstairs and walked out of the house and across the street toward the ocean. As he left the house, he could hear the sound of the waves in the distance. He walked beneath the trees, along the illuminated wooden path, between the sand dunes until he crossed Emerald Drive onto the ocean side of Beacon's Reach. He reached the top of the dunes and took a seat along the decking overlooking the shoreline. The breeze was strong coming off the ocean. It was a full moon, stars shining to the south and west; then there was a rumble from a thunderstorm that was brewing from the northeast. Lightning in the distance back over the rooftops of the hotels and cottages behind him. With the wind blowing through his hair, Travis stared at the ocean waves coming ashore. He felt the cool breeze against his skin, made sensitive by the sun's rays. The smell of salt air, the sound of the wind whistling between the blades of thick grass that lined the top of the sand dunes beside him. In the quiet of the moonlight he wondered to himself.

"Lord, how did You bring me here tonight; and was this really Your plan for me all along? And what about tomorrow?"

Then the quiet still voice whispered back to him in the breeze.

"Tomorrow, we leave for Charleston."

BIG DECISION

"Travis, I've got everything in the car; I'm ready whenever you are."

"I don't believe it," Travis replied.

"It's true." Sarah said. "It's all in there, just like she said."

Kathy then added, "You can't mess with us girls when it comes to packing."

"Everything she brought with her," Travis asked, "plus the new stuff she bought since we've been here. Even the sailboat picture she bought in Beaufort?"

"Yep, every bit of it." Mary Katherine said.

"What about my stuff?"

"It's in there too," Kathy said. "For a minute it looked like your stuff wasn't going to make it, but we got it in there."

"Alright then, I guess we're ready to go."

There were hugs and kisses as Travis and Mary Katherine began to make their way to the car. On the way out Ed pulled Travis to the side.

"Travis, have you decided what you are going to do?"

"Yes, Dad; I've got it all figured out."

"Are you nervous?"

"I am; but I'm going to do it anyway."

"Good, you let me know how it goes. Son, I love you, and I am so, so proud of you."

"Thanks Dad; I love you too."

The kids were on the road to Charleston. Travis and Mary Katherine drove down the Carolina coastline. They passed through Wilmington and Myrtle Beach, mostly talking about Travis being accepted to compete at the U.S. Open and the trip they would both now be making to New York in two weeks. The one subject that was not discussed was the big decision facing Mary Katherine. Was she going back to school after the U.S. Open, or would she leave N.C. State to travel and play the women's pro tour? It was obvious to Travis that the time had come for Mary Katherine to move on, to leave school and play professional tennis. But there was now a tension in the air. Mary Katherine did not want to leave Raleigh. She wanted to be with Travis. Being with him was more important to her than playing tennis. Travis did not want to see her leave, but he knew she needed to do it. So as they drove along the highway to Charleston, that subject was not discussed, but it was weighing heavily on both of their minds.

It was a little before 5 p.m. when Travis turned the Jetta in the Rawlings' driveway. Russell and his family lived in the Charleston suburb of Mt. Pleasant, just across the Cooper River Bridge from downtown Charleston. Market Street and the houses on "Rainbow Row" were just across the Cooper River from the traditional brick house and landscape nursery that Russell and his family called home. When Travis and Mary Katherine stepped out of the car, Russell was there to greet them. He was sweating like a pig, covered in dirt from head to toe, wearing a "Rawlings Landscape & Design" T-shirt and hat.

"Travis. Man, am I glad to see you." Russell said.

"Whoa! Looks like you've been going at it hard today Bro!"

"Man, you just don't know." Russell replied, "My dad is going to kill me when he finds out I look off early to meet you. But thank you Jesus! Today is my last day. I get one week off before we go back to school. So now that you're here, I'm on vacation too."

Mary Katherine asked, "Where is your Dad?"

"He's cutting roses somewhere. But he told Mom he would be home by 6. He's going to cook shrimp and salmon on the grill for dinner tonight, so Mom told him he had to be home and take a bath by 6:30. He's just like a little boy; he will not come inside if he can help it. Hey, let's get your stuff and get you all situated inside."

Russell walked toward the car. He looked inside.

"Goodness gracious! Look how much stuff is in that car! Travis, that's more clothes than we have in our dorm room combined!"

"Ha, ha, don't bother with it now, you're too dirty to be handling my clothes anyway. You need to take a bath, then you and Travis can take it all inside."

"Wait a minute," Russell said. "What about you superstar, aren't you going to help?"

Mary Katherine said, "No way. I've seen you two in action. You boys were more than willing to tote clothes and suitcases outside the girls' dorm at school that first day I met you. Remember? Besides, I'm company, and I'm on vacation!"

About that time Russell's mother Kim walked outside.

"Travis, Mary Katherine, we are so glad to have you visit. Mary Katherine I love your sundress!"

"Thank you Mrs. Rawlings, I am so glad to see you. I've been looking forward to our visit."

Russell was an only child so Kim was excited about having a young woman in the house.

"Mary Katherine, come on inside, let me show you your room. I've got lots planned for us this week. I want to take you down to Market Street shopping. Then we can tour some of the plantations, go to the beach, we are going to have the best time."

As the girls were walking inside Kim turned around and said, "Russell, you go on and get your bath. Then you can help Travis get their things out of the car."

Mary Katherine just smiled at the boys as she turned and walked with Kim in the house.

Russell said, "How does she do it?"

"I'm not sure." Travis replied. "But I'm working on it. She does that with my mom, dad, Sarah, and even Wesley. She doesn't say anything but yes ma'am, yes sir. Thank you ma'am. She is so polite and personable; she just draws you to her. Then the next thing you know, everybody is waiting on her hand and foot. She's even got me doing it now. I know I am spoiling her rotten, but I can't help myself."

"Well, you're in too deep now. The best thing for you to do is just do what she tells you as quick as you can."

"I know it, she's got me alright."

Russell and Travis followed the girls in the house. Russell jumped in the shower while Travis played with the family dog, a black lab named Buddy. Travis walked outside and he and Buddy sat down on the concrete patio that Russell Sr., or "Russ," as everyone called him, had built in the backyard. Russ had also built an outdoor grill. The family cooked out most nights in the summertime. Often times Russ would be out in the yard working in the rose garden while he was cooking on the grill. Kim was always after Russ about tracking dirt in the house so Russ built an outdoor shower where he would take a bath and change out of his dirty clothes before coming inside. It was Russ' way of keeping the peace; and besides, he liked the feeling of taking a shower outside anyway, so everybody was happy. Travis hadn't been outside for long before Russ drove up in his gray pickup truck.

"Travis Simpson, boy somebody told me you were going to play in the U.S. Open; is there any truth to that?"

"Yes sir."

Russ then said, "Russell told me Mary Katherine signed you up without telling you."

"She did, that girl is always up to something."

"Kim has been talking about Mary Katherine coming to visit all summer," Russ said. "With all boys in the house, she doesn't have anyone to shop with, do "girl stuff." She has told all her friends Mary Katherine was coming, so they all want to meet her. Looks like you are stuck with me and

Russell; that is unless you want to go shopping and sightseeing all week."

"That's okay; I believe I'll just hang with the boys."

Russ then turned toward his dog. "How's my boy Buddy doing, is he behaving?"

Buddy hopped up and Russ rubbed his head.

"This dog and me have spent a lot of time out here on this patio. We are both bad about making a mess in the house. I've got to give him a bath tonight since we have company."

Russ was covered in dirt that even filled the hair on his arms. He had a dark suntan and thick powerful forearms and hands from working outside. He reached over and put the leash on Buddy.

"Watch this Travis,"

Russ took Buddy and the two of them walked toward the den where Kim and Mary Katherine were sitting. As they walked toward the door, Kim could see them coming. By the time Russ reached for the door knob Kim was there waiting for him.

"Wait a minute Mister; where do you think you're going?"

"I'm going to take a bath, you told me to be home and cleaned up by 6:30."

"You're not coming in here looking like that, you and Buddy are both filthy! You're not going to mess up my clean house. I've got Jan, Liz, Joan, and Linda coming over after dinner to meet Mary Katherine and Travis. You and Buddy need to go out to 'your shower' and wash that dirt off both of you. You're not coming in here!"

"Kim, it's not nice to talk about Buddy that way, at least fix me a glass of lemonade. I would fix it myself but I don't suppose you'll allow me to walk in the kitchen."

"No, you and Buddy stay right here. Don't you two dare come inside!"

Kim then turned and walked into the kitchen and Russ smiled at Mary Katherine.

"Does your mom treat your dad like that?"

"Oh yeah. You know she does."

"I know it," Russ said. "They like to mess with us sometimes; it keeps life interesting."

About then Kim returned with the lemonade.

"Here you go. Now Russ, you go get cleaned up and make sure Buddy is dried off before you take his leash off him. I don't want him walking around shaking water all over everybody."

"Yes Mama."

Russ walked by Travis on the way to the shower.

"Travis, we'll play a little trick on those girls later, so we need to be good now so they won't expect anything. Come on Buddy, let's go get washed up."

After awhile Russ and Buddy came back to the patio. Russ was as clean as a whistle and Buddy was all dried off. Kim brought the salmon and shrimp and everyone came outside. Russ got the grill started.

"Travis, Mary Katherine, come with me," Russ said. "We've got to cut some roses for Mary Katherine's room."

Mary Katherine smiled and said, "Alright! Every girl loves roses!"

Russ then said, "Travis, long stem roses will help keep a man out of the dog house, but roses are expensive and I'm in trouble a lot, so I started growing my own. I've got all kinds. Depending on what I've done, I need different colors. I have yellow roses, white roses, pink roses, and a girl's best friend, red roses. Mary Katherine, which ones would you like?"

Mary Katherine's smile beamed as she walked amongst the rose bushes.

"They are all so beautiful; it's hard to choose."

"Take your time," Russ said.

As they walked along Travis and Mary Katherine held hands. Travis watched Mary Katherine as her eyes moved from one flower to the next. She smiled as she smelled the aroma of the roses, and the sweet fragrance of the Carolina Jasmine vines that surrounded the garden. Russ had a cut glass vase with some water in it.

"Travis, once Mary Katherine decides which ones she wants, we will cut off the leaves and I'll show you how to arrange them. That's important information when you're in a jam and you're trying to get out."

"That's good to know. Mary Katherine is always looking for inside information. I need some of my own if I'm going to keep her honest."

"I told you from the beginning I was high maintenance. I'm always looking for an advantage."

"Alright which ones will it be?" Russ asked.

"My mood changes a lot in a week, so can I have some of each?"

"That's an honest answer, and a good choice. Let's cut some of each. Pick the ones you want and then you and Travis can cut them."

For the next few minutes Travis and Mary Katherine walked along choosing twelve roses. They cut them, then sat down and removed the thorns and leaves; arranging the roses in the vase.

"They are so beautiful and they smell wonderful," Mary Katherine said.

Travis leaned over and kissed her.

"You are the most beautiful thing in this garden."

Mary Katherine smiled.

"If you keep talking that way, you'll stay out of the doghouse."

"Does that mean I will never have to buy you roses?"

"I'm still high maintenance, remember?"

After the roses were cut and arranged they all sat down around the table outside while Russ finished grilling the seafood. Before long dinner was prepared, enjoyed, and finished. Then they all sat outside after dinner and talked in the warm summer night air, as the sun slowly dropped below the horizon. Travis could hear the sound of the ocean waves in the distance.

"How far are we from the beach?" Travis asked.

"We're four blocks from the ocean." Russell replied. "We just walk down this path," as he pointed behind him.

"It takes us through the garden. Then we cross the beach highway and we're at the sand dunes and ocean access. Since this is an old residential neighborhood, there are no hotels or condominium projects here. The beach is very private. We can walk over there later."

"Yeah," Travis said as he reached out for Mary Katherine's hand, "That would be nice."

"Russ, you and Russell help me get these dishes cleaned up," Kim said. "The girls will be here in a few minutes. I have some tea and pound cake for us all when they get here."

Mary Katherine asked, "Mrs. Rawlings, can I help you with anything?"

"No, no, you and Travis just sit and relax."

In a few minutes the four ladies arrived, and when they did things got lively. Linda, one of the four said, "Mary Katherine, I swear you are prettier in person than you are on TV."

Jane then added, "Well, when you are as pretty as she is, you can get yourself a boyfriend that looks like this young man. Ain't he a handsome devil?"

Joan said, "Yes he is. Lord, him and that Russell Jr. in the same dorm room. I bet they have to dead bolt the door to keep the girls out of there just so they can get some sleep!"

Liz then added, "You know Russ was a pretty thing back in the day, that's how he landed Kim. Kim had all the boys after her when we were in school!"

"Alright you 'steel magnolias' don't go telling all your secrets and scaring the kids." Russ said. "This is just their first night staying with us."

Jane responded, "Hush Russ! We are in the South, you know we are always talking and carrying on about something. There ain't no way we can be but so quiet."

"Besides Russ," Liz added. "Everybody in Charleston knows you are always causing a ruckus. If you want quiet, you and Buddy can walk over to the beach. You can't expect six women to not make a fuss! We're going to say whatever comes to our minds!"

Russ said, "Alright, me and the boys will take Buddy for a walk so you girls can all get acquainted. But don't ya'll go messing with Mary Katherine. After all she is a young girl. Don't the five of you go talking bad about husbands and make things hard for poor Travis here."

"You just go on Old Man," Kim said. "But don't you let Buddy run in the ocean. I don't want him tracking sand in the house."

Russ got up and put the leash on Buddy and then the three boys and Buddy started walking down the path toward the ocean. They could still hear the women talking and laughing as they walked along through the nursery. Then Russ stopped.

"Let's have a little fun with those girls, what do you say?"

Russell said, "Fine with me, those women are crazy!"

Russ walked over and picked up the water hose and turned the water on and ran the water all over Buddy until he was soaking wet. Buddy liked the water so he sat there happy as could be. Then Russ yelled out in a loud voice,

"Kim, Buddy got off his leash. Call him and see if he'll come to you."

Kim yelled back, "Russ! How did the dog get off his leash? "

"It just came undone. He went running down toward the ocean. Call him, maybe he'll come if he hears your voice."

Kim looked at the other women and said, "Lord have mercy; those boys, what are we going to do with them?"

Then Kim yelled out, "Buddy, Buddy, come here boy!"

Russ held the leash on Buddy. Buddy was whining. He wanted to go to Kim. Then Russ and the boys started to laugh.

"Try it again Honey, a little louder!"

Kim really yelled this time. "Buddy! Buddy! Come here boy, come here Buddy!"

"Buddy, go to Mama boy, go to Mama."

Russ unclipped the leash and Buddy took off. Buddy went streaking toward the house. He was flying full speed across the back yard, tongue out and tail wagging. When Buddy reached the concrete he slammed on the brakes and skidded across the patio and landed paws first in Kim's lap.

"Buddy Rawlings! You are soaking wet boy! You've been jumping in the ocean you rascal! Get down!"

Buddy landed on all fours and shook for all he was worth. Water went flying everywhere and the girls went to screaming and laughing.

Russ yelled out, "Kim! Kim did you find him? Have you got Buddy?"

Kim screamed, "Russ, you are going to get it this time boy! I don't know how you did it, but this was no accident! You and Buddy had this planned; I know you did!"

"Kim. How can you say that about Buddy? Besides we have company!"

"You just go on; I'll get even with you later."

The girls all had a big laugh as they toweled off Buddy. Before long they were all settled down telling stores about tennis, college, boyfriends, and husbands. The girls all wanted Mary Katherine to tell them if the celebrities at tournaments were as handsome in person as they were on TV? What it was like to go to the parties and dinners at tournaments with the other players? How serious were she and Travis, and did she think Travis was "the one?" Mary Katherine enjoyed being treated like one of the girls. She was seeing more and more the joy of family, the simple life. Although she had the prospects of fame, fortune and travel in her immediate future, she was seeing more and more that friends and family were the things most important to her. Dinner with the Rawlings helped reinforce her decision that a life shared with Travis Simpson was the thing she wanted most.

Over the next six days Mary Katherine found Kim to be a woman of her word as Kim and the "steel magnolias" took Mary Katherine all over Charleston. Meanwhile, Travis, Russell and Russ hung out with the boys, their friends around town. At night the gang would all get together and go out to dinner somewhere in Charleston, or ride over to the Isle Of The Palms and walk along the white sandy beach enjoying the brilliant low country sunsets. Then Russell would take Travis and Mary Katherine into Charleston to visit the local nightspots and meet his friends. It was a great week, and all too soon it was Friday night, and Saturday morning Travis and Mary Katherine would be heading home to Raleigh. Russ and Kim had a cookout planned Friday with a group of about thirty friends and family coming over for the kids last night in Charleston. Russ cooked chicken wings on the grill, salad, watermelon, cantaloupe, strawberries, and assorted vegetables, pies and cakes for desert. Everyone had a wonderful time. Travis and Mary Katherine were not ready for the week to end. After dinner, the Rawlings, Travis and Mary Katherine sat outside talking until late into the night. After awhile Russ and Kim decided to call it a night; then Russell decided to go inside and give Travis and Mary Katherine some privacy. Mary Katherine looked over at Travis.

"These two weeks have been great. I don't want to see it end."

"Yeah, me too, I could get used to living like this."

Then Travis stood up and held out his hand.

"You want to go for a walk on the beach?"

Mary Katherine took his hand as she stood up and the two kids walked down the path between the garden that led out to the sand dunes and the ocean. The sky was clear and the stars illuminated the path, the sound of the ocean in the distance, the sea breeze from the Carolina shore blowing the smell of jasmine and salt water through the air. Not much was said as the kids held hands walking along the path. They reached the deserted beach. They took off their flip-flops and with the sand between their toes, the two of them walked quietly along the edge of the surf. Travis tried to make small talk about school, the past two-week trip, but it was obvious there was tension in the air, and they both knew it was there. Then Travis decided it was time to have a talk.

"Mary Katherine, I want to tell you something I have never told anyone else."

"Okay, what is it?"

"When I was in high school, the day before I was injured, my father and I met with a scout from the San Diego Padres. He told us that the Padres had decided to take me as the fifth pick in the draft. They were going to send me to Florida for a couple of months in rookie league, then transfer me to their double A minor league team. He told me what my signing bonus would be. They agreed to pay my college tuition and fees at the school of my choice. Everything I ever wanted was there for me, all I had to do was say "yes." That night before the accident, my father and I talked about the decision I had to make, to sign with the Padres or go to State. He told me it was my choice and that I would have to decide. The next day before the game in Raleigh, I had decided that I was going to sign with the Padres. Then in the last inning I was hit by the pitch, and everything changed."

Mary Katherine then asked, "I had heard the rumors that was true. Why have you never told anyone?"

"Because it is in the past. But it is important for me to tell you because you have a choice to make. I wanted you to know that I understand how you feel, and if I were in your shoes, I would leave school and play professional tennis."

Mary Katherine didn't like what she was suddenly hearing.

"Is that what you want? To see me leave school; what about us? How would that affect our relationship?"

"What if I weren't involved? What would you do then? Wouldn't you leave school and join the tour?"

"But you are involved, and that makes all the difference. I'm not going to risk losing you just so I can play tennis!"

With that Mary Katherine began to tear up, she turned and looked out into the ocean, as she wiped the tears from her eyes. Travis reached in his pocket and put his arms around Mary Katherine.

"Mary Katherine, Honey, look at me."

Mary Katherine turned around, with her feet in the surf, the ocean behind her.

"I know you have a big decision to make about playing tennis, but before you make that choice, I want to ask you to make another decision."

Then Travis took Mary Katherine's left hand, he bent down on one knee.

"Mary Katherine; I love you, I will always be here for you, no matter what you decide to do, no matter where you go. Mary Katherine, you are the woman I want to spend my life with. I promise nothing will ever change that. Mary Katherine Outland, will you marry me?"

Mary Katherine stood there in the moonlight; she put her right hand over her eyes. Her knees were shaking as her whole body trembled. She had worried for so long that her tennis career would come between the two of them. Now here she stood, that fear was leaving, and she was overcome with joy and relief. Then she dropped to her knees, and with the surf washing ashore the ocean waves beneath them, she put her arms around Travis.

"Yes, Travis Simpson, I will marry you."

Meanwhile atop the sand dunes, and in the ocean breeze blowing around them, the God of creation watched as the ocean waves came ashore around them, one after another, after another, after another.

"Sarah, is that all the bags?"

"Yes Dad, that's everything."

"Alright girls, let's get this stuff outside the terminal exit," Ed pleaded. "Travis and Mary Katherine should be here any minute."

As Ed, Kathy and Sarah pushed the luggage cart toward the US Air terminal exit they heard a familiar voice.

"Mom, Dad! Welcome to New York!"

They looked to their right and saw Travis and Mary Katherine walking in their direction.

"Travis, you're just in time," Sarah said. "These are some heavy bags."

"We've got a car waiting outside to take us all to the hotel." Travis said, "Dad they have so many parties and dinners for the players, you just won't believe it. They provide a courtesy van and shuttles to take us anywhere we want to go in the city. I could get used to this kind of living real easy."

"That's great Son. How have your practice sessions been going?"

"Good, I'm glad Jim came with us. He and I have kept our same practice routine. My serve is better than ever. I'm excited about playing tomorrow."

"Sarah, we have a big night tonight," Mary Katherine said. "There is a charity benefit dinner party at the tennis stadium ballroom. All the players and their guests will be there. There are so many celebrities and sports personalities here. You are going to love it."

"I can't wait!" Sarah said. "Mom, which celebrity would you most like to meet tonight?"

"I don't know Honey. I'm just excited to be here."

Once the family reached the shuttle they loaded up. Within an hour everything had been transported to the hotel and unloaded in their rooms. It was now a little past 1 p.m., so Travis and Mary Katherine changed into their practice clothes. The USTA had a court time reserved for all the players so they all went over to the stadium for their practice sessions. Mary Katherine's practice was scheduled for 2 p.m. Travis' practice time was at 4 p.m. When Mary Katherine arrived at the court there were reporters there waiting to speak with her.

"Mary Katherine, how do you feel entering your first tournament as a professional?"

"It is exciting. I'm glad the U.S. Open is my first professional event. Playing here two years ago was my first experience playing with the professionals, so this tournament is very special to me."

Then the reporter said, "I understand you have some other news in your personal life as well; is that an engagement ring you're wearing?"

Mary Katherine smiled. "Yes it is! The Lord has blessed me in so many ways. I am very thankful."

Then the reporter said, "I understand your fiancé is in the tournament too, Travis Simpson."

"Yes, Travis and I are both excited to be here."

After a few more minutes the interview concluded and Mary Katherine got to work. Travis and Jim worked with Mary Katherine as Rudy watched and coached Mary Katherine through her warm-ups and hitting practice. Meanwhile, Kathy, Rita, Ed and Sarah watched from the sidelines with the other spectators. Mary Katherine was just beginning the interview process of hiring a sports agent and a coach to travel with her on the tour. The family had decided that Rita would be traveling with Mary Katherine to tournaments for a while to help Mary Katherine get adjusted to life on the road. Rita had traveled with Rudy for six years when he was playing professional tennis; so Rita knew what it was like to live out of a suitcase. For the next hour and a half Mary Katherine worked on footwork and fundamentals, forehands and backhands, serves and volleys. Her practice session was solid. She was ready to compete with the best players in the world. After Mary Katherine's practice ended the families moved to another court in the tennis center where Travis was scheduled to practice. When they reached the court Travis was surprised to see the reporter from the sports channel waiting to interview him.

"Travis, have you got time to talk a minute?"

"Yeah, sure."

The reporter asked, "Travis, there has been a lot of interest in the sports world about your transition from baseball into tennis since your injury. It is truly remarkable. How have you been able to do it?"

"I played a lot of competitive tennis as a junior, so playing tennis is something I have done since I was a child. But the Lord has opened doors for me. He has placed Christian people in my life to help me, and I give God all the glory for what has happened."

Then the reporter said, "I also hear you are engaged to another pretty good tennis player; Mary Katherine Outland."

Travis smiled. "Yes, she will definitely be the best tennis player in the family. Mary Katherine and Coach Outland have helped me so much, as well as Jim Rose; my teammate and doubles partner at State. The Lord has truly blessed me."

"Anyone who could play professional baseball has got to have a strong throwing arm. I have been told you have one of the fastest serves in tennis. Do you want to hit a few serves on camera for us?"

"Sure, just let me get loosened up."

After working out with Mary Katherine, Travis was quickly ready to go, so the reporter set up the cameras and radar gun to film Travis' serve. After a couple of warm-up serves, Travis signaled to the reporter he was ready. Then he tossed the ball in the air. "Pop." It sounded like a gunshot as the ball exploded off the racquet and into the court, 133-mph. Then Travis hit ten more just like it, all of them over 130-mph.

"Man, that is fast." The reporter said. "Have you always been able to hit the ball this hard?"

"I've had a big serve since I was playing in the juniors, but with Coach Outland's help, I have learned to be more consistent, and hit my serve with more power."

The reporter then said, "We'll stick around and watch some more of your practice session, and good luck this week."

"Thank you, I appreciate you taking the time to talk to me."

Mary Katherine and Jim then began to go through the practice session with Travis. The practice was intense as Travis blasted forehands and backhands from the baseline, while the reporter continued to film parts of Travis' practice. About thirty minutes into Travis' workout, Tom Ham, another reporter who was covering the tournament stopped by.

"I see you're here watching Travis Simpson, how does he look?"

The television reporter said, "See for yourself, he can really put some pace behind that tennis ball, and he moves across the court like a ballet dancer. His footwork is amazing."

"I did a feature article on Travis when he was in high school." Ham said. "We felt like he had a legitimate chance to be an all-star in professional football and baseball. He was as good a two-sport high school athlete as I have ever seen. I am going to be following him this week. I've interviewed his coach, Rudy Outland. Rudy played on a national championship team at UCLA, and then played the professional tour for six years. He says that Travis is the most talented athlete he has ever coached, and has more tennis talent than anyone he has ever been around."

Then the television reporter said; "I knew Travis and Mary Katherine's engagement, and Travis' recovery from his hand injury, would make the two of them a great human interest story this week. But I honestly did not expect him to be this good."

"I'm not surprised," Ham said. "I have a friend who was in Florida earlier this year when Travis beat Steve Sloan, last year's NCAA singles champion. He told me Travis blew Steve Sloan off the court. Travis just overpowered the kid. That's the way he was on the baseball and football field. He was such a great athlete. He was a natural. So I'm not surprised he's this good. He would be great at whatever he did. The kid's a winner."

After the practice session concluded, Travis was walking off the court when he recognized Mr. Ham.

"Travis, it's good to see you again."

"Yes sir, Mr. Ham, it's been a long time."

"Travis, I was very sorry to hear about your accident, I know that must have been tough on you and your family. But I was excited to hear you are now playing tennis again."

"Thank you. It's been a turbulent time in my life. But through it all Jesus has been there for me. I have seen God bring Christian people in my life when I needed them the most, and that has made all the difference. I can see that now through it all, Jesus has never left my side."

"Travis, tell me, how did you get involved in tennis again? I remember when we talked a couple of years ago before the accident, that you had played at a very high level in junior tennis, but how did you come to play again?"

As Travis and Mr. Ham were speaking, the television reporter was standing there as well, and the cameras continued to record their conversation. Travis then said,

"Actually, I was just trying to get a date with Mary Katherine."

"Really? Tell me about it?"

Travis smiled.

"I first saw Mary Katherine outside her dormitory and she and I met, then the next night at Bible study I saw her again. She told me to meet her at the tennis courts, and the next thing I know, we were playing tennis."

"So you played against Mary Katherine on your first date?"

"I don't know if it would classify as a date. She beat me up pretty good. But that's how I got started playing again. Mary Katherine has helped me in so many ways. Not only tennis, but she has encouraged me, taught me to believe in myself again."

"Travis, what do you see yourself doing with tennis? Have you set any goals for yourself?"

"I am a part of a great tennis team at N.C. State. We have all stayed in Raleigh this summer to get ready for tennis season. Coach Outland has worked with all of us to improve our games. We have all our starters back from last year's team, which made it to the NCAA tournament. All the players have dedicated this season to the glory of our Lord and Savior, Jesus Christ. Helping the team win a championship is my only goal."

"I noticed that T-shirt you're wearing, "Play 2 Win-Live 2 Serve" John 3:16-17. Where did you get that?"

"Jim Rose, he is my doubles partner, he is here, that's Jim over there," as Travis pointed in Jim's direction. "Jim is our team captain. He designed the T-shirts as a way for the team to express our faith in Jesus Christ."

"Why is there a number '2' on the shirt instead of the word to?

"It's a witnessing tool; a conversation starter. It gives us a chance to explain the two choices we all have, to accept Jesus Christ as our Lord and Savior, or to reject Him. It also represents the two lives of the believer. The life we are born with, and then the life, the spirit of Jesus that we have living inside us."

As the cameras continued to film the reporters and camera crew, as well as the spectators standing near by, were touched by Travis' sharing of his testimony.

"Travis, when we first met, you talked about your faith in God. Talking with you today, you are still witnessing your faith even after all that has happened. Tell me; how has this experience affected your beliefs?"

"When I was injured, my faith was severely tested. As a Christian, I could not understand why a God who loves me could allow one of His children to be hurt. Not just the physical pain but the emotional pain, the doubt that you feel when suddenly your life is turned upside down. I struggled with questions and disbeliefs, I have had my doubts and at many times today I still struggle with the memories and fears of what happened. But this experience has made me more compassionate for others who are struggling. People like me who have experienced disappointments they can't understand. But over time I have seen God take this situation and teach me to love my friends and family more. I appreciate the blessings of health and the love of family I once took for granted. I have learned that life is fragile, and we need to thank God every day for the blessings in all of our lives."

"Travis, let me ask you one more question. After all that has changed in your life - the injury, the period of doubt, then playing tennis again, getting engaged to Mary Katherine - what is the thing you see yourself doing in the future with your life now, after all the changes, good and bad?"

Travis thought for a minute.

"I want to be a good husband and father, to have a family. I want to support Mary Katherine in her tennis career. This is something she has worked for and wanted all her life, so I want to help her achieve all her goals. As for me, I am looking forward to playing tennis and finishing school. My career plans are still very much up in the air. But in whatever I do I want to witness my faith in God, and teach people about the love and forgiveness offered through a relationship with Jesus Christ. After all that Jesus has done for me, I feel like sharing my love for Him is the least I can do in return."

"Travis, it's great to see you again. Congratulations on your engagement and good luck the rest of the week."

"Thank you Mr. Ham. It is good to see you again too."

Afterwards they were all headed back to the hotel to get ready for the banquet. Later that night when the families arrived at The Tennis Center the banquet room was filled with the other players, as well as sports and entertainment personalities. Sarah and Mary Katherine quickly began moving around the ballroom. Mary Katherine was busy introducing Sarah to the other women players she had met on tour. Travis and Jim were tagging along behind them while the two girls worked the room making introductions. There were many congratulations from the women players to Mary Katherine on her engagement. Travis, Sarah and Jim were quickly made to feel at ease by the other young women and their friends. As the night went on Travis met many of the other young men who traveled the world playing professional tennis. He felt comfortable with these new friends; after all, these were all young people who shared the love of sports. Travis had found that even though the sports were different, the love of competition was the same. He knew that being married to Mary Katherine, that professional tennis would be a part of his life. But now he was beginning to feel that he too might have a future in professional tennis. He was beginning to believe he too could compete with the best players in the world, that his God-given talents could still be used, in ways he never thought possible. The sting of what had happened to him was still there. But Travis knew now that talent was still there too, and expressing his trust in Jesus helped him to believe again. Believe that God was in control. That God was still leading Travis, and that through it all, God would work all things for good.

Later that night, after the banquet ended, Ed sat outside on the balcony of the hotel, enjoying the late summer night air. Kathy came outside to join him.

"That was some party tonight," Ed said.

"It was a special night," Kathy agreed. "Sarah had the best time. She and Mary Katherine are something when they get together. They will be great friends for one another."

"You're right. They were so beautiful tonight; and so were you."

"Thank you Honey, that's sweet."

"Who would have thought two years ago we would be here, at the U.S. Open? Travis engaged and playing tennis."

"I know, it still seems like a dream to me."

"Me too. We just never know where God may lead us. When I heard Travis give his testimony today to Mr. Ham, I was so touched by what he said, the young man he is becoming."

"I know, I am so proud of Sarah and Travis. The witnesses they are for the Lord. No matter what they may accomplish in this world, their Christian testimony will always be the thing I am most proud of."

"Me too Honey," Ed concluded. "Me too."

They sat there late into the night, talking on the hotel balcony overlooking the city, enjoying the blessing of family. Ed and Kathy had come to realize that although they could not control the world around them, and that they could not protect their children from the trials of this world, that God was in control of all things. That God had a plan for them all. That He was working in their lives, and that wherever the Holy Spirit led them, and whatever they faced, God would always be there with them.

QUALIFYING

"Travis, that was very impressive."

"Thank you Coach Outland."

"That's the best I've ever seen you hit the ball. I know you're going to play some great tennis today."

Travis collected his racquets and tennis bag, and then he and Rudy sat down for a talk. Travis was scheduled to be on the court for his first match in one hour.

"Travis, you know Steve Thompson, the kid you're playing today is another college player, he played number one for Stanford. He is a left-hander so you need to be prepared for some different spins, especially on his serve. I've talked with some of the coaches who coached against Stanford this year. They told me Steve is very sound fundamentally, but you should have an advantage physically with power and foot speed. I want you to play very aggressive today. To win in professional tennis you have got to hit winners. Players at this level will not give away a match. Everyone is going to make some unforced errors; but to win you've got to go for it. Play to Win."

"Yes sir, I understand."

After their talk Travis picked up his bag and then he and Mary Katherine walked over to the court where he would be playing and sat down on the bleachers.

"Are you nervous?" Mary Katherine asked.

"Yeah, I am."

"That's good, that let's you know you want it."

"I do. I can't wait to get out there."

"Travis, you are playing great. Just be super aggressive today. Just let it happen and that boy won't know what hit him."

While the kids were talking Mr. Ham walked up.

"Travis, are you ready to go today?"

"Yes sir."

"Mary Katherine, I'm Tom Ham, it's a pleasure to meet you."

"Yes sir, it's nice to meet you Mr. Ham."

"Mary Katherine, I met Mr. Ham when I was in high school."

"That's right, I wrote a magazine article on Travis. I am excited to see he has done so well with his tennis. Mary Katherine, Travis tells me you are largely responsible for his success."

Mary Katherine smiled.

"Travis has worked hard and I am very proud of him."

213

"Mary Katherine, I also want to congratulate you and Travis on your engagement. Have you set a date?"

"Thank you. Some time next summer, probably next June or July."

"Well, I'll grab a seat and let you two finish your talk. Good luck today Travis."

"Thank you, sir."

Mr. Ham then sat down on the bleachers. The stands began to fill as the match time approached, then the officials called the players to the court to warm up. After a short warm-up session the match was set to begin. As the match began the players both played consistent, solid tennis. Then with the score tied two all, Travis stepped in on a forehand and whistled a crosscourt winner to break Thompson's serve and take a 3-2 lead. When the players took their seats at the changeover, Travis took a deep breath to relax himself. He had worked his first set jitters out. After the break, Travis went back to the court, he took a deep breath, and signaled to Thompson he was ready to serve. Travis tossed the ball in the air and blasted a serve out wide for an ace.

Rita said, "Wow, he hit that one!"

The radar gun on the court flashed the serve speed at 136 mph. From that point on Travis dominated the match. He hit blazing serves, forehands and backhands. He just simply overwhelmed Thompson as he cruised to a 6-2, 6-1 win. After the match Mr. Ham came over to speak with Travis.

"You made that look pretty easy."

"Thanks; things just went my way today."

"That reminded me of watching you play football and baseball."

"Thank you. I'm just doing the best I can. The Lord has blessed me, and He deserves the glory."

"Congratulations on your win, I'll see you again tomorrow."

"Yes sir, thank you for coming."

After the match Travis received a round of congratulations from everyone.

"I tell you what Travis," Sarah said. "You keep playing like that and I'll have plenty of time to shop in New York, cause you will be here awhile. Nobody's going to beat you if you keep hitting the ball like that."

"Sarah's right," Rita added. "That was some great tennis Travis."

"Thanks, I feel like my game is really coming together."

"You just stay with it," Mary Katherine said. "I can see you getting better all the time."

Later in the day Travis and Jim worked with Mary Katherine while Rudy coached her through her practice session. Since Mary Katherine had played so well in the two previous U.S. Opens she was entered in the main draw and did not have to compete in the qualifying rounds. After Mary Katherine's practice was over the group went back to the hotel and later that night went to dinner. Then the kids- Sarah, Jim, Travis and Mary Katherine, went out to some of the parties held for the players around the city.

The next morning Travis was up early. He had a 10 a.m. match time against William Corbett. Corbett was a ten-year tournament professional, who had been ranked as high as twenty-five in the world earlier in his career. Over the past three seasons Corbett had been hampered with an elbow injury that had made it difficult for him at times to practice. Corbett, like Travis, was also a power player. He hit the ball hard, but agility was his weakness. So Travis' game plan was to move Corbett around the court early in the match to expose his lack of mobility. When the match started Travis immediately went after Corbett with a variety of heavy top spins and slices to move Corbett across the court and into the corners. Then once Travis had him out of position he would blast a flat driving forehand or backhand into the open court for winners. Jim had worked with Travis all summer to help add the spins and slice shots to Travis' game. Playing Corbett was the first time Travis had faced an opponent in a match where he needed to use these new weapons. It quickly became apparent that these new skills had taken Travis' game to another level. Travis' serve was also working as he had 12 aces in the match, hitting his first serve consistently above 130 mph. Travis' powerful serve and ground strokes were making news in the national papers and sports television so there was a considerable crowd on hand to see Travis handle Corbett, 6-4, 6-2.

When the match ended Travis received a warm round of applause from the crowd. As he came off the court Travis was met by Mr. Ham and several other sports reporters to get his comments on the match.

"Travis, your serve was really on today, was that the difference in the match?"

"Yes, thank you. Coach Outland has helped me become more consistent, that is really paying off, when I can get my first serve in; it's a real advantage for me."

Another reporter asked,

"Travis you hit a lot of top spins and slices today, is that something you've been working on?"

"Yes. I am trying to work on adding variety to my game. Against a player like Corbett, I knew I had to mix it up, to keep him from getting into a rhythm. He's too good of a player to just hit with him from the baseline."

Then another reporter said, "Travis, since they posted the main draw schedule this morning, how do you feel knowing the winner of your match tomorrow will play the number one seed Tom Williams; Saturday night on center court?"

"Really. Wow! Actually, I didn't know that. That would be exciting, playing the number one player in the world on center court at the U.S. Open. That would be something special, but first I will have to play another great player tomorrow, so I need to focus on one match at a time."

As the reporters finished asking their questions and the crowd thinned out, Mr. Ham made his way over to Travis. By now Mary Katherine, Jim, and the other family members where all standing there around Travis.

"Travis, congratulations, you did it again!"

"Thank you Mr. Ham. I really appreciate your coming today."

"Travis, I wanted to let you know that I am writing another feature article on you. I have been following your progress this year since your return to tennis. The magazine decided to feature you in the college tennis edition this year."

"Thank you Mr. Ham, that is wonderful news."

"I also wanted to tell you that I do some freelance writing for some Christian publications, and since our talk the other day I have contacted some people about doing an article about you. Covering your transition from football and baseball into tennis after the accident, and your personal testimony about your belief in God. That is the type of message Christian media is looking for. I believe it would be very helpful to young people who are looking for role models to help encourage them to witness their belief in Jesus Christ. Is that type of interview something you would be interesting in doing?"

Travis just stood there for a moment trying to take it all in.

"Yes sir, I would be honored to be a part of that type of an article, but Mr. Ham, my teammates, Coach Outland, Mary Katherine, my roommate Russell, all these people, these Christians are the reason I am here today."

"We would include them all in the article, your teammates at State, Mary Katherine. We would want to include the stories of the people who have helped you. Your family, friends at school. I believe it is a compelling story, and I have several sports magazines and Christian publications that are interested if it's something you would like to do. You just let me know once the tournament is over, and we'll set up a time for me to come to Raleigh so we can talk."

As Mr. Ham turned and walked away Travis was in a sort of fog. With everyone congratulating him on his victory, the news about Mr. Ham's assignment, to do a feature article in the sports magazine. Travis welcomed the opportunity to give his testimony in Christian magazines and to publicly witness his belief in Jesus, but everything was happening so fast. Travis was thrilled by what was going on around him. Yet in the midst of it all, it seemed as though what was happening, was happening around him, and not really to him. It was as though he was watching these things happen through his eyes, but to someone else. Travis was having a hard time believing this was real, that these wonderful things were happening to him, in his life. It wasn't that long ago that Travis had been convinced that he was born to be a professional athlete. He had imagined himself playing professional sports in New York. Making a play at shortstop in Yankee Stadium, or catching a touchdown pass at the Meadowlands against the Giants. Since the accident, so much had happened, good and bad. Now that things were going so well, Travis was still having trouble putting the past disappointments behind him. From a distance, even in the midst of the celebration, Ed could see that the doubts were there. Ed could see deep into Travis' heart, after all, they shared the same blood. Ed waited until things quieted down, then he went over to Travis and put his arm around his Son.

"I am so proud of you Son."

"Thanks Dad."

"Look Son, I know you are super busy today, with all that is going on; but there's something I need to get your advice on. Do you have an hour or so when we can get together and talk?"

"Sure Dad. Do you want to meet at the lobby of the hotel after I've had a chance to shower and change, say about 4 p.m.?"

"That would be perfect. I'll see you then."

It was a little before 4 p.m. when Travis walked into the lobby of the hotel. Ed was already there, eating some peanuts and reading the newspaper.

"Hey Buddy, thanks for meeting me. What time are you kids going out tonight?"

"Probably sometime around 8 p.m., Jim said he had something he was going to work on this afternoon. Sarah and Mary Katherine went shopping again, it's a good thing New York is a big city, 'cause those two can really cover some territory when they start shopping."

"You know your Mom and Rita went with them."

"I thought they might, but they didn't say much. I just looked around and saw that Mary Katherine and Sarah were gone. Did Mom say when they would be back?"

"No, your Mom doesn't have any conception of time once she and Sarah get in a mall. I just figure I'll get something to eat around 7 p.m. or so. She may be back by then, maybe not."

"Travis, I need your opinion on something."

"Sure Dad, what is it?"

"I've got this friend of mine who is in a complicated situation. I can tell he's a little confused about what to do, I think I know how to help him, but I don't want to step on his toes. I'm not sure if I should offer my help or not. If it was your friend, say Russell or Jim; what would you do?"

"I don't think you ever go wrong by telling the truth. I appreciate it when the people who I trust try to help me."

"I see, so you would want your friends to come to you in that situation."

"Yes, I would."

"Dad, why do I have the feeling that the friend you are talking about is me?"

"Well, I suppose that's because it is you we are talking about."

Travis laughed. "Dad, you know I always come to you for advice."

"Yes, that's it! You and Sarah do come to me, and I love to help you both any way I can. But often times when I try to help either of you without you asking me first things don't go so well. Now isn't that true?"

Travis smiled. "Yes, that's true."

"Look Son, it's complicated being a dad. When your kids are little, they tug at your leg as you walk out the door to go to work. As they get older you have to start to back away so kids can make their own decisions, good and bad. They have to learn to stand on their own. That's why now I don't like to offer my opinion unless you or your sister first tell me that you want to hear it. I trust you both to make good decisions, but sometimes as your father who has watched you all your life, I can see things a little clearer because I'm not the one in the middle of the situation."

"Dad, you have always made me feel confident in myself because although I have always known you were there, you have made me face things on my own. Any advice you have, I am always interested in your opinion, because I know you only want what's best for me."

"I love you Son, and one day when you are a father you'll better understand where I'm coming from. The thing I want to talk with you about is this, Travis you have had some wonderful, wonderful things happen lately, and sometimes good things can be just as overwhelming as bad things. Changes, even good ones, can seem surreal if they happen too quickly. I just sense that you are a little uncomfortable with these sudden changes. That it is all happening too fast."

"I am Dad. I am so thankful, please understand, I am not complaining. As a matter of fact, I am more thankful for my blessings now than ever before. After all that has happened; I'm having a tough time accepting that God is blessing me this way. I find myself worrying that it will all fall apart like before. That something bad will happen again. I know I shouldn't feel that way. I know that's not how God wants me to think, but I can't help it Dad. Those feelings are there, and I don't know how to make them go away."

"Travis, someone once said, 'courage is not the absence of fear, courage is doing what is right in the presence of fear.' Jesus understands what it is to be afraid. He experienced all the emotions we face. Things that we experience in our lives stay with us, they make us the people that we are. We can only choose how we react to things, we cannot prevent bad things from happening."

"Dad, I want so much to believe again, to have the kind of fearless faith in myself that I had before the accident. As wonderful as things are now I worry that something is going to happen and ruin it all. I used to expect good things to happen to me. Now, after all the disappointment, I'm struggling with believing in the good things. I see so many others who are struggling. I don't even feel deserving of the blessings. I wonder why am I so blessed with a family and friends who love me? Mary Katherine, she is everything I could have ever hoped for. Why me? Why has God blessed me again in this new way? And will it last this time?"

"Travis, first remember that none of us - you, me, any of us - are deserving of our blessings. We have not earned our families, our talents, our health, even our abilities. Those things are all gifts from God. They are His gifts, and we are to use them for His glory. They are given to us through grace. The fact that you don't feel deserving is a sign that you understand where your blessings come from. From God, and not your own accomplishments, and that is a good thing."

"Dad, I feel as though my faith is weak? Is it a sin to have doubts? To be afraid?"

"No Son, your faith is not weak. You have questions. Travis, I have questions for God. So many things I've seen in my life I don't understand. God knows our fears. He understands our doubts. God uses us in our weakness, to display His strengths. I want you to understand the importance of what you are doing. By doing your best, whatever that is, you are honoring God. I see God working in your life, and in Jim's life, in Sarah's life, all of our lives. Our roles may be different, but they are all equally important in God's eyes. Don't try to figure God out. His plan is too complex for us to ever understand. Just continue to give Him the credit no matter what happens, good or bad, then see where God leads you. Where He leads all of us. Just do the same things you've done all your life. Live one day at a time. It's Jesus' job to save the world. It's our job to praise Him for doing it, and to tell others about Him."

"Dad, I am thrilled to be able to profess my faith in God, but I don't feel qualified to be an example to others. I'm just a normal person like everyone else. I'm afraid I will make a mistake, or not do a good enough job. After all Jesus has done for me, how can I ever do enough to repay Him? I feel a great sense of indebtedness, and I don't want God to be disappointed in me."

"Travis, parents should always love their children unconditionally; that's the way God loves us. I can tell you as a father, nothing could separate my love from you and Sarah. God has blessed every person with special gifts. Every person will face trials, successes and disappointments. God does not expect us to always succeed, but He does expect us to try. To do our best, and give Him the glory no matter what, so that others may decide for themselves to explore a relationship with Jesus Christ. I don't know where God is leading you Travis, and I can't tell you what to do or how to feel, but I know what's in your heart, and God has His hand on you. Just go with it wherever He leads you. At times you might be scared, other times excited, happy, sad, just keep praying for God's will to be displayed in your life, and see where He takes you."

"Dad, I hadn't told anyone I felt this way. How did you know? Is it that obvious?"

"No Son, I'm your father. I've been watching you all your life, it's my job."

"Thanks Dad. I really appreciate it."

"Anytime Son."

The next morning Travis was at the tennis center at 10 a.m. for his warm-up. He was scheduled to play Paul Stancovich at 1 p.m.. For the past two days there had been feature articles in the New York papers about Travis' matches. Travis' powerful serve along with his relationship with Mary Katherine had gotten a lot of television coverage as well. Travis' comeback and transition into the tennis world along with his natural athletic ability and good looks had also caught the eye of the media photographers. Travis had quickly become a crowd favorite, so there was a large crowd of spectators at his practice session to watch him warm up, many of whom were not only tennis fans, but also attractive young women. Mary Katherine quickly noticed the obvious presence of the other attractive girls, and true to form, she quickly said what was on her mind.

"Seems like you are developing a fan club."

"I don't know, maybe."

"There sure are a lot of pretty girls here, I guess they came to see you!"

Travis said to himself, "*Oh boy, here were go again.*"

Then Mary Katherine walked up and put her arm around him, and gave him a kiss.

"Those girls are too late," as she looked at her engagement ring. "I don't have to worry about that anymore, do I?"

Travis took a deep breath and a sigh of relief.

"No, and you never did!"

With that, Travis began his stretching and agility drills. He started with short delicate topspins, slices and volleys. Then he moved to the baseline and blasted forehands and backhands as he floated effortlessly across the court. As he concluded his practice he hit serves, using tennis cans for targets. He pounded the ball into the service court drawing "oohs" and "aahs" and applause from the crowd. With every match Travis' confidence in his tennis game and himself was growing. As Rudy watched the practice session from the side court, he could see the once "diamond in the rough" beginning to emerge. Rudy knew what it took to be the best in the world, and it was obvious to him that Travis had the talent to get there. When the warm up ended Travis and Rudy sat down to discuss Travis' third round opponent, and plan the strategy for the match.

"Travis, you are ready. You are playing some great tennis."

"Thanks Coach, I feel good. I'm excited about today."

"When I was in Florida I saw Stancovich play quite a bit as a junior. He moved to the States with his family when he was thirteen. He has been here seven years now and his whole life has evolved toward a career in professional tennis. He is extremely fit, and he is very sound fundamentally. He is a very good baseline player. He likes to stay back and he's not going to beat himself. He does a very good job of running everything down, so you're going to have to play long points. He's like a backboard. He just hits everything back. He doesn't have an overpowering serve, but he is very accurate. He doesn't have great power but he is super quick, and he is very motivated so he will not quit. You're going to have to work to beat this guy."

"What should I do Coach? How should I play him?"

"His strength is in his ability to run the ball down. But running the ball down, playing defense all the time can wear you down in a long tough match. Paul is going to want to play long points and try to get you frustrated with his defense, so you need to be prepared for that. You will see him play behind the baseline, especially on your serve. But if you are patient and hit

221

hard driving ground strokes over and over, side-to-side, you will eventually wear him down. But you need to be aggressive hitting the ball with power. Don't get frustrated when he runs the ball down and hits it back. Let him wear himself out, then when you get a chance to hit a ball by him go for it. Just remember, the more balls he runs down, the sooner he'll get tired. Use his strength against him, then you will eventually break his will, then you'll have him."

"Yes sir, I understand."

It was 12:30 when the officials called the players to the court to begin their warm up. There was already a capacity crowd in the bleachers. One of the spectators in the stands was Tom Williams, the number one player in the world. Williams was there along with his coach developing a scouting report on Travis and Stancovich as he would be playing the winner of their match in Arthur Ashe Stadium in Flushing Meadows Park on Saturday night. When the match began Travis served first and easily held serve to take a 1-0 lead. Stancovich's service game went to deuce five times before Travis broke Stancovich's serve to take the game and lead at 2-0. Travis then served again. Stancovich moved well behind the baseline to give himself more time to return Travis' powerful serve. Travis played consistent powerful tennis and after a long intense game with several long rallies, Travis held his serve to take a commanding 3-0 lead. From that point on every point was closely contested. Travis stood at the baseline, blasting forehands and backhands deep into the corners of the court, moving Stancovich from side to side, but Stancovich was relentless, running everything down, hustling after every ball, with each man holding his serve until Travis built a 5-3 lead, serving for the set. As Travis toed the baseline and prepared to serve, he looked up and saw Stancovich a full three steps behind the baseline. Travis blasted a 140 mph serve out wide into the service box and Stancovich lunged to his right blocking the ball back deep into Travis' forehand. Travis then hit a series of powerful forehands driving Stancovich back behind the baseline. Stancovich continued to battle with everything he had until Travis finally miss-hit a forehand out wide to give Stancovich the point. The rest of Travis' service game was played with the same intensity until after almost 15 minutes and six deuces Stancovich won the game to put the match back on serve at 5-4. The next three games were played the same way, both players holding serve. Travis blasting shots from the baseline while Stancovich tirelessly sprinted after every ball until the score reached 6-6 and forced a tiebreaker for the set.

At this point Travis was beginning to become frustrated. He had held a commanding lead at 5-3 with the match on his racquet, serving to take the set. Then he saw his lead slip away along with his patience as he found himself in a tiebreaker. The tiebreaker was intense, each player protecting their service points until with the score tied 5-5 and Travis serving; he faulted by hitting his first serve out wide left. Then on his second serve he double faulted to give Stancovich his first lead of the match 5-6. Then on the next point Stancovich served an ace, only his second ace of the match. And just that quickly Stancovich won the point and took the first set 7-6.

Travis was furious at himself for losing the lead, and for also double faulting at such a critical time in the tiebreaker. He calmly walked over to the sideline and sat down. However, inside he was about to explode. He had been in total control. He had run Stancovich all over the court. Yet he sat there down a set, only one set from elimination. He was disgusted with himself, and he knew he had to quickly put it behind him or he was going to get beat. It was as simple as that.

While he sat there drinking some water and trying to compose himself, he looked into the stands and saw Rudy sitting there looking back at him. Rudy then pointed for Travis to look at Stancovich. When Travis looked over, he saw that Stancovich was sweating profusely, and that he was heavily drinking water and had changed his shirt to try and cool off. Travis looked back at Rudy who smiled back at him and gave Travis a "thumbs up." Travis then realized that Rudy's strategy was working. He was still upset because he had missed his opportunity to win the first set, even though he had controlled it from the beginning. However, Travis was still very comfortable physically, while his powerful ground strokes had drained the energy from his opponent.

When Travis went back out to begin the set he was determined that win or lose, he was going down swinging. He said to himself.

"I am going to run this kid to New Jersey if I have to. I'm going to throw everything I have at him."

Travis came out in the second set with both barrels blazing. Travis used his own exceptional foot speed and quickness to break Stancovich's serve and take a 1-0 lead. Then he blistered three aces in his service game to extend his lead. On Stancovich's serve he attacked at every opportunity, using heavy top spins out wide to move Stancovich even farther off to the side, then stepping up and blasting the ball by him into the open court. As the pace of Travis' shots quickened, the crowd got behind Travis as he simply wore Stancovich down physically and mentally to take the second set 6-2. Then as Travis came out for the third set the outcome was all but a formality as Travis made quick work of Stancovich 6-1 to claim the win, and reserve his spot on center court against the world's number one player Saturday night.

"Good morning Son, I see you made it back in one piece last night. What time did you kids get in?"

"It was late."

"I remember back when I was your age. If it seemed late to you, I don't want to know what time it was. Did ya'll have a good time?"

"Yeah Dad, we went to a party for the tennis players. There were so many people in that place, I think Sarah and Mary Katherine met everyone there."

"Those two girls can really work a room," Ed said.

"Jim and I just sort of hung out together. Every once in a while they would come and find us and start introducing us to all these different people they had met. If we stay here another week I believe they will know half of New York City."

"Well Travis, did you see any of the other players, any of the other men?"

"Actually, at one point when Jim and I were standing there waiting for Sarah and Mary Katherine, I had someone tap me on the shoulder, and when I turned around, it was Tom Williams."

"Really? What did he have to say?"

"He was very nice. He congratulated me on winning yesterday. He was very complimentary of the match, and he told me he was looking forward to tonight. He was there with some of the other guys on the tour. Tom told me that the players on tour spend a lot of time hanging out together as they travel. I never really thought about it, but like Tom was saying last night, there are no home matches in tennis. The tour travels all the time. All the matches are away from their homes. It's not like football and baseball where half the games are on the road, and half are at home. The tennis tournaments are played all over the world, and the season lasts almost all year, it never really stops. The players are traveling together all the time, so many of them develop their closest friendships with the other players they are competing against. It is a very unique situation."

"That's interesting. I'm like you, I never thought about it that way before, but that does make perfect sense." Ed then asked, "Where's Jim this morning?"

"Jim got up early. He said he had to go pick up something."

"What about the girls, have you seen them?"

"No, I haven't seen them, but I heard them."

"What do you mean, you heard them?"

"Earlier this morning I stopped by their room and knocked on the door. But they wouldn't get up. So I knocked on it a little louder, then a little louder, then I heard one of them yelling for me to leave them alone. So then I went in my room next door and called them on the hotel phone a few times. I could hear them in there fussing, and then when they picked up the phone and they realized it was me, one of them, I'm not sure, maybe both of them, were yelling that they were going to get me if I didn't leave them alone! After a few minutes I heard them laughing in there so I called them again."

"I see, so they never came out."

"No. I suspect they'll try and get me back later, but I imagine by now they are probably sleeping again."

"Your mom is taking it easy too, so why don't we go ahead and get some breakfast?"

"That sounds good."

Travis and Ed went into the hotel restaurant and as they went through the buffet line they both filled their plates to capacity. One of the many traits that Travis and Ed shared was that they both loved to eat. As they were sitting down Travis looked out the restaurant window and saw Jim walking into the hotel lobby carrying a box. Travis sat his plate down on the table and walked back out into the lobby.

"Hey man, what ya' got there?"

Jim turned around and smiled.

"I got you something partner."

"What have you gone and done now, Rose Man?"

Jim was grinning from ear to ear as he walked toward Travis. Jim then sat the box down on a chair in the lobby.

"I know you don't have a big endorsement contract like Tom Williams has, but you do have a 'powerful sponsor,' so I had you some shirts made with His logo on them."

Jim opened the box and took one of the shirts out and held it up.

"Well Travis, how do you like it?"

Travis' eyes lit up as he looked at the white shirt.

"Jim, this is too much! How do you come up with these ideas?"

"I don't know. I just like marketing. I wanted to make something to help promote the Lord tonight."

"Where did you get these made Jim? How did you do it?"

"The day before yesterday when we found out you would be playing Tom Williams tonight if you made it through the qualifying, I just thought what an opportunity to promote Jesus' message. So I went down the street and bought some white tennis shirts that did not have a sports logo. Then the concierge at the hotel helped me find a company that does embroidery work. I went over to see them and they made them for me. Turns out; the owner of the embroidery company is a believer too. They have been following your story in the news, so they embroidered the shirts for free! They even helped design the logo so it would really stand out tonight when you're playing."

The shirt was all white. On the right sleeve were the words; "Play 2 Win-Live 2 Serve." On the left sleeve was an American flag. On the left chest, right over Travis' heart, was an Ichthys symbol, the Christian fish.

"Jim, I don't know what to say. I am simply blown away by this."

Then Travis looked back in the box.

"How many of these shirts did you have made?"

"I had two made for you in case you decide to change shirts during the match. Then I had one made for all the rest of us too. That way while we are sitting in the player's box tonight, when you look up there during the match, you can remember that you are not alone out there. We are all in this together."

"Jim, this is so amazing. I will be so proud to wear this tonight. When you think how far the Play 2 Win-Live 2 Serve message has gone on those T-shirts, just by us wearing them around Raleigh, just think what the possibilities are with this match tonight on national television."

"Not just national television," Jim said. "The U.S. Open is broadcast all around the world; remember tennis is an international sport. The best players from all over the world are in this tournament. There is no telling how God may choose to use this opportunity tonight to promote Jesus. But I do know this; I can't wait to see you walk on center court tonight with the symbol of our Lord on your chest."

It was a little before noon when Sarah and Mary Katherine made their way out of bed and down to the lobby. The girls were headed into Manhattan to do some shopping before the match. That's when they had their first look at the shirts Jim had made for all of them. Mary Katherine and Sarah agreed, along with everyone else; that the shirts made a wonderful statement about faith and patriotism, and they were both excited to be able to wear them at the match.

With the match time at 8 p.m. Travis ate an early supper at 5:30. He arrived at the stadium at 6:15 with a warm-up scheduled at 6:45. Travis was focused and excited as he quickly went through his practice routine. Hitting the ball crisply and gracefully moving around the court. There was a large crowd on hand to watch his practice session. With every passing match Travis was gaining the respect of the knowledgeable New York tennis fans, as well as the sports media and other players. When the practice session concluded Rudy and Travis sat down to discuss the strategy for the match.

"Travis, your practice was outstanding. Every match you have played this week has been super. I can see that you are growing as a player, and I am extremely proud of what you have accomplished."

"Thank you Coach."

"Travis tonight when you go on the court, the environment is going to be very different from any tennis match you have ever played. I know we have hit balls on center court, and you've walked around out there, but when you are playing a night match in Arthur Ashe Stadium, the crowd noise is deafening. It's like being on the field at a college football game. The difference is the crowd for the most part is very quiet during the points. Then in an instant the crowd will erupt, the crowd noise can be very distracting even unnerving, if you are not prepared for it. Don't be surprised if it takes a few games to get your nerves under control tonight. Just be very aggressive, even if you make a few more mistakes early in the match. Just concentrate on finding your rhythm. Since these major championship tournaments are best three out of five sets, whatever happens in the first set, both of you will need to win at least two more sets to win the match. So be aggressive, play your attacking style of tennis."

"Tom Williams is a great player. At this point in his career, he may be the best American player of all-time. He can hit the ball on a dime. He's won ten major titles and he is at the peak of his game. He plays smart. He is going to test your game early in the match. He will go after either your forehand or backhand early, to try and find a weakness he can exploit. So if you start miss-hitting a few shots from one side or the other, don't be surprised if he tries to pound the ball at you until you prove to him you can hit all the shots, okay?"

"Yes sir."

"Tom is a professional in every sense. After watching you play yesterday, he knows you have the athletic ability and the technique to give him trouble tonight. I suspect he will move the ball around on you on his serve. He hits the ball big, he has plenty of power, but he does not have the kind of power you have, so I expect Tom to really mix it up on you tonight. Be looking for him to hit lots of slices and topspins trying to get you out of your rhythm. The key for you tonight Travis, is to focus on anticipating where the ball is going to be hit. Use your quickness and speed to get to the ball quickly; giving yourself time to hit an aggressive shot. Don't let Tom get you thinking too much. He's going to try and make you second guess yourself; become defensive. Just play the ball like you did when you played shortstop. Charge the ball every chance you get and move through the shot, try to make Tom play your game. You are stronger and faster than he is, and you hit the ball harder than he does. So that needs to be your game plan tonight. Forget about his ranking. He is the two time defending champion so he is expected to win. The pressure is all on him tonight. Take the energy from the crowd and just go for it; play all out, on every point."

"Yes sir."

Then Rudy reached over and put his hand on Travis' shoulder.

"Travis, there's one more thing you need to remember."

"What's that Coach?"

"The best men's tennis player in the world is going to walk on center court tonight, and it's not Tom Williams. It's you Travis."

"Travis, I knew there was something special about you the first day I saw you play with Mary Katherine. You have a rare and special gift. Go out there tonight and play with the Spirit of the Lord, give Him the glory, and remember God has His hand upon you, I am convinced of that."

"Thank you Coach, not just for tonight, but for all you have done for me. I could never tell you how much your support, and Mrs. Outland, Mary Katherine, what you all have done for me. How can I say thank you enough?"

"We all feel the same way about you Travis. As a father and a coach, I can say you are truly a blessing in the life of our family. Before you go out there tonight, let's give the thanks were it belongs. Let's pray." They bowed their heads and Rudy prayed.

"Dear Lord, we give thanks for the many blessing in our lives, for our families, our health, for our country Lord. Father, be with Travis tonight, and may your Son Jesus be glorified, and your will be done. In Jesus name, Amen."

Then Rudy stood up.

"I'm going to go out there and take my seat with your other 22,000 fans. You have fun tonight, and show Tom Williams what he's going to be up against once you start playing the tour all the time."

Travis just smiled and nodded back at Rudy. Travis believed deep down in his heart that all the things Rudy had said about him were true. But that was not something Travis would have ever said to anyone else about himself. Yet hearing Rudy say that he was the best player in the world, made Travis begin to realize that it was true. Travis knew Rudy Outland was an honest man. Rudy had never been anything but totally honest with Travis. So as Travis sat there, quietly thinking alone in the locker room, he decided that tonight when he walked through the tunnel and onto center court, that he would show the world that center court was where he belonged.

Travis and Tom met together briefly inside the locker room, they shook hands, wished each other good luck, then they left the locker room and walked together down the players' tunnel toward the court. As they approached the tunnel exit Travis could hear the stadium announcer's introduction. He could see the ball boys and officials on the court. Then as the two men stepped beyond the tunnel, the crowd noise echoed through the stadium. Travis looked up and saw the enormity of the stadium lit amongst the New York skyline, as the capacity crowd rose to its feet. Even though he had an idea of what to expect, he was still unprepared for the rush of adrenaline that pulsated throughout his body. Travis walked over to the players' chairs beside the court. He sat his tennis bag down and selected a racquet. He drank some water to compose himself and then he took a look up at the players' box where his family and friends were sitting. He unzipped the N.C. State tennis jacket he was wearing and walked out onto the court to warm up.

Meanwhile, the international television broadcast had begun, as the announcers previewed the match.

"Tonight we have a very interesting match-up. Tom Williams, the two-time defending champion, is a heavy favorite in this opening round match. But William's opponent tonight, Travis Simpson, has made a very positive first impression in this U.S. Open. Isn't that right John?"

"Yes Steve, he has. Travis Simpson is a young man who from his youth appeared to be headed toward a career in professional sports, but not as a tennis player. Simpson was injured in a high school baseball game and it appeared his dreams of becoming a professional athlete were over. He injured the fingers on his left hand; which made it impossible for him to continue to pursue a career in professional football and baseball. Simpson is an amazing athlete. He played shortstop in baseball, and wide receiver in football. So he has tremendous physical strength and speed, along with great hand-eye coordination. Simpson also possesses one of the most powerful serves in tennis. This match will not be a 'walkover' for Tom Williams. I believe Simpson will give Williams all the trouble he wants tonight."

"So John, you believe Simpson has a legitimate chance to win this match tonight?"

"I don't know if Simpson is ready to win this match tonight, but I am convinced he has the talent and determination to be one of the top players in the world. Simpson is a devoted Christian, he's a tough kid. I believe we will see some great tennis from these two tonight."

Back in Raleigh, Russell and Joe were over at the student center with Coach Clark, Stephanie, and a bunch of the other kids from across campus preparing to watch the match on television. As the announcers finished their preview, the cameras rolled over to a close up of Tom Williams, then to Travis. As soon as the camera flashed a close up of Travis, Russell immediately noticed the Ichthys symbol on Travis' shirt.

"Hey," Russell said. "Travis is wearing a shirt with the Christian fish on his chest!"

Joe then said, "That's an American flag on his left sleeve, and Play 2 Win-Live 2 Serve on his right."

Immediately text messages were buzzing on cell phones and BlackBerrys, as Travis' friends and classmates were spreading the word that the "Play 2 Win-Live 2 Serve" message was spreading. Christians sitting in their living rooms across the country and around the world were asking themselves; What does the number "2" stand for, and where can I get a shirt like that with the Christian symbol on it? Just like that, in an instant God was using a symbol on a shirt, worn by a young man in a tennis match to cause other believers to ask themselves how they too might quietly, yet powerfully witness their faith. Maybe through a T-shirt, maybe by wearing a shirt with a Christian symbol to the golf course, or a football game, or a PTA meeting? God was using a simple symbol to spread a powerful message. That God can make a mighty difference, through a simple act of praise, when we place our hope and trust in Him.

Following the warm-up, the players briefly met at the net. Then Williams came to the baseline and signaled to Travis that he was prepared to serve. The match was under way. Williams took a deep breath, then tossed the ball in the air and whistled a serve out wide to Travis' forehand. Travis quickly moved to his right and hit a deep return into the opposite corner, both players then continued the rally with deep solid ground strokes from the baseline, until Williams eventually forced Travis to hit a short ball, that Williams turned into a backhand winner to take the lead 15-love. For the next thirty minutes both players played sensational tennis, each man protecting his service games until Williams took a 4-3 lead. After the change over, Travis came out to serve and attempt to level the match, but Travis double faulted to open the game. It was his first double fault of the match to give Williams the lead at Love-15. The double fault seemed to unnerve Travis just enough, that he failed to get his first serve in on the next three points, quickly falling behind the attacking Williams. Travis dug himself too deep a hole and eventually lost his service game to fall behind Williams 5-3. Williams seized the opportunity, and then held his serve to take the first set

6-3.

As Travis walked to the player's chair to rest between sets, he was upset that he had lost the set, but he had proved to himself that he belonged. Then as he stood to walk onto the court, he looked up in the players' box and saw the Outlands, Mary Katherine, Sarah, his Mom, Dad, and Jim all cheering him on. He thought to himself how blessed he was, he looked around the crowd, he felt the electricity in the air. He felt his heart rate slow down, everything around him seemed to quiet down. Travis looked across the court at Williams; he seemed to realize that this all was real, that things were working out this way for a reason. Then he signaled to Tom that he was ready. Travis toed the baseline and blasted a 139-mph ace into the corner of the service box. 15-love. For the rest of the set both men put on a serving clinic, as each player easily held serve while the game score quickly reached 6-6; and forced a tiebreaker to decide the set. Travis served the first point; and after a long rally won the point to take a 1-0 lead. Then with Williams serving the players split the next two points to give Travis a 2-1 lead. Travis then blasted two 130-mph serves to widen the lead to 4-1. The players split the next four points giving Travis a 6-4 lead and an opportunity to serve for the set. With each spectacular point the crowd intensity had grown, now with the 22,000 New York fans on the edge of their seats, Travis whistled a 134-mph serve up the "T" for an ace winning the set, and sending a roar through the crowd and out into the New York skyline.

As Travis walked toward the side court, he looked up at the players box, everyone was on their feet screaming and yet he could distinctly hear Mary Katherine's voice above the crowd; yelling;

"That's my boy! Stay with him Travis! One point at a time, you can do it!"

Travis took a deep breath as he relaxed in his chair between sets. It was a mild night in New York, and as he drank a bottle of water; he could still hear the ringing in his ears from the thundering applause when he tied the match at one set apiece. Meanwhile, in the press box above him the television announcers where recapping the action.

"John, those have been two sensational sets, and Travis Simpson has proven he can play with the best player in the world."

"You're right Steve, what impresses me so much about Simpson is his footwork. He does such a great job of anticipating where the ball is going, and then he reacts so quickly. Just like a shortstop in baseball; he lowers his center of gravity as he approaches the ball, then he keeps his head down, watching the ball until it has left his racquet. That's why he hits the ball so consistently. You can also see the skills he developed as a wide receiver in football, the soft hands, the quick feet. Those years of experience playing football and baseball are very transferable into tennis. Simpson is demonstrating that tonight."

"Well John, where do you see this match going from here?"

"I think we will continue to see great tennis from these guys. I still don't know if Travis has the experience to win this match tonight, but he has shown us he can play with Williams. We'll just have to wait and see."

As Travis and Tom stood up to take the court to begin the third set, the crowd again rose to its feet and the deafening roar filled the stadium. Then as Travis came to the baseline to serve, the noise evaporated in the cool night air. Travis could hear the sound of the ball bouncing, as he prepared to serve, suddenly, it was as quiet as if he was just simply practicing on his own. It was as if no one else was there. Travis tossed the ball in the air, he watched the ball as it floated against the black New York skyline, then he felt the strings of his racquet compress the tennis ball, the sound of the "pop" as the ball left his racquet, then the "hissing sound" as the tennis ball sped away from him and into the court for another ace. The roar of the crowd, and then, another crescendo when the radar gun flashed the serve speed at 145-mph. Travis was in *"the zone,"* as he quickly won the next three games to take a 3-0 lead.

But Tom Williams was not number one in the world for nothing. Tom came out in the fourth game and responded the way a professional should, he stayed calm, and he stuck with his game plan. Tom continued to play his game, which was solid consistent attacking tennis. In doing so Tom quickly regained his rhythm as he proceeded to win the next three games to square the set at 3-3. Then with Travis still reeling, Tom dug in his heels to face Travis' serve again. Tom fought off four deuces and add-ins before finally getting an opportunity to win the game. Then after the fifth deuce, Williams finally won the deuce point. Tom then returned a 145-mph serve deep to Travis' backhand. Travis then hit a topspin backhand up the middle of the court. Tom moved inside the baseline and hit a delicate cross court drop shot to win the game and regain the lead at 4-3, again bringing the capacity crowd to its feet.

During the changeover Travis sat quietly drinking water, trying to regain his composure. He took a look toward Tom and he thought back to his early service break in the set. The way Tom had calmly responded, staying focused, then fighting back to win the set. Travis had witnessed firsthand the professionalism that made Tom the world's number one player. When Travis and Tom went back onto the court after the break, Tom held his serve to extend his lead to 5-3. Both men continued to hold serve and

Tom eventually took the set 6-4, giving him a two sets to one lead.

In the fourth set each man held serve until the set moved into a tiebreaker at 6-6. Then during the tiebreaker, Travis and Tom both played inspired tennis, but in the end, Tom's experience advantage was just too much for Travis to overcome, as Tom won the tiebreaker 7-4, winning the match and advancing Tom into the second round.

Immediately following the match, the television announcer met with the players for a live interview on court before the capacity crowd.

"Travis, I know you wanted to win tonight, but you should be very proud of the way you played, that was some great tennis."

With that said the crowd gave Travis a wonderful standing ovation, which caused Travis to back away for a moment to compose himself.

"Thank you all so much! The fans have been so supportive this week. I played as well as I could play tonight. Tom is a great champion, he played a super match."

"Travis, you've had a great week on the tennis court, and I understand you have something to celebrate in your personal life too, your engagement to Mary Katherine Outland."

The crowd again roared as they flashed a picture of Mary Katherine and Sarah on the giant television screen at the stadium.

"That's right, it's been a wonderful summer, the Lord has truly blessed me. I have so much to be thankful for."

"You're going back to school to play college tennis this year, but what about professional tennis, when will we see you on the professional tour again?"

"I'm not sure. I'm excited about our team at N.C. State this year, we have a great team and we are all focused on our upcoming season. Again, I know that the Lord has blessed me, and He deserves all the credit. So wherever He leads me, I will go."

Travis then stepped to the side and the announcer interviewed Tom Williams.

"Tom great match tonight, congratulations."

"Thank you. I'd like to congratulate Travis on the way he played tonight. We could all see what kind of player Travis will be by the way he played. You can see what kind of determination Travis has by the way he competes, and I also admire the way he is witnessing what he believes is important by the symbols on the shirt he is wearing tonight."

After a few minutes the interview concluded as the crowd applauded. Afterward, the two men walked together into the tunnel towards the locker room.

"Travis, can you do me a favor?"

"Sure Tom, what is it?"

"Travis, can you help me get some of those shirts?"

"Yeah Tom, we can work that out."

Once the two men reached the locker room they each spent some time speaking with the sportswriters discussing the match. Afterwards Travis took a shower and was getting ready to leave the locker room when Tom walked over.

"Travis, do you want to go out and grab something to eat?"

"Sure Tom, that would be great."

"Come on then, let's get going. There will be some fans outside the player's exit waiting for autographs. We'll need to speak to some of them and sign some autographs, so the sooner we get going, the sooner we can eat."

"Sounds good to me. I'm ready."

Travis gathered up his tennis equipment and the two men then headed out toward the exit. When they reached the stadium gate there was a crowd of over two hundred people waiting outside.

"My goodness," Tom said. "I can't believe this many people have waited over an hour for an autograph."

Just then Mary Katherine spotted Travis and Tom. She ran over to the two of them.

"Travis, the most amazing thing is happening. After the match, as we were all walking out of the stadium, we had all these people come up to us, congratulating us on how well you played, then thanking us all for wearing these shirts and witnessing our faith. Then some of the fans began to ask where they could buy the shirts, who made them, and why was the number '2' on the shirts instead of the word to? Suddenly all of us, Sarah, Jim, our parents, we were all standing outside the stadium talking about Jesus. The choice we all have to make, whether to except Jesus or reject Him. The life we are born with, and the new life of the believer. All these tennis fans are now here talking about Christianity. They all came to see a tennis match, yet God has used these shirts as a way to draw people to Him. Jim and Sarah have witnessed to who knows how many people tonight. I know the two of them have well over a hundred business cards with e-mail addresses of people who want to order the shirts. It is the most amazing thing."

Travis and Tom just stood there, amazed by what was happening. Then people began to approach Travis for his autograph. Believers, thanking Travis for his willingness to express his beliefs and publicly give his testimony, many of whom had been following Travis' story in the news. There were parents who wanted to thank Travis for the Christian example he was setting for their children. Travis began to see the role all of them were now playing in God's plan. How Jim had been given an opportunity to use his God given creativity to honor Jesus, while Sarah was using her communication skills to explain the gospel message. Ed, Kathy, Rudy and Rita were talking with other adult couples about raising Godly children. Sharing their stories of successes and failures, to encourage other parents who were also building their families on Christian principles. Travis began to clearly see how God had brought just the right people, in God's perfect timing, each with their own unique skills and abilities, to use them all to glorify Jesus.

For the next thirty minutes Tom stayed with Travis and the others as he too began to share his beliefs. Then once the crowd began to disperse Tom went along with Travis, Jim, Sarah and Mary Katherine as the kids went to eat a late dinner at one of the player socials in Manhattan. Once they got to the restaurant and ordered their meals, the topic of conversation again returned to a discussion about faith.

"I have been a Christian since I was a child," Tom said. "But I have never felt comfortable witnessing my faith to others. Tonight was a first for me. Openly talking about Jesus like that tonight was as exciting as anything I have ever done. It was the most awesome feeling!"

"Tom, I know what you mean," Sarah said. "I would like to be in more situations where I can witness for the Lord, but I am uncomfortable approaching people. I'm afraid people may not want to hear what I have to say. Wearing this shirt with the Christian symbol, it lets people know I am a Christian without me having to say anything. Then tonight, people came up to us! They started talking about Christianity, asking questions. You know, if I saw someone wearing a shirt with a Christian symbol I would be more comfortable approaching them, because I would know they are believers too."

"Jim, where did you get the idea for the shirts," Tom asked, "and the slogan Play 2 Win-Live 2 Serve?"

"Almost everything we wear today has a symbol on it," Jim said. "Like a sports company logo, clothing advertising everything from banks, restaurants, athletic clubs, college logos, sports teams, you name it. People identify with each other through symbols. Maybe they went to the same school, pull for the same sports team, use the same sports equipment, belong to the same club, or drive the same type of car. It just seems to me as

Christians we should identify more with one another, support one another, and encourage one another. I always notice if a girl is wearing a cross; that immediately tells me she is willing to express her faith. It's a little thing, but it means something to me. When I made the T-shirts for the tennis team, I just wanted to show people our team was united as tennis players and as Christians. I had no idea God would take it this far. But He is God, it's just exciting to try and imagine what God will do next."

"Judging from tonight," Tom said, "there is no telling what may happen."

Later that night after dinner, the kids went back to the hotel. Mary Katherine had a 1 p.m. first round match time on Sunday, so the kids got to bed before too late. When Jim and Travis got to their room Jim said to Travis, "Travis, I want to thank you for tonight."

"Jim, I'm the one who should be thanking you. You designed these shirts. If it wasn't for your creativity none of this would be happening."

"Travis, you may not be able to see it, because you are living it, but I can clearly see that God is moving in your life. God is placing people, Christian people, like Tom Williams in your life. Do you realize we just ate dinner and had a conversation about Jesus with the world's number one ranked tennis player? The guy's won ten majors, and it was as if we have known him all our lives! That didn't happen because I made a shirt; that happened because God is positioning you Travis. I want to thank you, and God, that He is allowing me to be a part of it."

"Jim, I may have been the one on the court tonight, but this is not about me, this thing that is happening is about God, it is about Jesus. Tonight as I was watching the crowd outside the stadium, I was amazed by what God is doing. He is using all of us to glorify Jesus. Just think about how God placed the players' draw so that my match was scheduled to play Tom tonight. God gave you the idea to make the shirt, and then the concierge at the hotel referring you to an embroidery shop who just happened to be owned by Christians. They had followed the tennis in the news, so they did the work for free. They wanted to be involved, to serve the Lord, so they went above and beyond to design these wonderful tributes to Jesus. Think of the role they played in what happened tonight, people whom I have never met. Jim, God is moving in a mighty way in your life too, in all of our lives. I thank God every day for what He is doing through all of us. I don't know where this is going, but I do know this, God will bring His plan to fruition, but it's not about us, it's all about Jesus."

When the boys cut out the lights, Travis lay awake in his bed thinking about all that had happened. The encouragement from Rudy, the match on center court, the opportunity to witness after the match, dinner with Tom, and now the things Jim had said. Travis could sense that something very special was happening. He felt the presence of the Lord again in his life. Travis could see more and more that he was not alone, that God was bringing Christians together to glorify Jesus. His confidence had returned. He was thinking clearer now than ever before, even clearer than before the accident. Travis knew that all these blessings were not happening by chance. That God was moving in a mighty way in all of their lives. Then, as he lay alone in the darkness, he told the Lord the only thing he knew to say.

"Thank you Jesus. Thank you Jesus. Thank you Jesus."

DINNER TONIGHT

Mary Katherine was up early Sunday morning. She said her prayers and then she took her Bible outside on the balcony to have her quiet time with the Lord. She ate breakfast at 9 a.m., changed into her warm-ups, and at 11a.m. she had her game face on when she walked onto the court for her practice session. Over the past week Mary Katherine, with Rudy and Rita's help had hired a sports agent to handle her business affairs. She signed endorsement contracts with a sports clothing line, a shoe company, and an equipment manufacturer. Rudy also had negotiations with one of the leading coaches in women's tennis about coaching Mary Katherine while she traveled the tour. Now with the business negotiations in place, she was ready to focus on tennis. Mary Katherine had played tennis matches since she was ten years old, but today's match was different. Today was the first match of her professional career, and she was ready to go.

When she got to the practice court, she, Travis and Jim began their stretching routine. Rudy and Mark Watkins, the coach Rudy was interviewing, watched from the side court. After the stretching exercises were complete, Mark began to work Mary Katherine through her practice routine. Travis and Jim hit balls with Mary Katherine as Mark gave her instructions and observed her warm-up. Mark had been coaching professional women's tennis players for fifteen years. He was well respected by the players and he had a reputation for developing talent. As the practice session moved along Rudy carefully watched the interaction between Mark and Mary Katherine. Rudy knew that Mary Katherine needed a coach she would feel comfortable with. Someone she could communicate with while she traveled, not just about tennis, but also the changes in her personal life, being away from home for extended periods of time. Mark was a Christian and that was important to both Rudy and Rita. Rita would be traveling with Mary Katherine for a while, but at some point Mary Katherine would begin to travel alone. Rudy had known Mark since the days twenty-five years ago when Rudy played the tour. So as the practice session concluded, Rudy was beginning to see that Mark was the man for the job. Rudy walked over toward Mary Katherine.

"You look great out there Buddy, I believe you're ready to go."

"Yeah, I feel great Dad. I've looked forward to this day for a long time."

Mark then reached over and put his hand on Mary Katherine's shoulder.

"Mary Katherine, I have followed your progress and watched you play since you were a little girl. You have grown up to become a fine young lady, and a great tennis player. You have a very bright future ahead of you in women's tennis."

Mary Katherine smiled. "Thank you Coach Watkins, that means a lot coming from you. I know you've coached some very successful players, and I respect your opinion."

Rudy stood to the side as Coach Watkins and Mary Katherine continued their conversation. Rudy knew the time had come for him to step back and let someone else coach Mary Katherine. She would be traveling with the women's tour and with Rudy's commitments at N.C. State, he would not be able to travel with Mary Katherine. Rudy also knew that now as a professional tennis player, Mary Katherine would be better served by having a coach who was not her father. Rudy understood that for Mary Katherine to reach her full potential she would need to be pushed, and as her father, that may strain their relationship. Mark was someone Mary Katherine had known and admired for a long time. So as Rudy listened and observed Mary Katherine and Mark discuss the strategy for the day's match, he realized that he was watching one of those milestone moments in a parent and child's life. Mary Katherine was all grown up now, and this new stage of independence in her life was beginning.

Once Mark and Mary Katherine finished their strategy session, Travis and Mary Katherine decided to walk around the grounds at the tennis center to kill some time before her match. While Travis and Mary Katherine were walking along the two of them were approached by fans and spectators asking for autographs, then after a few minutes they decided to stop and grab a couple of seats in the bleachers and watch a doubles match on one of the side courts. Travis turned and leaned over toward Mary Katherine.

"Since Jim and I will be going back to Raleigh in the morning, I thought you might want to take me out somewhere special for dinner tonight?"

Mary Katherine looked back at Travis with a little "smirk;" on her face.

"Wait a minute Buddy! You're the one who is suppose to take me out to dinner!"

Travis smiled back.

"Who says, you're a modern thinking, progressive young woman, an equal pay for equal days work kind of girl. You certainly don't believe in an old fashioned notion like the man should always buy dinner, do you?"

Mary Katherine then took her fist and popped Travis on the shoulder.

"I'm a traditionalist when it comes to tried and true dating principles, my view on that is, if it ain't broke, don't fix it!"

Travis grabbed his shoulder.

"Oow! That hurt!"

Then he looked back toward the elderly couple sitting behind them.

"Did you see that? She hit me!"

Travis looked at the woman and asked, "Ma'am, do you hit your husband like that?"

The lady never even smiled.

"All the time, I'm sure you deserved it."

Then the lady asked Mary Katherine, "What did he do Honey, is he cheating on you?"

"No, he just thinks I should pay to take him out to dinner tonight."

"Those pretty boys can be high maintenance."

Then the older man said, "Son, you're lucky she didn't hit you with her left hand, those engagement rings can cut you up bad. I suppose you're the one who gave her the ring?"

"Yes I did. I tell ya,' she's tough!"

"I bet she never hit you until 'after' you gave her the ring, did she?"

"No, come to think of it, she didn't."

"William, don't you be causing trouble for this poor girl," the lady said, "or you'll get a punch yourself!"

Then the lady looked back at Travis as she pointed to Mary Katherine.

"Well Son, what makes you think a pretty girl like her is going to buy you dinner?"

"She's the one with all the money. She's getting paid more money to wear that tennis dress than most people make in a year, plus extra money for the racquet, the shoes, the watch, the make up. She's loaded, and I'm just an unemployed college kid."

Then the older man said, "Son, a girl that looks like that, and she's got plenty of money too! I'll take her out to dinner and buy her some caviar and champagne to go with it!"

Mary Katherine smiled.

"See, a true gentleman. Travis you need to be paying attention, I'm a hot commodity."

Travis then looked at the older man.

"There's no point in arguing with them is it?"

"It's kind of fun to get them riled up once in a while," the man said. "But there's no point in arguing with them. Once they get their high heels dug in, you might as well surrender. It's all over then."

The lady nodded her head.

"It took me fifty-three years but I've finally got him trained."

Travis turned and looked at Mary Katherine as she smiled and nodded.

"That's it. So Travis, who's buying dinner tonight?"

"I suppose that would be me," Travis replied.

Then the older lady said, "He's learning, just keep working with him Honey, after a while you'll get him like you want him."

Mary Katherine looked at Travis.

"He's come a long way. He's not completely broken in yet, but I'm patient, I'll get him there."

Once Mary Katherine had established Travis would be the one buying dinner tonight it was almost 12:15, so the two of them got up to walk back to the court where Mary Katherine was scheduled to play. As she was leaving she looked at the older couple.

"Thanks for your help. I think Travis learned a lot."

Then the older man said, "Mary Katherine, what time shall I pick you up for dinner tonight?"

"William," the lady said, "I'm afraid those days are long gone for you. You are trained, but Travis here has more long term potential."

Mary Katherine smiled at the man.

"I do appreciate the offer, if Travis doesn't come around, I'll get back with you."

"I'll be right here," the man said.

Then the two kids headed off toward the stadium court, it was time for tennis.

When Mary Katherine reached the stadium court it was 12:30. She did some light stretching then she went into the locker room for a short talk with Rudy and Mark.

"Mary Katherine, your opponent today, Sara Collins, is a five-year tour veteran from Canada," Coach Watkins said. "She has had a solid consistent career since she joined the tour. I've seen her play many times; she runs well, she hits the ball hard, but she hits it hard all the time. She does not have a solid finesse game, and at times she can become inconsistent if you make her play long points. Your advantage today will be using your all-court game. Mix it up with her- slices, heavy topspins, you can hit her some flat driving shots, but remember, she likes to take the ball early and blast it back at you, so keep her off balance. Don't go out there and just bang the ball back and forth with her, that's her strength. Make her play all the shots, and you will see she doesn't have the complete game you have."

Meanwhile, Travis, Jim, and Sarah were sitting together in the stands before the match when Tom Williams walked up.

"I thought I might find you here Travis."

"Hey Tom, thanks for coming."

"Sure. I wanted to see Mary Katherine play, especially since this is her first match as a professional. I remember I was as nervous as a cat in my first professional match."

"I don't know if she's nervous or not, she seemed like normal before the match, she was as feisty as ever."

"Mary Katherine is a cool customer," Sarah said, "nothing seems to phase her."

When Mary Katherine and Sara Collins walked on the court to warm up, they received a warm reception from the stadium crowd. As the match began, both players were all business, and after four well played games the match was tied at two games apiece. Then with Collins serving, Mary Katherine began to move the ball deep into the corners of the court, as she extended the length of the points in an effort to frustrate her opponent. As the two women began to play points with longer rallies, Mary Katherine spun the ball deeper and deeper into the court. She took the net out of play, and as Collins continued to try and blast flat ground strokes just above the net cord from well behind the baseline, Collins made three unforced errors to drop her service game and fall behind Mary Katherine, 3-2.

After the changeover Mary Katherine came out to serve and continued to control the points with topspins and slices, until she got a ball she could step in on and then she blasted the ball into the open court for winners. Mary Katherine was in her element. She was in total control as she made quick work of her Canadian opponent, 6-2, 6-1. Mary Katherine's first professional victory was in the books.

After the match she was interviewed by the sports channel announcer.

"Mary Katherine, your first win as a professional, what does it feel like?"

"It feels great. First though, I want to give Jesus the glory, it all comes from Him."

"What was the key to today's match?"

"Sara is a great player, she hits the ball hard so I knew I could not get into a power game against her. So I tried to mix up my shots, and I was fortunate today things went my way."

"I see your boyfriend Travis Simpson is in the stands today; are you two going out tonight to celebrate?"

"Actually," Mary Katherine said as the crowd applauded, "I believe

Travis is going to take me out somewhere special for dinner tonight."

The announcer then looked toward Travis.

"Is that right Travis?"

Travis smiled as he looked out toward the announcer and nodded.

"Yes."

It was about quarter past six when Travis checked his watch, as he waited for Mary Katherine in the lobby of the hotel. Travis was wearing a coat and tie as he read the sports page. He was finishing one of the articles about the match he and Tom had played the previous night, when he heard a familiar voice.

"Well don't you look nice. You must have a hot date tonight."

Travis looked up over the paper.

"Yes ma'am she is a hot commodity. My date is one of the contestants in the U.S. Open. She won her first professional match today, so I have something special planned for dinner tonight. The only thing is she's running a little late, and I don't want to miss our reservation."

"She may be taking her time so she looks especially nice tonight, since it is a special occasion. If she has on a new dress and took some extra time to braid her hair, have her nails done, you could forgive her for being a little late, couldn't you?"

Travis stood up; he walked over to Mary Katherine, put her arms around her and kissed her.

"You know you have me wrapped around your little finger, don't you?"

"I like to think so, but I don't take it for granted. I know I have a good thing in you, so I want to keep you happy too."

"You look beautiful. I guess the new dress, shoes and pocketbook are from one of you and Sarah's shopping trips this past week?"

"Yes. Do you approve?"

"I do. Are you ready to go to dinner?"

"Yes sir, I am."

Travis took Mary Katherine's hand as they walked toward the concierge's desk.

"We have a dinner reservation for 6 p.m., Simpson, party of two."

The concierge replied, "Yes Mr. Simpson, right this way,"

Then he led Travis and Mary Katherine into the hotel elevator.

"Where are we going Travis?"

"You'll have to wait and see."

The concierge led Travis and Mary Katherine to the top floor of the hotel. He took them through a private elevator to the hotel penthouse, then out onto a balcony courtyard overlooking Manhattan. There was a waiter who was there with the dinner table prepared for two.

"Mary Katherine, how do you like the view?"

Mary Katherine's smile resonated.

"I love it, it's perfect."

The two of them had a wonderful candlelight dinner. Afterward they sat together on the penthouse terrace late into the night. Mary Katherine would be staying in New York for the next two weeks with the tour while Travis would be leaving in the morning for school. They would not be spending as much time together as they had been, so they decided to make the time they would have together special. There were new and exciting things happening in both of their lives. As they sat there in the moonlight, they were both thankful, thankful for all the blessings in their lives. Thankful for the times that the Lord had already blessed them with, and excited, as they looked forward to the "special moments" that were yet to come.

LEADERS

"You know Travis, traveling is nice, but whenever the plane stops at the terminal gate I'm always glad to be home."

"You're right Jim. When the wheels touched down on the runway just now I was thinking the same thing."

The boys unbuckled their seatbelts and they stood up to get their bags from the overhead compartments. Afterward, they waited in line as the passengers filed out of the airplane, and then they made their way into the terminal waiting area. Once they got through the crowd, Jim spotted Russell and Joe leaning up against the wall. As usual, they were talking to a group of attractive young girls. Travis walked up behind Russell.

"I thought you guys were suppose to be here to pick me and Jim up, but it looks like you two may not have room for us."

Russell then turned around and whispered.

"Actually Travis, Joe and I were using you as bait again."

Joe then put his arm around one of the young girl's shoulders he was talking with, a stunning blonde coed, whose flight had just arrived from Knoxville, Tennessee. She was a goalie for the University of Tennessee women's soccer team. They were on their way to Durham to play the Lady Blue Devils.

"Angela, this is Travis Simpson," Joe said. "Travis, this is Angela Short. Angela thought Russell and I were just hanging around trying to pick up girls. We told her we were here to pick you up, but she didn't believe us. Imagine that!"

"Angela," Travis replied, "you are obviously a very perceptive girl. You need to be careful around these two."

"Girls have to be careful these days, especially around two charmers like Joe and Russell. I thought they might be pulling my leg when they said they were here to pick you up. I thought, these two guys could be waiting for their girlfriends for all I know. Travis, I'm glad to see you're real and not just an excuse they made up to meet girls."

"These two are too smart to do anything like that," Travis said.

"Never in a million years will we do that again," Russell agreed.

It took about twenty minutes for Joe and Russell to wrap up their "interviews" of the Lady Volunteers, as the two boys made their plans to attend the women's soccer game in Durham the following night. Then Russell and Joe helped Travis and Jim get their luggage and tennis equipment in Russell's Sentra, and the four of them headed back to campus.

By the time the boys got back to the dorm and dropped their luggage off in their rooms, it was time for lunch. They grabbed a bite to eat in the cafeteria in the athletic dorm, then they all headed off to their afternoon practices. Later that night the boys met back at the dorm and they went to Bible study. It was the first meeting of the fall. Coach Clark and Stephanie met the boys at the door. It was also the first time Travis had seen either of them since his trip to New York.

Coach Clark said, "Well, if it isn't Jimmy Connors! My goodness Travis, I thought you were going to take out the number one ranked player in the world. You played great. I am so proud of you."

Stephanie spoke up and echoed Coach Clark's sentiments.

"Me too. Travis you played so well, from the commentators, to everyone I've spoken to who saw the match, your talent is obvious. I am just so happy for you. Oh by the way; I hear you are engaged. Congratulations!"

"Thanks Stephanie. It's been some summer."

"Yes it has," she agreed.

The boys then made their way into the classroom and took a seat. Russell looked around the room.

"We have a bunch of new folks in here tonight. There is hardly an empty seat in here, and class doesn't begin for another fifteen minutes."

As the boys sat there looking around, they noticed several students wearing the "Play 2 Win-Live 2 Serve" T-shirts. While they waited, there continued to be a steady stream of students making their way into the classroom, right up until it was time for the class to begin. When the class started there were no empty chairs, and a crowd of almost fifty students left standing.

"There must be four hundred people here tonight. These classrooms have a three hundred fifty-seat capacity, and there are people sitting and standing in the isles. I wonder why there is such a big crowd tonight?"

"There has been some type of article in the paper or on the news about Travis playing in the U.S. Open every day for the past week," Russell said. "There were stories about the Play 2 Win-Live 2 Serve shirts, and information about the Bible study in The News and Observer, and the student paper. I've had people around campus asking me about the shirts and Bible study all week. I thought we would probably have some extra people tonight, but I wasn't expecting this kind of a turnout, especially for the first class."

When the class began the students all stood up together and recited the Pledge of Allegiance, then Coach Clark led the group in prayer. Coach Clark then went through the gospel rotation, explaining the goal for every student to complete a study of the four gospels during their time in school at

State. He told the group that this year's study would take the class through the Gospel of Mark. Coach Clark told the students that they all had been blessed by the Lord to have the ability to learn. That their ability to study, to gain an education, the intellect they all possessed to graduate from high school, the ability to meet the entrance requirements and be accepted into the university, all these abilities, these talents, were gifts from Jesus. He challenged the students to not only develop their God-given academic gifts, but also to develop and use their God-given spiritual gifts. To study and learn God's Word, the Bible. He challenged the students to commit to serve their campus community in witnessing the love of Christ. Then Coach Clark read the class Mark Chapter 4: 26-27.

"He being Jesus" also said; "This is what the kingdom of God is like. A man scatters seed on the ground. Night and day, whether he sleeps or gets up, the seed sprouts and grows, though he does not know how. All by itself the soil produces grain, first the stalk, then the head, then the kernel in the head." (NIV)

Coach Clark went on to explain that the mission, the charge of Jesus to all Christians, is to plant seeds. We never know how a single seed we plant today, may produce a mighty harvest for the Lord. Then Coach Clark held up one of the Play 2 Win- Live 2 Serve T-shirts. He told the class how the message on the shirt started as a simple act of praise, designed to show unity among a group of Christians on the tennis team. Yet, in three short months, they had sold over a thousand shirts to raise awareness of the teachings of Jesus. They also had plans to use the money generated from the sale of the shirts to help support Christian missions in the community. How this simple act, was a planted seed, and that when we plant our seeds of praise, talents and creativity, to glorify the Name of Jesus, then we are responding to the call of discipleship, in service of God.

After the class was over Travis and Russell walked back together to the dorm room, it was the first time the boys had a chance to talk alone in a while. It gave them a chance to sit down and catch up on things, and there were a couple of questions Russell had on his mind.

"Travis, what's it like to be engaged?"

"It's nice. I'm excited. I feel so much more relaxed now that I don't have to worry about losing Mary Katherine to some other guy. But it is kind of weird."

"Yeah, I'm happy for you. But it's hard to believe you're getting married. It's hard for me sometimes to believe I'm out of high school and twenty-one years old, but married, man! My parents are married, that's great for them, but I can't imagine me being married."

Then Russell said, "Tell me about those women tennis players. Do they look as good in person as they do on TV?"

"Better! You wouldn't believe it Russell."

"Look Travis, you've got your tennis player, Mary Katherine looks like a supermodel, so do you think you and Mary Katherine can hook me up with some of those other women tennis players?"

"Russell, you just said you weren't interested in settling down."

"I didn't say 'one' of them, I said 'some' of them! After all, I don't want to leave any of those girls out. I want to make myself as available as possible. Besides, these sorority girls around campus have taken it real hard since the word got out you're engaged. I'm afraid if I got engaged too, it could really cause problems amongst the coed population. Who knows, it may even reduce our enrollment."

"Lord have mercy Russell, I'm not talking about this anymore. I'm going to sleep before God strikes you with a lightening bolt!"

The boys joked and laughed for a while longer. Then it was time to turn out the lights and get some sleep.

The next day things began to get back into a routine again for Travis. He was up early and off to breakfast, and then to class. There was tennis practice in the afternoon, and a couple of nights cooking fish in the kitchen at 42nd Street Oyster Bar. The cooking part made Mary Katherine very happy! Meanwhile, Mary Katherine continued to win matches in New York, as she made her way into the round of sixteen. On Wednesday Travis received an e-mail from Tom Ham regarding a date when he could come to Raleigh to interview Travis and the other kids and parents for the feature article he was going to write for the Christian news publications. They decided on the week of October 23rd. That week, the State tennis team would be playing in a tournament at Duke University in Durham, N.C. Also, that week, the Wolfpack football team would be hosting Florida State in a nationally televised Thursday night game. Mary Katherine would arrange her tournament schedule so she could be in Raleigh for the week, and her brother Joe, who was a student at Florida State, would be in Raleigh as well to watch the Seminoles take on the Pack.

As the week progressed, the football and tennis teams were each preparing for important games. The football team had it's first conference game of the season on the road Saturday against Wake Forest. The tennis team was scheduled to play host to the University of Georgia on Sunday afternoon. So there was, as was normally the case with college kids, a lot to do to get ready for the weekend.

On the football field, Russell and the Wolfpack were extremely focused on practice as they designed their game plan to take on the Demon Deacons. Wake Forest and the Wolfpack were both 2-0 on the season. The Deacons had an excellent team, coming on the heels of four straight bowl appearances. It had been five years since State had last beaten Wake Forest. So this was a big game, especially for Joe and the other seniors. Wake was the only Atlantic Coast Conference rival that the seniors had never beaten, and that made Saturday's trip to Winston Salem very important.

It was a humid September morning as Travis and the Wolfpack football team boarded the bus to make the trip up I-40 to Winston Salem. The sky was overcast with a stiff breeze blowing from the southeast as a tropical depression was passing up the coast toward Myrtle Beach and Wilmington, making its way north. The weather was expected to deteriorate over the course of the day, with kickoff scheduled at 3:30. Once the team arrived at Grove Stadium on the campus at Wake Forest, the wind was whipping with gusts up to 40 mph and light rain. The players dressed in the visitor's locker room at the stadium, and before the Wolfpack took the field, Coach Clark met with the offensive players.

"Alright men, we are in for a very physical game today. These windy, wet conditions are going to make it difficult to throw the ball downfield. Both teams are going to have to protect the football and keep the game plan simple. We are going to have to win the battle at the line of scrimmage today. We're going to establish our running game and throw short quick passes to move the football. So buckle up your chinstraps, because in this kind of weather it's going to be a street fight. This game will come down to who wants it the most."

When the Wolfpack took the field to warm up, the offense practiced short passing routes, quick out patterns, and slants over the middle. In the blustery conditions, the quarterbacks were having trouble controlling the ball in warm-ups, even on the short pass plays. Coach Clark called Russell over to the sidelines before the kickoff.

"Russell, you are going to have to call most of the plays at the line today. Read the defense and try to run the ball into the gaps in the defense whenever possible. The ball is going to get away from you some passing in this wind today, so be patient, and understand you're going to have more incompletions than normal. But remember, the weather is bad for both teams, just keep the guys focused, and fighting for it!"

The Wolfpack won the coin toss and decided to defer to the second half, so Wake took the opening kickoff and returned the ball to their own thirty-one yard line. On its first possession Wake ran three plays and was forced to punt. That was the way it went for both offenses in the first half. It was a physical, hard-fought first half. Highlighted by a hard-hitting defensive struggle, as State took a slim 10-7 lead into the locker room at halftime. When the teams came out in the second half the rain had stopped and the sun had come out, but the wind had picked up. The breezy conditions helped to dry off the field, but the wind was playing havoc on the kicking and passing game. State received the kick-off to begin the second half and returned the ball to the twenty-seven yard line. From there Russell led the Pack down the field behind a power running game, and timely passes. Then with 6:32 to go in the third quarter Russell ran an option play on third and goal from the two-yard line, and he dove into the end zone to extend State's lead, 17-7.

From that point the defenses again began to take control, and with the score still 17-7, and just 7:12 remaining to be played, Wake was forced to punt again from its own 34-yard line. The Wake Forest punter, with the wind at his back kicked a high spiraling punt that forced the State return man back to the State 15-yard line. In the swirling winds, the Wolfpack receiver misjudged the flight of the ball, and fumbled the punt. The Wake Forest defenders recovered the ball on the State 13-yard line. Three plays later, on second and goal from the eight-yard line, the Deacons ran a sweep to the wide side of the field and scored cutting the State lead to 17-14 with 5:17 left in the fourth quarter.

With the wind at his back the Wake Forest kicker kicked the ball out of the back of the end zone giving State a first and ten on their 20-yard line. Russell brought the Wolfpack offense onto the field and the Pack began a methodical drive down the field. State proceeded to pick up four first downs, running the clock down to 2:09 before calling a time-out with third and seven on the Wake Forest 23-yard line. Coach Clark met Russell on the sidelines to discuss the play call.

"Russell, we need this first down, we're going to have to throw for it. Keep it simple; let's run a quick slant. If we don't get the first down, we'll kick the field goal."

When Russell got back to the huddle, he called a quick slant play designed to go to his freshman wide receiver, Jordan Smith. Jordan was lined up out wide to Russell's left, with Joe in a slot back position between them. When the ball was snapped, Joe ran down field toward the corner of the end zone to draw the defenders away from Jordan, as Jordan cut toward the middle of the field. Russell took a quick two-step drop; then turned to his left and fired a pass toward Jordan. As Jordan was approaching the pass he could sense the presence of the Wake Forest strong safety coming in his direction. The charging safety distracted Jordan just enough, that it broke Jordan's concentration, and he hesitated. Causing the ball to go right through his hands and float up into the air. The Wake Forest safety, seeing the play in front of him, picked the ball out of the air and raced eighty-five yards down the field for a touchdown. Just that quickly State trailed Wake, 20-17. In the windy conditions the Wake kicker missed the extra point, keeping the Wake lead three points.

When the Wolfpack offense reached the sideline following the interception, Coach Clark huddled the team together. The Pack had one timeout remaining and they needed to reach the Wake thirty-yard line to have any chance at a field goal to take the game into overtime. The Wake kicker, kicking again with the wind at his back kicked the ball deep into the end zone. Forcing State to start from its own twenty-yard line, with only 1:54 to play. The Wolfpack offense came onto the field. Russell lined up in a shotgun formation, and began to throw short passes. The Wolfpack worked their no huddle offense, calling pass plays at the line of scrimmage to save time on the clock. They quickly moved the ball down the field to the Wake Forest thirty-seven yard line. Then, with just fourteen seconds to play, following an incomplete pass that stopped the clock, the Pack faced third down with one time-out remaining. Coach Clark signaled a play in from the sideline and the Pack broke the huddle. Russell came to the line, Joe split out wide to the right. The ball was snapped as Joe broke toward the middle of the field. In the face of a heavy pass rush, Russell planted his feet and whistled a pass in Joe's direction. As Joe reached forward to catch the ball, he was drilled head on by a Wake Forest defensive back knocking Joe's helmet off, and Joe to the ground on the Wake twenty-eight yard line. Somehow though, Joe managed to hold onto the football, and quickly signaled time-out to stop the clock with six seconds to play. It was a gutsy play. Joe sacrificed his body to make the catch. He was a team player who was not afraid to take a hit. The Wolfpack then sent the field goal team on with a chance to tie the game. The State players huddled together on the sideline, as the kicking team lined up to attempt a forty-five yard field goal, dead into the wind. The holder knelt on one knee as the lineman set in place. The ball was snapped, then placed down and kicked. Both teams and the capacity crowd held their breath as the kick sailed up into the wind, and just wide right. The field goal attempt failed, and Wake escaped with the victory, 20-17.

After the game, the State locker room was quiet. The coaches praised the players for their effort, but the loss was a bitter pill to swallow, especially for Jordan. Once the team returned to Raleigh, they met together briefly in the locker room before the coaches dismissed the players. As Russell and Travis were leaving the locker room, Russell walked over to Joe.

"Joe, come with me and Travis. I need to talk with Jordan, then we'll all go down to Char-Grill and get something to eat."

Russell then left the other two boys and went and sat down beside Jordan. Jordan was sitting alone beside his locker. He looked as though he had lost his last friend in the world. Russell reached out and placed his hand on Jordan's shoulder.

"Jordan, I want you to come with us and get something to eat."

"I'm surprised you would want to do anything with me after I missed that pass and cost us the game. I am so sorry Russell. I feel awful about it."

Jordan just sat there hanging his head. Russell could remember back to the game he threw a fourth quarter interception against Virginia Tech. He knew how Jordan felt, and he wanted to help. Travis and Joe stood across the room watching Jordan and Russell. They both knew what Russell was doing.

"Russell is a winner," Travis said. "He is a born leader."

"Russell is a winner," Joe agreed, "because he is always leading. He cares more about others than he does himself, that's why people are willing to follow him. He leads by example."

"Jordan, if you play long enough you're going to make mistakes," Russell said. "At this level the competition is so fierce, almost every team in the country, even the very best teams are going to lose some games. We win as a team, and we lose as a team. Nobody blames you for losing this game. We all could have played better, so don't beat yourself up about it. Now get your head up, and let's go get something to eat."

The smile then returned to Jordan's face. The four boys headed outside, got in the car and headed down Hillsborough Street. The conversation changed from dropped passes to college co-eds as the boys "wolfed down" some Charburger steak sandwiches and a couple of milkshakes apiece.

Later that night Travis called Mary Katherine on her cell phone. With "unlimited weekend minutes," their conversation lasted well into the night. Mary Katherine had a 6 p.m. televised match on Sunday against the number four seed, and Travis was excited about the tennis team's home match against Georgia. It had been a long day, so there was a lot to talk about. When the conversation wrapped up, Travis decided to go for a walk. He made his way around campus and over to the tennis bleachers. He leaned back on the bleachers and looked up as the limbs and leaves of the giant oak trees were rustled together by the stiff breeze gusting from the southeast. Travis said his prayers that night, as he praised Jesus for all his blessings.

Travis had learned so much about himself by watching others. How Joe was willing to sacrifice his body for the good of the team. How Russell reached out to Jordan when he needed a friend. Travis thought back to all the times God had placed people in his path to aid him in his recovery. Travis took off his cap and prayed.

"Lord, I am so amazed by what you have shown me. You have taken my broken spirit, and made it new. Lord, give me the courage and wisdom to praise You, and share your goodness, and may your will be done, Amen."

Then as he gazed up at the clouds being blown quickly past the stars by the breeze, Travis' soul was being shaped, to spread the message of his leader, Jesus Christ.

ROLE MODELS

Travis met Jim and the rest of the tennis team in the cafeteria of the athletic dorm at 6:30 for breakfast. Once the team finished eating, they went as a group to an early church service being held at one of the churches within walking distance from campus. After church, the team walked back and changed into their tennis uniforms. Then they went through a strategy session with Coaches Taylor and Strader before the match. Rudy was still in New York with Mary Katherine and Rita, so Coach Taylor and Coach Strader would be coaching the match against the nationally 6th ranked Georgia Bulldogs. Today's match was the first of the season as the State men faced another nationally ranked opponent. The Wolfpack men, coming off their strong previous year's record, and with all six of their starting singles lineup returning, were also ranked, at 16th in the nation.

The team walked onto the court at noon and began with some light stretching exercises. From there they ran agility drills to get their blood pumping, and work out their pre-match jitters. It was a beautiful September day in Raleigh, not a cloud in the sky. The humidity was low, with a mild breeze blowing from the northwest. The passing storm from the previous day had pulled all the moisture out of the atmosphere, as the tropical depression swept north leaving the Raleigh area with temperatures in the 70s. It was a perfect day for tennis. As the team continued to progress through their pre-match drills, Travis could not help but notice the large crowd of spectators gathering around the tennis courts. By the time the match was set to begin, the viewing area above the courts was filled. The bleachers were full. There were people in folding chairs, and sitting on blankets covering the hill above the courts, and all the area surrounding the courts on every side. The State players were all amazed by the extremely large turnout for the match. Jim looked around at the crowd and saw that many of the fans were wearing the Play 2 Win-Live 2 Serve T-shirts.

"I can't believe this crowd. Two years ago we didn't have this many fans at all our home matches put together. Travis, this is awesome!"

Just then Coach Strader called the young men together.

"Men, we have practiced all summer to get ready for today. Let's make this day a day to remember; leave it all on the court. I've seen great improvement in each one of you over the summer. Let's go out there today and give these State fans something to cheer about. But before we do anything, let's give thanks to our Lord, Jesus Christ."

The team formed a circle. The young men, coaches, and trainers, they held hands, bowed their heads, and prayed. When they finished praying all the young men put their hands together in the circle.

"Gentlemen together on three," Coach Strader said. "One, two, three; Play 2 Win-Live 2 Serve!"

Then as the capacity crowd came to its feet, the Wolfpack men took to the court. Their season had begun.

When the three N.C. State doubles teams walked onto the court, the doubles lineup was the same as the year before, but it quickly became apparent that their tennis games were much different. Stephanie's conditioning program, and the hard work each man had put in playing and practicing over the summer, had turned the boys into men. It was apparent in the way they moved across the court. They were all faster, their agility was better, they covered the court easier, and there was a noticeable spring in their step. The young men simply moved to the ball better, and when they hit the ball, the sound was different. With the improved strength and agility, they all hit the ball harder, with more control and accuracy. They were the same players, but they were all better athletes, and that was transforming a good team into a great team. The Wolfpack made quick work of the Bulldogs, easily winning the doubles point and taking a 1-0 lead in the match.

After the doubles were completed, the players met with Coaches Taylor and Strader to review their game plans for singles. There was a sense of electricity among the team and the crowd. There was also a new unity among the players; they were focused, they played with an intensity that had not been there before, and Coach Strader could feel it.

"Fellas, let me tell you, you guys are so much improved. You were focused, you guys played smart, and you played hard. I'm just proud of every one of you. Now let's go out there and finish the job! These guys aren't going to roll over for us. We have got to go out there and continue to play hard, play to win!"

When the Pack took the court to begin the singles, the players up and down the line had on their game faces. The team came out playing fast and hard as the Wolfpack simply overwhelmed the Bulldogs 4-1. When the match concluded Travis met with several members of the sports media including local news reporter Paul Durham.

"Travis, great match today."

"Thank you. The whole team played great today, it was a total team effort."

Paul then asked, "The team seems much improved since last year. The guys all seem quicker and stronger, is it just another year's maturity and experience? Is that the cause for the dramatic improvement?"

"The year's experience has certainly helped, but all the guys stayed in Raleigh this summer and worked out and practiced together. We have all been on a workout program Dr. Stephanie Clauson designed to improve our strength and agility. It is a combination of things."

"Georgia was the sixth ranked team in the country; beating them 4-1 has got to be a big confidence boost for the team as you look forward to the rest of the season?"

"It was a great win today. We are all thrilled by what is happening with this team. We just want to give Jesus the glory for giving us an opportunity to be a part of the team, and the university. All the praise, we give to Him."

After the interviews were finished, Travis walked over where Jim was standing. Jim was talking to a man with two small boys. Travis knew he had seen the man before, but he couldn't remember where. Once Travis reached them, one of the boys said,

"Travis, I saw you on television. Are you a TV star?"

Travis reached over and rubbed the boys head.

"Nope, I'm just a normal guy, just like you."

Jim then turned to Travis.

"Travis, this is Tom Corbett. We met Tom at the Char-Grill with Tom Jr. and Will, remember?"

"Oh yes, I remember. Mr. Corbett it's nice to see you again; thanks for coming out today."

"I had a great time today. You guys played super!"

"Yes sir, thank you sir."

Jim then told Travis, "Mr. Corbett has an idea he wanted to run by us about how to promote the gospel using the Play 2 Win-Live 2 Serve shirts."

"That's great, what's your idea Mr. Corbett?"

"Our youth group at church is always looking for ways to raise money to support mission trips, provide supplies for their activities or other mission opportunities within our church or the community. The church leadership is also looking for ways to help inspire the youth and adults to witness their faith, to go out into the community to spread the message of Jesus. I was thinking that our youth group at church could use these shirts as a fundraiser. We could go out and take orders from people who would like to buy a shirt. Then our youth group could collect the money for the shirts and purchase the shirts at a discount. That way the shirts would be distributed in the church and the community. The youth group could use the shirts as a way to start a discussion about Jesus, and the money the youth made from the sell of the shirts would go to help fund other youth activities, like mission trips or youth supplies. Is that something you guys would be interested in?"

Jim looked at Travis.

"I think it's a great idea. What do you think Travis?"

"Yeah, it is."

"Mr. Corbett we want to spread the gospel message," Jim said. "If these shirts help Christians to express their faith and possibly lead people to Christ, that would be fantastic. If your youth group, or any other Christian organization can use these shirts as a way to promote the gospel we want to help support them in doing it."

"That sounds good to me guys. Let me go talk with our youth advisors to see if they are interested. We already have a bunch of kids and adults in the church who have asked me where they could get one of the shirts, so I'm pretty confident they will want to do it, but I wanted to talk with you guys about it first."

Jim reached out and shook Mr. Corbett's hand.

"Thanks for your input Mr. Corbett. We really appreciate your support."

"I want you guys," Mr. Corbett said. "I want your whole team to know, how much I appreciate what you guys are doing. Our young people today desperately need leadership. They need to understand that there are other people who are proud to say they are Christians. These are more than just T-shirts, they are a statement of what we believe. Christians today more than ever, need to step forward and profess what we believe. There are people everywhere we go who need to hear the message of forgiveness and acceptance that Jesus preached. If we can encourage Christians to reach out and share their faith, then we are doing the work He called us to do. By wearing one of these shirts, Christians young and old, may have an opportunity, possibly for the first time to explain the gospel message. And once they see that they are not alone in their beliefs, their faith will grow. Then whether they are wearing the shirts or not, they will know that God is with them, and that people want to hear the good news about Jesus. You young men are role models, especially for young children like mine. What you are doing is very important, maybe more important than you or I may ever know."

After their conversation was over Mr. Corbett and his sons left. Jim and Travis went into the locker room and changed. Russell, Joe and Jordan had come to the match, so they hung around outside waiting on Jim and Travis. Then the boys all went down the street to grab a bite and hang out for a while. Once they got their food, Jim and Travis told the other guys about Mr. Corbett's idea. They all agreed that if the shirts could help raise money to support church youth groups that they should try and support it anyway possible. Also, they began to talk about the ways the boys themselves might witness to the youth. Possibly make a list of ideas to help the kids explain the gospel message. To explain to the kids the meaning behind the number "2," and why the scripture verses were John 3:16-17 instead of just verse John 3:16 that we see so often. They discussed ideas about how they could help youth leaders develop other outlets to encourage young people to witness. The boys all agreed that they had benefited in their teen years by other people having courage and witnessing to them. So they wanted to give back. They began to see their roles differently. Their talk with Mr. Corbett had opened their eyes to new areas of service. As Christian athletes, they began to realize the platform they had been given by Jesus. They began to see that there was another reason for their athletic gifts, by being athletes; they had a unique opportunity to reach young people for Christ. So while they ate their barbecue sandwiches, fries and drank sweet tea, they discussed their ideas about how they could Play 2 Win, and Live 2 Serve Jesus.

After the boys finished eating, they walked back over to campus. They ended up at the student center, where they met with some of their other friends to watch Mary Katherine's match. Mary Katherine was playing Evana Frankel, a five-year tour veteran from the Czech Republic. Frankel had risen to number four in the world after winning the French Open earlier in the season. When the match began both women played intense competitive tennis with the first set going into a tiebreaker which Frankel won to take the set. In the second set Mary Katherine, playing with her back to the wall, broke Frankel's serve twice to take the set 6-3 and level the match at one set apiece. Then in the third set Frankel, leading one game to love, broke Mary Katherine's serve to take a two games to love lead. From that point both women held serve the rest of the way as Frankel took the final set 6-4, and won the match two sets to one. The loss capped what had been a great week for Mary Katherine. She was disappointed she had lost, but Mary Katherine understood that in professional tennis with a field of over one hundred entries every week, that only one player a week would win all their matches. Making it to the round of sixteen was a great accomplishment, and it was also her first payday as a pro. She had a lot to be thankful for.

Once Mary Katherine reached the locker room, she sat down and dialed the number of a young man in Raleigh.

"Hey, you played great Mary Katherine, I am so proud of you!"

Mary Katherine was still a little emotional after the loss.

"Thanks. I wanted to win, but all these girls are great. I'm just thankful to be here."

"I know you like to have your way, and you don't like to lose, but you are always a winner in my book."

At that point the conversation changed from tennis to the other subjects kids discuss. There were lots of "I love yous," and "I miss yous." There were wedding plans to be discussed. There was a date to be chosen. How many bridesmaids and groomsmen should there be? What color should be chosen for the bridesmaids' dresses? What style tuxedos? The time of the wedding, should it be 2 p.m. or 6 p.m? Where should the reception be held, and of course, a destination for the honeymoon? Mary Katherine did a lot of the talking and suggesting, while Travis wisely did a lot of listening and agreeing. Once the two kids had talked long enough, they said their goodbyes. They both had a busy week ahead.

SHARE YOUR LOVE OF JESUS

"I want to start out by telling you guys how proud I am of each and every one of you," Rudy said. "Coach Strader and Coach Taylor have told me how hard all of you have been working in practice these last three weeks while I was gone. I want to congratulate you all. That was a great win yesterday against Georgia. The Dawgs are one of the top tennis programs in the country. That was a super win for this team, and the tennis program at N.C. State. Men, I believe something very special is happening with this team, both on and off the court. I just want you guys to know that I feel truly blessed to be a part of this, and I can't wait to see where this team is going. Now before we get started, let's come together in prayer."

The teamed formed a circle. As the men held hands Rudy led the team in prayer.

"Heavenly Father, we thank you Lord for the gift of life. The opportunity to be a part of this team, Lord, bless these young men as they each seek to know You more and more each day, and may our efforts glorify You, and your will be done. We ask this in the name of Jesus, Amen."

Then the men placed their hands together in the circle, "On three, one, two, three, "Play 2 Win-Live 2 Serve!" Alright let's get to work."

The players began with footwork and agility drills, then they moved into the finesse shots as they played mini-tennis. From there they worked on volleys and short balls, then they moved back to the baseline to hit forehands and backhands. Afterward they played singles and doubles matches. Rudy was a model of the concept, "teacher coach." He believed in helping develop solid fundamental skills in all his players. He was interested in more than just banging balls. Rudy understood that wisdom and knowledge were the keys to success, and he was willing to try new ways of doing things, as long as it did not go against his fundamental values of teaching technique and developing solid work ethics within his players.

While the players were going through their practice routine, Stephanie came out to the courts and met with Rudy.

"Hi Stephanie, I appreciate your coming over today."

"You're welcome Rudy. I came to the match yesterday, the guys played super!"

"Well Stephanie, you're a large part of that. The conditioning program you designed has improved the athleticism of all our players, and that has been an important part of their overall improvement. I really appreciate your help. The reason I wanted you to come by today is that I need some advice."

Stephanie was always anxious to help any of the State coaches. It made her feel involved in the athletic program and the success of the teams, so Rudy's interest in her opinion meant a lot to Stephanie.

"I'm not much of a tennis player, but I'll be happy to give you my input."

"Stephanie, you may not be a tennis player, but you are the finest athletic trainer I've ever worked with, and you are very observant."

"Thank you, that's very kind. Tell me, how can I help you?"

"Stephanie, tennis played at this level is a very demanding, physical sport. Once the matches begin there is no substituting. Most of the time tennis is played on hard courts, a type of asphalt or concrete surface, and the tennis strokes- forehands, backhands and serves- are repetitive movements. While playing on hard surfaces with repetitive movements, often times tennis players have a tendency to develop knee or ankle problems, as well as joint injuries, like rotator cuff or elbow problems."

"Like tennis elbow?"

"Exactly Stephanie. Players need to practice to improve and be ready for matches, but it's not good for them to play too much because they can become injured or worse, burnt out mentally, then they don't want to practice or even play at all. Stephanie, let's sit down and watch the singles matches the boys are playing."

Rudy and Stephanie sat down on the bleachers and quietly watched as the six singles matches were being played on the courts beside them, after a few minutes Rudy spoke.

"Stephanie, in your opinion, by watching the guys play tennis, what type of drills and exercises would best help the players improve their athletic abilities needed to play tennis?"

Stephanie looked out onto the courts as she studied the way the boys moved. She focused on the quick foot movements, the stopping and starting, the jumping necessary in the service motion. Stephanie made a mental note of the need to accelerate quickly, and the muscles in the arms and shoulders required to hit the ball with power, and the cardiovascular endurance needed to play long points in close matches. Once she had watched the practice for about fifteen minutes Stephanie asked,

"Rudy, is this something you want them to do every day, or every other day? Is this going to be a part of the practice, or is this something you want done in addition to practice?"

"Stephanie, I have been amazed how much the conditioning program we did over the summer has helped our team. I would like to have a regular tennis practice one day then devote the next practice session totally to conditioning. That's what we did this summer and it has worked so well I want to continue it. I would just like you to think of tennis specific exercises, now that you see what we are trying to accomplish, I believe your expertise will be very helpful."

"Rudy, I am flattered that you are interested in my opinion. Let me sit and watch the rest of practice today. Then by the end of the week we can sit down and go over what I will put together, and come up with what works best for you and the team."

Rudy then thanked Stephanie again for coming, and she sat quietly observing the rest of the practice while Rudy resumed coaching the team. Once the practice ended, Travis went back to the dorm room and showered. He hooked up with Russell and Joe then they grabbed some dinner and went to Bible study.

When the boys entered the building where the Bible study was held they walked up a flight of stairs, then they turned down the hallway headed toward the classroom. Once they entered the hallway they saw a line of people standing along the wall. Russell, always the first one to express himself commented.

"They must have added another class the same time we have Bible study. I wonder where their professor is? There must be a hundred kids locked out of the room."

When they got closer to the line of students the boys noticed a lot of the kids waiting were holding Bibles. Once they reached the classroom and turned to go inside they could see all the seats were filled and students were sitting in the isle and standing along the walls of the classroom.

"My goodness," Russell said. "This place is packed, all those folks outside are waiting to get in here."

The three boys walked on into the room and up to the front where Coach Clark, Stephanie and Jim were standing discussing the situation. Coach Clark looked toward the filled classroom.

"I never thought I'd see this, did you guys?"

"No Coach," Jim said. "This is my fourth year, as a freshman we sometimes wouldn't have a hundred people in the class. Tonight we have that many or more waiting outside to get in."

"I'm thrilled we have this kind of a turnout," Coach Clark said. "But I'm not sure what we're going to do with all these kids. There's no way we're going to turn anyone away. Does anyone have any ideas?"

The six of them stood together for a while discussing their options, then after a few minutes, no consensus had been reached. Then Stephanie spoke up.

"Let's turn it over to the Lord. Let's pray about it."

The group of six formed a circle and asked the students inside the classroom, and the ones waiting outside to commit to pray, that the Lord would show them where to hold the class to accommodate everyone. They asked the students outside to remain, that no one would leave. Then they all bowed their heads together and began to pray. After about five minutes of silent prayer, Coach Clark lifted his head.

"Ladies, gentlemen, pick up your Bibles and notebooks and follow me."

Coach Clark led the students out of the classroom and down the hallway, down the stairs and then they exited the building. They walked through the parking lot and down one of the streets that cut across the university, until they reached the lighted athletic fields near the middle of campus. There were flag football and soccer games being played on the fields, but there was also a set of empty bleachers near the road that was well lit, and plenty of room for the students to stand or sit down. Once they reached the bleachers, Coach Clark and Stephanie, along with the other faculty leaders, stood atop the bleachers while the students situated themselves either standing or sitting in the grassy area.

Coach Clark stood up on the bleachers and welcomed the new students who were attending for the first time. Then he asked everyone to stand, they prayed and then they recited the Pledge of Allegiance together. Afterward Coach Clark asked everyone to take a seat and he began the lesson. The lesson was from Mark 6:30-44, the story of Jesus feeding the five thousand men who came to hear Him preach. Coach Clark explained that Jesus desires to meet all of our needs, that Jesus is Lord of all things. He provides for our spiritual salvation and forgiveness of sins by His giving up His physical life as atonement for us. In addition to that, He also wants to be involved in providing for our physical needs as we walk this road of life in our human bodies. Our need of food, clothing, shelter, Jesus is the giver of all the things we have and enjoy, and the Lord loves to provide for His children. That God's blessings are not limited to what we see in our human eyes, that when we bring what we have to Him with a thankful heart, all things are possible.

As Coach Clark was speaking, standing on the bleachers talking to the students in the cool night air, there was a steady stream of people walking by. While the students sat there together in the twilight, the crowd of students began to grow. There were people walking by who saw the group of students, they stopped to listen, to see what was going on. Then before long the crowd multiplied as the passersby joined the group. They began to take a seat among the students in the grass to hear the gospel message. There were others who were playing intramural football and soccer who once their games were finished, then came forward to stand or sit among the group. While Coach Clark was speaking from his position standing in the bleachers he could see the students walking steadily in all directions to join the group. He at times felt almost overwhelmed with emotion, as he witnessed God draw the students to the group, to draw them to Himself.

Coach Clark told the students that Jesus told the disciples to gather what they had to feed the multitude of people. The disciples returned with "five loaves and two fish." Jesus then took the food, looked to heaven, He "gave thanks" and blessed the food. Then the disciples distributed the food among the people, there was such an abundance of food left over that there were twelve baskets filled with bread and fish. Everyone there was satisfied. Coach Clark, made the point that before Jesus did anything He took a look at what He had received, and then He gave thanks to God. That in every situation, in the midst of every circumstance, before we do anything we must always give thanks to God. We must thank Him for what He alone does for us every day. We must thank Him for what we already have, and give praise to Jesus for whatever we have been given. Then, we must ask God for His blessing, and when we turn our situations over to Jesus, all things are possible.

Coach Clark then told the students that God was working a mighty miracle within their class. He explained that the students being there was a blessing. They normally in years past planned for a group of around 150 students a night. This year in the first class, they had 378 students, and tonight there were so many students they had to move the class outdoors. On top of that, Jesus had used moving outside as a way to draw even more people to Himself. That all during the lesson, people who were simply passing by were drawn to the hearing of God's Word. Coach Clark asked the other faculty members to separate the crowd into ten groups and they counted the group. When the count was taken, there were 796 students in the group who that night had heard the gospel message. Then they all prayed. They thanked God for what He had done, bringing them all together. Then they prayed that God would lead them. That God would bless their efforts, and that through the name of Jesus, their efforts would help spread the gospel message across the campus, and out into the world.

Wednesday afternoon when Travis got to tennis practice, Jim told him that he had received an e-mail from Tom Corbett. Mr. Corbett told Jim that he had spoken with the youth advisors at his church and they wanted to organize a fundraiser using the Play 2 Win-Live 2 Serve T-shirts. Mr. Corbett's church had a regular Wednesday night supper, followed by a Bible study. Mr. Corbett wanted to make an announcement about the fundraiser after the dinner. Also, Mr. Corbett invited Jim, Travis, Joe and Russell to the church for their youth group meeting on Sunday night. That would give the boys a chance to meet the youth advisors and church officials and speak briefly about how the shirts were first made, and the boys' hopes for how the shirts may help the church membership to witness for the Lord.

Sunday night the boys got to the church around 6:15, the spaghetti supper was scheduled for 6:30. When the boys got to the church fellowship hall, they were greeted by Mr. Corbett and the Senior Pastor, Johnny Sullivan.

"Hello fellas," Mr. Corbett said. "I really appreciate you guys coming over tonight."

Jim reached out and shook Mr. Corbett's hand.

"We're all excited to be here. I know I'm a little nervous about speaking to a group of fifty teenagers, but I guess there's a first time for everything."

"Jim you don't need to worry about speaking to fifty teenagers tonight," Pastor Sullivan said. "We've got a crowd of around three hundred here already!"

"Three hundred!" Jim said. "We only brought fifty shirts."

"When we announced at the Wednesday night supper you guys were coming tonight," Mr. Corbett said. "We had kids coming from other churches who wanted to hear you guys speak. I wish ya'll could come every week."

The boys followed Mr. Corbett and Pastor Sullivan as they entered the fellowship hall. There were parents, teens, visitors from other churches filling the dining hall, with the smell of spaghetti and fresh baked bread coming from the kitchen. Once the boys got the boxes of shirts situated at their table, Pastor Sullivan opened the program.

"Friends, tonight we have a special treat and some very special guests. We have with us four student athletes from N.C. State visiting with us tonight. These young men are actively professing their faith in Jesus Christ. They are here to talk with our youth about ways they have shared their faith, and to help our young people learn how they too, can share the Gospel of our Lord. Before we have our dinner, let's come together in prayer.

"Heavenly Father, we thank You for these young people who are gathered here tonight. We pray Lord that You will open the hearts and minds

of our youth, the visitors who they have invited here to be with us tonight, our parents who are here supporting these children, and these four young men who have taken their time to come and fellowship with us tonight. Now Father, bless this food to our bodies, and us to thy service, in Jesus name, Amen."

After the blessing, the boys got in line and served their plates. The spaghetti was piled on thick, with the baked bread smothered in butter. These boys were all young and fit, so they piled on the food. Once everyone had eaten everything in sight, the program got started. Mr. Corbett took the stage and introduced the boys. The four boys had decided that Jim would do the talking for the group. Then after Jim's talk, all the boys would spend time answering questions from the group of teenagers. When it was Jim's time to speak, he approached the podium, thanked Mr. Corbett and Pastor Sullivan for the opportunity to join them for dinner, introduced the other three boys, then he began to give his testimony.

"I want to tell all the high school kids who are here tonight that I am excited to be here and share with you all some of the exciting things I have witnessed God doing in my life, and the lives of my three friends who are here with me tonight. But before we go any further, I want to make one thing very clear; it is all about Jesus. God has brought people together with different skills, at just the right time, to bring His plan together, and again, it is all about Jesus. Our tennis team last year was made up of ten Christians who decided to come together with the goal of winning a national championship. We want to take the tennis program at N.C. State to another level, and we want to do it, while serving the Lord. We made these shirts with the simple message, Play 2 Win-Live 2 Serve; John 3:16-17, as a way to honor God. To say a small thank you for all He has given to us. The number 2 stands for the two lives of the Christian Believer, the life we are born with, and then the new life of Christ that lives in every Christian. It also stands for the two choices we all have, to accept the offer of Jesus, or we will reject Him. Then we added the 17th verse in John 3:16-17 to the popular verse John 3:16, we so often see and hear. That was important, because we want everyone to know that no matter their history, their circumstances, their successes or failures, that Jesus laid down His life for us all."

"For God did not send his Son into the world to condemn the world, but to save the world through him." John 3:17 (NIV)

"We believe it is especially important in this often times cynical world we live in, for people to know that Jesus came to save the lost, and we are all welcome at the foot of the cross. My prayer for you all is that you would develop a deep abiding love for Jesus. That you would seek to know Him, that you would dedicate your life to Him, and that you will share your love of Jesus with others."

Once Jim finished and the boys had spent some time meeting with and speaking to the young people in attendance, they hopped in the car and headed back to campus. On the drive back to the dorm, Travis thought about how comfortably and powerfully Jim had witnessed his love for Jesus. There was a powerful, convincing quality in the words Jim had spoken. Travis could see God's Hand at work. He thought about his three friends, they were far and away the closest friends he had ever known, and yet, this time two years ago, he barely knew any of them. Travis' mind raced as he thought back to all the changes in his life over the past two years. He began to realize that while his life was changing, the lives of his three friends were changing as well. That God was somehow working in all their lives, using them together yet separately at the same time, to develop the gifts and talents He created in all of them for His glory. Travis wondered about the young people in the church, which ones God was grooming, developing, molding to do His will? What His will for them might be? What role might they play? And what role did God have in mind for Travis?

Soon he would see.

QUEEN FOREVER

"Russell, man you better hurry up. If we're late picking up Mary Katherine and Mrs. Outland I'll never hear the end of it!"

"Alright Travis, let me get my shoes on and I'll be ready to go. You can tell Mary Katherine we had to stay late at practice. She'll understand we've got a short practice week this week trying to get ready for Florida State Thursday night."

Travis shook his head at Russell.

"Russell, you know Mary Katherine is never late. Well, I take that back, actually she's late sometimes, but somehow when she's late it's okay. It's when I'm late, that's when being late is a problem."

"And what's this present she's suppose to be bringing me anyway? You know she likes to mess with me, she probably just got some extra luggage for me to tote."

"Well whatever it is, we better get there on time or she'll tease us about it until we're sick of hearing it, so let's get moving."

Travis and Russell left the dorm and drove over to the Outland's to pick up the family Suburban. They both knew there was no way they could get all of Mary Katherine's and Rita's clothes, luggage, and "Lord only knows" what else they could have bought while being gone for three weeks in Travis' Jetta. Rudy had attended a booster club dinner that was being hosted by the athletic department, so Travis had enlisted Russell's help. And besides, Mary Katherine had sent word she was bringing "something special" for Russell, but she wouldn't tell either Travis or Russell, what the "something special" was.

Once the boys got to the airport they parked the Suburban in the parking garage, then made their way into the airport terminal. When they got to the terminal gate, Travis could see the airplane taxing up the exit ramp. Travis then took a deep sigh of relief, the boys had made it on time. Travis and Russell then positioned themselves near the entrance into the waiting area and soon Mary Katherine came bounding out of the exit ramp and jumped into Travis' waiting arms. Rita was following close behind, there were hugs and "welcome homes," talk about the flight and detailed instructions for Travis and Russell regarding the luggage.

"Now what's this about my gift? The something special you brought me," Russell asked.

Mary Katherine had been waiting for Russell to bring up the subject, and she knew exactly what she was going to say.

"Russell, I never said I was bringing you a gift. I said I had something special for you. I never said it was a gift, or that you could keep it!"

Russell was now convinced Mary Katherine was playing a joke on him.

"Well, what exactly is this something special and where is it?"

"Russell, before I tell you what it is, you have to promise not to embarrass me. And when you see what it is, you have to promise you'll treat me like a 'queen' for the rest of my life for bringing it to you."

Russell laughed.

"No way Superstar! I'm not promising you that when you won't even tell me what it is!"

"Whatever," Mary Katherine replied. "You can thank me later. Now turn around and don't embarrass me. I brought you a date for the weekend, Maria Lopez."

Russell laughed and shook his head.

"Maria Lopez, the tennis star, slash, swimsuit model! Come on Mary Katherine, that's not funny."

"Russell. I'm not kidding, she's here, and she's walking up right behind you. Now turn around and behave yourself!"

"If Maria Lopez is behind me, then I'll ..."

Just then Mary Katherine's smile lit up.

"Maria, I'm so glad you could come visit this weekend. You remember Travis, and Maria, this is Travis' roommate I was telling you about, our friend Russell Rawlings."

Russell turned around, his jaw dropped to the floor, as there standing in front of him was the most beautiful creature Russell had ever seen. She held out her hand.

"Russell, Mary Katherine has told me so much about you. I want to thank you for agreeing to be my escort for the weekend."

Russell just stood there speechless; he was in shock. Mary Katherine snapped her fingers.

"Russell, Russell, it's alright, she's not going to bite."

Russell then snapped out of his trance.

"Maria, I don't know what to say. I can't believe it's really you, I thought Mary Katherine was joking. It's a pleasure to meet you."

Maria just smiled. "Russell that's sweet. You know Mary Katherine, Russell is even cuter than you described him."

Then Mary Katherine walked over to Russell as she put her arm around him.

"Now Russell, do you owe me big time or what?"

Russell smiled as he nodded.

"Yes ma'am. Mary Katherine, you will always be a queen in my book!"

Once Russell started to breath regularly again, and was able to regain some control over the grin on his face, the five of them walked down the terminal hallway to the baggage claim area. Travis then told the girls. "You all wait here and we'll go get a luggage cart."

Mary Katherine quickly informed the boys. "You better make that two carts, Mom and me did some shopping while we were traveling."

Then Maria, in her broken English added, "Better make that three carts."

"That's no problem at all," Russell replied. "We've got plenty of room in the Suburban, don't we Travis?"

Travis could barely compose himself.

"No problem. The first thing Russell and I ever did together was help some students at State move their luggage and clothes in their dorm rooms, wasn't it Russell?"

"Maria, as a matter of fact," Rita added. "Travis met Mary Katherine when he offered to help her move into her dorm room at State. Isn't it a coincidence that the first time you meet Russell he is helping you with your luggage?"

Russell just smiled, he didn't say anything, but he was thinking. *"If I could only be that lucky."*

The boys managed to secure three luggage carts which were soon loaded beyond capacity. Then with the assistance of Rita's expert packing ability, they got everything inside the Suburban and headed over to the Outlands'. By the time they got to the Outland's house Rudy was already home. There were another round of reunions, after which the men got the girls' things to their rooms. Once the girls were settled, they all went outside on the back porch and had some lemonade. Before it got too late, Travis and Russell called it a night so the girls could get some rest.

On the way back to the dorm the boys decided to go down to the Char Grill to get something to eat. Russell was still on cloud nine.

"I tell you bro', I really owe you one."

"Mary Katherine brought Maria home, not me."

"Yeah, but if it wasn't for you, I wouldn't know Mary Katherine, and Maria wouldn't be here!"

"Russell, if you feel that strongly about it, why don't you buy me a Charburger and a milkshake?"

"No problem."

Then there was a buzz on Russell's cell phone. He opened it and read the text message, laughing as he told Travis, "I took a picture of me and Maria on my camera phone and sent it to Dad. He sent me back this reply:

"College life sure looks rough; does Maria have a sister? My dad is crazy."

There was plenty of activity crammed into the next couple of days as the football team put its game plan together for the Thursday night game against Florida State. Travis and the men's tennis team were also busily preparing for their weekend trip to Durham to play in the Blue Devil Fall Championships. The Wolfpack men would be playing three nationally ranked opponents as each of the four participants played a round robin tournament over the course of three days. On Friday, the Pack would play Texas Tech, then on Saturday they would face Notre Dame, and on Sunday the Pack would square off against arch-rival Duke. Meanwhile, away from the athletic fields, Mary Katherine, Rita and Maria were visiting bridal boutiques, bakeries, florists, printers, caterers, and so on and so forth. Travis, who knew he was better off leaving all the decisions up to Mary Katherine, relied on the five magic words Ed had taught him whenever Mary Katherine asked him anything, about anything.

"When it comes to the wedding," Ed had told him. "You really don't have a dog in the fight Son. And then once you are married, unless it is something you feel really strongly about, always say the five magic words that every woman wants to hear:"

"Honey, whatever makes you happy!"

So every time Mary Katherine asked Travis a question about the wedding, Travis' reply was always the same.

"Honey, whatever makes you happy!" And just like magic, Mary Katherine was happy.

Thursday afternoon Russell, Joe, and the rest of the Wolfpack football team met at 4 p.m. at the football field house to review some game film and go over their offensive assignments. Tom Ham, who had arrived in Raleigh earlier in the day, was there with the football team as well, beginning his research for the feature stories he was doing on Travis. The articles for both the sports publications and the Christian magazine, would feature Travis on the cover of the December edition. So while one magazine was focusing on Travis' athletic comeback, and the other publication was being developed around a spiritual theme, both articles would hit the newsstands right before Christmas.

Before the game Travis sat quietly with Russell and Joe while Coach Clark reviewed the offense.

"Men, we are going to have to put some points on the board tonight if we're going to win this ball game. The field is dry and fast, the temperature tonight is going to be in the high 50s, with little or no wind, it is a perfect night to throw the football, so that's what we're going to do. Florida State has an excellent defense. They get a good push up front from their pass rush so we want to work primarily out of the shotgun, late in the game that should wear their defensive line down. Offensively they are going to score some points, so if we're going to stay with them, we've all got to do our part tonight."

It was 7:05 when the Wolfpack huddled together in the tunnel exit underneath the field house. The capacity crowd of 65,000 Wolfpack faithful was already worked into a frenzy, while the players nervously shuffled underneath the bleachers, as the sound of the stadium crowd chanted together in unison; "WOLF"; "PACK"; "WOLF"; "PACK"; then the fireworks exploded, sending streams of light and smoke into the air as the Wolfpack players ran through two lines of cheerleaders. The crowd roared, and the band played the Wolfpack fight song. They were ready for some football!

Russell and Joe walked with the two N.C. State defensive captains to the middle of the field for the coin toss, while Travis stood beside Coach Clark looking on from the sidelines. Mary Katherine, Maria, and Sarah were in the grandstands sitting in the student section. Sarah grabbed Maria's hand to get her attention amidst the deafening crowd noise and yelled out.

"This place is rocking!"

Down on the field Florida State won the coin toss and deferred until the second half. Russell and Joe returned to the sideline and gathered with the other offensive players as the State return team took the field with Jordan Smith back deep to receive the kick, standing on the State five-yard line. The crowd was on its feet as the Seminole kicker approached the ball and booted a high end over end kick, that Jordan fielded on the two-yard line. Jordan ran the ball back up the middle of the field to the twenty-yard line, where he saw a running lane open up to his right. Jordan quickly darted between two Wolfpack blockers and ran down the sideline in front of the State bench. Suddenly there was only one Florida State defender between Jordan and the end zone. Jordan then stiff-armed the would-be FSU tackler as he went ninety-eight yards for a touchdown, and the Carter-Finley crowd went nuts!

After the extra point the Wolfpack defense came on with their "ears pinned back" as they attacked the FSU offense and quickly forced a punt. The Wolfpack offense took possession on the State twenty-nine yard line. Russell and the Pack broke the huddle with Russell in the shotgun. Russell from there began to quickly fire passes as he led the Wolfpack to four first downs. Then on second and six from the FSU thirty-one yard line Joe got a step behind one of the Seminole defensive backs and Russell lofted a pass down the right sideline that Joe caught just inside the pylon for a touchdown extending State's lead to 14-0. Later in the first half the Seminoles scored their first touchdown from seven yards out to make the score 14-7. Then with just seven seconds to go in the half FSU added a thirty-six yard field goal cutting the State lead to 14-10 at halftime.

During halftime Sarah, Mary Katherine and Maria met the Simpsons, the Outlands and the Rawlings underneath the grandstand, where they introduced Maria to Kathy and Ed, and Russell Sr. and Kim. It didn't take long before Russ was telling Maria all about his rose garden as Kim and Kathy rolled their eyes while Russ and Ed smiled at Maria like little boys in a candy store. Meanwhile in the locker room the Wolfpack coaches were exhorting on the Wolfpack players on both sides of the football. They all knew that this was anybody's ball game, and State needed to stay focused on offense and defense if they were going to come out with a victory.

When the teams came back on the field, Florida State took the second half kickoff and proceeded to march down the field, scoring a touchdown that gave the Seminoles their first lead, 17-14. On their next possession Russell and the Wolfpack offense behind Russell's strong right arm took the ball eighty-yards down field, and on third and goal on the FSU one-yard line Russell scored on a quarterback sneak, as the Pack regained the lead 21-17. At that point the defenses on both sides began to dig in their heels, and the third quarter ended with the score still State 21, FSU 17. After three quarters Russell was 20 of 26 passing for 273 yards. When the fourth quarter began Florida State had the ball third and twelve on its own twenty-six yard line. The FSU quarterback dropped back to pass, but was flushed out of the pocket. When the FSU pass protection broke down, the quarterback took off down the State sideline where he was eventually run out of bounds on the N.C. State forty-seven. After the FSU quarterback had clearly stepped out of bounds he was drilled from behind by an over-zealous defender, and knocked into the State bench, drawing a 15-yard penalty for unsportsmanlike conduct, taking the ball all the way down to the State thirty-two yard line. Then on first and ten, the Seminole quarterback hooked up with his tight end on a pass play over the middle of the field for a touchdown: FSU 24, N.C. State 21. State received the kickoff and ran the ball back to its twenty-four yard line. The Pack then proceeded to pick up two first downs. On second and four from the FSU forty-six, Russell hit Jordan on a crossing route. Jordan then broke two tackles as he galloped into the end zone. But the State celebration would be short-lived as an offensive holding penalty brought the play back, taking the go-ahead touchdown off the scoreboard. At that point the State drive stalled, and the Pack was forced to punt, and Florida State took over first and ten on its own thirteen-yard line with 9:42 to play. FSU then turned the ball over to their running game, and behind the Seminoles' mammoth offensive line, they started on an eleven play drive that ran 6:32 off the game clock before facing third and nine on the Wolfpack twenty-one. The Seminoles broke the huddle and lined up in an I-formation then the FSU tailback went into motion toward the FSU bench. When the ball was snapped the tailback broke down the sideline as the FSU quarterback lofted a pass toward the back corner of the end zone. As the ball came down the FSU tailback and two N.C. State defenders leaped into the air. The ball was batted around before being hauled in by one of the State defenders for an interception. Stopping the FSU drive, and giving the Pack first and ten on the State twenty-yard line, with just 2:40 to play.

Coach Clark and Russell quickly discussed the situation as the Pack offense prepared to take the field.

"Russell, we've got two time-outs, we have got to reach the thirty-two yard line to have a legitimate attempt at a field goal. Work the ball down the sidelines, and stay in the shotgun. Use our no huddle offense, we'll signal the plays in from the sidelines."

Russell and the Pack offense lined up on the ball and Russell immediately began throwing five-to ten-yard passes as the Pack moved the ball down field. After picking up four first downs, while using none of its time outs, the Pack had a third and two on the FSU twenty-four, with only :19 to play. Coach Clark signaled for Russell to call time out. Coach Clark removed his headset as he walked out onto the field to meet Russell, and discuss the play call.

Coach Clark said, "This is some ball game ain't it!"

Russell, whose eyes were as wide as quarters agreed, "Yes sir, it's awesome!"

Coach Clark then put his hand on Russell's shoulder.

"I don't want to leave this up to a field goal and overtime, what ya' say we take a shot at the end zone?"

Russell smiled back; "Sounds good to me Coach."

"That's my boy! Alright; send Joe in motion right, Z-fade to the back pylon, and Russell, take your shot if it's there, and Play to Win."

"Yes sir Coach."

When Russell reached the huddle he knelt on one knee in the middle of his offensive players.

"Let's don't depend on the field goal team, let's end this thing right here! Z-formation, motion right, fade to the pylon, on two. Let's get this done right now! Men, together on three, one, two, three; Play to Win!"

The Pack broke the huddle with Russell lined up in the shotgun and Joe split out in a slot on his left. Russell then signaled Joe in motion to the right. As Joe passed the end of the line of scrimmage the ball was snapped. Joe broke straight down field until he reached the ten-yard line, then he cut toward the back corner of the end zone. When Joe cut toward the pylon, Russell floated a soft spiral toward the corner of the end zone. Joe and the FSU defensive back raced stride for stride toward the football. Then at the last possible second, Joe leaped into the air, and wrestled the ball away from the Seminole defensive back and into his arms for the go-ahead touchdown. Sending shockwaves through the 65,000 N.C. State fans! The touchdown gave State the victory, 28-24.

What a great way to start the weekend!

MOVE OVER WESLEY

It was Friday morning, a little past 10 when Travis met Jim and Mr. Ham for the first time to discuss the concept behind what was now becoming the "Play 2 Win-Live 2 Serve" movement. Over the past seven weeks since their previous meeting in New York at the U.S. Open, the "Play 2 Win-Live 2 Serve" message, through the inspiration of the Lord had taken on a life of its own. While the kids were busy playing tennis, football, and going to school, the simple seed that began as a slogan on a T-shirt for the men's tennis team had become a powerful message to witness the gospel, a message that was helping Christians young and old to witness their faith in Jesus.

The tennis team had a 3 p.m. match in Durham, so Travis and Jim met with Mr. Ham at the N.C. State Athletic Center to talk about how all this had begun. When the boys met with Mr. Ham, he had a series of questions he wanted to discuss with Jim and he wanted to also get Travis' input on the topics. Mr. Ham's first question was for Jim.

"What was your motivation to make the shirts in the first place?"

"I wanted to do something for the guys on the team who committed to stay in Raleigh for the summer. These guys are like family to me, it is so different now than it was two years ago. Before Coach Outland got here our tennis team was very different. Not just in wins and losses, but in the attitude, the unity of the team. We had a good team and a good coach and players, but it was different."

"How so Jim, can you be a little more specific?"

"At practice we worked hard, but the practices were not as focused. We did not work on technique and learning the game the way we do now. Coach Outland spends more time teaching tennis. The instruction he gives us during our practice matches, especially the doubles, has drawn the team closer together. As the only senior on the team, I wanted to do something for Coach Outland and the other players, so that's why I made the shirts."

"Why the Christian theme for the shirts? After all, this is a college tennis team, not a Bible study group, so why all the emphasis on faith?"

"Because this team is about more than just tennis. Over the course of the last year all of our team began to attend Bible study together."

"The Monday night Bible study on campus?"

"Yes sir. Travis and I both went the year before however we really didn't know each other at the time. But over the past year, as we became friends and doubles partners, we often spoke about Bible study at practice. The other guys became interested in the class and before long, we were all going."

"So Jim, you made the shirts for the tennis team, as a way to say thank you, but also because you're a senior, I suppose to lead by example?"

"Yes sir."

"Why do you think leadership is so important, and Jim why do you personally feel the need to be a leader on this team?"

"Leadership is critical to success in any situation. Like I was saying about Coach Outland, he leads by example. He is calm and confident. He is very open about his faith. We all have great respect for him on and off the court. I just believe we should all do our part. The T-shirts were a simple gesture. I love being a part of this team. I just wanted to let the players and coaches know how much this all means to me."

"Jim, when did you make the decision to accept Christ as your Lord and Savior, and how has your faith in God grown since you came to school at N.C. State?"

"I grew up going to church with my family. There was not a special moment for me when Jesus suddenly became real. For me, my faith has grown over a long period of time. When I came to school at N.C. State I was already a Christian, but the weekly Bible study has taught me so much. It was the first time I studied and discussed the Bible in detail. Also, being a part of a study group with kids my own age has made the class fun and made the Bible more real to me. That knowledge has given me more confidence to begin a conversation about Jesus."

"How so?"

"Sometimes as a college kid or teenager you can be made to feel uncomfortable about your faith, about being a Christian. The news media and society in general can portray being a Christian as odd, or even silly. But being in this Bible study has shown me that there are lots of Christians out there. Kids just like me, that want to learn more about the Bible. Kids who want to come to know Jesus on a personal level but they don't know where to begin. The weekly Bible study was that beginning place for me. I wish every kid had an opportunity to be a part of a program like we have here at N.C. State. The information I have learned by studying the four gospels and the other Biblical passages taught me the message Jesus preached. Now that I know more about Him, I want to share what I have learned with others, so hopefully they will want to then learn more themselves."

"Last year you guys had an excellent season. You made it to the NCAA tournament and lost to the eventual national champion, UCLA. Jim, you missed almost half the season and the ACC and NCAA tournament when you contracted mono, how did that experience affect you? Watching your team play without you?"

"Not being able to play was very disappointing. Particularly when we lost. When you're a part of the team, it's hard to watch your teammates out there competing and you can't help them."

"You guys have had a super fall season so far, that was a huge win over Georgia. What do you think this team is capable of?"

"We have a talented team. If we stay healthy, I believe we can play with anybody."

"Is this a championship team?"

"This team has the talent to win a championship. We just have to go out there everyday, work hard, and see where it takes us."

Then Mr. Ham had a few questions for Travis.

"Travis, what did you think when Jim first showed you the T-shirt, and he explained the slogan and how the shirts could be used as a witnessing tool?"

"I was excited about the shirts, as Jim said they were a gift so I was thankful Jim cared enough to make them. All the guys were excited. Jim is just a very thoughtful person. Then later that same day after practice Jim and I went to the Char-Grill to get some lunch. While we were there in line waiting for our food a man who was there with his two sons came up to us and asked what the '2' stood for? When I listened to Jim explain the symbolism of the '2,' the two lives of the believer and the two choices we have, to accept Jesus or reject Him, it just sounded so simple, so natural. Then when the man asked Jim if he could get some shirts like that for his little league team. I knew right then it was something special."

"Travis, the night you played against Tom Williams on center court at the Open, when you took off your jacket and I saw the shirt you were wearing, I got goose bumps just watching. What was it like to wear that shirt, that night?"

"So many things that night seemed surreal. Even now I have trouble sometimes believing it really happened. It was great. It was scary. It is very humbling to think about it."

"How was it scary?"

"To be blessed to have an opportunity to play tennis at that level, especially after the accident. It seems to good to be true. Sometimes I have to pinch myself to make sure I'm not dreaming. Then to be blessed to wear that shirt with the Christian symbol on it, the American flag, the words "Play 2 Win-Live 2 Serve." I wonder, why me? Lord, why have you chosen to bless me this way? I want to honor God, to glorify Jesus. It's scary sometimes because I want so much to be a good disciple for Jesus. I do not want to do anything that does not bring glory to God."

"Last question, where do you want to see this go? What are your hopes for this from here on?"

"I want to see Jesus glorified," Jim replied. "I hope what has happened with this simple slogan will encourage other Christians to do something themselves. This didn't start out as a big idea. But who knows how far it may go. I want people to understand this isn't something we're doing, this is something God is doing, and Jesus is the one who is to be praised."

"Travis what about you, what do you think will happen with this message?"

"I see God using these shirts as a way to draw people to Jesus. I also see more clearly now how we as student athletes have a platform through playing sports to reach people, especially young people. When you play sports- high school, college, professional, people want to hear what you have to say. I hope Christian athletes will be motivated by the way God is moving through these shirts. Hopefully other kids will want to become involved, to witness their faith when the opportunity presents itself. Honestly, I have no idea where this is going, but I am anxious to find out."

It was 3 p.m. sharp when the Wolfpack men took the courts at the tennis center on the campus of Duke University. It was a mild afternoon, with overcast skies and just a hint of breeze. The conditions were perfect for tennis. Texas Tech's team was made up primarily of foreign players. As is the case with many of the top college tennis programs, the Red Raiders lineup had a distinctly international flavor. The number one singles player for Texas Tech was Aaron Topkov. Topkov was a junior, he was originally from Poland, but he had spent the four years before entering Texas Tech at a private school in Dallas, designed for junior tennis prodigies who aspire to play professional tennis. Topkov had a solid all-court game. He made it to the semifinals of the previous years NCAA singles championship. So his match today against Travis was the feature match-up, and there was a huge crowd on hand to see the action.

Also in the crowd today were the Simpsons, Rita, Sarah, Mary Katherine, Maria and Russell. Russell, who was grinning from ear to ear sat close by Maria's side, more than willing to perform his duties as her escort for the weekend. Once the girls got situated, it didn't take long for the tennis fans in attendance to begin approaching Mary Katherine and Maria for their autographs. Russell, who was used to being the center of attention was more than willing to watch Maria and Mary Katherine attract the bulk of the limelight from the fans. After all, he was still the boy getting to sit next to Maria.

When the matches began the N.C. State men jumped out to an early lead in the three doubles matches. Then with continued solid play in all the matches they cruised to convincing wins in the number one and two doubles, taking a 1-0 lead into the singles. After the doubles concluded the two teams took a twenty-minute intermission before beginning the singles matches. The break gave Travis a chance to visit with Mary Katherine.

"Hey, you guys played great," Mary Katherine said. "You and Jim have really come together in doubles. I believe that's the best I've ever seen the two of you play together."

"Thanks, we've worked hard this summer, and it's really paying off now. Tell me, how are things going off the court, up in the stands with Russell and Maria?"

Mary Katherine smiled.

"Maria is having a great time, she really likes Russell. We had a lot of fun at the game last night, and Russell is actually behaving himself. The boy can be a real gentleman when he wants to be."

"Russell has been talking about Maria non-stop since she got here, I tell ya' Mary Katherine, Russell has never acted like this over a girl before, not that I've seen anyway."

"Maria is a special girl. She's obviously beautiful, but she is just as lovely on the inside, and I'm telling you, she likes Russell a lot."

After their little chat, Mary Katherine went back to the stands. Travis then met with the rest of the team as the singles matches were about to begin. When Travis and Topkov took the court to warm up before the match Mary Katherine paid close attention to Travis' strokes and his footwork. This was the first time she had seen Travis play since the U.S. Open. Mary Katherine had an observant eye. She always watched the little things, the things Rudy had taught her over the years. Mary Katherine could see that Travis' star was on the rise. Since his performance at the Open, his confidence had risen to another level and so had his tennis. Travis moved across the court with such ease that he appeared to be gliding to the ball. Then in the blink of an eye his quick hands would send the tennis ball into the other court with power like Mary Katherine had never seen. Maria, who was also watching the warm up in-between her conversation with Russell, also noticed the improvement in Travis' game.

"Mary Katherine," Maria said. "Travis played very well in New York, but he seems different, more confident than before, and he looks to be hitting the ball harder now."

"I know, he hit it hard before, but now he seems more relaxed."

"Mary Katherine, I have a cousin who played professional baseball on the Cuban National team. He reminds me of Travis. His hands were so fast and he moved like a cat. He would play tennis with me sometimes when we were younger. He was not very good at tennis. He could not keep the ball in the court. But he could hit the ball so hard, it was amazing. He could just flick his wrist and the ball would explode off his racquet. It would go by me so fast I could barely see it."

Once the singles matches began, it quickly became apparent that Mary Katherine and Maria were correct. Travis had improved. So much so, that once the match started, it quickly ended. Travis' serve was all but untouchable and his ground strokes, volleys, and finesse game were just as exceptional. As Travis pounded Topkov to the tune of a 6-1, 6-0 win. Travis left little doubt that in the world of college tennis, he was at the top of the class. Meanwhile the rest of the Wolfpack men were also having their way in the other matches as the team closed out Texas Tech 4-1.

Later that night Travis and Russell took Mary Katherine and Maria out to dinner and a movie. There was an obvious chemistry developing between Russell and Maria. Russell, who was captivated by Maria from the moment he saw her was going above and beyond in performing his duties as Maria's escort. He was polite, charming, extremely thoughtful, and unusually quiet, which was very surprising to Travis. While waiting for a table at the restaurant, the girls went to the ladies' room. While they were gone Travis broached the subject of Russell's sudden interest in listening, rather than speaking.

"Russell, man you haven't said two words all night. I've never seen you this quiet before, what gives?"

"Travis, you know sometimes I can get excited and stick my foot in my mouth."

Travis rolled his eyes then he smiled at Russell.

"Really, I've never noticed."

"Ha, ha, you know how I can be when I get to talking too much. It's going great with Maria, so I don't want to say something and mess it up. Besides, she and Mary Katherine are talking enough for all four of us."

"You've got a point there, but at some point you've got to say something to her."

"Not yet. I'm going to just listen for a while. Then once I know she wants to see me some more, I'll start talking. You know Travis, Proverbs says, '*Even a fool appears to be wise, when he is silent!*' And hey, are they really interested in what we think anyway?"

"Another good point. Mary Katherine and I get along great as long as I agree with her, but when I don't, it's not pretty."

"Travis, have you ever noticed how when our mothers talk, our fathers just say, 'Uh huh,' or 'yep,' maybe 'O.K. Honey, whatever you say.' They're not really listening to them at all and they almost never say anything to our moms first. My dad sometimes will pretend he can't even hear mom. Boy, that really gets her fired up."

"My dad told me unless it was something life threatening, or morally incomprehensible to just let Mary Katherine do whatever she wanted. Dad told me Mom hasn't changed her mind ten times in twenty-five years to go along with him when Mom thinks she's right."

"So he doesn't say anything if he can help it, does he?"

"No, he doesn't."

"There you go, you know those 'old guys' are smart. I'm not chancing it. I'll talk to you all you want. Otherwise, I'm just going to tell Maria how beautiful she looks, and I want to see you again. Other than that it's, Uh, huh, and yes ma'am for me."

The rest of the night Russell was true to his word. He was charming and extremely quiet. By the end of the night, Maria was very impressed, and so was Mary Katherine. As they were walking out of the restaurant, Mary Katherine whispered in Travis' ear.

"There's something different about Russell."

Travis, choosing his words wisely replied.

"Really, I haven't noticed."

"I'm not sure what it is, but it's a big improvement."

"Uh, huh."

"You know, he hasn't said anything in two days that wasn't just right to Maria."

"Uh, huh."

"That's just not like Russell, normally he's always embarrassing me."

"Uh, huh."

"I really like this new Russell, how about you?"

"Honey, whatever makes you happy."

On Saturday when Travis and the rest of the Wolfpack team arrived at the Duke Tennis Center to warm up for their match against Notre Dame, there was already a large crowd of spectators there to observe the warm-up. There had been excellent news coverage of the previous day's matches, including an article in the morning paper highlighting the Saturday matches and also the Sunday match to be played between Duke and State. The Simpsons along with Jim's parents, Jim and Rhonda Rose, and the parents of several other players had come to Raleigh for the weekend to see the team play. Rudy and Rita had invited the players and their dates and families over to their house for a cookout Saturday night. It was something the players and their families had looked forward to since school had started in the fall. Russell's parents had also decided to stay in Raleigh for the weekend. Since they had come up for the game on Thursday night, they decided to stay over and visit with Kathy and Ed and the other tennis families. Friday morning before State had played Texas Tech, Ed, Russell, Big Russ and Mary Katherine's brother Joe, had played golf at the Duke University golf course. Ed and Big Russ had won a couple of bucks off of Russell and Joe, so the "Old Guys" were really rubbing it in before the tennis match started.

"Russell, did you boys tell Mary Katherine and Maria how you guys lost to a couple of senior citizens yesterday?" Big Russ asked.

"No. Besides, we'd have beat you two to death if you hadn't played from the ladies' tees!"

"Those are the senior tees," Ed replied, "and that's no way to talk to your elders."

Joe then spoke up.

"You two should be ashamed of yourselves, both of you hit the ball just as far as we do. Travis told me you were a two handicap Mr. Simpson, and Mr. Rawlings, you made every putt you stood over!"

Big Russ fired back.

"Don't think we feel sorry for you guys. We're old! Just think about it, you guys go to school and play ball all day. Russell Jr., he's going out with a supermodel, while me and Ed are just trying to stay out of the dog house."

"That's it," Ed added. "We've paid to raise you kids; we've earned a few privileges. But, I tell you what Russell, you let me take Maria out tonight and I'll give up the senior tees. What ya' say?"

"Nope, can't do it. Being Maria's date for the weekend is a tough job, but I believe in finishing what I start, so I'm sticking with her. You can just cuddle up with Wesley if you have to."

It wasn't long before the players for State and Notre Dame had finished their warm-ups, and the two teams took the court for doubles. The Fighting Irish had an excellent team and one of their strong points was their doubles. From the outset the doubles matches were all closely contested, with lead changes taking place in every match. Rudy had always coached aggressive doubles play. He understood the necessity to win the doubles point in college tennis, but the Irish were no pushovers. As the doubles matches progressed the Garcias pulled ahead on the number one court, and took the first win of the match. Then the Irish took the win at number three, leaving the doubles point to be decided by Travis and Jim's match. Travis and Jim were playing well, but they just could not get the cushion they needed to control the match. The games went back and forth with long rallies on every point. Finally, Travis and Jim broke the Irish's serve to take a one-game lead. Then with Travis serving, they closed out the match giving State the doubles point. Once the doubles point was decided, the Pack came out firing on all cylinders in singles, as they swept the Irish 4-0.

Once the match was over, Travis, Ed, Kathy and Sarah sat down for a conversation with Mr. Ham.

"Congratulations Travis, you guys are really coming together."

"Yes sir, this is a great bunch of guys."

Mr. Ham then began to discuss the information he needed for the article with the Simpsons.

"Kathy and Ed, I know you must be very proud of Travis."

"We are so proud of him," Kathy said. "He's a wonderful son."

"I know Travis' injury was a blow not just for Travis, but for the whole family. How was it for you two as parents seeing something like that happen to Travis?"

"It was shocking," Kathy replied. "You know, that was the first injury other than simple bumps and bruises Travis ever had. While he was lying there on the ground I was numb all over. It was just a nightmare."

"Ed, what was going through your mind?"

"When it first happened I was actually just thinking about getting him to the hospital," Ed replied. "I could tell he was hurt, but until I got down on the field and saw his hand up close, I had no idea it was that severe of an injury."

Mr. Ham then asked Sarah.

"Sarah, you were at the game that day, how did seeing that happen to Travis affect you?"

"I had seen Travis get hit by pitches before," Sarah said. "I had seen him get tackled hard in football games. At first, I thought he would just bounce back up like before, but when I realized what was wrong and the doctors told us he would never play football or baseball again. I just couldn't believe it. I know how much he loved to play; his future was set. I was really afraid for him. I wondered how would he recover from that kind of disappointment?"

"Ed, who told Travis he would never be able to play baseball again?"

"Dr. Hamilton, at Wake Med."

"What did you do as a family to get through this?" Mr. Ham asked.

"We prayed," Ed replied. "We just tried to hold onto each other. It was the toughest pill I've ever had to swallow. I wanted so much to help Travis, but it was out of my control."

"Kathy, how did you cope? What kind of emotions, questions did you have as Travis began his recovery?"

"Why God? How could You let this happen to my Son? What good could come from this? Day after day I watched him hurt. Not just physically, but mentally too. We are Christians. We all have accepted Jesus. As a mother who had raised our children to glorify the Lord, I just could not see God's plan being accomplished by Travis getting hurt."

"After Travis' injury," Mr. Ham asked, "could you ever in your wildest dreams have imagined you would be here today watching Travis playing tennis?"

"No, not in a million years," Kathy said. "Looking back at it now, I can see all the ways God has moved in Travis' life. Bringing new and wonderful things into all our lives. I have seen Travis grow so much as he has battled to recover. I can't tell you how proud I am of him."

"Ed, what about you, what were some moments that stand out in your mind? Moments that you now can see God was working, using all this apparent tragedy for good?"

"When Travis first met Stephanie Clauson and they discussed Jesus and trusting in Him. Then when Travis told me he and Russell were going to Bible study, and Travis would tell me all he was learning about the four gospels. I began to see his smile come back. But the biggest thing was the night he told me he met this girl who played tennis at State. Then he saw her again at Bible study, and the next day they were going to play tennis together. Somehow when he told me that, I knew this girl would be important to him. So I drove up to Raleigh the next day to watch them play. Then after they finished playing, when I listened to Travis talk about Mary Katherine, I could see his eyes sparkle. He was really excited again. It was the first time I'd seen him that happy since the accident."

Kathy then popped Ed in the shoulder.

"Hey Ed, you never told me you went to Raleigh that day."

"Yes, I did."

"No, you didn't!"

Travis just sat there; he wasn't getting involved in that. Travis remembered Ed had snuck up to Raleigh to get a Charburger that day and watch the tennis, so Travis did what Russell was doing, he stayed quiet. Ed then tried to change the subject.

"Sarah, when did you notice the improvement in Travis?"

Kathy quickly jumped in to let Ed know he had been caught.

"Ed, I thought Mr. Ham was the one asking the questions? Just for the record, I know you're trying to change the subject to get yourself out of trouble."

Ed mumbled under his breath.

"*Move over Wesley.*"

"What did you say Ed?"

"Whatever makes you happy, Honey."

Travis just smiled. He knew Ed needed more than the five magic words this time.

WHO COULD SAY

"Aunt Mute and Aunt Annie, I'm so glad you two decided to come up today to watch us play, and I'm especially glad you all decided to stay for the cookout tonight."

"Awe Travis," Aunt Mute said, "We wouldn't have missed it for the world, would we E.R.?"

"No way," Uncle E.R. replied. "Travis we've had a great time today. Mute and Annie went shopping over at the Crabtree Mall, and me and your Uncle Ernie have been knocking around taking it easy."

"Travis, where is that Mary Katherine," Mute asked. "She sure is a pretty girl, and smart, I tell you what, there ain't "no flies" on that girl. I don't think she'll put up with no junk will she?"

"No, Aunt Mute, that's for certain, she likes to have her way alright."

"Your Daddy told us," Mute said, "Mary Katherine told you, she wanted you to learn how to 'cook fish' at the restaurant! Ain't that the funniest thing Annie?"

"I'm glad to hear somebody can make that boy behave," Annie replied. "I tried to straighten you out when you were little Travis, and I've got the scars on my knees to prove it! You would fuss and kick at me with your cowboy boots when you couldn't have your way. We all just spoiled you rotten, but I don't think that's going to work with Mary Katherine, do you Mute?"

"No way! I bet that Mary Katherine has some cowgirl boots of her own! I tell you Travis; she's a pistol. She's going to snap you into shape Boy; and I love it!"

About that time Ed walked over.

"What are you doing Aunt Mute, I know you're up to something?"

"Ed, you always ask me 'What am I up to?' What makes you think I'm the one causing the trouble? Why not E.R., Ernie or Annie?"

"Because you are always the one who's up to something. Aunt Annie told me you were the one always getting her in trouble for something when ya'll were growing up, isn't that right Aunt Annie?"

"Yes Lord!" Annie replied. "Mute is always starting something. Talking, she is talking a mile a minute. There ain't no 'mute button' on Mute! But we love each other, that's for sure."

Travis had a wonderful close family. His Grandfather Travis had four sisters, and they remained very close after his death. Seeing his great aunts helped Travis stay connected to the memory of the grandfather who was his namesake, but he had never met.

Rudy and Rita had hosted the parents of the players for most of the afternoon once the team had finished the match against Notre Dame and returned to Raleigh. Rita, who possessed a love of gardening and a very capable green thumb had transformed her back yard into an outdoor restaurant. Rita had planted confederate jasmines all along the wooden privacy fence that surrounded the back yard. She also loved fragrant teacup pink roses, gardenias and camellias. The bushes were spread across the landscape to add fragrance and beauty to the yard. Meanwhile, Rudy had fired up the charcoal, and the smell of barbecue shrimp and chicken wings filtered through the air as the dinner guests began to assemble around 6:30. There were tiki torches lit, tables set up with salads, fruit trays, baked beans, boiled potatoes and coleslaw. Freshly baked lemon and chocolate pound cakes, pecan pies, lemonade and sweet tea were also provided. It was a Southern buffet, and all in attendance were in a festive mood, ready to enjoy the food and fellowship.

Mr. Ham was also a guest at the party and as he mingled amongst the crowd he could see the special bond that existed between the tennis players and their families. There was a bond there that was unlike anything he had seen before while covering other sports teams. There was more than just a shared love of tennis; there was also a love of the Lord that Mr. Ham could feel as he moved throughout the crowd. Mr. Ham began to recall all the different athletes he had met over the years who off the record had expressed their beliefs in God. He began to wonder about all the other families he had interviewed who had openly witnessed their faith in Jesus Christ. While he walked around that night he remembered, and made a mental checklist, of the tremendous number of successful coaches, administrators, sports agents and sports executives who openly prayed and expressed their commitment to Jesus. He began to wonder, "Why he had never noticed the connection before?"- the obvious relationship between these different people from across the country and around the world.

It was as though he had been brought to this place, at this time, to tell this story. He thought about all the young people in America and in the many other nations around the world where he had covered sports. Mr. Ham knew the powerful influence of the media. For some time now he had been concerned about the growing negativity of the news, and programming that was shown on television, on the Internet and in the print media. He realized that the vast majority of people he had met and seen in his travels were good people who loved their families, who did the best they could every day. Mr. Ham began to see the importance, the power to facilitate change, by spreading that message. How important it was for people to see, to realize that we all have more in common than we might think.

The simplicity of the message on the T-shirt, "Play 2 Win-Live 2 Serve." The simple symbol of the fish, the Ichthys symbol used by the early Christian church. "Ichthys" is an acrostic word, a combination of Greek letters. A word made up of the first letters of a combination of words, the words "Jesus Christ, God's Son, Savior." How the early believers when meeting another person, someone they did not know to also be a follower of Jesus, they would draw one half of the fish symbol, often times on the ground. Then, if the other person also followed Jesus, they would complete the other half of the fish symbol, to identify themselves as followers of Christ.

Now today, these kids on a college tennis team had placed this simple symbol on a shirt, openly declaring themselves as followers of Jesus. Publicly professing what they believed, without ever saying a word. Now God was using this ancient symbol, first used two thousand years ago to protect the identity of the early church to save them from persecution, to now lead people to Jesus. That today, instead of writing one half of this symbol in secrecy to protect their identities, these Christians were displaying the Lord's symbol on their chests, above their hearts, to openly display their belief in Jesus. And now others who shared their beliefs were reaching out to them as well, who could say how far it might go. While Mr. Ham was making his observations, and mingling throughout the crowd, there were lots of conversations going on around the back yard.

Travis, Jim and Russell were talking college football. While Mary Katherine, Maria, Sarah and Jim's girlfriend Joanna, were talking fashion; particularly wedding fashion. Sarah, whose bubbly personality made her a crowd favorite at parties, was giving Mary Katherine her two cents worth on the topic of bridesmaids' dresses and shoes.

"Now Mary Katherine, you know I love clothes, my Dad will tell you, 'I am a professional' when it comes to shopping. When you go picking out your bridesmaids' dresses you need something stylish, yet affordable. Most of us girls have to pay for our own clothes, we don't get paid to wear clothes the way you supermodels do. We have to work for a living."

Joanna chimed in then.

"That's right. We want you to pick out something we can wear again, not just a one shot deal."

"That's it," Sarah concluded.

Maria then spoke up.

"One of the clothing companies I do some modeling for told me if I am ever in a wedding or get married myself, they would like to do a photo shoot after the wedding. Who knows, they might give us the clothes Mary Katherine if you let them photograph the dresses."

"Now hold on!" Sarah announced. "That's a different story. Free designer clothes! Maria girlfriend, I knew I liked you the moment I laid eyes on you."

From there the crowd of young girls began to grow as they started making plans. They were laughing and giggling, they had a big time. Meanwhile, the boys began to congregate around the grill with the dads eating up the chicken wings and shrimp as it came hot off the grill. The moms began to move toward the lounge chairs and stretch out on the patio with chocolate pound cake and lemonade in hand. The wives began to discuss the common tendencies shared by their husbands. Kim spoke up first and got the conversation rolling.

"Rita, this is a beautiful yard."

"Thank you Kim."

"Has Big Russell offered to prune or plant anything for you," Rita asked. "I'm telling you the man loves to play in the dirt like a little kid."

"As a matter of fact," Rita replied. "He gave me some suggestions of how to fertilize my rose buses so they would produce more blooms. Mary Katherine told me Russ cut fresh flowers for her room every day when she was in Charleston."

"Yeah," Kim said, "that Russ is a charmer. Ya'll should have heard him telling Maria about his rose garden. Those men still think they're twenty-years old."

Kathy chimed in.

"Ed and Russ are two peas in a pod. Ed Simpson can ruin a pair of pants or a shirt working in the yard before you know it. That man can tear a hole in a shirt in a minute. I need to hose him down sometimes before he's fittin' to come inside. Then he'll leave his clothes and shoes all over the place. Don't ever pick up after himself!"

Those comments received a course of "uh huh's" and a rousing "you got that right girl!" from the other wives.

Meanwhile, over at the grill, the dads were holding a discussion of their own. Russ Sr. was the first to bring up the topic of women; and then it was on.

"Kim was on me all day reminding me to be on time tonight. Then, I sat on the bed in the hotel room for thirty minutes while she changed clothes four times."

"Tell me about it," Ed replied. "Kathy will get dressed and ask me what I think? Man, there ain't no way I'm going to say I don't like what she's wearing! But she'll walk up to me and say, 'You're not going to wear that are you?' I ain't saying nothing if I can help it."

"That's it!" Russ agreed. "What ain't discussed, ain't argued about."

"You got that right!" Rudy added. "With Rita and Mary Katherine, as long as they are happy, I'm happy. You young guys will be wise to remember that. If Momma ain't happy, nobody is happy. So when Momma ain't happy, you better go cut the grass, or hit some golf balls or something."

"Look boys," Ed continued, as the "old guys" instructed the younger boys, "it's like this, men and women are like night and day. You can't have one without the other. If a woman gets her mind set on something the best thing to do is just let her go on and do it, that is unless it's life threatening!"

"Yeah!" Russ agreed. "You got to draw the line when it's life threatening."

"But like I was saying," Ed continued, "otherwise, let her do whatever she wants, and you go do something else until she calms down."

"That's why the Lord invented tennis, golf, television and ball games. So we will have something to do when they get fired up at us!" Rudy advised.

"That's it!" Russ stated. "Now boys, a wife don't think a husband knows how to do anything without her telling him how to do it. When Kim gets her mind made up, I go to digging or planting. When I was growing up I hated to do yard work, but since I got married that rose garden has got me out of a lot of jams, let me tell you."

"Yep boys," Ed agreed. "Every man needs an ace in the hole, somewhere to go and hang out when it gets too hot in the house. Now we all know we wouldn't take anything for the women in our lives, so if you know what to do when they start after you, things will go a lot easier for you."

"Now boys," Rudy instructed. "Just say you're sorry as quick as you can whether you know what you did wrong or not. Then get out of the line of fire. Cause whether we want to admit it or not, we wouldn't take anything in the world for those girls."

"That's it," Ed said. "It's as simple as that."

By now the "young single girls" had made their way over to the pecan pie and lounge chairs, and Aunt Mute and Aunt Annie were explaining young men and husbands to Sarah, Maria, Mary Katherine and the rest of the girls.

"Mary Katherine," Mute said. " I believe you got Travis Simpson wrapped around your little finger. Don't you agree Annie?"

"Yes ma'am I do!" Annie replied. "Mary Katherine, if you ever have a little boy, whatever you do, don't buy him any cowboy boots."

"Lord have mercy," Mute agreed, "those Simpsons are a kicking bunch. Now Sarah, are you going to settle down, or play the field for a while?"

"I don't know Aunt Mute," Sarah stated. "You know there are a lot of fish in the sea; I think I might just take my time."

Rita jumped in.

"Don't rush it girls, a husband is a whole lot of responsibility. One grown man is harder to look after than three little boys."

"Boy, ain't that the truth," Kathy agreed. "You can teach a little boy something, or at least send them to their rooms. But a husband, let me tell ya,' once they get their minds made up there ain't no changing it."

"You got that right," Kim said, "and I tell you, they think we can't do anything without them telling us how to do something!"

Rhonda jumped in then.

"Big Jim will ask me what I think, but I try not to say anything. No way I want to disagree with him. Boy that gets him fired up."

"That's it," Kathy said. "When that happens the best thing to do is just leave them alone. Just get out of the way."

"That's why the Lord invented lounge chairs, swimming pools, shopping malls, and aerobic classes," Rita concluded.

"That's it," Kim agreed.

"Now girls," Kathy summarized, "we wouldn't take anything for those men. But when they get in one of their 'moods' you just need to know how to handle them. Always remember, when it seems like you can't live with them, it's still a lot better than trying to live without them!"

Later that night once the party had wound down and Travis and Russell had gotten back to the dorm room, Travis decided to go for a walk. He grabbed his tennis ball and baseball cap and strolled across campus and took his seat on the bleachers looking down on the tennis courts. As he sat there beneath the giant oak trees, he prayed. He thanked God for all of the blessings in his life. At the party that night, there had been three adult generations of his family there. Travis enjoyed talking with his great aunts. Even though there were two generations, and almost fifty years between them, Travis was amazed by what they had in common. They were as much fun to be around as any of the kids his age, and they loved him unconditionally. He also enjoyed being with Ed and the other dads. He thought about how similar Russell and Big Russ were. They talked the same way; they had so many of the same likes and dislikes. How all the dads had the same observations about their wives, the same way of coping with the obvious differences between men and women. How while the men were talking about the way the wives were always telling them how to do things, Mary Katherine had told him the women were sitting in the lounge chairs saying the exact same thing about the men. How if "men are from Mars, and women are from Venus," that Mars and Venus are really closer together than we realize. That nobody likes to be told what to do by somebody else. But at the same time everybody wants to help the people, the family they love. It's just sometimes we are all not sure exactly what to say or how to say it. That the most important thing to remember is that every person has his or her own opinion and we all need our own space sometimes. If we can all just not take ourselves so seriously, and do what Jesus said, "treat others the way we would want to be treated," and learn how to laugh at ourselves sometimes, we'd all get along a lot better.

Travis also thanked God for the adult leaders in his life- his great aunts, his parents, the parents of his friends, his coaches and his teachers. Now that Travis was becoming a grown man himself, he was beginning to see the value of experience. That just because something was new, did not make it better. That all the years of experience that these older adults had gave them a wealth of knowledge that Travis could use if he chose to. His Mom and Dad had taught him things all his life because they loved him. Tonight, as he mingled with Ed and the other fathers, he could see the dads were just like the sons; they were all still little boys. It's just the dads were a little older. That none of them were right all the time, because none of us are perfect. But Travis felt safe and secure when they were together, and the dads and sons needed each other more than they realized. He thought about how much Mary Katherine and Rita had in common, just like Kathy and Sarah, they were so much alike, sometimes they didn't get along because they were so similar. But tonight at the party when they were all together, the moms and dads, sons and dads, and the moms and daughters, Travis began to see that just like night and day, you couldn't have one without the other. That whether we are male or female, young or old, we are all part of God's creation. We are all God's children. And that God created all of us differently, with different imperfections, so that we would all need each other, and that was a good thing.

Meanwhile, as Travis sat there praying, Jesus sat close beside him listening. And though Travis could not see it, or feel it, Jesus had His hand on Travis' shoulder. That all those nights before when Travis had made this same walk, and sat on these same bleachers, that Jesus had always been there, every step of the way. So tonight as Travis sat there thinking, through

Travis' thoughts Jesus was teaching. Jesus was preparing Travis to teach God's message to God's other children, other children like himself.

ONE ON ONE

"Travis Simpson, how are you doing boy?"

"Jacob Hackney, I know you love seeing me today. I'm a sure thing for you."

"Come on now Travis, you're anything but a sure thing, and hey, I'm not the one who took a set off of Tom Williams at the U.S. Open."

"Maybe not Jacob, but we've been playing tennis together since we were ten-years old and I've never beaten you once. Not one time!"

"Come on Travis, we both know things are different now. Back when we were playing in the juniors you were playing baseball and football, while I was just playing tennis. That made a big difference back then, but things have changed. We had four close three-set matches last year, and whenever we played this summer it was always close."

"Close yes, me winning no! Jacob, you realize it's not good for my confidence for you to beat me over and over like that? Don't you think you should 'throw me a bone today?' Let me win just this once?"

"No Travis, I can't say that I do. Besides, you're going to beat me plenty before it's all said and done, but you're going to have to work for it."

"Jacob, changing the subject, have you seen Big John lately? I heard he has a good chance to make the Braves forty-man roster this spring."

"John talks to Dad pretty regularly. He hasn't been home to Burlington in a while. I suspect he'll be coming home soon since the professional baseball playoffs are over. I've heard the same thing you have, that the Braves are very high on John. Dad says if he doesn't start out next season in Atlanta with the Braves, he should make it up there sometime next year."

"Well when you talk to Big John," Travis continued, "tell him I was asking about him. Are your mom and dad coming today?"

"Yeah, they should be here anytime."

"My parents are coming too, so is Mary Katherine and Sarah, so take it easy on me. It's not nice to whip up on somebody in front of their family, especially their fiancée!"

"Travis, please, you should be ashamed of yourself poor mouthing like that."

"Alright Jacob, you play good today, I know you will."

"You too Travis, and tell Jim and the other guys good luck as well."

Travis and Jacob had known each other since the time the boys were in the junior ten-year olds. They had first met while playing junior tennis. Often times when the boys would play in junior tournaments together they and their parents would watch each other's matches. And the families would meet and go to lunch or dinner together when the kids were playing out of town. Jacob's father, John Hackney, was the head baseball coach at Burlington Williams High School. John and Ed Simpson had become good friends over the years as they followed the boys around the junior tennis circuit. John had called and visited with Ed several times following Travis' accident. Even though their sons had competed with one another over the years, the two fathers understood that their role as parents was to train sons, not develop tennis players. John and Ed both stressed integrity, fair play and hard work to their sons. They were not caught up in wins and losses, the way so many parents are today. They each taught their boys to play to win, but more importantly, they taught their children that doing the right thing, good sportsmanship, giving it your all, was what being a winner is really all about. So win or lose, Travis and Jacob loved to play tennis together. Now that Travis himself was also a "year round" tennis player, the matches between the boys were more competitive than ever. Today's match would be no exception.

Rudy gathered the team together after the warm-ups. The Wolfpack men had played some excellent tennis over the previous two days. Their pre-match warm-up had been crisp, so Rudy expected the boys to play well. He knew they would have to play their best if they were going to beat the Blue Devils.

"Fella's," Rudy said, "you guys look real sharp out there. We're going to have to play our best again today if we're going to beat Duke, so stay focused and go for your shots, and play to win! Now let's give thanks before we take the court."

Rudy then had the boys form a circle. The young men held hands while Rudy led them in prayer. They broke the huddle and headed out onto the courts, it was time to play doubles.

From the very beginning of the doubles, the tennis played by both teams was excellent. All twelve of the young men representing the two schools were also among the teams' top six singles players, so each player possessed very strong service games. As the doubles matches continued to develop it became clear that all three matches were a toss up. There were lead changes on every court, with each team protecting their service games. Duke drew first blood in the match as it won at number three, then Travis and Jim leveled the doubles as they won at number two. But in the end, Jacob and his partner, took the win on the number one court, beating the Garcia twins. It was only the second time the Garcias had lost a college doubles match. Giving the doubles point to Duke.

During the doubles matches, the capacity crowd on hand became more and more drawn to the action by the well-played, and enthusiastic tennis on both sides of the net. Then, after the brief intermission before the singles matches began, Rudy called the team together.

"Guys, we played some great tennis in those doubles matches. Every one of those matches could have gone either way. Let's just keep our chins up and stay at it. This thing is a long way from over. Now let's go out there and win this thing! On three, one, two, three, Play 2 Win-Live 2 Serve!" Then the team took to the court.

One of the neat things about playing college tennis is that while you are playing tennis, unlike most sports, the matches are one on one. While you are playing for a team score, you play individual matches. During the singles match you are concentrating only on your opponent. You study their tendencies, their strengths and weaknesses. There are no protective pads or equipment to cover your opponent's face, so you watch their facial expressions, for signs of confidence, or signs of fear. Over the years, Travis and Jacob had played countless times. Jacob was a very bright young man and he did an excellent job of evaluating his opponent's strengths and weaknesses. He was a two-time first team All-American, so he had all the physical skills to play with anybody. Jacob also was a lefthander, so his spin moved the ball inside on his right-handed opponents. His style of play gave Travis trouble. The bottom line was, Jacob had "Travis' number." Jacob just seemed to be able to win the big points when he needed to against Travis.

When the singles matches began, the intensity level on the courts and in the large crowd on hand was at a fever pitch. Up and down the line the points were all hotly contested. In Travis' match he and Jacob each held serve throughout the first set until the game score reached six games a piece. The two boys then played a tiebreaker to decide the set. Then, with the tiebreaker score at 6-4, Travis blasted a flat driving forehand down the line to win the tiebreaker and the set. Meanwhile, on the other courts, the Wolfpack won the first set on courts six, three and two.

The second set for Travis and Jacob continued to be dominated by great serving. As the games progressed, Jacob began to back deeper and deeper behind the baseline. Jacob began to extend the points by hitting deep spinning shots to Travis' backhand. With the game score 5-6, and Travis serving to take the set into another tiebreaker, Jacob played exceptional defense, giving himself a set point at 30-40. On Travis' first serve, Jacob returned a deep slice to Travis' backhand. From there a long rally ensued before Jacob was able to approach the net and volley the ball into the open court, winning the second set and tying the match at one set a piece. On the other courts, the second set in each match was close, but all the matches were decided in two sets. So as Travis and Jacob took the court for the deciding third set, all the players, coaches and fans were focused on the action on the number one court.

Once the third set got under way, both players began to "read" each other's serve. The game scores became closer, with many of the games going to deuce before being decided, and each player breaking the other's serve once before the game score reached 4-5, with Travis serving to level the set at five games apiece. Then, with the game score at ad-out, Travis hit his first serve up the "T" and Jacob blocked the ball back toward Travis' right, Travis quickly moved across the court and hit a spinning forehand forcing Jacob to lunge to his right, slicing the ball back toward Travis. Travis quickly moved toward the net, preparing to volley the ball into the open court and win the point. But as the ball approached the net, it barely clipped the top of the net cord causing the ball to drop just over the net and onto Travis' side of the court. Travis then dove toward the ball, trying to slice the ball back over the net, but the ball bounced a second time before Travis could reach it, and Travis lay sprawled out on the court. Jacob had gotten him again. The crowd then rose to its feet and gave both players a rousing round of applause. It was a great match. Travis and the Pack played super, but the ball didn't bounce their way today, as the Blue Devils escaped with the victory. Then after the match was over Travis sat down on the bleachers to have a one-on-one talk with Tom Ham.

"Travis, that was some match today."

"Yes sir it was. Jacob is a heck of a player, he has beaten me every time we've played since we were ten-years old!"

"Maybe you'll get him next time. Travis, I've had a great time these last few days. It's been a pleasure talking with your family, Mary Katherine and the Outlands, David Clark, Stephanie, Jim and Russell. I feel like I've learned a lot about you from talking with them."

"Every one of those people has helped me so much. I don't know where I would be without them."

"Travis, after your injury, when you first came to school here at N.C. State, what were you expecting?"

"I was very nervous about leaving home and going to school. After the accident I just felt uncomfortable everywhere I went. I had spent a lot of time at home with my parents, and my dog, Wesley. Honestly, I didn't want to go to school at all."

"Did your parents know how you were feeling?"

"I suppose they did, but we never talked about it. I knew they were hurting too. I knew I had to go. It was the only thing to do, so I didn't want to give them anything else to worry about, so I kept it to myself."

"How did things go once you got here? Was it as tough as you thought it would be, and how long did it take before you felt comfortable again?"

"As soon as I got to school, Russell sort of took charge. He got me out of the dorm and started introducing me to people. He invited me to go with him to Bible study. At the same time, Coach Clark sort of made me his assistant at football practice and on the sidelines on game days. That kept me involved with Russell and the rest of the football team. All the players and coaching staff went out of their way to support me. I could never tell you how important that was to me."

"How so?"

"Because when you have a drastic change like I had, nothing feels normal. I felt as though I didn't fit in anymore. Not that anyone was ever rude to me, or anything like that. It's just that all my plans changed over night. It wasn't anyone's fault. It just happened, but once it did, all I wanted to do was isolate myself. Russell and Coach Clark, along with Stephanie, they kept me busy and involved in the football program and that helped me see that my life wasn't over."

"Travis, did you feel like your life was over?"

"Yes sir, I did."

"You were only what, eighteen-years old, you had your whole life ahead of you. Why did you feel like your life was over?"

"I guess because before the accident I thought I had everything I ever wanted. I loved what I was doing. I believed in God. I believed in myself. Then when I injured my hand, all those dreams vanished overnight. The mental pain was so profound. It made me afraid of being hurt again. I questioned God. How could God allow this to happen to me? Questioning God made me feel my faith was weak. I was ashamed. I felt that I wasn't trusting God enough. But when you are afraid and hurting inside, it's hard to trust."

"Travis, what were some of the key moments, when you began to feel your confidence returning?"

"The Bible study, going every Monday night, it helped get me into a routine. Watching Coach Clark, the way he carries himself. Just being around him made me feel safe. I can't really describe it any other way. He just reminds me a lot of my dad. Also, the exercise routine Stephanie designed for me. Being active physically helped me relieve my tensions, and being in shape made me feel normal again. Stephanie also had me mold images with clay to help regain the dexterity in my fingers. There is something very spiritual about molding things out of clay. I still make things out of clay, it helps me relax."

"Tell me about Mary Katherine," Mr. Ham asked.

"What can I say, I love her. She has helped me in so many ways. She supports me and encourages me. Mary Katherine challenges me to be the best that I can be."

"Travis, if you had not injured your hand, have you ever thought how would your life be different? And would it have been better or worse?"

"Actually, I think about it a lot, and my life is much better because of the injury."

"Really, can you explain?"

"Before the accident, I had decided to forgo college and play professional baseball. I've never told many people that, but I think it's important now to tell you."

"Why now?"

"Because, if I had not hurt my hand and I had signed a long-term professional baseball contract, I would not have come to school at State. I would not have gotten to know Russell, or met Stephanie Clauson, Joe Moore, Jim Rose, Coach Outland and Mrs. Outland. I would never have met Mary Katherine. Then playing tennis again. Playing at the U.S. Open. Being a part of the Bible study on Monday nights, and all I have learned from that. Watching Jim make those T-shirts. Seeing what is happening with the Play 2 Win-Live 2 Serve message. I would not be sitting here with you today if it had not been for the accident. God has taken that accident, which at the time looked like the worst thing that could have ever happened to me, and turned it into so many things more wonderful than before. I can see now being injured was the best thing that ever happened to me."

"Travis, we're talking about what every one else has done, but tell me what was your part in all this? What did you do to help yourself? What would you tell someone else to do in a difficult situation, to help them get through it?"

Travis thought for a few minutes, as he searched for the right words.

"First, I would read my Bible and pray for wisdom and discernment to make good decisions. I would then count my blessings. Be thankful for the things you do have. Thank God for the blessings He has already given you. Then pray that the Holy Spirit would open your eyes to God's purpose for your life. Ask God how can you use your difficult period of testing to help others? Then wait. Wait on the Lord to open the doors. Then pray for the wisdom to see God moving in your life. Do the very best you can day by day, and glorify Jesus in all that you do. Remember, God is in control, and in His perfect timing, He will bring you through."

Later that night, before Travis got in the bed, he knelt down beside the bed, and on his knees he prayed. Travis thanked God for all the blessings in his life. Then once he laid down, he wiped a tear from his eye, as he thought about all that had happened. Travis was having a hard time believing that God had chosen to bless him in such a way. Travis could clearly see that God was shaping his life. And as he lay there thanking God for what He had already done, he wondered what was next.

PLAYING 2 WIN WHILE LIVING 2 SERVE

It was the first Monday in December, a little past 9 a.m. when Travis' cell phone started buzzing. Magazines had just begun arriving at mailboxes and newsstands. Pictures of Travis on the cover of the nation's leading sports magazine and Christian publications under the title, "Playing 2 Win While Living 2 Serve," were being read across the country. At approximately the same time, Sarah, Jim, Russell, Mary Katherine, Coach Clark and Stephanie all began to receive congratulatory phone calls, e-mails and text messages, inquiries from friends and family. Over the next several days they also began receiving requests from other Christians, many of whom they had never met before, wanting more information about the shirts. Sports teams, high schools, colleges, summer camps, church choirs, youth groups, Sunday school classes, all types of Christian organizations that wanted to use the shirts to help support their Christian outreach programs and expand farther out into their communities. Travis, meanwhile, was receiving invitations to attend local and national radio and television broadcasts to talk about his return to tennis, and give his personal testimony. Now that the magazine articles had been published, the story of Travis' remarkable comeback and the T-shirts, originally made simply to inspire a single college tennis team to witness its faith, had caught fire nationwide. And from here, there would be no stopping it. On the athletic fields, the college football regular season had concluded, with Russell and the Wolfpack football team finishing the season 8-4. The Pack accepted a bid to the Gator Bowl in Jacksonville, Florida, New Year's Eve against Oklahoma State.

The Wolfpack tennis team continued their excellent play, and as the university completed exams and closed for the Christmas break, Rudy and the Wolfpack had broken into the top ten. The Wolfpack men were ranked 9th in the country as they headed into the spring tennis season. Mary Katherine, meanwhile, was continuing her solid play on the women's professional tour. Mary Katherine had made it to the quarterfinals in three tour events, and twice advanced into the semis. So as the holidays approached, there was much to celebrate on and off the court, as the kids looked forward to Christmas and the New Year.

The weekend before Christmas, Mary Katherine went to Wilson to spend the weekend with the Simpsons. On Friday night when Travis and Mary Katherine arrived at the Simpsons' home, Ed and Wesley were next door in the Richardsons' driveway. Mike and Ed were drinking a Coke, leaning against Mike's pickup truck, while Ryan and Madeline were circling the driveway on their bicycles. When Travis turned the Jetta into the driveway, Wesley broke for the car pulling Ed for all he was worth, trying to get to Travis. With Wesley's leash and Ed's arm fully extended, Wesley's feet and toenails skid atop the concrete. Wesley's legs were moving as if he were running a hundred miles per hour, but he couldn't budge Ed who outweighed Wesley by a good two hundred pounds. Travis got out of the car and he looked over toward Ed.

"Hey Dad, I see Wesley is excited to see us."

"Yeah," Ed replied. "Wesley still believes he can drag me across the yard if he tries hard enough. I love to watch him try."

"There ain't no quit in Wesley," Travis agreed. "I believe he'd wear a hole in that concrete before he'd give up."

Ed then turned to Mike.

"Mike, did I tell you they had to start sedating Wesley at the vet's office when we'd take him to get his hair cut and toe nails clipped?"

Mike laughed. "No, what for?"

"Wesley doesn't like anybody messing with his feet," Ed said. "Especially his toenails. He won't even let me cut them."

"What did Wesley do when the vet tried to cut them?" Mike asked.

"He tried to bite him! The dog has never been aggressive before in his life. He doesn't even bark. But boy, he doesn't like it when you mess with his feet."

Meanwhile Wesley's legs were still churning in place, and you could hear his nails scratching across the pavement.

"So I went and got some shears from the pet store," Ed continued, "and started cutting his hair myself, but this," as Ed pointed to Wesley still grinding his nails across the concrete.

"This is how we trim his toenails. Wesley 'self grinds' his own nails. Ain't that dog crazy! I tell you, everybody in our house has issues, even the dog."

About that time, Ryan pulled up next to Travis and Mary Katherine on his bicycle. He adjusted his bicycle helmet, looked toward Travis and smiled.

"Travis, is Mary Katherine your girlfriend?"

"I guess so Ryan, we're suppose to get married next summer."

"Will she be your girlfriend once you get married?"

Mike then broke in.

"Ryan, Mary Katherine is Travis' fiancée, she will be his wife once they get married."

"I know that! I want to know if she'll still be his girlfriend!"

Mary Katherine then spoke up.

"Ryan, you look pretty good on that bicycle. How long have you been riding your bicycle?"

"My dad took my training wheels off on my birthday last year, you want to see me ride down the street?"

"Wait a minute Ryan," Mike said. "Your mom is going to have to go with you if you go out of the driveway."

Ryan took off inside the house and got his mom; Mary, to come go for a bike ride. Meanwhile, Mary Katherine got a bicycle out of the Simpsons' garage. Then Ryan, Madeline, Mary Katherine and Mary headed off around the block. Once the four of them got started on the bike ride, and things quieted down a little.

Mike said, "Travis, you're becoming a full fledge celebrity aren't you boy!"

"I guess so, it's really pretty weird."

"Well weird or not, we are all real proud of you."

"Thank you Mr. Richardson."

"But even though we're all proud of you," Mike continued, "I don't think that's going to stop Ryan from trying to steal Mary Katherine away from you. Ryan's pretty sweet on Mary Katherine, and you know how persistent a six-year old can be."

"I don't know that I can compete with Ryan. Mary Katherine's been talking about Ryan ever since we got in the car to come to Wilson."

About that time the four cyclists turned into the driveway with Ryan leading the pack. Once the other three pulled up next to the garage Ryan said, "Mary Katherine, do you want to go inside and play Battleship?"

Travis, realizing Ryan was making a move on Mary Katherine said, "We better get going before Ryan takes Mary Katherine away from me. I tell you what Ryan; you're a smooth operator."

"We do need to get moving Travis," Ed said, "We're suppose to meet your mom and Sarah at Dick's Hot Dog Stand in fifteen minutes."

Mary Katherine then looked at Ryan.

"I better get going Ryan, but I'll be here all weekend, maybe we can play Battleship tomorrow?"

That wasn't exactly what Ryan wanted to hear, but Ryan, like Wesley, was determined. He wasn't ready to give up on Mary Katherine just yet.

By the time Ed, Travis and Mary Katherine got to Dick's, Kathy and Sarah were already there in a booth waiting for them. When Travis walked through the door, he was greeted by the restaurant owner Lee Gliarmis, and later by his son Soc and daughter Chrisanne. Mr. Gliarmis' son Soc had played high school football with Ed. The Simpsons had taken Travis and Sarah to eat at Dick's since they were children, the same way their parents had taken Kathy and Ed when they were kids thirty years ago. Mr. Gliarmis, who had coached Ed's little league teams, always made a point to be informed and supportive of the local kids.

"Travis Simpson, we sure are proud of you boy, and who's this young lady you have with you?"

"This is Mary Katherine Outland, my fiancée."

Mr. Gliarmis then reached out and shook Mary Katherine's hand.

"Mary Katherine, we know who you are. It's a pleasure to have you visit us tonight. I tell you Travis, she's a pretty girl."

"Yes sir, she's something special alright."

Travis, Ed, and Mary Katherine took a seat with Kathy and Sarah. Then Chrisanne came over to get the family's food order and say hello.

"Travis, it's good to see you. We miss seeing you since you've gone off to school."

"Thank you Chrisanne, I miss you too."

"I see your Grandma Prince on Sunday's after church," Chrisanne replied, "and Ed comes by to get a hamburger steak about once a week. But we don't see you or Sarah too often."

"Chrisanne," Ed said. "I want you to meet Travis' fiancée, Mary Katherine Outland. Mary Katherine, I've been coming in here to eat since I was a little boy."

"Soc and Ed, Kathy and me, we've known each other since we first started school. They're a good family. I'm sure you will be a great addition to it."

"Travis tells me he gets the same thing every time he eats here," Mary Katherine said. "Two fried ham sandwiches plain on a bun, French fries and sweet tea."

"That's right," Chrisanne replied. "What would you like Mary Katherine?"

"I'll take a hotdog with ketchup, fries and a Coke."

Chrisanne then proceeded to get the rest of the family's order. The conversation amongst the girls then turned to the wedding arrangements. About that time Soc came over and he, Travis and Ed began to talk sports. Then once the food was ready Chrisanne came back, pulled up a chair and sat down with the other girls as they all discussed the upcoming wedding. The girls talked about life on the women's tennis tour and how tough it was for Mary Katherine to travel the world playing tennis. Then the Gliarmas'es and Simpsons proceeded to fill Mary Katherine in on the ins and outs of the Wilson community. They showed Mary Katherine the pictures lining the wall of the restaurant. The photographs of high school and little league teams, as well as celebrities that had visited the restaurant when passing through Wilson. As the Simpsons were finishing their dinner, Mr. Gliarmas got the two families together along with Mary Katherine and he took a picture to later frame and hang on the wall.

Dick's was one of the few places in Wilson that Travis had felt comfortable after the accident. The Gliarmas family had been so supportive of Travis over the years. He just felt at home whenever he was there. The environment inside the restaurant exemplified the importance of community. Dick's represented all that is so special about small town America. It was the friendship shared with the Gliarmases that made Dick's such a special place to Travis and his family.

Later that night, when the Simpsons got back to the house, the girls popped some popcorn and spread out in the den. Ed, Travis and Wesley grabbed a Pepsi and went outside on the back patio. Ed lay down on his lounge chair. Wesley jumped up on the end of the lounge chair and lay down too. Travis then took a seat in one of the wrought iron rockers on the porch. It was a mild night for December, the kind you have in the Carolinas sometimes. There wasn't a cloud in the sky, temperature in the mid 50s.

"What a beautiful night," Ed said.

"I know Dad, I love to be outside at night. It is so peaceful. Something about it makes me feel safe."

Ed could tell Travis was uncomfortable with all the sudden attention he was receiving, but he waited for Travis to bring it up.

"Me too. When I am outside, especially at night, it helps me remember God is in control. There is something spiritual, holy, about being outside at night."

"Dad, I know God is in control. But sometimes, even though I know God is in control. I am still afraid."

"Me too. I don't think there is any person who is not afraid sometimes. I know I am afraid at times."

"Dad, what kinds of things frighten you?"

"Lots of things. For a long time, I was afraid of dying. After my dad died so young, I was afraid it could happen to me too. I really began to think, even worry about it once you and your sister were born. I didn't want you two to hurt the way I did when my dad died, so I thought about it a lot. Too much actually."

"Dad, dying is not something any of us can control. So why do people worry about it?"

"I don't know Son, maybe we worry about dying because it is

something we can't control. It's hard to accept that there are some things that no matter how hard we try to affect the outcomes, they are simply out of our hands."

"Dad, I've had a lot of really wonderful things happen to me lately. I should be trusting God more, after all the ways He has blessed me. But I find myself worrying about failing and letting God and everyone else down."

"Son, what kind of things are you worried about?"

"Dad, I've got these people calling about interviews, to talk about my faith, what I believe. They want to know how I was able to overcome what happened to me, the secret to my success. But Dad, I don't feel like I've overcome anything, at least not on my own anyway. Whatever I've achieved it's with God's help. I don't want any credit for that. Honestly, I don't like to talk about what's happened."

"Travis, why don't you want to talk about it?"

"I don't like to look back. What happened was so traumatic. It upsets me to think about it. Besides, it is in the past. If I keep talking about it, it scares me that something like that could happen again."

"I see Son, that's certainly understandable. Let me ask you something though; are you a better person because of what's happened? I know it was a very painful thing, for you, for all of us. But you have learned and grown so much these past three years. What about all the good that has come from it?"

"Dad, I have learned so much from what happened. The truth is, what happened has enriched my life in so many ways. But I don't feel like I should be the one talking about it. I want to help people any way I can. But I'm uncomfortable telling my story. It's not my story. I feel like God is doing all this, and here I am, people asking me how I did this, and how I did that? But that's not how I see it. I just feel so blessed. So thankful that God has blessed me so. I do not want to misrepresent God. I want to do my best. It's nice to be recognized for doing your best at something. But I've learned that without knowing Jesus is beside me, I couldn't do anything. I am thankful for these new blessings and opportunities God is bringing into my life. I'm just not sure how to respond to all the attention, and I want to do exactly what God wants me to do. I'm just not sure what that is."

"Travis, I'm like you. I don't like a lot of attention either, but the reality is as an athlete, you perform in a very public arena. And when you do, there are going to be a lot of people watching you. That just comes with the territory. Being in the public eye gives you an opportunity to do some wonderful things if you use that platform for good."

"Dad, I want to serve God. I want to do my part. But I am afraid I will make the wrong decisions, or not represent God the right way. I want so much to do the right thing. But I feel unworthy, inadequate to try and explain to people who God is, and what God wants us to do. I see how much Jesus has done for me. I am so thankful, I feel like I owe God so much, how can I ever repay Him for all He has done for me?"

"Travis, none of us can repay God for what He has done for us. We are only human, and He is God. God created the world. He set the moon, the stars and planets in place. None of us are worthy of our blessings. It's by God's grace that we even exist. How could I repay Jesus for all He has done for me? Repay God for you and your sister, for the love of your mother? Travis, none of us can repay God. God knows that. God is omnipotent. He exists on His own. Everything belongs to Him, and is under His control. Yet God chooses to work through us to reach out to others to accomplish His plan of salvation. He does that because He loves us."

"Dad, I believe God loves me. And every day I feel a desire growing inside me to teach other people about Jesus. Sometimes these thoughts are so powerful, I can't think of anything else. I wonder, is God calling me into the ministry? I'm uncomfortable just being a college kid, and yet I want to follow Jesus 100%. I'm just not sure what God wants me to do."

"Travis, I'd like to tell you I have the answers for you, but I don't. After fifty years, I am still searching for answers myself, but I believe that's just a part of life. It is one of the mysteries of faith. Travis, you know the difference between right and wrong. You have made the decision to accept Jesus as your Lord and Savior; those are the things you can count on, place your trust in. The fact that you know what God has done for you, and that you want to do your very best to honor Jesus, that is what God wants from everyone. When someone asks you about your faith in God, when you tell them what you have told me tonight, you will be an awesome witness for Jesus."

"But Dad, there is so much I don't know, and I am ashamed to say I still have doubts and fears."

"Travis, Jesus was referred to as the 'Truth.' Whenever we tell the truth about how we feel, we are honoring Jesus. God doesn't need witnesses who claim to be perfect, who say they are never afraid. God wants us to be honest, and the truth is none of us are perfect. As Christians we need to share our fears and imperfections, we know we are still saved, not because of what we've done, but because of what Jesus did. That is what God wants. People need to understand that God will accept them just as they are."

"Dad, Russell and Jim are naturally gifted when it comes to speaking in front of people. Sarah, she has never met a stranger. They just draw people to them with the way they express themselves. But me, I have never been comfortable speaking in front of people. I wish one of them could do the interviews and public speaking, and I could just be in the background doing something else to help out."

"Well Travis, apparently that's not what God wants, because you are the one being called for interviews. You remember the story of Moses, when God called Moses to go to Egypt and free the Israelites?"

"Yes, I do."

"Do you remember, Moses was determined not to go? He told God he did not speak well, didn't he?"

"Yes Dad, he did."

"But God told Moses He, the I AM, would be with Moses, and Moses became a great leader of his people. But it was God's strength working through Moses that made all that possible. If God calls you to do something Travis, then God will not abandon you. God will give you the talents and abilities you need, to do the work He has called you to do."

"Dad, I know, and you know, I don't like speaking before groups, and I am so happy playing tennis again. But Dad, I feel God is calling me into ministry. I feel a tremendous desire in my heart to serve Jesus, but honestly I do not want to be a minister. I want to play tennis."

"Travis, every Christian is a minister. We are all disciples of Christ. You don't have to work for the church as a preaching minister to have a ministry. Your ministry may be as a professional tennis player. You mother and Sarah have a ministry, a mission field in their classrooms, and in their schools. David Clark has a ministry on the football field, and leading your Bible study. My mission field is in my business. If the gospel is going to be taught, we as Christians can't expect full-time ministers to carry the load alone. I have no doubt God is speaking to you Travis. Just stay open minded to whatever possibilities present themselves, and God will show you the way."

Later that night, once everyone else had gone to bed, Travis got up and went outside on the back porch. He laid down on the recliner. Travis looked at the stars suspended above the tops of the pine trees that framed the Simpsons' back yard. He listened to the wind as it gently blew against the tops of the tall pines, the sounds of the squirrels as they scampered along the sides of the trees. In the solitude of the cool night air, as the gentle breeze blew across his face, Travis prayed and searched for God. While Travis was thankful for the blessings in his life, he was apprehensive of what lay ahead. He was afraid of being hurt again. He was still battling the feelings of loneliness he had felt since the accident. Yet, the reality was all the while,

Travis was not alone. Jesus, sat in the chair nearby him, quietly listening to his thoughts. Meanwhile, the Holy Spirit living inside Travis was molding him, preparing Travis to teach the gospel of Jesus Christ.

CHARLESTON

Christmas holidays and New Year's quickly came and went. Russell and the Wolfpack football team lost a heartbreaker to Oklahoma State in the Gator Bowl, 23-21, on a last-second field goal. Russell, however, had another outstanding game going 20 of 27 passing. Throwing for 324 yards and two touchdowns. Then, after the conclusion of the bowl series Russell was named first team All-Atlantic Coast Conference, and second team All-American. Russell was also rated as the number two quarterback by the leading professional NFL scouts. So as the deadline approached to enter the NFL draft, Russell had a decision to make. Either return to State in the fall to complete his eligibility, or enter the draft and move on to professional football. Russell, who had red-shirted his first year at State would be graduating on time in May with a degree in communications. Either way, Russell's education was complete. So as the spring semester was beginning, Russell had a lot on his mind.

The first week of January Mary Katherine and Rita boarded an American Airlines flight bound for Australia. This time Mary Katherine would be playing in her first Australian Open as a professional. By now Mary Katherine was beginning to get somewhat accustomed to life on the women's tour. She and Maria were now both being coached by Coach Watkins, so they generally worked out and practiced together. Mary Katherine and Maria had also joined a Bible study that was formed amongst the players, coaches and some of the other corporate sponsors and associates who were involved in women's tennis. The Bible study helped Mary Katherine and Maria stay connected to their faith while they were away from home. It also helped Mary Katherine meet and develop friendships with other believers. It gave her a sense of normalcy. The life of a professional athlete, traveling from place to place, with all the parties and special privileges could become a great temptation to the players. The pressures of constantly being in the spotlight at times seemed overwhelming. For Mary Katherine, the Bible study helped her to remember that while playing professional tennis was her occupation, she was still just a twenty-year old kid. A young woman about to be married, even though the scenery changed every week, God was in control, wherever she went.

Back in Raleigh, Travis, Jim and the rest of the Wolfpack tennis team were moving into high gear as they began their spring season. For the previous two months Rudy and Stephanie had worked together to develop a tennis-specific conditioning program for the team. Rudy was convinced that Stephanie's expertise could help the team win, so he listened carefully

317

as Stephanie stressed the need for increased flexibility and agility to prevent injuries. Also, Stephanie showed Rudy some innovative drills she developed to improve hand-eye coordination, a skill that was especially important in tennis. Rudy knew all the kids could hit the ball. Their forehands, backhands, serves and volleys were solid. Rudy decided to gear the team practices around developing control. Teaching the players how to hit the ball wherever they wanted, whenever they wanted. Then they worked on situational tennis. Teaching the players how to better structure points. To develop a strategy designed around each player's individual strengths, while continuing to improve in the areas where they were weak. So as the spring season was getting under way, each player and the coaches had the same two goals in mind, winning a championship, while leading people to Christ.

"Fellas, I want you guys to know I have never been as excited about a tennis season as I am this year." Rudy then went on to say, "When I was a junior at UCLA we won a national championship. We had a chemistry, a sense of unity on that team. That is the same type of togetherness I feel with this team. But in addition to that, we also have a special unity off the court, as witnesses of Jesus. I am so proud of each and every one of you guys. Another thing this team has going for it is the expertise of Stephanie Clauson. You all know how much Stephanie's off-season conditioning program has helped us already. For the past two months Stephanie has been kind enough to visit our practices and attend our matches. Stephanie has developed a tennis specific exercise program that we are going to implement as a part of our practice routine. So I'm going to turn it over to Stephanie so she can explain the benefits of these exercises."

Rudy then took a step back while Stephanie began to explain the routine to the players. Rudy had great respect for Stephanie's professional ability, as well as her personal integrity. Rudy watched the players and his two assistant coaches as they listened intently as Stephanie gave her presentation. Stephanie was a young woman in her late twenties, yet she carried herself with the dignity and grace of a seasoned veteran. Rudy also noticed the cross that Stephanie always wore around her neck. Stephanie exemplified the example of discipleship for young women. And being the father of a young woman himself, Rudy understood the importance of Godly Christian women. When Stephanie finished her demonstrations, Rudy thanked her again for all her help and support of the team. Then the team got to work.

Once the season began, the Wolfpack men went through their

regular season schedule like a "hot knife through butter." By the time Easter break rolled around the Pack was 22-0, and ranked third in the nation. Rudy had scheduled an open week in the Wolfpack schedule so the team could take some time off and visit their families before the ACC and NCAA tournaments. The women's professional tour was playing in Charleston that week. The Family Circle Cup matches were being contested on Daniel Island, just across the Cooper River Bridge from downtown Charleston. So the Outlands and the Simpsons took the week off and the families went to Charleston to watch Mary Katherine play.

Russell, who was out of school for the week, also went home to watch the tournament. Russell wanted to see Mary Katherine play too. But he also had his eye on another tennis player, Maria Lopez. Russell and Maria had for the last six months developed a long distance romance of their own. He and Maria had double dated with Travis and Mary Katherine during the weeks the girls were not playing tournaments. It was obvious to everyone that Russell and Maria were now much more than just a passing thing. Russell had fallen hard for Maria, and it appeared the feeling was mutual. So when Russell and Travis met Rita and the girls at the Charleston International Airport, Russell found himself in the same situation as his roommate. Maria had Russell wrapped around her little finger, and there was no point in hiding it.

While Russell and Travis waited for the plane to arrive, Russell had some questions for Travis.

"Travis, what do you think about this getting married stuff. Are you nervous?"

"Yeah, a little bit. I'm not looking forward to getting up there in the church in front of all those people."

"Well, what about the being married part, are you nervous about that?"

"No. I don't have any reservations about being married. It's just the wedding, the getting married part that scares me a little. But the wedding is a big deal to Mary Katherine, her mom and my mom. All that ceremony stuff doesn't make much difference to me."

Russell then asked Travis, "Were you nervous when you asked Mary Katherine to marry you? Were you sure she would say yes?"

"I was pretty sure, but there's always a chance she could say no? What do you think Russell; are you nervous about asking Maria?"

"What makes you think I'm going to do that?"

"Russell, please."

"Is it that obvious?"

"Yes." Travis replied. "And why wouldn't it be, I mean the girl is drop dead gorgeous, she is the sweetest Christian person you could ever hope to meet. I mean what guy wouldn't be crazy about her?"

"I know you're right. My dad says he would ask her in a skinny minute. I want to ask her I'm just not sure she'll say yes."

"Russell, this week at the tennis tournament there will be guys everywhere watching these women tennis players. I mean all these girls are smoking hot. Maria travels the world with men asking her out all the time. If you don't tell her how you feel, some other guy will."

About that time the plane landed and the boys greeted Rita and the girls. Then the boys loaded up the luggage, which took some special packing skills. Once all the many bags were secured, some inside the Suburban, and still others on top of the luggage rack, they all headed to the Rawlings' house.

On the way Mary Katherine posed a "question" to Travis.

"Travis, I've been thinking about something?"

By now Travis knew that really meant, "I've got something I'm going to do, and I'm about to tell you about it."

"Okay Honey, what is it?"

"Since I grew up in Orlando, and I only lived in Raleigh a year before traveling the tour, I don't want to get married in Raleigh with a big church ceremony."

Travis thought, *"Okay, that sounds good to me."*

Mary Katherine went on to say, "I would like to have a private ceremony with the wedding in the seaside garden at the Rawlings' house. How do you feel about that?"

Travis was so happy he could barely contain himself. But he remained calm and said, "Honey, whatever makes you happy."

At that point Travis was showered with a chorus of "I love you's" and "isn't he the greatest" and other compliments like that. Russell looked at Travis as if to say, *"is that all there is to it?"*

Travis smiled and nodded as he looked toward Russell, then "in silent man sign language replied."

"The five magic words, they'll never let you down."

Over the next week the families relaxed and caught up. Russell had "a talk" with Maria. And though nothing was official, the couple decided to take their relationship to the next level. Russell told Maria he wanted to visit with her family as soon as possible, because he had something to discuss with her father. Travis and Mary Katherine began to discuss where they would like to live once they got married. They both agreed that Charleston was at the top of their list. The beautiful downtown historic district, the ocean, the low country lifestyle made Charleston a great place to live and raise a family. And since Charleston was the place Travis proposed to Mary Katherine and they would also be getting married there, it seemed the perfect place for the couple to call home.

Mary Katherine and Maria both played well in The Family Circle Cup, with each girl advancing into the quarterfinals. During the week Travis helped with the girls' practice sessions to stay sharp. Then on Sunday Travis headed back to Raleigh.

It was time for the college tennis playoffs to begin, and Travis and the Wolfpack were ready to get started.

GOD SAID IT

Monday at practice, Rudy gathered the team together for a talk.

"Men, we have just come off a fantastic regular season, 22-0 is a record we should all be very proud of. But I think we would all agree, we had one goal for this team before the season started, and that was to win a championship, an ACC championship, and an NCAA championship. Starting today let's focus on the task at hand, play fast and loose, 'Play 2 Win, and Live 2 Serve.' Let's get to work."

For the next four days the team had intense, competitive practices. On Friday the Pack faced Virginia in the first round of the ACC Tournament, with the Wolfpack beating the Cavaliers, 4-1, to move into the second round. Wake Forest was the next hurdle for State, and the Pack handled the Demon Deacons, 4-0, to advance to the finals against the University of Miami. With the team now focused on hitting on all cylinders, the State men made quick work of the Hurricanes, 4-2, to claim the ACC championship. Meanwhile, Travis was named the tournament most valuable player and the ACC Player of the Year.

In the first round of the NCAA tournament the Wolfpack played Wisconsin with the Pack easily advancing by a 4-1 margin. Then in the second round State squared off against the University of Louisville, as Travis and the Wolfpack were again in total command, beating the Cardinals, 4-2. Once the Wolfpack reached the round of sixteen all the matches were played at the Dan Magill Tennis Complex on the campus of the University of Georgia, in Athens. When the team arrived they were greeted with a warm reception from the fans on hand for the sweet sixteen. As the season had progressed, the N.C. State men had developed a following as they traveled around the country. The articles about Travis in the Christian and sports magazines published before the Christmas holidays, had shone a spotlight on the entire team. It seemed everywhere the team went to play, Christian sports fans had come out to support them for their willingness to openly express their commitment to Jesus Christ. Athens would be no exception.

When the team arrived for their first scheduled practice there were local and national news media on hand requesting interviews. There were also numerous fans in attendance who were wearing the "Play 2 Win-Live 2 Serve" T-shirts. N.C. State had played Georgia earlier in the fall, and Jim had made a point to share the idea for the shirts with other players on all the teams the Pack had played during the season. By doing that, the shirts had spread to over fifty other NCAA Division One schools, as many of the teams began to help spread the "Play 2 Win-Live 2 Serve" message. The

University of Georgia had a wonderful history of Christian discipleship, and outstanding leadership in their athletic department. So the Bulldogs and their fans had been very supportive of what Rudy and the N.C. State team were doing. When the team arrived the university and the Athens community quickly adopted the Wolfpack, and the "Play 2 Win-Live to Serve" message as it spread amongst the fans in attendance and throughout the community.

When the Wolfpack took to the court for their round of sixteen match against the University of Michigan, the N.C. State men found themselves in a dogfight with the Wolverines. From the beginning of the doubles matches, each match was intensely played. The capacity crowd on hand was treated to some exciting, well-played tennis. The Pack hung tough and after three close matches the Wolfpack men were able to secure the doubles point, then hold on to advance to the quarterfinals with a 4-3 victory over Michigan.

The quarterfinals opponent for the Pack was the sixth-ranked University of Alabama. The Crimson Tide, who had won the Southeastern Conference championship, had a sensational team. The Wolfpack men again quickly found themselves in a fierce battle for the doubles point. But Rudy's emphasis on doubles play, and the conditioning program designed by Dr. Stephanie Clauson, helped the Wolfpack again take the doubles point, as the Pack overcame the Alabama Crimson Tide, 4-2. Qualifying State for the semifinals, and a match-up with the nation's number-two ranked team, the University of Texas.

Later that night after the quarterfinal win over Alabama, the team went out to dinner. Once dinner was over and the kids got back to the hotel, Jim and Travis went out by the pool to relax and get some air. The boys pulled up a couple of lounge chairs and sat down next to the pool to take it easy.

"Travis, I've got something I've been praying about, and I'd like to get your opinion."

"Sure Jim, what is it?"

"This is my senior year. It has gone by so fast. It really doesn't seem possible that my time as a student at State is over. I've thought and prayed a lot lately about all that I've learned while I was here at N.C. State, and the thing that stands out the most is being a part of our Bible study class."

"I agree 100%. I don't think I could overestimate the positive impact the study of the gospels has had on my life. And being a part of a group made all the difference for me."

"I know what you mean, Travis. There is something very special about being a part of a group, or a team. Doing something with other people who share the same goals and interests, it really keeps you motivated. Keeps you on track."

"Exactly. I tell you what else. Being a part of the group Bible study helped me fit in when I came to school at State. After I injured my hand, everything was so different for me. I didn't feel like I fit in anywhere. But when I went to the Bible study and started to study God's Word with the other kids in the class, it helped me get a sense of normalcy again. For me, studying the Bible helped me find myself again; it changed my life."

"Travis, I feel so blessed to be a part of this tennis team, to be able to represent the university, to be able to attend the Bible study. Jesus has given me so much, I want to do something to give back to others, for all God has given to me."

"I feel the exact same way, Jim. Jesus has done so much for me. I don't begin to know how to ever repay Him for all the ways He has blessed me."

Jim continued. "I've thought of an idea I want to share with you. Our Bible study, the four-year rotation through the gospels, that class has helped us so much, I would like to see the class expanded to other colleges using the same text and lectures. That way the same gospel lessons would be taught at colleges and universities across the country at the same time. Kids in California, South Carolina, Texas, Ohio, they could all communicate back and forth week to week about the same lessons. Lessons relating the Bible truths to subjects like being away from home for the first time, community service, managing money and developing relationships. It would teach the gospels, while also bringing students together."

"Jim, that's a great idea."

"I also thought, it would be helpful to expand the classes to high school students. Starting in their freshmen year, high school students could begin the gospel rotation. The high school kids would study the same scriptures, with the lessons applied to the issues facing high school kids. Issues like underage drinking, peer pressure, discipleship and honoring parental authority. It could be taught in Sunday school, Christian youth groups, school organizations designed to promote Christianity. What an advantage that knowledge would be for kids in their teen years. Before they graduate from high school and go out on their own.

"We could also design a class for parents," Jim continued. "With the lessons applied to topics like parenting and managing financial resources. They would rotate through the same scriptures, all three groups would be studying the same text, but teaching life lessons applicable to each age group. It would give Christians, parents and kids something they would have in common. Something they could talk about and discuss together. It would help them communicate better. Develop closer relationships. What do you think Travis?"

"That's awesome Jim. How do you think we could get something like that started?"

"I thought we could talk to Coach Clark and Stephanie, also Pastor Sullivan and Mr. Corbett. Get Russell and Mary Katherine, Sarah and Maria involved, talk with our parents, Coach and Mrs. Outland. Then we commit to pray about it. See where it takes us. Who would have ever thought we'd be in Athens, Georgia, with people in the stands from all over the country wearing 'Play 2 Win-Live 2 Serve' T-shirts. But it's happened. If we commit to explore new ways to teach people about the redemptive love of Jesus, who knows what might happen, Travis, will you commit to begin to pray about it?"

"Yes, I will, let's go for it! Let's see what Jesus will do next."

The next day the team practiced in the morning to prepare for the following day's semifinal match against Texas. The practice was sharp, as the kids focused their attention on the Longhorns. Off the court, Jim began to share his idea about expanding the Bible study. Everyone agreed that the idea was a good one, and they all committed to pray that God's Will would be done, and that He would open the doors to turn the good idea into a reality. Before long the off day quickly passed, and it was time for the Pack and the Longhorns to "hook up" on the court.

It was an overcast mild morning when the Wolfpack men arrived at the tennis courts to warm-up for their semifinal match with Texas. Both teams found themselves just one win away from the NCAA Championship match. So there was no doubt that both teams were going to bring everything they had to the courts, because it was a win or go home situation for both teams. In the other semifinal match, the defending national champions, the UCLA Bruins, ranked number one in the nation, and 27-1 on the season, were playing the University of Tennessee. The Vol's were 21-6 on the year and ranked fifth in the national rankings.

Before the Wolfpack began their stretching exercises, Jim looked around the stadium and saw that a large percentage of the fans in attendance were wearing the "Play 2 Win-Live 2 Serve" shirts. The local media had interviewed Travis constantly since the time the team arrived in Athens. It seemed that with each passing match, the crowd support for the Wolfpack had grown, and today against Texas, the Pack would need every advantage they could get if they were going to advance into the finals.

Once the doubles got under way, Texas came out with both guns blazing as the Longhorns took an early lead in all three matches. With the intensity building with every point, Texas rode the momentum of their early leads to victory, as they closed out the first two doubles matches to take the doubles point, and a 1-0 lead into singles. It was only the second time all season the Wolfpack had lost the doubles point. So now the Wolfpack had to win four of the six remaining singles matches, or their season and hopes of winning a national championship would be over. Before the singles began Rudy called the team together.

"Fellas, I know we would all like to have those matches to play over again. But, that's over now. We have to put that behind us and move on. Texas has a great team. They are going to come out and try and take their early momentum and jump on us in these singles matches. So we need to turn this thing around. Focus on what you are doing. Play one point at a time, and go for it! Let's jump on them right out of the gate. Encourage your teammates on the court next to you. This thing is a long way from over, but we've got to come out ready to play. Alright; together on three, one, two, three, Play 2 Win-Live 2 Serve." The Pack broke the huddle, and went out to do battle with Texas.

When Travis took the court for his singles match, he knew the team needed a lift. So as he toed the line to serve to start the match, he decided he would go for every shot to try and get the crowd into the match and take that 1-0 lead away from Texas. Travis took his game to another level as he pounded his first serve in over and over. He hit crisp spinning forehands and backhands while gliding across the court hitting winners from all angles. In what took only 55 minutes, Travis had beaten his opponent 6-0, 6-1 to take the first singles point and level the match at 1-1. Travis' inspired play lit a fire under the rest of the Wolfpack players, and when Steven Anderson hit a forehand crosscourt winner on the number six court to win his match, the Pack had rallied to a 4-3 come from behind victory, advancing the Wolfpack into the finals.

Later that day UCLA beat Tennessee 4-2, completing the national championship pairing, a rematch between N.C. State and the team that had knocked the Wolfpack out of last year's NCAA Tournament, Rudy's alma mater, and defending national champions, the UCLA Bruins.

The night before the national championship match, the university held a dinner for the Wolfpack team and their fans in the hotel banquet room where the team was staying. Athletic Director Lee Matthews and the university chancellor, along with several members of the athletic department, made the trip to Athens in support of the team. Rudy and the other coaches and players each spoke briefly thanking the university, parents and fans for their support throughout the season.

After the dinner ended the players spent time with their families before turning in for bed. Travis had a lot on his mind, so he couldn't get to sleep. He decided to get up and go outside for a while. He got up and put on his N.C. State baseball cap, grabbed his tennis ball and walked out to the pool. As he was walking toward the lounge chairs he saw a familiar figure lying out by the pool, looking up at the stars.

"Are you out here counting stars?"

"No Son, I'm counting my blessings."

"Dad, I thought I might find you out here."

"That's funny, I was thinking the same thing about you."

"Mind if I join you," Travis asked.

"No, go ahead and grab a chair. It seems sort of strange being outside without Wesley."

"I know it. It's amazing how attached you can become to a dog isn't it Dad?"

"Yes, it is. Wesley is just like a person to me, he is a part of the family, that's for sure. I tell you, that was a nice dinner tonight. I'm mighty proud of you kids. You all have had a great season."

"I know Dad. I want to win tomorrow, but more than that, I hate to see it end. It's bitter sweet either way."

"I know what you mean. When you take off that uniform for the last time, that's a funny feeling."

"It is Dad. You know, when I took off my football and baseball uniforms, I had no idea those would be my last games. I guess you just never know, do you Dad?"

"No Son, you don't."

"I know after tomorrow, that will be my last team match. From here on out it will be matches for myself, singles and doubles. I won't be on a team anymore. I'm really going to miss that."

"You know Son, when you and your sister were little, I wanted you both to play team sports, but I wanted you two to play an individual sport too. Something you could play all your life. Something to play after the team sports ended, tennis or golf, and you both chose tennis. I always thought Sarah chose tennis because more girls in Wilson played tennis. And I thought you chose tennis because Sarah did, and you always wanted to do whatever your big sister did. That is except for the times when you two were fighting like cats and dogs."

"Come on Dad, we didn't fuss that much, did we?"

Ed just rolled his eyes then he said, "You'll find out what that's like when you have kids."

"Dad, have we really been that much trouble?"

"No Travis, you and Sarah have never been trouble. You have both been great kids. I wouldn't trade the two of you for anything in the world. But having kids can be so stressful. You just can't explain what it's like."

"Is it that tough?"

"Yes! It's the toughest job in the world!"

"Dad you just said you wouldn't trade us for anything?"

"I know. I wouldn't!"

"Then how can it be so tough?"

"Son, when you love something, the way a parent loves a child, you worry about them all the time. When a baby comes into your life, it dominates every thought you have. Suddenly, there is this new person in the house, and they are totally helpless. Your child depends on you for everything. Day and night you care for them. You get them up in the morning. You give them a bath. You change their diapers. You feed them, rock them to sleep.

"Then they learn to talk. They learn to walk. Diapers change to pull-ups. You teach them how to tie their shoes, ride a bicycle, to say their prayers. Then there is preschool, kindergarten, elementary and middle school, high school then college. All the while, you watch everything they do and somehow in the midst of all that, you try and figure out how to slowly back away, so that they can learn to stand on their own. Trying to say enough to help, but not so much that you interfere. And the longer you live, the more you want to teach them, but you know you have to let them stand on their own. Just the way your parents did with you. No, I wouldn't trade being a Dad for anything in the world, but after being a Dad for twenty-one years, I still haven't figured it out."

"Well Dad, I think you've done well so far."

"Thanks Son, I've done my best anyway."

"Have you got any advice about tomorrow?"

"Are you asking my opinion?"

"Yes, I am."

"It's two great teams taking the court tomorrow. You know there are ebbs and flows in every ball game. It could go either way. But I've got a good feeling about it!"

"Me too."

"I tell you what though," Ed continued. "Win or lose tomorrow, I've never been as proud of a group of kids as I am this team. You kids have really started something by praying before the matches and wearing those T-shirts. The way the Christian community has come together in support of Jesus. Every day since we got here I have had people asking me about those T-shirts, where I am from, talking about Jesus. The fans, they are talking in the stands about how to organize Christian rallies and exhibits at sporting events, it's amazing to me. And it all happened because you guys did something. I know no one expected all this to happen. But I've begun to wonder myself what I might could do? I mean dawg gone, when we start something to glorify the Lord and then God decides to bless our efforts, nothing can stop it! But if we all sit back and wait for somebody else to step up and do something, nothing good can ever happen.

"People today desperately need something good to believe in! These T-shirts have taught me that anything is possible if we try, but nothing is possible if we don't try. It sounds so simple, but that's just the way it is."

"Dad, what do you think about the idea to expand the Bible study?"

"Again, it's a great idea. But like we were saying, somebody has got to take the bull by the horns and do something. I was thinking the other day about all the responsibility that falls on the shoulders of our ministers. Visiting the sick in hospitals, budget meetings, choirs, managing office staff, pre-schools, Sunday schools, weddings, funerals, community organizations, counseling, revivals, all those responsibilities and we haven't even talked about preaching and teaching the gospel, much less a detailed Bible study.

"We, the church, we have placed too much responsibility on these ministers. They have families too. We no longer teach the Bible in our public schools. The church is overwhelmed with social and economic issues. Travis, my generation, myself included, I am ashamed to say, I believe we have dropped the ball when it comes to teaching the Bible, the 'Good News' of the gospel. There is nothing to lose and everything to gain by making Jesus Christ the Lord of our life. But sadly, we as Christians have not done a good enough job of teaching that message. We are all so worried about offending somebody, that we aren't helping people. People need to hear the message of the gospel, but how can they hear it, if we Christians don't effectively teach it. I believe God is moving in what you kids are doing, and if God wants it to happen, then it will happen. No doubt about it."

It wasn't long before Travis and Ed agreed it was past both of their bedtimes, after all, they did have a big day tomorrow.

The next morning at breakfast the team was extremely quiet. So much so that Rudy didn't know what to make of it. Once they got to the tennis courts the boys began to relax and the mood lightened a bit. Then the team went through their warm-ups and stretching exercises to get loosened up for the Bruins. When the doubles matches began, Travis and the rest of the Wolfpack came out and played the best doubles they had played all year. Easily sweeping the first two doubles matches, sending their confidence soaring, and the capacity crowd into a frenzy. Taking a decisive 1-0 lead into the singles matches.

Rudy was ecstatic, but he tried to remain cautious. He knew that UCLA was a veteran team, and he wasn't taking anything for granted. So before the singles began, he brought the team together, to try and bring everyone's emotions back down to earth.

"Now fellas, that was some exceptional doubles play, and I am really proud of you guys. But we need to remember, we lost the doubles point to Texas in the semis, but we came back and won the match. These guys are the defending national champions. They are not going to quit and give up. So fight for every point. They are not going to give this to us. We've got to go out there and take it! Alright; together on three; one, two, three, Play 2 Win-Live 2 Serve."

Then the boys took to the courts with a national championship to be decided.

When the singles began, Travis played consistent solid tennis as he quickly won the first set, beating UCLA's number one player, All-American senior Eric Thomas, 6-3. In the other matches, UCLA won the first set on courts two, three, four, and six, while the Wolfpack won on five. In the second set Travis jumped out to an early three games to one lead, and felt he had the match under control. Then Travis went through a stretch of unforced errors that allowed Thomas to level the match at the three games apiece. From there Travis began to struggle with his concentration as the game score progressed to 6-6, forcing a tiebreaker for the set. Meanwhile UCLA was rallying on the other courts, winning the second sets on courts two and four to regain the match lead at 2-1.

Jim Rose won the set on court three to force his match into a third set. N.C. State won at court five, ULCA won at court six, and the match score moved to 3-2 UCLA, with Travis' and Jim's matches yet to be decided. During the tiebreaker with Travis trailing 5-6, Travis stepped in on a short slice from Thomas and blasted a forehand into the top of the net to lose the point and the set. So Travis and Jim now both needed to win their third sets, or the National Championship Trophy would head back to California with the Bruins.

In the third set Jim came out and played fantastic. He covered the court, hitting the ball cleanly and crisply, quickly moving out to a 5-3 lead and serving for the match. Travis meanwhile continued to struggle with his consistency, with the match on serve at 2-3, and Travis serving to level the match. Then, just as Travis was about to serve to start the sixth game, Jim hit a backhand down the line on match point to win his match and tie the team match at three all, and the crowd went nuts. Travis himself got caught up in the moment. He then played a few sloppy points and before you know it, he lost his serve to fall behind 2-4. The UCLA veteran Thomas calmly held his serve to take a commanding lead at 2-5.

At the change over Travis walked over and sat down. He took a drink of water, trying to figure out what had just happened. After all, Travis had been in command the whole match. Now, he took his mind off what he was doing for just a few minutes, and things had gotten away from him just that quick. Travis knew if he lost one more game, it was all over.

While Travis was sitting there, looking like he'd just lost his last friend, trying to regain control over his emotions, Rudy came over and sat down in the chair next to him. Rudy patted Travis on the shoulder.

"I bet you're glad you and Mary Katherine are going to get married at Russell's house so you don't have to get married in a church in front of all those people aren't you?"

Travis, who was taken aback by the timing of the question smiled and replied. "Yes sir, I am."

"Me too, I don't like being up in front of a crowd of folks, especially in church."

"I know what you mean."

"I reckon you've decided to make this thing exciting today, your match I mean?"

Travis then was able to relax a little as he smiled back at Rudy.

"Yes sir, I reckon so."

"Well Son," Rudy said, as he again patted Travis on the back. "What are you going to do about it? It's up to you, you know."

"Up to me?"

"Of course. The best player always determines who wins the match. We both know who the best player in this match is, so what are you going to do?"

Travis felt himself calm down; he knew Rudy was right. Then Travis looked Rudy in the eye.

"I know what to do."

Then he walked back on the court.

Travis walked behind the baseline, took a deep breath, then he prayed, *"Lord, your will be done."*

And he stepped forward and toed the baseline one more time. Suddenly, everything began to slow down. The sky became brighter. The crowd noise grew quiet. Travis then held up the tennis ball to signal Thomas he was ready to serve. He bounced the ball three times. He bent his knees and took the racquet back. He tossed the ball and watched it float into the clear blue Georgia sky. Then, as he watched the racquet compress the tennis ball, Travis' mind drifted away. Away to that special place of concentration, *"The Zone"* where mysterious and magical things happen. And over the next thirty minutes, Travis had a near out-of-body experience. Those times in sports, and in life, where everything is just as it should be, when time stands still.

Four games and two changeovers later, Travis found himself sitting there again drinking water, leading 6-5, and about to serve for the match. Travis calmly stood up, picked up his racquet and walked back onto the court. Three points later, leading 40-Love, Travis again bounced the tennis ball three times. He tossed the ball in the air, and in what seemed like a millisecond, the ball bounced into the service box, and up against the fence beyond the back of the court. Ace. Game, set, match. The crowd stood to its feet and roared. The Wolfpack players, coaches and fans stormed the court. As Travis fell to his knees, the photographer's cameras flashed. Travis lifted his hands over his head in a symbol of praise, there were no need for words. Travis had led the Wolfpack to a National Championship, and God had led Travis all the way back.

Travis didn't need to say anything. After all, Travis knew God had said it all.

THE ORIGINAL AMERICAN HERO

Travis was deep in thought as he sat there. So much so that when Pastor Sullivan opened the door, Travis just sat there rubbing his palms together. He was looking down at the once injured left hand that had brought so many changes into his life. Then Pastor Sullivan spoke up.

"Are you thinking about what you are going to say tonight?"

Travis, at first startled a little, gathered himself.

"No, I was just counting my blessings."

"That's always a good thing to do," Pastor Sullivan replied. "As a matter of fact, we have already been blessed tonight."

"Really; how's that?"

"Normally Friday night is our smallest crowd whenever we have our youth revival. Most folks have something planned on the weekends in the summer, when the kids are out of school. So we ran an ad in the paper and the church bulletin advertising that you were going to be our speaker tonight. And now the sanctuary, which holds 1,500 people, is filled to capacity, and we've set up 300 chairs in the church gymnasium for the overflow kids just so they can listen to your sermon over the intercom. This is by far the largest revival crowd we've ever had. Isn't that a blessing?"

Travis, who already was scared to death, then felt like he would faint, but he forced a smile.

"Oh yes sir, that's wonderful news."

Pastor Sullivan knew Travis was nervous because Travis had already told him he was afraid.

"Travis, this large crowd tonight is not by accident. The Lord has brought all these kids here tonight because you have something to say that God wants these kids to hear, you're going to do just fine. I know you will. What do you say you and I say a prayer before we go inside the sanctuary?"

Pastor Sullivan then reached out and put his hand on Travis' shoulder and they prayed.

"Heavenly Father, we thank you for Travis. For the way You are using Travis' life to spread the message of the gospel. For the young people who are here tonight to learn more about Jesus. Lord, I pray that You will be with Travis as he teaches Your word tonight. Let his message reach these young people, and may the Holy Spirit draw Your children to Jesus. It is for the glory of Jesus we pray, Amen."

A few minutes later Travis and Pastor Sullivan entered the sanctuary. Travis took a seat in the chancel beside Pastor Sullivan. From there he could

335

see the capacity crowd. He also saw his family, Mary Katherine, Russell and Jim, Coach Clark and Stephanie Clauson also in the audience. He was scared stiff, but he knew there was no turning back now. The service began with announcements. Then there were hymns. An offering was taken. Awards and recognition for the teachers and participants who attended and worked in the weeks vacation Bible school and youth revival. Then it was time for Travis to deliver the sermon. Travis tried as best he could to appear confident, as he approached the podium. But his knees were still shaking when he placed his hands on the lectern. He quickly said a silent prayer for courage as he took a deep breath.

"Please stand for the reading of God's word. Our Old Testament lesson for today is Genesis Chapter 1 versus 1-2 and versus 26-27.

"The Beginning. In the beginning God created the heavens and the earth. Now the earth was formless and empty, darkness was over the surface of the deep, and the spirit of God was hovering over the waters." (Genesis Chapter 1 versus 1-2, NIV)

"Then God said; "Let us make man in our image, in our likeness, and let them rule over the fish of the sea and the birds of the air, over the livestock, over all the earth, and over all the creatures that move along the ground.' So God created man in his own image, in the image of God he created him; male and female he created them." (Genesis Chapter 1 versus 26-27 NIV)

"Then from the New Testament, the gospel of John, Chapter 1 versus 1-5 and Chapter 3 versus 16-17.

"The Word Became Flesh. In the beginning was the Word, and the Word was with God, and the Word was God. He was with God in the beginning. Through him all things were made; without him nothing was made that has been made. In him was life, and that life was the light of men. The light shines in the darkness, but the darkness has not understood it." (John Chapter 1 versus 1-5 NIV)

"And from John the third chapter.

"For God so loved the world that he gave his one and only son, that whoever believes in him shall not perish but have eternal life. For God did not send his son into the world to condemn the world, but to save the world through him." (John, Chapter 3 versus 16-17 NN.)

"The word of God, for the people of God, thanks be to God. Please be seated."

The sanctuary crowd took a seat as Travis took another deep breath to compose himself, then he began his testimony.

"I've often wondered what made them do it. Why would people board a ship with their families, whatever possessions they held near and dear, and set sail off into the unknown? What kind of courage must a person possess to undertake a journey like that? And why would you want to? Was the promise, the reports of the new world that wonderful? Were the prospects of life in the new colonies that promising? Or was the life you were leaving so bad, so oppressive, that the unknown no matter what it was; was more appealing than what you were leaving behind? After all, few if any of these travelers had ever seen the 'New World' to which they were heading. Yet, they boarded a ship in South Hampton England, on September 16, 1620. The 102 passengers plus the ship's crew boarded and sailed off toward the west and the sunset on the horizon. Off on a voyage that would eventually lead to the foundation of the first American colony, and the nation of America we now call home.

"A voyage, a journey like that would have required planning and a skilled crew and captain. There was the need for food and supplies to make the 66-day trip. Provisions to battle the elements. There were undoubtedly days when the seas were calm, and nights when the moon and stars illuminated the sky. Then there must have been times when the ship was pitched to and fro from the ocean winds, with waves washing water atop the ship deck. No, this was not a journey for the faint of heart. It was a journey made by courageous men and women. Our ancestors. In search of religious freedom, they took a stand for what they believed in, that God, the creator of heaven and earth would watch over them, provide for them. It was a journey of faith.

"Today the world we live in, it is still a world of faith. A world still controlled by the God who created the heavens and the earth, God the Father, the God of Abraham, Issac and Jacob. Who called Abraham to leave his home and his family, to set out on a journey of his own, a journey to the promised land. A land that he had never seen, a land he had only heard about. Heard about in a quiet whisper. From a God he knew existed. Abraham knew because he believed. Abraham believed, by faith. And God made a covenant with Abraham. That he would make Abraham the father of a great nation. That through his seed the world would be blessed. That his descendants would be like the sands, to numerous number. That they would dwell in the land God would give him, forever.

Then from Abraham's descendants, Isaac first and then Jacob, who God changed his name to Israel. Then came Joseph, and Kings David and

Solomon. Then through the work of the Holy Spirit, our Lord and Savior Jesus Christ was mysteriously placed in the womb of the Virgin Mary. Born in a manger, because there was no room for Him in the inn. No room for the creator, the sustainer of life. Jesus humbled himself. He took the form of a lowly servant. He lived among us, experiencing all the joys, pains and trials that we face. Yet doing so without sin. Then at the age of thirty he began his ministry. For three years, he taught and molded twelve ordinary men into teachers themselves, and somehow after these men, who had abandoned Jesus at the cross came together again, those men then in the face of opposition and persecution the likes of which few of us could ever imagine, these men spread and taught the message of the gospel, and changed the world forever.

"It is interesting to think that none of the disciples Jesus chose were ministers, at least not in the way we think of ministers today. They were not ruling elders or deacons in the church. They were not educated in the Hebrew law. They were not chosen from among the Pharisees, the leading authority on church doctrine. No, they were twelve ordinary people. People just like you and me. Then somehow with no internet, no cell phones, no fax machines, no television satellites or radio communications. No print media, no modern transportation, no established churches, no protections under the law for freedom of speech, or freedoms to even practice their new religion, or express their beliefs. These men came together and they did it.

"And their reward for that was to be martyred. Eleven were executed for their beliefs, and the other, the apostle whom Jesus loved, who through the Holy Spirit pinned the words of John's gospel. He found himself a slave of the Roman Empire. Imprisoned on the Island of Patmos. Where he later received a vision from the angel of the Lord, and wrote the book of prophecy, The Revelation.

"Certainly, when these twelve men first left everything they knew to follow Jesus, they couldn't have known what wonders and terrors they were to face. Yet, they ventured to take a walk with Jesus. They walked with Jesus out into the unknown. They too took a journey, a journey of faith.

"Sadly, many people in our America today seem to think they have no need of God. They are dependent on their intellect. They are dependent on their own strengths, wisdom or abilities. They somehow believe their gifts, their privileges, are of their own creation. They seem to think that they have evolved on their own, that Darwin's theory of evolution, the idea of a person, a man no different than you or I; somehow this man is right, and the creation story of the Holy Bible is wrong. As for me, I chose to believe that I myself was created by God, in God's image, and have not evolved from an organism or an ape. Some people even believe that the Earth and solar system somehow created itself. But I will put my faith in the fact that the Holy Spirit of God hovered above the waters. That the creative mind of the I Am, through the Word, the person of Jesus Christ, spoke the world into existence. That Jesus is the sustainer and keeper of all life, and He, God alone is in control, and He will be, until God sends his Son Jesus Christ again to call His believers to Himself.

"Then after a seven year period of great tribulation on the earth, during a time when satan, working through the antichrist and the false prophet will lead the nations of the world to rise up against God's chosen people. Jesus Christ, will then again return to this world. But this time, His Kingdom will come on the clouds, and He will crush the nations that stand against His people. Then every knee shall bow, and every tongue will confess, that Jesus Christ is Lord, and He shall reign forever. His Kingdom will never end.

"Three years ago, in a baseball stadium not far from here, I said a silent prayer and stepped into a batter's box. I prayed the words, '*Lord thy will be done.*' Little did I know, that I would never hold a bat or step into a batter's box again. I couldn't have known, but Jesus knew. Then over a period of tribulation, an unexpected journey in my life, God taught me what it meant to depend on Him, and not myself. I found myself like the pilgrims, on a voyage to the unknown.

"The reality is we are all on a journey into the unknown. Every day when we get up, none of us knows where that day may lead us. We make our plans. We chart our course. We take provision and make preparations as best we can. But as Jesus said,

'*We should not worry about tomorrow, because each day will have enough trouble of its own.*'

"The truth is, we don't know where we are going, but we don't have to go it alone. If you choose to study and prayerfully consider Jesus' teachings, and make the decision to make Jesus Christ the Lord of your life, Jesus will go with you every step of the way. I have seen Jesus take my shattered hand and broken dreams, and lead me on a journey more glorious than I could have ever planned on my own. He placed Christian witnesses along my path, at just the right places, at just the right time. He walked and sat with me on lonely nights. When the quiet was so loud, that my mind could not determine which way to go, or who to trust. Then Jesus led me to a Bible study where He taught me the scriptures. He whispered His wisdom to me, when no other counsel could help me. He rekindled a passion in my life that I had long ago forgotten. Then He brought a new love into my life, and mended my broken heart. He did all that without anyone else knowing He was there. He did that for me, and He will do that for you. But you must ask Him. You must choose. Jesus will not force you to choose. But choose you must. You must choose to accept the redemptive offer of Jesus, or you will reject Him. The choice is yours, but you must choose. And deciding not to make a decision is a choice. It is a choice to reject Jesus.

"Earlier today, I was eating lunch in a local restaurant. I heard people talking around me, some reading the local paper, others discussing the weather or the economy. It made me think, we all have time to do so many things. Yet we make so little time to study God's word, the Holy Bible. We spend more time researching a purchase for a cell phone, computer, new house or a car, than we do studying and researching the instruction given to us by the creator of the universe. There is so much wisdom to be found in the Bible, yet most of us spend so little time reading it. The indexes in the back of your Bible will refer and direct you to passages of such wisdom and insight to help guide you in any situation. Yet how many Christians even know how to find them? Our calling as ministers and individual disciples of Jesus Christ is to spread the message of the gospel. The gospel is a message of hope. Jesus came into the world to save the world. He came because He loves us. The people He created.

"Today in our country, our world, people are desperately seeking leadership, a safe port in the storms of life. You and I, we as Christians, we are not here by chance. God created us to be right here, right now to accomplish His purpose, to save the lost for His glory. And is that really so much to ask of us? After all, Jesus went to the cross for our sins. Is it so much to ask that we as Christians share the good news with a world searching for a savior?

"I don't know who you are, or where you may be in this walk we call life. You may have never accepted Jesus Christ as Lord of your life. If not, would you prayerfully consider the offer of Jesus? You know, Jesus will not condemn you for your sins. No matter what you may have done, or whatever may have been done to you, we are all welcome at the cross. Jesus Christ died for my sins, and for yours. He did it because He created us, He sustains us, and He loves us. Maybe you have already made the decision to accept Jesus. You have already given your life to Him. If so, would you commit to study the life of Jesus, the lessons of the Gospels? By studying God's word the Holy Spirit will fill you with wisdom and a confidence that will help you lead the lost to Christ. Would you commit to pray about it?

"As for me, I have made my decision about the cross, and I have placed my hope in the person of Jesus Christ. I can honestly say from experience that I have no idea what God may have in store for me. I no longer want to be a leader myself. I want only to be a follower of Jesus. And tomorrow morning I plan to get up and see where Jesus takes me.

"And wherever I go, and whatever I do, I will play fast and loose, play hard but play fair. And I will always Play 2 Win as I Live 2 Serve, my Lord and Savior, Jesus Christ."

From the Author

I would like to thank you for investing your money and your time in the purchase and reading of this novel. I understand the importance of a person's time and financial resources, so I truly appreciate you reading this story. When I set out to write this book, I had no outline or target market for this story. I simply prayed and wrote, and prayed and wrote, until the story came to a conclusion. As you recall from the story, there is no profanity or overtly explicit sexual content in this book. For some time now, I have been troubled by what I see in the content in our movies and on television. Images of defeat and failure bombard our society, and especially our young people. Profanity and explicit sexual behavior give us all a false sense of what is acceptable, and what is not. The reality is, that unlike what we would be led to believe in the media broadcasting, our country is filled with young people like the ones in this story. Kids that do the right thing, succeed in the classroom, and worship Jesus Christ in the way they live their lives every day. These are the qualities we should be celebrating in our television broadcasts and in movies and print media. Not the isolated images of sensationalism, that have taken the place of what used to be the respected and dependable field of journalism.

If you enjoyed this story and agree with me, that you yourself are disappointed in what you are seeing in the misrepresentation of our young people, I would appreciate you recommending this book to a friend. Also, if you go to our website, www.play2winlive2serve.com, you will see that we have made the t-shirt worn by the characters in the story. When I started writing this story, I had no idea the t-shirt would be a part of the book. But as the story developed, the t-shirt and the witnessing aspect of the shirt became a reality. I am praying that the shirt will become a witnessing tool in real life just the way it is in the story. That people wearing the shirt will be led to explain the Gospel message through wearing these shirts in their daily walk of faith.

After completing this book, I now find myself wondering how this message will be received, and where this book will lead me. However, I am convinced that you can have an unpredictable storyline, with an openly Christian message. And that our mainstream media is simply missing the boat by believing that our society has grown tired of storylines with characters portraying reality, whom exemplify honesty, integrity and truth in books, television programming and movies. I want to thank you again for taking the time to purchase this book and read this story. My prayer for you; is that you may begin to explore new and exciting ways to live out the Gospel message. And that as you do, that God will abundantly bless you as you live out your faith in service to our Lord and Savior, Jesus Christ.

Donnie Prince